'Unsettling, addictive, and razor-sharp, Francesca Reece is a
devastatingly compelling new voice in literary fiction'
Louise O'Neill

'Tense and sultry . . . addictive . . . With a complicated
love triangle, glamorous settings, a cast of enigmatic
characters and a mystery that will keep you guessing
right until the end, it's a genuinely thrilling read'
Stylist

'A sultry, summery book . . . devastatingly witty,
compulsively readable . . . like Sally Rooney meeting
Martin Amis in Paris'
Francine Toon, author of *Pine*

'From Paris to the South of France, with narrative strands
that wind beautifully through London's Soho and the
hot streets of Athens, *Voyeur* seems as though it may be
your standard airport novel: scandals in sunny climes.
But Francesca Reece's stirring debut is much more
than the sum of its wanderlust parts'
Harper's Bazaar

'A gripping debut'
Irish Examiner

'Set to rule the literary summer'
Sunday Times Style

D1347292

Francesca Reece

VOYEUR

TINDER
PRESS

First published in Great Britain in 2021 by Tinder Press
An imprint of HEADLINE PUBLISHING GROUP

First published in paperback in 2022 by Tinder Press
An imprint of HEADLINE PUBLISHING GROUP

1

Cataloguing in Publication Data is available from the British Library

ISBN 978 1 4722 7221 8

Designed and typeset by EM&EN
Printed and bound in Great Britain by Clays Ltd, Elcograf S.p.A.

Headline's policy is to use papers that are natural, renewable and recyclable
products and made from wood grown in well-managed forests and other
controlled sources. The logging and manufacturing processes are expected
to conform to the environmental regulations of the country of origin.

HEADLINE PUBLISHING GROUP
An Hachette UK Company
Carmelite House
50 Victoria Embankment
London EC4Y 0DZ

www.tinderpress.co.uk
www.headline.co.uk
www.hachette.co.uk

To my mother, and to Jess

One might simplify this by saying: men act and women appear. Men look at women, Women watch themselves being looked at. This determines not only most relations between men and women but also the relation of women to themselves. The surveyor of woman in herself is male: the surveyed female. Thus she turns herself into an object – and most particularly an object of vision: a sight

John Berger, *Ways of Seeing*

All of his portraits of me are lies. They're all of Picasso. Not one of them is of Dora Maar

Dora Maar

Oui, quelquefois la vie est monotone et quotidienne, comme aujourd'hui où j'écris ces pages pour trouver des lignes de fuite et m'échapper par les brèches du temps

Patrick Modiano, *L'Herbe des nuits*

One

PARIS

She was bitterly conscious of her failure, at a couple of years over twenty, to build up a coordinated life for herself

Muriel Rukeyser, *Savage Coast*

1

Leah

My association with Michael Young began with an advert in *FUSAC*, the monthly listings paper known (and resented) by most of the Anglophone population of Paris. Its header (in a smug, paternalistic blue) symbolised unemployment, homelessness and a general cul-de-sac of misfortune. It was an endless grid of minuscule apartments you'd never get and the same three jobs on an infinite loop: English-speaking babysitter; waitress for a 'diner-style café' or the ubiquitous 'manager of an Australian bar, ready to be part of *a fun, crazy team*!'. *FUSAC* was the leery expat landlord who would offer a rent reduction if you happened to be into reflexology. It was the greasy-haired bohemian youngest son of a Texan businessman who had come to Europe to start his fanzine on John Cassavetes and was touting for (unpaid) content. It was an unlikely zombie from the pre-internet age, and the original cornerstone of the gig economy.

Around that time I'd got into the habit of taking long, aimless walks around the city. I kept returning to the same places – my feet would carry me there mechanically – places I'd gone before, when I hadn't felt so astronomically useless. They existed in a constellation around Paris, anchors that pierced through layers of time and could root me back to various landmarks in my memory. They existed as proof that time wasn't some sort of horrifying linear and kinetic beast, hurtling past me in an unstoppable trajectory. I was three years out of university and I was floundering. I felt already like I'd peaked; like my promising adolescence had been an anomaly – or at the very least had given me false encouragement, because it had panned out in the *provinces* (for all my self-loathing, I was also a snob).

On Monday mornings I went out around the same time the real people left for work. We'd share pockets of time in the lift together from the top floor. They were generally men in sharp suits and *foulards* with expensive briefcases, normally attractive but almost universally depressed, with deep bags under their eyes. The speaker played snatches of a string quartet (the same three phrases on rotation, phrases that would inexplicably drift in and out of my mind years later, and that I'd hum all day before realising when it was that they had lodged themselves there). We'd greet each other with a nod or a half-smile, and sometimes I'd make a dull attempt at chit-chat: *fait froid aujourd'hui*, or *j'ai toujours cet air dans ma tête!* I wondered what they made of me. If they thought I was still a student, if I filled them with longing for scruffy youth, or if they just wondered how someone so shabby had made it into their building. At the front door we'd offer a curt *bonne journée* and exit swiftly from each other's lives, existing on top of each other in mutual, wilful ignorance.

The streets were packed with more real people. I'd cut through them as if I too had a timetable and a tangible destination, over the *buttes* and south towards Abbesses, down Rue des Martyrs and then veering east into the 10th, with no particular plan and not much thought, just a faint instinct to carry on towards some kind of central point – to the Seine with its gravitational pull. On that particular Monday morning, I sleepwalked over the Pont des Arts and into Saint Germain-des-Prés. On the boulevard I felt the pleasurable twinge of nostalgia that had become the point of these route marches. Here, across from the bottle-green awning of Les Deux Magots and its hordes of gaudy tourists, I could be a student again. Feeling full of the light absence of responsibility, I made my way down Rue des Saints Pères, and into a café where boys in blue shirts and red chinos with beautiful floppy hair and impeccable jawlines talked about the European Union and internships in New York.

I'd sloped in with my hands thrust deep into my coat pockets, like a spare uninvited guest skulking around the edges of a dinner party. The light was grey that morning. The Seine had been grey, the imposing buildings of Sciences Po, slicing the space of the street by half, had been grey. The only colour in the room besides the strip of muted neon along the zinc was the institutional blue of the *FUSAC*s piled up by the door. I slipped one into the stack of papers in my bag and took a seat in the corner. I turned to the first page, *Annonces d'emplois*. A dull fog of the same words again and again: *babysitting, business English, hostel receptionist*. Then all at once my eyes found an inconsistency in the middle of the page – the block capitals of a grandmother writing a text message: WRITER SEEKS ASSISTANT.

'*Mademoiselle!*'

'*Je prends un p'tit café, s'il vous plaît,*' I muttered, automatically.

> WRITER SEEKS ASSISTANT TO HELP WITH
> ARCHIVING/RESEARCH FOR A NEW NOVEL.
> Don't bother to apply if your name is Shakespearean
> or classical. PARIS AND SOUTH. PART-TIME.
> MICHAEL: 01. 14. 24. 60. 86.

I read the advert through about four times and felt the lump that rose in my chest every time something with potential presented itself. I started to invent tenuous reasons not to call the number. What did 'and south' mean? When was this issue dated anyway? This sort of thing would have surely been snapped up by now. Then, as it was prone to, my mind started swimming with good omens: 24 *was* my lucky number; '86 was the year my parents were married; Michael was the name of the man who'd done my braces when I was thirteen – and my teeth had been largely successful ever since. It was a pleasant-sounding name. The *A*s and *E*s looked good next to each other on paper, like the swell of a tiny bump in the pavement. On the other hand, if 'Michael' were in any way legitimate, why would he be resorting to an advert in a chronically naff listings magazine? I self-consciously circled the advert, relishing how cinematic the action felt, and stuffed the paper back into my bag, where my lack of actual action was out of sight.

*

'Darling, the thing is, I do just feel like I'm a special person.'

I nodded in earnest agreement.

'I'm just so open. Sometimes I feel like a new page in a notebook, just waiting for the world to write their ideas on me so that I can make them better.' Romain stroked the silver chain around his neck between his forefinger and his thumb, and with his free hand shovelled a spoonful of lurid pink pomegranate into his mouth. 'You know what I mean?' he demanded insistently.

'Totally,' I said, having no idea what he was talking about. He pursed his lips and placed one of his sublimely moisturised hands on my knee. His muscles strained against the deep V-neck of his white T-shirt. 'This is why you really are my *perfect* English teacher.'

I glanced down at the exercises I had painstakingly composed for him the previous evening and felt a fleeting pang of guilt at how little English he had ever learnt with me, and how, other than buzzwords like *le marketing* and *un selfie*, the only English to pass his lips in the entire two hours we'd spent together today had been 'Ariana Grande is sexy dance girl.'

Romain was one of the three jobs keeping me afloat in what I considered to be this strange limbo period of my life. He was a minor celebrity fitness guru, whom I'd met at five o'clock in the morning in a cloakroom queue, his pupils dilated into big black pools in his pretty, vacant eyes.

'*T'as un accent*,' he'd said, grasping my hands and rolling his lips under his teeth in delight. I – in a similar state – had beamed in satisfaction and, stretching my hands towards the ceiling, marvelled at how *kind* human beings were, how *great* the music was, and how *thrillingly* tactile his leather trousers were.

'*Anglaise*,' I'd sighed, shoulders pushing against the tangible pulse of the beat and eyes closed in ecstasy.

'*Mais c'est trop bien!*' He grabbed my hands again. 'I'm looking for an English teacher.' (A pause to chew his mouth.) 'I feel we have a real connection.' I felt I had a real connection with everyone there at that point in the night – all of us bound together by the same divine beam of perfect human energy.

He'd thrust his phone into my hands and the keys had all seemed to jump around and shimmer before my eyes. On the third attempt I'd managed to type my number and had sealed my fate. Our schedule was erratic. Some weeks he'd try and convince me to spend multiple four-hour sessions with him at the Starbucks at Métro Saint-Paul; other weeks I'd hear nothing, and then, suddenly, a relentless onslaught of manic texts (often at three in the morning) insisting that we absolutely *had* to see each other, and how he absolutely *had* to be fluent in English within the fortnight and that his career absolutely depended on it. Our 'lessons' usually ended up in me translating messages on his Grindr account, watching YouTube videos of his workout routines or listening to his spiritual-lite meandering soliloquies, such as the one he was about to launch into.

Besides Romain, I was muddling along with one job in a hip café and another teaching a group of pre-teen girls 'English through the medium of song', which had allowed me to become frighteningly well versed in the oeuvre of Justin Bieber. I wasn't unhappy at all. It was more that I constantly felt the burden of time. I felt keenly that I didn't have a lot of it and more than anything I saw myself as out of step with the time to which I supposedly belonged.

Apparently though, my malaise was a distinctly millennial one. Most of my friends from university had stayed in London and were determinedly forging careers. They fell into two distinct groups: the ones who'd had parents to support them through endless unpaid internships and were now slowly starting to get textbook 'cool jobs', and then the others, who'd disappeared seamlessly into the City and whose lives seemed more and more alienated from my own – Friday-night cocktails in Soho and Shoreditch, pristine wardrobes from COS, conversations that seemed to be made up entirely of snappy acronyms. That said, even the more enviable jobs left me cold, with talk of *clickbait* and *reaching out to creatives*; though in this instance I suspected that the coldness was probably underlined with a squeak of jealousy.

I'd moved back to Paris – where I'd studied in my third year – on the basis that here, I could get a cheaper room and work less than in London, thus freeing up vast swathes of time to 'find myself', or whatever it was I thought I'd be capable of doing. As time sprawled out in front of me, though, I was starting to get the impression that I was genetically unambitious, and in short, I was coming to terms with the fact that I really wasn't that special.

I thought a lot at that time about how I would have done university differently. Although I'd been largely unaware of it then, I could see now that I'd spent the first two years in dumb awe. I'd arrived from a small village in Cumbria, a sad satellite of a town that was slowly dying – full of empty shops and bus shelters with sun-bleached obsolete timetables. The last time I spoke to my mother, she reported that they'd even shut the ATM.

It was the sort of place that wasn't sufficiently glamorous in the midst of kids who'd grown up in places like Oxford, or Bristol, or Wimbledon, or even New England, and who had opinions on Russian novelists, kimchi, government legislation and the comparative merits of various long-haul flight operators. Their parents worked for the BBC or for NGOs. My mum worked in a primary school and my dad was one half of a 'skidder team' – a skilled and increasingly obsolete forestry profession that I romantically translated to 'lumberjack' for the benefit of my new friends. I still remember quite acutely how I'd worn that accolade like a badge of honour at freshers' week, how it had been fetishised by the kids whose parents did jobs that I didn't even understand. One son of Dulwich socialists had almost creamed his harem pants when he'd found out. 'A *lumberjack*?' he'd cooed. 'Ah mate, that's a *real* job – that's getting back to the *land*.'

Having been an intensely productive and ambitious teenager, I found that the creative endeavours that had been the solace of my claustrophobic adolescence (the things like music and literature upon which I had hinged the very idea of my personality) became fraught with insecurity. I became an obsessive diarist instead, recording everything and reading voraciously in an attempt to catch up with my peers. I was still smarting from the moment when the boy I lost my virginity to (trilingual, international school stock) had judged my carefully curated film collection as 'so clichéd'.

Losing said virginity had been like shedding an ill-fitting skin, only for it to be replaced with a straitjacket. I was terrified of my own body – of my pubic hair, of my untidy labia – and above all I was desperate to impress the boys who (as I saw it) deigned to sleep with me. I wanted so much to be seen as sexually liberated and naturally gifted that in the end my sole aim was that he (*he* being a whole parade of dazzlingly self-assured middle-class boys in baggy jumpers) should enjoy himself. I thought I was giving myself some kind of education, and I suppose in a way I wasn't far off the mark. I think over the course of two years I had one single experience that hinted that sex could do for me what I could do for myself, but it was sordid and laden with guilt, with the ex-boyfriend of a friend on a creaky old sofa in his damp basement room on Chatsworth Road. The next morning when he'd walked me to the Tube, I'd felt almost as if my legs were going to give way through the shame of the act that I'd committed. I was overwhelmed by the desire to go home and wash.

In Paris, everything had changed. Removed from the veiled and insidious ache of the class system (which I'd only discovered still endured when I'd got to London), I had felt a swell of self-worth. I was approaching the city as a Londoner, not as a hick. Paris, which I'd initially viewed as a museum piece, suited me beyond belief, with its resistance to moving into the future; it was just about as stagnant as I was. I was doing almost no work at all, living off the novel bounty of my Erasmus grant rather than having to wait tables, and writing entirely for myself.

In Paris, I made my most important (and admittedly predictable) discovery: sex. Sex in France, especially when the days started to stretch out that little bit longer, was everywhere. It was the filter through which life panned out. I learnt that it was absolutely normal behaviour to undress someone with your eyes on the Métro, or for the man at the *papeterie* to say that the new spring day was only almost as beautiful as you were. French men were frank and unfazed, and I realised finally that I was an object of sexual desire – and that it was an asset that could be weaponised.

*

It was spring. Everyone was out on the terraces but still wrapped up in coats and ostentatiously large scarves. On the canal, the wisteria bloomed. Emma took a drag of the cigarette we were sharing. 'So are you going to call?' she asked.

Emma was one of my more successful friends; in fact, arguably the most successful, as she had managed to remain a human being despite becoming a fully functioning adult with both a cat and a live-in boyfriend. She worked for an online art media platform and miraculously didn't induce homicidal leanings in me when she talked about *watching the sunrise from the roof terrace of a Renaissance palazzo during the Venice biennale with 'Pakistan's second most important artist'*. She was possibly the most stylish person I knew, despite that fact that every garment she wore looked like it was purloined from a reclusive octogenarian. On my right-hand side was Alex, who worked in a clothes shop that required a forward-thinking and well-curated Instagram profile to get so much as an interview.

I puffed out my cheeks in a gesture I'd learnt from the French that denied any scrap of responsibility or self-determination. 'Well I don't know,' I sighed. 'It seems a bit futile, you know?'

'You should still call. It could be cool.'

In all honesty, given what Emma had described as the *quasi-performative vagueness* of the advert, none of us really knew exactly what the job even entailed. 'Archiving/ research' were suitably meaningless indicators. We had made our judgement based on the fact that it clearly fell under the nebulous umbrella of 'a job in the arts', and in our insular universe of arts and humanities graduates, that vapid categorisation gave it irresistible allure and status. We were all complicit in this bourgeois mania for fetishising jobs in cultural industries. For all we knew, Michael (we could assume that he'd dispensed with a surname altogether, à la Madonna) could be looking for someone to water his plants, make his tea, or even just massage his ego (still preferable to actual massage, after all). The point was, if I could introduce myself as a *writer's assistant* at parties, my social capital (and presumably my self-esteem) would boom. Later, I would appreciate that it was this sanctification of a certain kind of labour that gave the arts establishment its dangerous power.

'To be honest, the advert does make him sound like a bit of a wanker,' Alex said, looking up from the screen of his phone, which he then dropped to his lap. 'I mean, the Shakespeare bit? Really?' Alex deemed most straight white males to be wankers.

'No, no,' I protested. 'That's the bit that really got me. Maybe he's fed up with all the Cressidas and their relentless domination of the arts – with their unpaid bloody internships and their houses in fucking Stockwell . . .' I could see from Alex's grimace that he'd rather I didn't embark on a social justice rant, and neither did I want either of my friends to suspect how deeply I'd already inwardly aligned myself with this absolute stranger. Over the course of forty-eight hours I'd imagined several different versions of our first encounter, only two of which involved the first hints of what would most certainly be a slow-burning seduction. As if reading my mind, Alex groaned. 'Oh God, and if you do get it, you'll obviously sleep with him – and he'll be some smug dad-bod baby boomer . . .'

'He probably has a daughter called Cressida,' Emma added. I mustered up faux-indignation but could barely even convince myself.

'But you *should* ring,' Alex said after a moment's silence. 'I mean, it's paid. Maybe this is your gateway out of the café?'

We often talked about my *gateway out of the café*, some kind of abstract *deus ex machina* moment over which I had pleasingly little control but that would miraculously transform my life into something more coherent: a job; a man. I'd even started buying scratch cards at the *tabac* on my street.

'I know, I know,' I said earnestly. 'I mean I'll definitely *ring*, at least.'

Duly, the second *pichet* of Corbières arrived. I was already feeling the delicious loosening of my limbs from the first. Emma passed me the end of the cigarette.

*

On the morning of Easter Sunday, I couldn't quite bring myself to leave my apartment. I woke up late and hung-over, into one of those limp, sprawling days, and felt acutely that I lived alone. I put the radio on and listened to a slightly surreal feature about the female celebrities who supported the decision to hold an EU referendum. Apparently, sometime in the nineties, Ginger Spice had been less than enthusiastic about those dastardly bureaucrats in Brussels. I ate two boiled eggs, thought about Jesus and got through half of a slim French novel about a literary young man observing an appropriately non-verbal, enigmatic and troubled heroine. Finally, at about half past five, when I could no longer bear the space between my four walls, I made an emphatic decision to leave. The fat, amphibian husband of the concierge was hovering in the corridor in his greying wife-beater. I offered him a chirpy greeting and he looked vaguely offended by my existence.

'You have to stop leaving your shoes outside your door,' he grumbled. 'Even if it's raining.'

Monsieur et Madame la concierge held me in utter contempt because I lived in a tiny *chambre de bonne* in the eaves of the building and shared a squat toilet with my neighbour, Farouk, an amiable, chatty and largely absent student who, needless to say, the concierges also despised. The seventh floor was a necessary stain on this otherwise money-spangled *co-propriété*. I had often witnessed the concierges' faces twitch into pained, unnatural smiles when greeting the sixth-floor families, so I knew that they were capable of social niceties. Madame was currently holding my post hostage to punish me for leaving my bike in the courtyard. I'd assumed that today of all days they'd have absented themselves in a fervour of religious devotion. No such luck.

Outside I walked briskly, past packed Sunday terraces and well-dressed children trailing *trotinettes*. I was listening to an old BBC interview with Morrissey, and as I slipped into the cemetery through the tall green gates, I lingered in his soft northern burr: *I just can't understand how people can do nothing with their lives when they know how finite time is.* I felt momentarily persecuted, but then I didn't really understand how a man who wrote such convincing lyrics about being gentle and kind could simultaneously write ones about keeping England for the English. It seemed to confirm my suspicion that successful people were all hiding disturbing perversions.

I was alone. The Cimetière Saint-Vincent was a twisted knot of roots, spindly iron and sun-bleached heads of cut hydrangea, a heap of spare parts left over from the necropolis down the road at Place de Clichy. I came here when I felt at my most adrift, because it reminded me of an ex-boyfriend. A long-haired grey cat eyed me briefly and I read the names emblazoned on the crypts (FAMILLE CAILLEBOTTE, FAMILLE LEGRANDE). The ground was dusted with brown pine needles, like my grandparents' garden had been when I was a child. Everything was some shade of dense green: the aquatic colour of the surface of a garden pond; or the ink-spill blotches of the lichen on the tombstones; or the tinge of light when it filtered through the stained-glass windows in the church at school service. I resolved to call Michael.

Perched on one of the high bar stools at L'Etoile de Montmartre, I went over all the possible outcomes of the phone call: A curt *position already filled*. Magnetic telephonic attraction (the faint impression that divine providence was at work, proven in a couple of snatched, chummy jokes). Heavy breathing, a couple of ludicrous phrases lifted straight from a porno and the realisation that I had been duped. I stared at my wine glass, swirling the purplish liquid around and around, and willed myself into action. Eventually, if only to avoid the advances of the middle-aged man next to me, poised to engage me in conversation, I dialled the number. The phone began to ring and after an eternity of seconds:

'*Allô?*' It was a woman's voice. She wasn't French.

'*Oui, allô, je vous appelle par rapport à l'annonce d'emploi. Pourais-je parler avec Michael, s'il vous plaît?*'

'He's not here,' she replied abruptly, in English, 'and I'm afraid the position is no longer open.'

'Ah.' Disappointment – along with a cowardly twinge of relief – worked its way through my body, draping itself softly on my shoulders. 'OK, well, thanks so much for your time anyway.'

'Yes, goodbye,' sighed the faceless voice, irked at the effort of the three syllables. She hung up, leaving the tone of the line to ring in my ears. I held the phone for a second as if she might ring back, and felt the silent weight of it in my palm.

'*Donc vous êtes Américaine?*' The man to my right had seen his chance.

'British,' I said, simpering sweetly. I swallowed the dregs of my glass and let a handful of coins drop on to the counter. '*Ciao.*'

*

After the abortive phone call, I wandered aimlessly around the *quartier* until well after sunset, trying to work out what on earth I could do with my life. The idea of working in an office filled me with legitimate horror, and by now I knew myself to be an intensely low-pressure creature. At the age of twenty-four I could still be swamped with paralysing guilt at the memory of letting a teacher down in secondary school. I thought about a friend working in financial PR who, bristling with pride, had told me that one day, the fortunes of entire companies would depend on her. I often felt that even having myself depending on me was pretty tedious. I came to a standstill, noticing that I was in front of a familiar wine bar, and I knew all at once exactly what would make me feel better.

I pushed open the door into a tightly packed little room that looked like someone's back kitchen. The walls were yellow and sparsely decorated with old Deyrolle-style illustrations of things like the different species of grape, pig or poultry found in the various regions of France. The floor, where you could see it, was terracotta-tiled, and the lighting was low and intimate. I jostled through the crowded tables towards the bar at the back, making sure that it was indeed him working. A faint glimmer of recognition – or rather a question of recognition – flickered across Benoît's face as he registered me sitting across from him.

'*Mademoiselle*,' he addressed me, shamelessly appraising my appearance. I asked for a glass of Saumur and took the paperback novel out of my bag. Five minutes later, he sidled over to my end of the bar. 'What are you reading?' he asked, in French. I showed him the Patrick Modiano novella I'd half finished that afternoon and he snorted. '*Et alors?*'

'You know it?' I asked. He smiled and, pulling out a dusty bottle from beneath the counter, filled up my glass and his own. 'I can't talk about books today, sweetheart,' he said. 'I'm far too hung-over.'

He had been hung-over the first and last time we'd met, about a year previously. I'd gone to the bar with the cemetery ex and Benoît had decided that we were going to distract him from his 'Dionysian punishment'. That really was the way he spoke. He was in his thirties; tall, skinny and charismatic enough to appear infinitely more attractive than he actually was. He was a spectre of what I myself could surely become in a decade. He worked in bars and wrote films – though he hadn't finished one for over five years. I'd told him I'd been a literature student. He had a master's in philosophy and asked me who I liked to read. Once we'd proven ourselves conversationally, he began to top up our glasses freely until all three of us were fairly drunk – me more so than anyone else, as I was wont to be. Fortunately, it was a Sunday night, and after ten o'clock or thereabouts, the bar started to empty. Conversation had gone from literary to sexual, to all-out vulgar.

'The reason your flatmate is having such loud sex is because he's clearly sodomising the bird,' Benoît said to us, piling paper-thin slices of *saucisson* onto the huge plate of cheese and charcuterie he was assembling. 'You two just have to do it better and louder.'

At that juncture, a bawdy wink in my direction. He'd been unashamedly flirting with me in the same way that the best shoplifters steal plasma televisions from retail parks by carrying them brazenly through the shop door. When my ex had been in the bathroom, though, and Benoît had lit my cigarette – holding my gaze for longer than was comfortable – I realised how entirely sincere his intentions were and, drunk and flattered, had reciprocated whilst exhaling the first long draw of smoke.

'You don't recognise me at all, do you?' I said now.

He narrowed his eyes, taking in the details of my face. 'Help me out here.'

'I was with someone last time,' I said. 'Business school type.'

He wrinkled his nose, and then the penny visibly dropped. 'Yes! Yes. You're the one who wants to be a bloody florist when she should be writing her thesis, aren't you?' I laughed. 'Did you go to floristry school?' he asked.

I confessed that floristry had ended up as yet another abandoned dream in my vastly growing cemetery of ambition. 'Good,' he said definitively. '*Est-il possible d'être revolutionnaire et d'aimer les fleurs?*'

Five hours later, the place had emptied out completely and I was drunk enough to think that going back to Benoît's apartment was an immensely appealing idea. As he closed up, I leant against the bar in a way that I imagined would be alluring and stabilising in equal measure; later, I stood out on the kerb in the cold, waiting whilst he dragged the metal shutter down across the vitrine.

'*T'as froid?*' he asked, seeing me shiver, arms folded tightly. I nodded, assuming he was going to gallantly drape his jacket over my shoulders. Instead, he slapped the jangling metal of the grate and turned to face me. '*Bon,*' he said, and, placing an unsteady hand on my shoulder, pulled me close enough for his bottom lip to brush against my forehead. 'We'd best get inside then.' His face creased into a smug half-smile.

Around dawn: 'What happened to your boyfriend then?' he asked blearily, absent-mindedly trailing a finger along my forearm.

'I can't seem to keep boyfriends,' I said into the mattress.

Benoît laughed. '*Tant mieux.*' I was lying flat on my stomach, naked on his bed. The room was devoid of any decoration. Piles of books were stacked on the floor with dirty mugs and wine glasses, some lined with ash and yellowing cigarette ends, the one on the bedside table now serving as the receptacle for the flaccid knot of the condom. My gaze lazily registered the words on the spines: Boris Vian, Henry Miller, Philip K. Dick, Hermann Hesse. Norman Mailer's smirking face on the top of the pile was half obscured by the torn Durex wrapper. Benoît's index finger had reached the small of my back and he paused for a moment before, with a flat palm, slapping my arse. '*T'as des très belles fesses,*' he enthused, and I felt a sharp stab of hollow pride, even if, from personal experience, an arse compliment was about as de rigueur as offering coffee the following morning.

'*Oui,*' he repeated, '*des très, très belles fesses,*' before adoringly enumerating my composite parts in a sort of Ronsardian *blason* that would have rendered my nineteen-year-old self helplessly infatuated. I lay in silence with my eyes closed, wondering if it was normal to view my conquests with such indifference, bordering on contempt.

*

I didn't think about Michael for a few weeks after that, and honestly, I probably would have forgotten about him entirely had it not been for Anna's exhibition opening. It was Emma who had dragged me along, to save her from 'the art wankers'. She'd sent me the event on Facebook, *Anna Young: Lenses/Perspectives*, along with an old article she'd dug up on her from the *Guardian* archive. It was dated 1998 and opened with a description of her studio: *At first glance, it would be easy to mistake Young's studio as one of the pioneering new restaurants in the area, valiantly attempting to bring focaccia and grilled vegetables to SE1.* All I wanted to do was lie on my bedroom floor listening to Lana del Rey and polishing off the bottle of wine I'd been saving for cooking. Fate, apparently, had other plans.

2

Michael

She walked into the room and it was like I'd slipped through some kind of channel directly into my own past. The girl wasn't *like* Astrid, she *was* Astrid. She had most of her face hidden behind a curtain of hair, but I could see it straight away; I felt it like an electrical surge.

'Darling, are you all right? You look a bit peaky,' said my wife, touching my elbow lightly.

My gaze was fixed on the girl, who must have been real; she was kissing a stranger's cheek, so she occupied tangible space. Anna's voice was remote and I wondered for a second if I hadn't gone into a different room, if she wasn't speaking to me through a closed window or even from the edge of a swimming pool. I was under the surface. Even the space around the girl seemed to occupy another, older sphere of existence. The light was the way light had looked in 1968, in the corner, by the basin in the flat on Charlotte Street. It brushed her eyelids in exactly the same way it had brushed Astrid's.

Anna hissed my name, increasing the pressure on my arm. Some kind of mechanical impulse allowed me to jerk my head in her direction. Somehow she was a physical thing next to me. I grimaced.

'Yes? Yes – sorry. I felt really strange there for a moment. I'm going to go and get myself a drink. Would you like anything?' My voice was full of forced cheer.

'Another glass of white,' she said, diminished a bit.

Astrid was making her way towards the bar too, and I

quickened my pace, ignoring a group that I faintly recognised as my French translator and his acolytes, one of whom called my name, *Mee-kay-elle, Mee-kay-elle!* They inhabited a realm I'd escaped. I was with Astrid, at the student union bar on Malet Street. I could smell the lingering mustiness of academic buildings cut through with beer and stale cigarette smoke. I felt almost as if, had I touched the skin on my face, it would be smooth and taut, like it had been then.

She was close enough to touch now and I reached my hand out to grasp her shoulder. She whipped around, and a fleeting expression of alarm was replaced by a fixed, polite smile. I searched her face for some kind of illumination, and then was struck by an uncharacteristic social anxiety. I felt a nervous laugh rise up and catch in my throat as I realised I was still gripping her shoulder; I could feel the heat of her body collect in my palm. I awkwardly let go, patting her like some sort of estranged stilted father attempting to show affection. Grasping clumsily at the first idea that came to my head, I cleared my throat and said, limply:

'Didn't you go to university with my daughter?'

She looked at me with what I registered quite horribly to be thinly disguised pity. How dreadful. She thought this was something sordid. I wanted so much to run my thumb along her bottom lip, to see if it felt the same.

'I might have done, I guess,' she said. 'Where did she go?'

'I'm sorry?' I asked, slightly dazed, and then, remembering what I'd said, added, 'Oh. Oxford. St Catz. Clarissa.'

The girl looked at me blankly, and then, as if remembering some kind of social obligation, said breezily, 'Huh. Like *Mrs Dalloway*? Or the Samuel Richardson one? Or that TV show with Sabrina the Teenage Witch?'

I looked hard at her features and there wasn't a single fault; but now her voice wasn't quite right, and she was referencing bloody Samuel Richardson, which didn't make any sense at all.

'James Baldwin, actually.' A little defensively.

'Well – can't be me. I didn't get in to Oxford.'

'Michael?' The familiar cadences of my wife's voice were the death knell of the unsettling shimmering hallucination. She pressed her slender body against mine proprietorially. 'Who's this?'

I turned and registered her, smiling sweetly at the girl. The unanticipated intrusion of blunt reality helped me regain my composure. Putting on my 'affable conversationalist' hat, I draped an arm around Anna and said, 'Well that's precisely what I'm trying to figure out. I'm sure we know her from somewhere; I could have sworn she'd gone to university with Clarissa.'

Anna was studying her coolly. 'I can't say she looks familiar,' and then, extending an elegant long-fingered hand, 'Apologies for my husband. I'm Anna Young and he's Michael.'

'Leah,' the girl replied, now visibly relieved that Anna was so expertly piloting the situation. Gesturing at the room at large, she added, 'Congratulations. It all looks – um – I mean the *work* looks . . . *fantastic.*'

Anna simpered. 'Thanks. Are you an intern at the gallery?' Her voice was brimming with warmth, but the question was a not-so-subtle assertion of power.

'No, no, not at all. I'm here with a friend who writes for a magazine about the art market. I know almost nothing about art. I mean, not nothing, obviously, but . . .'

She squirmed with embarrassment. Anna beamed charitably. 'What exactly do you do then?'

Leah grimaced. 'Ugh, I don't know really – as little as possible as is required to pay the rent. I work in a café at the moment,' and then, sensing this response was inadequate, 'I'm thinking of applying to do a master's.'

I could see she was looking for a get-out, which Anna would be glad to give her. I was determined that she wouldn't get away. I had to work out why the universe had given her to me.

'Well, you should come and work for me,' I spluttered, not even realising quite what I was saying. I could feel Anna's eyes burning into me.

'Excuse me?' Leah said.

'Yes,' I charged on, now led by absolute conviction. 'Yes, I was actually half-heartedly looking for an assistant a while ago—'

'Oh my God. Anna Young. Michael *Young*, of course. God, I'm an idiot. You're *the* Michael Young. The writer. *Richard, Falling*. You put an advert in *FUSAC*, didn't you? No posh names. That was you, wasn't it?'

Amazed now, and buoyed – the universe clearly *was* working for me – I nodded enthusiastically. 'You saw it?'

'I even rang! But the woman who answered said the position had been filled . . .' Her enthusiasm tapered off and she looked sheepishly at Anna, clearly aware of her potential gaffe. Of course my wife would have said that. She certainly wouldn't have wanted my assistant to be female, after all.

The warm smile stayed pinned on Anna's face. 'Well isn't this just perfect?' she said. 'How *great*.' She took my hand. 'And to think how much you resent coming to my parties. What a stroke of luck, hey?' She looked back and forth between the two of us, and then, taking Leah's hand in her free one like a sort of benevolent queen, said, 'Michael, I really have to go and mingle. Why don't you two set up a meeting?'

A meeting, yes. This whole weird, phantasmagorical experience wouldn't be an isolated one-off. She would exist outside of this evening. Placing my hand on the small of Anna's back, I kissed her cheek and said, 'Not a bad idea at all, darling. Do you still want a drink?' and then, turning to Leah, 'And what are you drinking?'

Anna could barely conceal her rage.

*

My daughter is a bitch – or at least she certainly is to me. She was a spoilt and arrogant little girl. I think Anna was so desperate to make up for the fact that she wasn't her mother that she just doted on her. She had this way with her – totally alien to my generation – where she was always telling her how special she was. *Oh darling, you have such an artistic soul*, or *oh darling, I really think you just feel music more than the other children.* Clarissa got used to thinking her opinion was important. Of course, she is clever; Christ knows she better be after all I forked out on her education. What I can't get my head around is how seriously she takes herself.

When I was her age all I wanted to do was to fuck and feel things. I was ambitious, but ambitious in a swaggering, adolescent way. Our ideas on ambition are so diametrically opposed. There's something so bloody puritanical about the way she works. She was always getting the right internships, staying at the office late and, perish the thought, *networking*. I had just always assumed that I was destined for greatness, and for a while it seemed I was. The thing about Clarissa is she's so prim and contrived. I can't imagine her having any kind of satisfying sex life. I get the impression that she doesn't really feel things at all – regardless of how bloody demonstrative she is about everything. They really are the generation of exclamation marks, aren't they? When my agent insisted I get Twitter, I was just inundated with this din of entitlement, with the assumption that I was even remotely interested in their opinions on Palestine, or women in art, or their home-made bloody quinoa salads or whatever. I wasn't surprised that Clarissa was there, leading the hashtagging ersatz revolution. I just feel this discord with her that doesn't strike me as much with her brother. With her, it feels like some kind of performance.

That was what I adored about Astrid. She was what Clarissa would have called 'a basic bitch'. She didn't have any particular aspirations. She just wanted to live. She was pure and unanalytical. She liked to eat Wall's vanilla ice cream straight from the tub, hanging over the kitchen sink in her underwear. She liked Princess Margaret because she was 'sort of naughty' and she'd renamed herself Astrid when she was trying to make it because it sounded chic and exotic. That was the only thing she ever felt the need to do to *curate* some sort of brand.

*

'I want the piece to be about *writers in exile*,' the boy said, consciously pausing before the last part and verbally italicising the words. 'Or not necessarily *exile*, but like, in a state of *expatriation*. Byron, Keats, Durrell, Hemingway . . . *you*.'

People were still writing magazine pieces about this shit? I nodded slowly and tried to work out when he must have been born. The end of the eighties? Was he older than Clarissa? He was wearing round tortoiseshell glasses and a light blue shirt. His cheeks were dusted with a sparse three-day shadow.

'I read this really interesting thing in the *New York Times* about a writer claiming his craft had benefited from living in Italy for thirty-five years and it just got me thinking. He talked about the internet and about how you just can't really be linguistically isolated any more. How does that change the language of the expatriated writer? I mean, I've been living and working in Berlin for four years now and I still can't speak any German. I'm not exactly reading Böll and Grass.' He smiled. 'Is the *concept* of an expatriated writer even relevant in our global community?'

Unable to help myself, I scoffed. He looked a little embarrassed, but, recovering himself quickly, as whichever public school or nice redbrick he'd been to had trained him to, said, 'I mean, that's why I wanted to speak to you. I wanted . . . an "exchange of ideas".'

Why did young people have this habit of putting everything they wanted to say in speech marks, as if it was going to be the title of their next blog post?

'I see,' I said unenthusiastically.

A plaintive little nod on the screen. 'That's why I'm just so grateful that Clarissa put us in touch and that I could reach out to you on Skype.'

I felt a nauseating wave of hatred for my agent for agreeing that this interview would be beneficial, and even more so for myself for acquiescing.

'Well,' I said at last. 'It sounds absolutely fascinating and I'd be happy to be involved.'

'Brilliant!' the boy enthused. 'That's brilliant. I mean, I know you have an appointment at two, but maybe I could even run a few ideas by you now?'

I made a vague, non-committal gesture of agreement and he started rattling off a long list into which I drifted in and out.

'Is it absurd to think your English can shift into something else abroad when we live in a world that speaks English? Has your subject matter changed? Can you still write about England when you're removed from it? Considering your writing was so typical of your generation and the sphere that you guys existed in – London, the late seventies and the Thatcher period, right up to Cool Britannia . . . I mean, how can you write *that* from Paris? Is that why you stopped writing novels?'

My face must have betrayed what I'd felt as he'd come to an abrupt standstill, and now, although I could barely make out the individual sounds he was saying, I could hear that he was backtracking nervously. *Is that why you stopped writing novels? Your writing was so typical* . . . Now he was waffling on about the virtues of 'taking time on your novel in this era of instant gratification'.

I cut across him. 'Listen, Jake, it's been a real pleasure to talk to you but I must go or I'll be late. How about you send me over those questions and I'll try my best to answer them, if I can still remember how to type.'

He shrank in visible humiliation.

'Michael, I—'

'As I said – a real pleasure. Send them over and I'll get back to you.'

'I—'

I clicked on the little phone icon on the screen and his face vanished. No doubt an angry message from Clarissa would follow – if he was brave enough to tell her. Sighing, I looked down and realised the silver track pad of the computer was washed with rivulets of bright red blood. The nail bed of my right thumb was covered in it and my palm was damp and sticky. I got up mechanically to fetch a tissue and wondered if Leah would notice when she arrived.

3

Leah

If it hadn't been for another morale-obliterating day at the café, I'd have probably made some implausible excuse and abandoned the dubious meeting altogether. His behaviour throughout the first encounter had been erratic to say the least, and his wife now clearly had it in for me. She, according to Emma, whom I had later mined for information, was a model-turned-artist and was commercially successful but critically panned. Rémy, Emma's comically bitchy colleague, had sneered between drags of a cigarette that she'd have been better staying on the other side of the camera where she belonged.

Warning signs aside, I felt like I had to see this through. Having actually met them, I was certainly more confident about the legitimacy of the job. I could now discount the idea that Michael was a writer of erotic Harry Potter fan fiction, for example, or an amateur biographer of Denis Thatcher. Michael Young was the real deal. His voice had been part of the genetic make-up of the English literary landscape since the end of the seventies, when his first novel, *Richard, Falling*, had appeared. Right up until the millennium, he'd consistently churned out cynical modern classics, and was adored in equal measure by both the old-guard establishment and the erudite, poser rebels that I'd gone to university with – the type who went to film-society screenings of *Apocalypse Now* and abbreviated David Foster Wallace to DFW. On my break at work, I'd messaged a university friend in London who worked in publishing to ask her if she knew him. She said she'd never come across him personally but that her boss had known him before his self-imposed exile and apparent retirement. Rather worryingly, she'd described him as 'not the kind to suffer fools'.

Later she'd messaged me to say that another mutual friend had worked with his daughter, whom she'd described, cryptically, as 'exactly how you'd imagine'. I'd guiltily searched for her on social media, terrified the whole time that I'd accidentally add her or, worse still, like something she'd posted. We had three mutual friends. A boy from my halls in first year whom I'd almost dated but had been a bit too scared of (self-styled dandy, boarding school, drama society); a girl I barely knew who'd been in my early-modern literature seminar; and finally, a friend of a friend who'd been at Central St Martins and was now (according to a quick perusal of his page) an editor at *Dazed & Confused*. So far, so predictable.

Michael and his wife were renting an apartment around Denfert-Rochereau, 'the unfashionable end of the 14th', he'd said with pride, leaving me wondering where exactly the fashionable one was. It was true that the neighbourhood was a little less eye-wateringly moneyed than the ones to the north and west. Denfert was one of the purest chunks of Paris left in the city. Its main thoroughfare, Rue Daguerre, was a long cobbled stretch of red brasserie awnings and market stalls, and as I wove my bike through old ladies in headscarves and mackintoshes, the tangy smells of cheese and then the fleshy saltiness of the fishmonger's perfumed the air. On the pavement outside the florist's, a bored old man in a green apron was sitting on a stool surrounded by buckets full of wilting lily of the valley. Someone had told me once that it was Bob Dylan's favourite street in Paris.

Michael lived on Rue Boulard, between the *tabac* and the second-hand bookshop. I locked up my bike and fished the scrap of paper with his codes on it from my coat pocket. My hands felt clammy. I wiped them furiously on my jeans and glanced down at my watch. I was ten minutes early. I walked the length of the street and back. Five minutes early. Five minutes, I assured myself, was the boundary between earnest and polite. The door opened onto a little courtyard trailed with wisteria and what I took to be the concierge's washing. It was flooded with greenish light and smelt of fabric softener. I re-read his instructions for the hundredth time. *Fifth floor, batîment B.* Within was the usual sweeping staircase with a mock-Persian runner, and a tiny cage of a lift, which I decided to take to avoid any further risk of perspiration.

He took a while to come to the door, and when he did, he opened it slowly, like a teacher deliberating whether or not to let a pupil into the staff room. When he saw my face, though, his expression softened and he pushed the door wide, throwing great shafts of white light into the shadowy stairwell. He contemplated me in silence for a second or two, then he sighed, *well, welcome*, before standing aside to let me in.

'Wow.'

'Yes, it's a rather big space, isn't it?' he said, hands thrust into his pockets. 'Tea or coffee?'

'Tea, please.'

He nodded and disappeared off into the kitchen, leaving me standing awkwardly on my own, leaning on the arm of a huge 1970s sofa the colour of tomato tapenade. The room was vast and airy, giving on to a balcony that ran the length of the apartment.

'Yeah, we've been here for about five years, I s'pose,' he called from the kitchen. 'When we first came out, Anna wanted to live somewhere trendy like the 11th, but I was still holding a candle for the Left Bank of my student days, and this was the closest we could get. I like it round here. There's not too many godforsaken expats.' He reappeared in the doorway carrying a little teapot and two mugs. 'Let's go into the study, shall we?' I obediently followed. 'I mean, we've still got the house in Highbury, we're only renting this place. We keep saying we'll go back, but somehow we end up renewing the lease.'

The study was poky and lined with books, save another big, rickety old window – open and looking out onto the courtyard. He made an expansive gesture as he placed the teapot on his desk. 'Take a seat.'

I sat on the edge of an old day bed covered in threadbare throws and pillows.

'Why did you move here?' It had been so long since I'd spoken that my voice sounded like a caricature of itself.

'Oh I don't know. I was tired of London. I needed a break. Anna wanted something new. The kids had both left home . . . I mean, not that they ever lived with us – they were with their mother in Cambridge – but still . . . We had the place in Saint-Luc and we were thinking of just packing it all in and going there, but Anna was so afraid of becoming that awful cliché of the jaded English artists who can't hack urban life any more and go to the Mediterranean to become all soft like rotting fruit. So we came here. It seemed like a good compromise. How did you end up here?'

'Well, I graduated and found myself ambitioned out of London.' Friends had told me that admitting to lack of ambition was deeply unstrategic in a job interview. I was still banking on Michael being eccentric. 'I got a year's contract working in a school and I somehow ended up staying afterwards. Now I'm just sort of loafing, I suppose.'

He smiled at me and made unnervingly intense eye contact. 'Good. I feel you don't get enough young loafers any more.'

'We seem to be a dying breed,' I agreed, pleased with my choice of tactic.

We talked a little about my academic experience, my eclectic employment record and what I liked to read. At last, drumming with flat palms on his knees, he said, 'Yes. Yes, I think you'll do very well. I like the idea of this.'

'Good?' I replied hesitantly.

'Yes, very.' He stood up and walked over to the window-sill, leaning on the rail of the Juliet balcony. I took a good look at him in the soft light of the afternoon. He was very tall and wiry, with thick grey hair and dark eyes.

'I'm sure you're probably aware that my last novel came out at the turn of the century,' he said, not looking in my direction. 'What you probably don't know is that I'm actually working on something new.'

He paused as if waiting for my appropriately impressed reaction. I obliged.

'Consequently I'm sort of snowed under at the moment. On a boring daily basis I'm looking for someone to deal with my correspondence. I get sent a lot of book proofs from editors wanting a sycophantic flyleaf sound bite or newspapers wanting reviews. It'd be nice to have someone to sort through them and work out which ones were actually worth my time. I get a lot of invitations that I have to turn down – I'm quite bad at replying to emails. Other than that, there's some bits of research for this new project, and then above all, this summer I'm looking for someone to type up my personal journals.' He cleared his throat and looked vaguely uncomfortable. 'There's this period of about two years in the late sixties – probably when I was about your age – I'm just sort of stuck on them. I want them made into something coherent . . .'

I pitched my features somewhere in between nonchalantly composed and keen.

'You said you write?' he asked.

'Um, *ish* – no, yes, yes but nothing serious,' I said, trying to remain cool.

He was looking at me intently again. 'God, it really is quite astonishing.'

'It is?' I asked.

He ignored the question. 'The name Christine Parker doesn't ring any bells for you, does it?' then, seizing on my silence, 'No, don't worry. It's nothing.' He smiled at me again, as if I'd said something surprisingly funny or clever, even though I hadn't said anything at all.

'We moved the bulk of our stuff to Saint-Luc when we left London so we could rent our house out. That's where all my old diaries are. We normally spend most of August there – it's a big old farmhouse that we share with one of my oldest friends, Jenny, and her husband. You know the drill – we're that horrible *bobo* English family trailing guests and children and drunk friends who don't speak a word of French. You'd start on a very part-time basis over the next couple of months – doing the emails, the reading – and then, well, if it all worked out, I suppose you'd come with us this summer and take on the diary project . . .' He was chewing the edge of his right thumb as he spoke. 'I didn't think I'd find anyone. I didn't just want to ask one of my kids' friends. They're too close and they've already got a whole ruck of dazzling career opportunities. I put that ad in

FUSAC on some stupid whim, but I didn't expect to actually get anything out of it . . .'

I let him speak, nodding at what I considered to be appropriate intervals, though now he seemed hardly aware of my presence.

'I've never really been much of a one for superstition,' he said, 'but when I saw you, I just . . . something just *clicked*.' He moved away from the window and came and sat next to me on the day bed, our knees almost touching. Scrutinising my features – for what was probably less than five seconds but felt like an eternity – he placed his hand on my thigh and smiled. The disconnect between his facial expression (unthreatening, apparently engineered to inspire confidence) and the pressure of his uninvited palm jarred. I told myself he was just being friendly, and as if to confirm it, he raised the burning hand into a matey tap. It was an age thing, clearly.

'Anyway, I read through your CV and the email you sent me and you seem to have the right sort of profile.' He thrust his hands back into his pockets. 'What do you think?'

I looked at him directly and valiantly crushed any dissenting voices. 'I think it sounds perfect.'

A wave of visible relief appeared in his eyes and he relaxed. He stood up again.

'Splendid. Yes – splendid.' He moved back to the desk. 'I've already got a couple of proofs for you, if you're ready to start now?'

*

'Mate, he sounds like a fucking weirdo.'

Emma grimaced in sympathy. 'Admittedly, the situation doesn't sound great. Well, the job itself does. You get paid to read books and write emails and then eventually read

Michael Young's secret-fucking-diary. That is quite cool. But then also weird. No offence, babe, but why do you think he's interested in *you*, specifically?'

The three of us were perched on the end of a long communal table, mopping up the remains of what had been a creamy swell of burrata slicked with olive oil and oozing onto a bed of plump cherry tomatoes.

'I want another one,' Alex just about managed to articulate through a mouthful of sourdough.

'Do you think that was shavings of turnip on the top?' Emma asked. 'It tasted like root vegetable.'

'So he's just a creepy old lech then?' I asked, directing the conversation back to me.

'Yes. Obviously,' groaned Alex, running his finger along the terracotta to get the last smudge of oil. 'He touched you and he's not even French. He wants you to read his old diaries and he doesn't even know you. He's a perv.'

I sighed dramatically. 'But it's the coolest job ever. And it's *paid*.'

I hadn't admitted to either of them that the thigh-touching-incident had actually thrilled me a little bit – that it had given me a guilt-laden indication of potential power.

'How awkward will it be when his kids come out there with all their mates and you're, like, their father's mistress?'

'I really don't think it's like that,' I protested weakly. 'I think he's just a bit demonstrative.'

'Just work with him here for a bit and see how it goes,' Emma said. 'Have you actually read anything he's written?'

I cringed a little. 'I actually did read his first novel the summer before university. It was very . . . ugh, you know that whole school of swaggy young men talking about fucking and pissing and the fall of patrician society?'

'Ah.'

'But then I also listened to his old *Desert Island Discs* and on that he said he couldn't even read his juvenilia any more.'

'Did he actually use the word *juvenilia*?' Emma asked.

'He's literally the worst,' Alex said.

'He's a *writer*,' I said. 'Writers are inclined to use big words.'

'He was on *Desert Island Discs*.' Emma whistled, visibly impressed.

'Exactly,' I said.

About a month after my first meeting with Michael, Anna invited me over for dinner. So far the work had been fairly consistent. Although he hadn't produced a novel in years, a regular slew of reviews, columns and even the odd script-consulting role in TV and film had ensured that his profile hadn't diminished enough for people to leave him alone entirely. I'd been spending about an hour or two a day politely declining invitations on his behalf and reading science fiction proofs (he'd had a dystopian moment in the eighties and had been suffering the consequences ever since).

When Emma and Alex had heard about Anna's invitation, they'd made the predictable jokes about the wife checking out the potential mistress. In reality, Michael and I saw each other briefly about once a week to check in. I did most of the work from home or in cafés, smug that I had somehow turned into the aspirational freelancer figure I'd been used to serving from the other side of the counter. Despite the ominous start, I'd fallen into a comfortable relationship with the job and even felt confident that I had genuinely been chosen on the basis of my suitability rather than anything more sinister.

I arrived in the 14th unnecessarily early again and so had to sit on a terrace in my plastic mackintosh, refreshing my Instagram feed, until it seemed appropriate to go up. Anna greeted me effusively at the door. She smelt amazing. Rich people always smell incredible. When I was a teenager, mainlining TV series about wealthy New Yorkers and Californians, all I could think about when watching the endless party scenes was how good they all must have smelt. Before I could stop myself, I heard the words 'Wow, you smell brilliant!' tumbling out of my mouth. She smiled serenely.

'Oh, my perfume? You know, I think I might have put on Michael's by mistake.'

I'd started talking about how I'd always wanted to be the kind of woman who wore men's scent before realising that the doorway was an inappropriate place to start a conversation, and that maybe I sounded sycophantic anyway. I let her lead me into the apartment, seamlessly seat me on the orange sofa and kit me out with a glass of wine. She sat opposite me, legs elegantly crossed, leaning forward with composed enthusiasm on one of those stylish mid-century and undoubtedly Danish chairs.

'So I hear you'll be joining us in Saint-Luc this summer?' she cooed.

She really was quite beautiful. She had thick corn-coloured hair that she'd pinned up, wisps escaping artistically and framing her face. She was probably about my mother's age, though of course the two were incomparable, Anna being the epitome of metropolitan chic. She wore smart black trousers that grazed her tanned ankles, a crisp man's shirt, minimal jewellery and bare feet.

'It'll be wonderful,' she continued. 'Clarissa's coming for about a fortnight and Lawrence'll be dropping in and out too. He's in Greece at the moment, volunteering with the refugees.'

'Lawrence?' I asked,

'Our – well, *Michael's* eldest.'

I hadn't noticed that Michael had come into the room. He strolled over to his wife, bending to kiss the crown of her head.

'Lawrence is a bit all over the place,' Anna explained. 'He graduated from SOAS about five years ago and he's been a bit unsettled ever since. He lived here with us for about six months, didn't he, darling?'

Michael shook his head. 'Lad's been everywhere. Here and Saint-Luc to start with. Then he went cycling off around Europe and ended up somewhere bizarre for a while; one of those old Soviet countries – which one was it again, darling?'

'Croatia, I think. That's when he was DJing.'

I groaned inwardly: *Lawrence, from Cambridge, who went to SOAS and was a DJ.* I'd known so many of his type at university. Admittedly, I'd been friends with a lot of them. He'd probably be fun. They tended to have a good sense of humour; funny, well-educated, interested in cool stuff; more than a little pretentious and totally out of touch with any kind of reality. They were the kind of boys I'd worshipped like gods as a gauche, parochial eighteen-year-old.

'Yeah, he was there for a while. Then there was a period when he looked like he was about to grow up. He went to live with one of his mother's friends in New York and was interning for a production company—'

'And then he buggered off to India,' Michael interrupted.

'Nepal,' Anna corrected.

'Yes, that's it. Nepal. What's he interested in now? Composting or something?'

'Christ knows, I can't keep up. He moved back to London in January and stayed for about a week before going off to Calais with some old school friends.'

I could feel myself easing up. These people were comfortingly familiar types. They were the people I'd learnt to negotiate – aspired to emulate even – when I'd first arrived in London.

At the table Anna began to tell me how she and Michael had met. 'It was around the time I was doing my first solo exhibition, so about 1998, I suppose. Michael was writing a piece about it for the *Evening Standard* and he went with that unbearable tag that all the papers swallowed about me being some kind of muse-turned-artist.'

'It wasn't a question of swallowing it – it was the truth!' he said.

'It was *not*,' she insisted. 'I was an artist before I was a model. I studied at the Slade and I was just doing the modelling thing on the side to help out some friends . . . then of course that erupted.'

'Obviously,' Michael snorted.

'. . . and I ended up dropping out and had a bit of a wild ten years . . .'

She'd said the words *wild ten years* for effect, I thought. She wanted to prove how she'd once been edgy, even if now she was more likely to be featured in the lifestyle section of the Sunday papers with tips about interior design.

'And then I found my medium.'

Michael rolled his eyes discreetly.

'Michael, however, didn't think so.'

'Oh no?' I asked hesitantly.

'Well, he trashed the exhibition, as he was wont to do.'

'It wasn't *that* bad,' he protested.

'And then three weeks later he started chatting me up at a party!' She laughed and Michael feigned a shamefaced expression. Anna twirled a ribbon of pappardelle onto her fork. 'But then, I suppose – as he wrote – I *was* nice to look at.'

She maintained this level of pleasant, elegant chit-chat throughout the evening, and it was only as I was leaving that she dropped her guard long enough to send out the vaguest ripple of concern. She insisted on accompanying me out of the front door to call the lift, as if we were in an old Hollywood film and I was incapable of pressing the button myself. The little square of hallway was cold, and away from Anna's poised small talk, the gentle clinking of cutlery and the artfully curated mood lighting (still just visible as a sliver of warmth from the door), I felt some of my initial awkwardness trickle back. The second's silence was broken by the lift lurching into place.

'Well then,' I said. 'Thanks so much again – it really was lovely.'

'Leah, I . . .' She stepped forward, close enough for me to smell her perfume again. Her movements were a little stilted and I realised for the first time that she was drunk. 'I really am so glad we met you. You know, Michael's like a man transformed since my opening night. He's been working every day; I can hear him hammering the computer keyboard from the study.' She was contemplating my face. 'At first I wasn't so sure. I thought it was . . . Well, you know how men can get. I thought it was some tacky mid-life crisis or something.' She laughed a little too enthusiastically. 'Michael can be . . . *tricky*. But I don't think it's like that at all, is it?'

Unsure of what to say, I agreed discreetly that it certainly wasn't.

The doors of the lift were about to slide back into place and she beamed at me with what I felt was sincere tenderness.

'Well then,' she said. 'Goodnight.'

*

Alex and Emma remained sceptical, but I couldn't shake the idea that my involvement with Michael and Anna might lead me to something. I couldn't help but be seduced by the theatre of their lives: the art on the walls, the mid-century furniture, the walls of dog-eared paperbacks, the Bauhaus wine glasses.

The following evening, I sat, mostly naked and cross-legged, in a little pool of sunlight on the floor of my ten-square-metre apartment. I contemplated my reflection in the mirror – where the ends of my dark hair fell below my collar-bone and grazed my nipples and the soft round of my belly – and I imagined, as I often did, that I was being looked at by a man; that I was a desirable object. I wondered, with a little swell of pride, whether Michael had imagined me naked. Of course, if he *did* ever try anything on, I'd never let it happen, would I? Although my ego had been flattered by his initial attentions, I'd felt relieved when it had become apparent that my enduring employment didn't hinge on my sex appeal. But still, it was nice to feel that he'd thought about it, that he'd wondered what it would be like to press the angles of his body (softened by age, I supposed, a little loose) into mine, and to kiss the nape of my neck.

I picked apart a triumphant head of artichoke and dipped each leaf into an old yoghurt pot full of olive oil and sea salt flakes. It was the end of their season and there were piles of them at the market under the railway bridge at Barbès. Boiling an artichoke on the camping stove that sufficed as my kitchen was easy. I liked the feel of tearing it apart with my fingers, and the repetitive action of dipping each leaf, then dragging my teeth along its rough surface to suck out the flesh at the tip. Each mouthful was a salty, oily reward for effort. I googled photographs of Saint-Luc, drained a glass of Pinot Gris, and felt I could just about burst with plenitude. Everything was coming together.

4

Michael

Astrid had worked in a café on Frith Street. It was a greasy spoon owned by a fat, old Italian man called Giorgio and I'd got into the habit of going there because I thought I was in love with a girl, Kathy, who lived across the street. She was a folk singer, and I found out years later that she'd ended up getting caught up in some cult in the States and had spent most of the seventies in orange robes. I looked her up with Anna's Facebook this morning. She was a music teacher at a secondary school in Bristol now, and posted almost exclusively about the Labour Party and lost dogs in the south-west. In her photograph she had her hair pulled back in a sensible plait and was wearing earnest sandals. She had a husband who looked like the kind of man who had a shed and could name garden birds.

It was a Thursday morning and it must have been the autumn, because I remember trudging through piles of soggy, brown leaves in Soho Square. There was a light mist rising off the pavements and I still felt all jittery from the coke I'd taken the night before. I couldn't quite face going back to Kathy's. Careering and arrogant from the drugs, I'd pressed myself against her best friend in the pub and told her that she looked like Brigitte Bardot. They were both cerebral types, though, and it didn't wash at all. She'd probably rather be like Doris Lessing, I'd sneered to a friend later, smarting.

I'd made it as far as Kathy's front door when I remembered that Giorgio's opened at seven. I thought I could maybe get a cup of strong dark tea and kill some time until I had the strength to catch the number 25 back to mine. The Everly Brothers were playing when I got there. I remember, because it was 'Cathy's Clown' and I almost turned back around and walked out again. Instead, I slunk in like a criminal and slotted in at one of the Formica tables. Opposite me, a huge poster of Sophia Loren stared me down with her alarming feline eyes. It was an expression donned to seduce, but I got the impression that she was about to devour me, like a grinning she-wolf.

The place was half full already. Next to me were a couple of girls I took to be hookers, eating scrambled eggs and smoking furiously, raucously sparring about a man they referred to simply as *his Lordship*, with more than a smack of contempt. Opposite them was a table of monosyllabic builders. One of them had the fresh, round face that denounced him as a rookie. He kept snatching furtive awed glances at the girls between hasty gulps of tea. The older lads largely ignored his presence. The leader of their pack was soliloquising about West Ham. In a shadowy corner by the telephone, a man in a suit was dozing on his briefcase. His tie was undone and his hair askew. I wondered if he had a wife in Guildford, sitting at the breakfast table in her curlers and housecoat, reading the *Daily Mail*.

My reverie was briefly broken by a distinctly terrestrial East End accent.

'Ready to order?' it said without enthusiasm, and I didn't bother to look up.

'Cup of tea, please. Milk, no sugar.'

Mrs Guildford would be called Susan or Caroline and she'd have one of those very English faces – a stroppy little pink mouth, a snub nose with a smattering of freckles, light brown hair and flushed cheeks. The housecoat was a sort of insipid coral colour that didn't suit her but grazed the outline of her breasts. She'd be so desperately bored.

The waitress returned and placed a mug on my table. 'Not eating, then?'

I looked up at last, and found myself unable to speak. I fancied myself an aesthete at that time, and she was quite remarkable – 'a twentieth-century Tess', as I pretentiously scrawled in my diary later that day. She had large brown eyes that, in the same hackneyed way, I'd described as 'fresh and innocent', and long, thick hair piled on top of her head in a way that struck me as deeply unfashionable and verging on Edwardian. Her nose was small and perfect, like a child's, and her mouth excessive. I stared at it as she spoke.

'No thank you . . .' I scrabbled desperately for an excuse to keep her. 'Are you new here?' I fished for a cigarette in my pocket, because an ex-girlfriend had once told me I looked sexy when I smoked.

She seemed momentarily disarmed by the attention I was paying her, and flashed me a knee-weakening smile.

'Yeah,' she said, 'it's my third day.'

I maintained direct eye contact with her, in a way that I found always worked with girls, and said, 'Well I suppose we'll be seeing a lot of each other then.'

She shifted nervously and raised her eyes to meet my gaze. I gave it a week.

Over the course of the following fortnight I made a point of going into Giorgio's on an almost daily basis. Inadvertently, I discovered that the uniform stacks of pappy white bread with bacon, eggs and disturbingly smooth sausages were a mere shopfront. At lunchtime the little room filled up with what felt like the entire Italian population of Soho, and out came plates of coiled spaghetti, seasoned with pepper that they ground right there and then, and glistening with golden drops of olive oil. It was an entirely new sensual experience.

I would sit in the corner, where I had a perfect view of the counter and the pass, and pretend to write or study. Mostly I was just writing a journal of my infatuation with Astrid, as she'd introduced herself at last, on day three. The last time I read it, it was excruciatingly adolescent, but at the time I thought I was being frank, perfectly balancing my natural artistic tendency to romance with a refreshingly sordid cynicism. I wrote paragraph after paragraph of faux-philosophical erotica (Kathy was reading Anaïs Nin and had rapturously read me a short story about fucking at an execution and thinking of Dostoevsky), and little by little, I started to eke out more details of Astrid's life.

She'd grown up in Mile End and her father was a musician. Her mother worked as a dressmaker. When she was a teenager, she used to sing in her father's band but had ended up having a 'terrible falling-out' with him. She was such easy pickings. I presented myself to her as a sort of tortured artistic type, and although I made sure to flatter her ego by letting on patent, if wordless, interest, in equal measure I knew I had to move slowly and build some kind of solid foundation before making any real move. I watched as she primly brushed aside the advances of other customers: sleazy Italians, maladroit workmen and sinister City types *à la* Mr Guildford. There was a moment when I thought maybe I could curry favour by intervening, and I'd started to prepare myself for a sublimely violent display of virile peacocking; but then, I reasoned, was it really worth getting myself barred when I'd only just discovered *arrabbiata*?

Every evening I would go across the road and fuck Kathy, and imagine as I was unbuttoning yet another paisley chiffon sack that I was unbuttoning Astrid's tight little gingham blouse that strained across her small, pert breasts.

*

'Michael, I don't want to see you any more.'

Kathy was barefoot, perched on her windowsill and dragging from a badly rolled joint. Layers of unflattering cheesecloth grazed her ankles but she looked unbearably pretty in the soft morning light. I sat up in her bed. 'Excuse me?'

She wasn't looking at me. 'It's over.'

I let out a snort of outrage. 'What do you mean, it's bloody over?'

She looked at me frankly then, in a way that unsettled me, and said, 'Michael, you're raining on my fucking parade.' I sat in stunned silence. 'Patty told me about what you said to her about *Brigitte Bardot*. I really don't mind if you sleep with my friends, but you sound like someone's seedy uncle – like you work in advertising or something.'

'Babe,' I said limply, 'that wasn't even me. I'd taken a lot of—'

'You're just one of those intellectual types who sees every seduction as another brushstroke in your masterpiece. I should have seen it when you wanted to go down on me the first time you came back here.'

She took a long drag on the spliff. I saw her as such a docile, non-confrontational creature that for a moment I was softened when I thought of the courage she must have mustered to do this. Then she closed her eyes and I felt my heart hammer in my chest as I realised she was being utterly serious. I surveyed the chaos of her room as I pulled on my clothes.

'What the fuck have you been reading?' I hissed, slamming the door as I left.

I was already drunk when I turned up at Giorgio's at twenty past two that afternoon. I'd been intending to spend the whole day at the library, but had got waylaid at the student union with a comfortingly stocky girl from Derbyshire who was reading French literature. Her barrel-esque proportions by no means belied her capacity to hold her drink and I soon realised that the effort to keep pace with her was giving me speckled vision. By midday I'd become dangerously truthful. That was always a real worry for me with booze – as soon as I was drunk I felt this desperate need to tell everyone everything I'd ever thought about them. I told my new friend that I was going to walk to Soho and tell Astrid exactly how I felt. She insisted that we toast the occasion with a final nip of whisky. 'Right on!' she giggled, her accent tainted with the tiniest Midlands burr. 'Love is all you need!'

I veered chaotically through Bloomsbury and onto Tottenham Court Road, unable to coordinate even lighting a cigarette in the persistent dirty drizzle. I suddenly felt quite sure of what I was about to do, but above all ravenous. A heroic portion of *spaghetti all'amatriciana* would sort me right out.

The last of the lunchtime Italians were slowly filtering out of the café and the vitrine was opaque with condensation. The green awning buckled under brown pools of rainwater. I sidled in and slumped against the white tiles of the wall. Every noise felt overwhelming: the hiss of the milk steamer behind the bar, the patter of rain against the windows and the spray of puddles slapping the pavement in the wake of the traffic. I sank into the undulating cadences of the last dregs of the conversation around me, and the gentle tinkle of the piano playing on the radio. I could feel my eyelids drooping. It was so hot in there after the damp chill of the street.

I was woken up by the flat palm of Giorgio colliding with my head.

'*Ehi ragazzo!* Rise and shine!' He was a second-generation immigrant and even his Italian was spoken with an unmistakable London twang.

My vision was bleary. I groaned. There was a plate of cold spaghetti next to me.

'Where's Astrid?' I asked.

'She's off this afternoon,' he replied, wiping down a table.

I sat up and attempted to twirl a string of dry spaghetti around my fork. I recalled the stages of the miserable day, from Kathy's rejection, to the Derbyshire girl, to me peeling off in elated determination. 'Giorgio,' I began, 'you couldn't happen to tell me where she lives, could you?'

She was lodging in the spare room of a wizened old Soho publican, who was thankfully absent when I arrived. Hammering oafishly on the front door, I'd seen her twitching the curtains above. It was raining properly now, and my hair was plastered to my head. I'd left my coat at the student union and I was starting to feel miserably sober. I hoped that I at least looked dashing and cinematic.

When at last she came down, she opened the door to me in her peignoir, which I judged as a remarkably positive sign; a girl willing to come to the door like that couldn't be all that prudish. Her hair was wet, and as she bustled around, a bundle of frenetic energy, she apologised for her state. She couldn't quite make eye contact with me.

'I've just got out of the bath. I was coming home from an audition and I got absolutely soaked.'

I sat at the kitchen table in silence whilst she boiled

water for tea and let her talk herself into a frenzy. When she stopped and made eye contact with me, I stared directly into her face. I watched her squirm under the weight of the silence.

'Why are you here, Michael?'

The kettle began to whistle and I stood up. She was rooted to her spot next to the gas ring. I went and stood in front of her, so close that she was forced to press herself against the lacquered work surface. Next to her I felt very tall, and was buoyed after the morning's attack on my self-esteem. Beneath the wafer-thin fabric of the peignoir I could feel the soft curves of her warm body, and I noted, smugly, that her nipples were hard. I cupped her chin with my right hand, drawing her face up to mine, and forced her to meet my gaze. I ran my thumb along her bottom lip and said, 'I came here because I had to see you.' She stared up at me, unable to speak. Mustering all my willpower, I drew away. 'I'll see you tomorrow,' I said quietly, walking towards the front door. The kettle was still whistling.

Outside, the rain had cleared and the streets were washed grey with feeble diluted sunlight. I headed jauntily towards Oxford Street to catch the bus, and felt my mood swell with victory.

5

Leah

The first weeks of summer were characterised by terrible weather and even worse politics, and everyone started bandying about the same arbitrary statistic that it hadn't been this damp since 1882. The rare sunny days were muggy and the air pollution was high. A palpable feeling of unease seemed to sweep across Europe, and in Paris everyone had become hunched over and bent into themselves. The only people left unfurled were the roving gangs of English football supporters, who marched in packs, unfazed by the rain and singing loudly in an unintelligible language of drunken swagger.

Earlier that week, a student at Stanford on a swimming scholarship had come out of county jail after serving a six-month sentence for dragging an unconscious freshman behind a skip and attempting to rape her. He was about to embark on a summer-long tour of the States, promoting temperance. I couldn't shake the image of his globular blue eyes and perpetually damp mouth, bulging with grinning teeth. The papers all used his yearbook photo instead of his mugshot. His face was fleshy and salmon-coloured. Apparently alcohol had thwarted his Olympic dreams.

One evening, as we were locking up our bikes in her courtyard, Emma turned around to me and said, 'I don't just feel apocalyptic; it feels more like we have a whole parade of apocalyptic outcomes to choose from.' We'd just cycled silently through the makeshift village of half-flattened tents under the railway bridge at Jaurès. The *piste cyclable* had

been crowded with barefoot men sitting on the hard concrete, smoking. Neither of us had said anything.

A week before Michael was due to leave for Saint-Luc,
he announced that Clarissa would be 'making an appearance' in Paris. He was in a vile mood. 'Anna thought you
might like to come over again to meet her,' he grumbled.

I felt a lump of nervous energy rise in my throat and
found myself replying with a nonchalant affirmation that
that would be cool and that I would keep Tuesday night
free. I spent the day leading up to the dinner in a state
of mild panic. What if she didn't approve of me? (A very
likely reality, judging by a couple of barbed comments from
Michael.) Arrogantly, I was looking forward to the eventual
introduction to Lawrence; boys, I told myself, were easy.
Maybe he'd even be attractive, I thought hopefully. I'd
guiltily attempted to find him on social media along with his
sister, but no amount of sleuthing could uncover a Lawrence
Young. He'd be the type to have one of those fake names;
he'd be too cool to over-share on the internet. He'd be a
Law Rence or a Man Go, or a Laurent Jeune or something
along those lines. Maybe he didn't even have Facebook.
Maybe he was *that* kind of guy.

I arrived at the Youngs' apartment in a state that wasn't
quite tipsy, but was undoubtedly buoyed by one ill-advised
glass of wine. As usual, I'd got to the 14th stupidly early and
so had gone to peruse the second-hand bookshop on Rue
Boulard. The bookshop was a glorious relic of how people
imagine Paris to be. It was owned by Léo, a wiry old veteran
of Mai '68 with wild white hair and a cigarette permanently
clamped in his distinctly Gallic mouth. Idly I flipped through
the rows of old novels; *editions folio, poches*, tatty old *pol-
iciers* with stark covers in garish primary colours. At last,
obliged to buy something so I didn't look like a philistine,

a poseur youth or, worse still, an Anglophone, I fell upon an attractive hardback copy of *Le Marin de Gibraltar* and handed it to Léo, who'd been leaning, framed by the open doorway, eyeing me coolly through intermittent plumes of smoke. He turned the book over in his hands.

'*C'est pas mal,*' he said, before telling me that he remembered going to see the film in a cinema in the Latin Quarter when he was about – a pause to appraise me – my age.

'*Z'avez un accent, mademoiselle. Z'êtes d'où?*'

The willingness of Parisians to comment on my foreignness never failed to amaze me – although of course, being British and above all white, their comments usually signalled curiosity rather than hostility. If anything my accent was a safety net. It let me off the hook when I was too drunk or tired to participate in deep conversation; it avoided any kind of unwanted depth, really, which had been convenient in a lot of my previous relationships. In French, I had discovered multiple new variations on my personality. The first had been a sweet, unthreatening one, the pliantly 'feminine' version of myself that men, unsurprisingly, seemed to appreciate. Later, I learnt that it could serve as an invisibility cloak and a lazy party trick in equal measure. Eventually, more confident in myself and less desperate to please or prove myself, I liked the detachment and subsequent freedom that speaking in another language offered me. It was no coincidence that I'd got comfortable talking dirty in French long before I could in English, or that I'd had the courage to break up with people in French, or to give in to confrontational road-rage impulses whilst cycling. In short, I was less invested. Words didn't have the same power that they did in English, and so I could be more careless with them.

Sliding a second filterless Camel out of the packet and offering me one as he did, Léo began to tell me about how he'd lived in Oxford and had been a rower. Had I ever been to the Boat Race? I confessed I hadn't, and, undeterred, he began to describe the spectacle with the relish of a novelist, digressing halfway to ask if I'd like a glass of wine (it was that time of day, after all) and disappearing temporarily into his papery den only to emerge with a dusty old bottle and three glasses. He placed them all on his makeshift bar (a pile of dense tomes about Lascaux) and poured: one for me, one for him, and one for his friend François, soon to arrive and bearing *saucisson*. My head was already faintly fogged with the tobacco that tore unhindered through my throat. At least, I told myself, I would be animated at dinner.

'He-*llo*!' Anna cooed enthusiastically, pulling me into extravagant *bises* at the threshold. 'You look gorgeous! I like your hair like that.'

My hair looked the same as it always did. 'I put coconut oil on it last night?'

'Yes! It's exactly that. You look like a show pony!'

Unsure if that was in fact a compliment, I followed her into the warmth of the apartment. The girl I took to be Clarissa (or rather knew to be, from extensive research on social media) was sprawled across the orange sofa. She was attractive in an unmistakably English way. Her thick blonde hair was cut straight, halfway between her shoulders and her earlobes, and her face was so pretty (pale blue eyes, nose-job nose, strong dark eyebrows) that her baggy, unflattering 501s and shapeless acrylic jumper looked dazzling. I felt instantly that I was in her territory and went with the only tactic I knew – deferential beaming.

'Hi!' I sang with unbridled enthusiasm. 'It's so nice to finally meet you!'

She smiled back at me, not showing her teeth.

'You see, Michael!' Anna called into the kitchen, defusing

Clarissa's emphatically non-verbal response. '*Meet*. They categorically do *not* know each other.' She turned to her stepdaughter. 'We told you, didn't we, that your dad was convinced Leah was one of your friends from university.'

Clarissa smirked. 'Right, as if Dad knows *any* of my friends from university.'

I carried on beaming through the awkwardness and said, inanely, 'You grew up in Cambridge, right?'

Michael cut across our weak line of conversation to greet me.

'Leah,' he said, 'you're not ten minutes early for once. What waylaid you?'

He'd noticed that I was always early? I explained that I'd been distracted by Léo downstairs.

'That grumpy old scrote? He never gives me so much as a *bonjour* and I spent a bloody fortune in there on some book about Walter Gropius for this one,' he said, gesturing at his daughter.

'That's because you're not a young woman, Dad,' Clarissa said. 'Old white Frenchmen are, basically, the single perviest group across the whole of society.' Just as I could feel myself smarting, she turned to me and, with the first glimmer of camaraderie in her eyes, said, 'Seriously, it was only my inability to speak French that stopped me getting trapped by him. He offered to carry my suitcase. You wouldn't get that kind of shit in London.'

The meal was a strained affair, made even more awkward by the dialogue that emerged between Anna and myself in response to the near silence maintained by both father and daughter. Anna attempted valiantly to coax them both into conversation, to which Michael replied in monosyllables and which Clarissa largely ignored. Occasionally she would engage with me, delivering faintly wounding blows wrapped up in a dazzling, disarming smile: 'I think it's really wonderful that you're not at all bothered about trying to have a career', or even 'London is just a bit too intense for some people in the end'. My personal favourite was her pronouncement that she was actually 'quite jealous you get to just work in a café. I wish my job were so chill I could switch off my brain, so I could focus on what I really want to do, you know?' I didn't ask her what exactly that was.

It was only later, in the small kitchen, when the two of us were alone clearing the plates, that she showed the slightest bit of warmth or genuine interest.

'So what are you doing after this?' she asked in a low voice, swallowing the dregs of a wine glass. 'I have to get out of here. Anna drives me fucking crazy.'

I had to think fast. I had work the following morning at seven and wasn't intending on doing anything more thrilling than going home and scrolling through my Instagram feed. Unfortunately Clarissa brought something of the nervous eighteen-year-old out in me and I found myself desperate for her to think I was sufficiently cool to be considered an equal.

I shrugged. 'I dunno. I've got work pretty early. I've got some friends who are having drinks at theirs, but to be honest I kind of can't be—'

'That sounds perfect!' she said. 'Let's go like, asap. This flat is killing me.' Evidently clocking my expression, she continued, 'Don't worry about seeming rude; Anna will just be happy that we're getting on, and Dad hardly gives a shit anyway.'

I scrabbled desperately for an excuse. The said friends who were having a drink were hardly an inviting prospect – it was in fact one friend, Salomé, whom I had already flaked on in favour of this dinner, and the host was a guy I'd once had a brief, self-esteem-lowering fling with.

'The only thing is, I can't really leave my bike here because I have work tomorrow morning.'

'Oh come on,' she said. 'You can get the Métro and come and pick it up tomorrow.'

I felt a slight pang of dissent, but knew in the end I was obliged to agree with her.

'It's also *really* far away,' I said, 'They live in this old warehouse thing outside the *bord périphérique* at Aubervilliers.'

'Paris is tiny,' she said definitively, and with an air of sternness. 'Nothing is far away.'

*

It was my second phone call to Salomé.

'Hugo says he's just going to come and find you. Stay where you are! You are by the petrol station, right?'

Having got off the train, we'd now spent half an hour wandering around the outer sprawls of Paris in what felt like a dystopian industrial estate punctuated with greasy neon *chickin* shops and the odd seedy *tabac*: sun-bleached maroon awnings and squalid little terraces with plastic chairs advertising soft drinks; men smoking in silence, playing lotto and watching endless muted matches of football.

'So is this like the Parisian equivalent of Deptford?' Clarissa asked.

'Getting there,' I answered, willing Hugo to arrive and for her to stop speaking English quite so loudly. The man at the petrol pump was staring at us, chewing gum with an open-mouthed smirk. Every now and then he would address a single accented word or phrase to us in broken English: *beauty girls*, or *how are you*, or, more jarringly still, *oh my God!* I fumed inwardly and nodded politely.

At last Hugo appeared, irritatingly attractive, on his old blue Peugeot fixie. He'd shaved his head since I'd last seen him, but he had such a good face, the face of a real Gaul – olive skin, full mouth, impossibly square jaw – that he only looked sexier.

'*Léa!*' he called, standing elegantly on one pedal. 'You should really get a bike!'

I sensed this was going to be a night of inward fuming.

We spoke in English, for Clarissa's benefit, though I was in little doubt that it was rather more so that the boys could show off. When Clarissa complimented Hugo's linguistic skills, he shrugged and said, 'I mean, to be honest it's just fucked up in this day and age *not* to be able to speak English. How do people think they're going to cope in the world without it? *Everyone* should speak English.'

I exchanged wide eyes with Salomé. Hugo was the internationally schooled child of diplomats – of course he couldn't understand how you could not. His flatmate, Clément, nodded earnestly. '*Ouais. Grave.*'

'Maybe refusing to speak English is a form of resistance,' said Salomé, whose own other language, Creole, had never quite been accorded the same kind of cachet.

Narrowly avoiding swallowing his cigarette in his haste to exhibit his progressive credentials, Clément insisted that he could totally see her point, but that above all, in this time of nationalism and political fragmentation, we had to prioritise the easiest channels of communication.

'Easiest for everyone,' said Salomé flatly. The irony was lost on Hugo.

'I like this music,' Clarissa said, taking in her surroundings. The boys lived in a converted industrial building, a vast open space with a couple of mezzanines and a few curtained-off rooms to give the impression of privacy. The concrete floor was spread with faded Persian rugs, and trailing plants hung from the huge beams. There were records and bicycles everywhere. The speakers were industrial. Clément, of course, was an artist-slash-producer. '*Il y a un peu trop de basse par contre, Hugo,*' he said in a theatrical aside, before addressing Clarissa. 'You do?' he said. 'Thanks – it's one of my mixes.'

I was standing, a glass of cheap wine in hand, snooping shamelessly through the bookshelf. I was suddenly aware of a presence behind me.

'*C'est fou,*' Hugo said softly, 'we haven't seen each other for years.'

God, I know, I thought, and how I'd hoped it would stay that way. The last time we had actually seen each other had been tragic. He'd invited me around to his apartment to make margaritas, which at the time I had sweetly thought meant we were going to make pizza. After three cocktails I'd been so drunk I'd lost control of my limbs and the last thing I remember was begging him to put on 'Gracias a la vida' and sitting in a heap on his living room floor attempting to sing along in Spanish and weeping intermittently – partly because of the music, but mostly because I'd just found out that he'd also been sleeping with my flatmate.

I smiled up at him and nervously ran a hand through my hair. 'It has been a while.'

He stared at me, shameless and unflinching. 'I missed you,' he said, grazing my arm. Ignore electricity, ignore electricity, I willed myself; for God's sake ignore electricity.

'Hey, *mec,*' Clément called, 'shall we roll another *pétard*?'

'I've got a better idea,' said Hugo, not taking his eyes off me. 'Let's do some lines.'

*

I had been a *huge* hit with Clarissa, I told my reflection in the bathroom mirror, a reflection that really was unbelievably attractive despite the tightly clenched jaw and the pooling pupils. I'd just taken another line off the boys' dirty, cluttered dining table and I could feel the acrid drip trickle down the back of my throat. Next door I could hear her laughing. She thought I was rebellious and unusual and free, with cool friends who lived in industrial spaces and took coke on Tuesday nights. I became aware that my reflection was baring its teeth at me and realigned my facial expression into one I felt more seductive and flattering. Hugo absolutely wanted to sleep with me. He was such an idiot that he'd even hung on every word of my incoherent monologue about how God's existence could be proven in certain hues of sunsets and phrases of music. To sleep with him and feel nothing would surely be an act of sublime vengeance on behalf of my twenty-year-old self. It was basically my obligation as a feminist. I tied my hair into a knot on the top of my head and pulled a couple of strands loose until I looked artfully dishevelled. I was young and did not need to sleep before work.

I went back into the room. Clément was enthusiastically showing Salomé and Clarissa a heap of ballpoint pens and torn-up adverts for life insurance companies that he called the start of his installation. 'So you work in a gallery in London?' I heard him say to Clarissa. 'That's really fucking cool.'

'What exactly is your artist's manifesto?' I heard her reply, mechanically.

Hugo was sitting by the laptop, controlling the music. 'Come and sit with me,' he ordered. I obliged. 'This coke is pretty good, huh?'

I nodded eagerly. 'Yeah! It reminds me of this coke we used to get in London from this guy called Dozer who used to keep his drugs in his ear stretchers.' I was aware that I was talking so fast that I probably sounded as high as I felt.

Hugo smirked and put a hand up to my cheek. 'You're still so sweet and adorable,' he said, pulling my face towards his. He smelt of cheap beer and tobacco. His breath was warm on my earlobe. 'I still think of you a lot, you know,' he whispered. We both knew he was lying. I'd seen on Facebook that he'd been in a relationship with an attractive blonde girl for the best part of the past four years.

'Me too,' I half lied – I still often thought about most of the boys I had slept with.

'*Petit soleil.* I think you should just stay tonight,' he said, kissing my earlobe and burying his fingers in my hair.

*

Later. All of us coming down, Hugo rolling a joint:

'It does feel a bit weird here, the atmosphere,' Clarissa agreed, inhaling deeply on the end of Clément's cigarette. 'Like police everywhere and the people checking your bags . . .'

'We've basically become a police state, that's why,' Clément snorted. '*13 Novembre – putain de Nuit des Longs Couteaux.*'

Hugo, jiggling and fidgeting and clasping his hands, added, '*Non, mais*, seriously, France is *fucked*. We're all fucked. Global governance, man. Europe is *so fucked*. I mean, I really hope the UK does vote to leave. Fuck the EU, fuck the IMF . . . Fuck big organisations, you know?'

Salomé groaned. '*Non, mais Hugo, t'es vraiment trop con quoi—*'

'*I'm* an idiot? Are you fucking serious? Do you understand anything about what's going on in the world right now?'

I felt a bubble of uncharacteristic anger rise in my chest and said, 'Yeah, but is the answer really to hand the country over to a bunch of fascists?'

He gave me a patronising, indulgent look. 'Who do you think controls it right now anyway, *ma poule*?'

Clément nodded smugly. '*Voilà*,' he said. 'If the UK goes out of the EU it'll be an important step towards smashing up a rotten system.'

I breathed in a toke of the joint that Hugo had just handed me. 'Guys, it really wouldn't be some kind of righteous revolution against capitalism; it would be one last arrogant ejaculation of a withered nation clinging to an embarrassing colonialist past that it thinks gives it some sort of status.' I took another drag and felt vaguely proud of myself.

Hugo glared at me. 'I just don't think you girls understand what's going on,' he said. 'If you'd been to the camps—'

'*Quoi, comme vous?*' Salomé laughed.

'And what exactly are *you* doing?' he asked accusingly. '*Léa*, you talk about fascists in your country; well, I know what I'd be doing if Marine Le Pen got power over here—'

'You'd be doing fuck all.' Clarissa spoke at last. She was eyeing him coolly. 'You'd be sitting here in your little utopian commune that Mummy and Daddy pay for, smoking weed and talking about the Baader–Meinhof gang.'

A stony silence descended on the room. Clarissa's eyes met mine and I felt gripped with a certainty that I absolutely wanted to be her friend. She'd silenced the boys in one blistering mouthful.

She yawned. 'Should I call an Uber then? I'm actually super-tired and I feel all misanthropic now I'm coming down.' She stood up decisively and smiled serenely in a way that reminded me of Anna. 'Thanks so much for having us, though. It's been so fun.'

The smile was all Anna, but when she'd shut Hugo down, I couldn't help but notice how much of Michael had shown in her face.

*

The following afternoon, exhausted after a ten-hour shift on approximately half an hour's sleep, I went back down to Denfert to collect my bike. There was a note tacked to the saddle in handwriting I didn't recognise: *Thanks so much for last night! Shame about the end but it was actually pretty fun (even if Clément's 'art' was deeply questionable . . .) See you in Saint-Luc. xxx*

I'd absolutely cracked her, I thought, before the image of her first, painted, closed-mouth smile flashed through my mind.

6

Michael

With the exception of the peignoir incident, it was the first time I'd seen her in anything other than her work uniform. She was in a pale blue tailored coat with an excessive fur collar and she'd rimmed her eyes with kohl, which made her look even more like Bambi than usual. She was leaning on the park railings, waiting for me. I was twelve minutes late. I stopped for a while to look at her before she clocked me. It was also the first time I'd seen her in the dark. It was getting on towards the end of September now and the days (iridescent and grey) blanched out into night earlier and earlier. Her pale face was illuminated in the lamplight and I noticed how sad her features looked in repose. I'd imagined her so many times: bathed in such half-light, her hair spread about the pillowcase and her dewy mouth half opened in pleasure. Her eyes were always closed. I'd never thought about the way lamplight would reflect in them. She spotted me and broke into a disarming, childish smile that was all teeth. I decided not to apologise for being late.

'Where are we going then?' she asked. The melancholy had vanished and she looked (I noticed victoriously) excited. I'd been intending to take her to the student union, where a friend's band was playing, but had realised as soon as I'd seen her that I didn't want her to become a tangible reality yet. I didn't want to hear her name made concrete in the mouths of the real, earthly people who configured in my life.

'Do you like jazz?'

'Of course,' she replied, which pleased me, because she represented a certain nostalgia for me already – I liked to think of her as a ghost from the previous decade, a daughter of the wholesome 1950s.

'There's a jazz club on Old Compton Street we could go to. It's full of people our parents' age, playing old standards and talking about how they saw Charlie Parker in New York even though they've clearly never been much further west than Slough.'

She giggled. 'That sounds perfect.'

I smiled and took her hand, which I noted was a little bit clammy. How endearing.

*

'I just think that version is a little bit over-arranged, that's all.'

'Billie Holiday? *Over-arranged*?' I was scandalised.

'I mean, obviously Billie is a goddess, no one compares . . . But the thing about the Chet Baker version is how simple it is. I just love that moment when the percussion comes in, the brushes on the snare . . . It gives me goose bumps!'

She'd spent the walk to Old Compton Street in gauche silence, which had suited me perfectly. Then, as soon as we'd come in off the street into the dark, smoky basement, she'd seemed instantly in her element. She'd walked through the crowd directly to the bar and had ordered a neat Scotch before turning to me and calling (in the broadest Bow accent), 'What you drinking then?'

For the first two whiskies she still hadn't spoken, but this new silence wasn't remotely bashful. She was perched on the bar stool, eyes closed, bopping blissfully to the music. It was a kind of self-possession I hadn't imagined her to be capable of.

She finally spoke when I lit up a cigarette, 'Oh, go on – give me one then!'

'You smoke?'

'I'm a part-timer,' she stage-whispered. 'My dad used to play hell with me if he caught me, said it'd ruin my voice.'

I handed her a cigarette.

'His mates all said my voice would get better for it, that I was too sweet otherwise. But Dad likes things to be his way, you know?'

'So your dad is a jazz musician?'

'Well, my dad's a chippie,' she laughed, 'but he's a trumpet player first, yeah. He met my mum playing with his band down the Underground at Bethnal Green in the Blitz. They used to take their instruments every night and play through the air raids.'

I felt a sudden wave of nausea at how entirely comfortable she was. London was part of her DNA. I thought back to when I'd first moved here after an unremarkable childhood in the north of England and three years at Oxford. I'd wanted nothing more than to consume London and to be consumed by it. I wanted to be baptised in the Thames and for my roots to twist into the same earth as the ubiquitous plane trees. I wanted a timbre of voice whose vowels and pauses and cadences chimed with Pepys, with Dickens, with gentlemen's clubs at St James's and barrow boys and the bells of Old Bailey. I wanted, in short, to be like Astrid. What was more, though, and what I absolutely hadn't been expecting, was her affinity with the music. I'd wanted to educate her, but here she was humming along to every tune. After a few plucked, tenebrous notes on the double bass and a couple of opaque broken chords, she leant towards me (when had she become this confident?) until her lips were brushing my cheekbone and sighed, 'Oh I absolutely *love* this one; this one is my favourite.'

'Billie Holiday,' I'd murmured in agreement. 'Classic.'

'Oh *no*,' she'd sighed. 'Chet every time.'

I couldn't bear to admit that I wasn't entirely familiar with that version and she took my silence as dissent.

'It was Billie I used to try and sing it like, though, when I was little.' She shuffled nervously in her seat, embarrassed that she'd challenged my point of view.

Now the singer was singing about the hurt of unkissed lips. Now was so obviously my moment. I took the cigarette out of her hand and stubbed it into the little Ricard ashtray.

I'd expected her, perversely, to taste of strawberries – the Tess fantasy had taken firm root in my precocious (yet immature all the same) brain and I'd wanted her to taste like fruit grown fat with warm Dorset sun. I'd almost been expecting to find little seeds in her teeth. Instead: tobacco, whisky, the jarring synthetic vanilla of the lip balm she was wearing. I'd kissed her chastely at first – a soft, closed-mouth kiss; but then without any pressure she'd gently parted her lips (pillowy, soft, pornographic) and kissed me back. Nervous delight passed over her features and she reached furtively for my hand. I felt an involuntary grin spread across my face. I wanted keenly to kiss her again. She was looking at me in adorable disbelief. I pulled her towards me, steadying her so the bar stool didn't tip, and I kissed her on the forehead.

'I do agree about the Chet Baker arrangement,' I said.

*

Years later, at a little cinema not so far from that bar, I watched the Bruce Weber film about Chet Baker. The bar had turned into that great monster of the 1980s, a wine bar, and last time I walked past it was an almost-trendy burger joint, packed with hordes of kids. I sat on my own at the back of the cinema and let the aching black-and-white footage flood my senses. I watched the parade of Chet's betrayed loved ones offer jigsaw pieces of their tragedy to the audience, and then, spliced between them and fragments of his gilded past, was the man himself, a toothless old junkie; a faded sociopath. Like his abandoned, inarticulate children with their diluted traces of his beauty on their faces; like his worshipping mother and like every discarded lover and friend I too found myself utterly charmed by him, despite the dull, glazed eyes and gummy, withered speech. He was Apollo. He was a favourite of the gods and he'd become their sport. I was his willing servant.

7

Leah

I woke up on my penultimate morning in Paris to find my little *chambre de bonne* flooded with soft bluish light, the shadow of the Juliet balcony rendered in blurred curlicues across the pale sloping parquet, and a sliver of rainbow cutting a slice out of the peeling wallpaper above my bed. The windows were flung open and I'd been bitten to death in the night. After the relentless weeks of dirty rain, summer was reasserting its grip on the city. The streets in neighbourhoods like mine were slowly beginning to empty with the annual bourgeois exodus. Only the immigrants who couldn't afford to leave stayed past the first week of August, and on the bend of my road, vast cages of scaffolding had appeared overnight as part of the annual effort to retouch the magnificent, ageing face of the *quartier*. I'd noticed that serendipitously, the *boulangerie* on the corner closed for the summer the day after I was due to leave, and as soon as I heard the clatter of its grille from the street, I slipped on a pair of espadrilles and sloped downstairs. The Polish builders greeted me in their heavily accented French:

'*Miss! T'es pas encore partie?*'

'*Non,*' I replied cheerily. '*Demain.*'

Despite the vague stab of treacherousness, in truth I was more than a little relieved to be joining the ranks of the local bourgeoisie. Paris in August had only ever been for me an agoraphobic wasteland of self-analysis and insomnia. The blank canvas of the empty city and the oppressive white heat buttressed the excruciating hours, portioned out in a slow drip. Too much space to think in and yet at the same time all thoughts hemmed in by the Haussmannian echo chamber of the city's very planning. Paris in August made me small-minded and jealous. Social media became an unbearable catalogue of my own lack of achievement. Why wasn't I cycling around Tuscany with my sensitive yet practical long-term boyfriend, or writing sickening odes to Mexican avocados, eaten for breakfast with a photogenic local child? Since beginning university I had spent each summer in the sticky heat of either London or Paris; perpetually drunk, inevitably waitressing and invariably entangled in a moribund, ill-advised almost-relationship.

In the weeks leading up to my departure I'd been uncharacteristically organised. I'd managed to find a sub-letter for my flat, a frighteningly earnest American. She'd let out a veritable squeal of delight when I'd opened the door to her a fortnight before.

'Taylor?' I'd asked, rather stunned.

'Oh. My. *God!*' She'd clasped her beautifully manicured hands together in glee. 'It's like the freaking *Aristocats* in here!'

I'd grinned manically, attempting to match her zeal, and awkwardly shifted my weight between my feet as she surveyed the room in rapture. I'd offered her a glass of wine.

'Oh, no thanks.' She'd smiled brightly. 'I'm on a cleanse!'

'Ah,' I'd said, feigning comprehension.

'I was working on an organic farm in Italy and I just ate so much mozzarella, and it was, like, amazing because I was really embracing the culture – like, my great-great-grandmother was from Sicily, and I swear to God I could just totally *feel* it in my blood – you can probably see it actually, right? Everyone says I look really Italian around my eyes!'

I nodded and hummed a few consonants of agreement.

'So anyway, I was eating all this cheese, which is kinda weird for me because I'm actually almost a vegan normally, but you know, when in Rome, hey? Ahaha, *literally* in Rome! Well, I mean, not *literally* because I wasn't actually *in* Rome . . .'

She pushed a sheaf of sandy hair behind her ears and carried on whilst I discreetly drained my glass.

Yes, my overall feeling had been one of relief. I thought back to Michael's description of the house, of *the horrible* bobo *English family trailing guests and children and drunk friends*. This was the summer I'd been dreaming of since adolescence. Summers at home had been ones of binge drinking in the Tesco car park or in a farmer's field; of boys with questionable haircuts strumming 'Wonderwall'; of sweet, synthetic, fluorescent ice lollies eaten in the bus shelter to avoid the rain, and of *anticipation*: anticipation for the moment when life would begin.

*

'It's actually really funny that you should say that, because my life's going down the drain too, HA-HA-HA.'

It was just after midnight and everyone in the small, smoke-filled apartment was either elastic-limbed drunk or coked up to the eyeballs. I'd found myself cornered when trying to refill my plastic cup with eye-watering ti' punch. She was moonfaced, unmistakably English, and was telling me (unblinking, and jaw fixed into a neurotic smile) everything about her life.

'It's just *absurd*!' she bellowed, 'I keep thinking to myself, I have a first from Edinburgh and I've spent the last two years mixing caipirinhas for graphic designers! HA-HA-HA.'

I scanned the room for support and managed to find no one I knew. Those of us that were left in the city had spent the evening liquid-picnicking on the Canal de l'Ourcq and had inexplicably ended up at the *pendaison de crémaillère* of a total stranger near the Buttes-Chaumont. Rhian (or was it Bethan? Or Megan? She'd definitely had a Welsh name, but had pronounced it in an emphatically English way) sucked determinedly on her cigarette and reached for my hand.

'Hey, do you know anywhere I could pick up some coke?' she asked, inhaling furiously. Hoping to use this as a means to get rid of her, I started to make a big deal of finding the number of Papa, a man I'd once picked up from who now sent me weekly messages advertising his *nouvos promos*.

Undeterred, Rhian retraced the thread of her monologue. 'Anyway, so I'm thinking of maybe doing a master's here, 'cause it's free . . . in, like, *communications* or something . . .'

It was then that I noticed that I was being studied from the other end of the room. He was tall and wiry, with hollow cheeks and slender, muscled arms that were all sinews. He was attractive in an exhausted kind of way. I took advantage of my new friend taking a breath to excuse myself. 'Oh, Bethan, one sec, I've just seen my friend over there.'

'*Hey*, no worries at *all*!' she sang through gritted teeth. 'I'll see you in a bit!'

I prayed otherwise and, running a hand through my hair in the way my sister had taught me aged fifteen ('so you don't look like the girl from *The Ring*'), approached him.

'*On se connaît déjà?*'

'Hi.'

'You're *English*?' I asked, slightly incredulously.

'Should I not be?' He half laughed.

'Well you just have a very direct gaze. It's very . . . Gallic,' I said.

He shrugged. 'There is quite a strong English presence here tonight, isn't there?'

'I think one of the flatmates is from Manchester or something.'

'Oh yeah! That guy – I just saw him coming out of the bathroom in a dress, like, *ay oop, Ah spilt beer all o'er me shirt!*'

I cringed: southerners trying to do northern accents always sounded like Joseph from *Wuthering Heights*. I asked him again if we already knew each other, in English this time.

'Not that I can think of,' he said, scanning my features again impassively, and then, with a smile, 'I guess I was just feeling moved to Gallic behaviour by our surroundings.'

I looked around the room and laughed. It felt as if I'd slipped down a torn channel through layers of time, right back into a house party at university. The Parisians there stood out as if illuminated, mostly by their enduring ability to stay upright. Other than that, the room was packed with foreigners: a pair of floppy-haired boys in rugby shirts; undoubtedly English girls with their telltale theatrical make-up and high-waisted jeans, or the braver ones with weird and wonderful but ultimately disfiguring sartorial choices (art students). Next to them, an eastern European in patterned tights with hair dyed plum red; then Americans, bright-eyed, brazen Americans, glowing with exhausting good health.

I decided to chance it. 'Fancy . . . well, leaving?'

He smirked. 'I see the spirit of *la française* moves you too.'

His accent was so bad that he was undoubtedly just here on holiday.

'Let me show you a bit of Paris,' I said, motioning to the door.

Outside, the thick heat of the day had lifted, leaving a

night that was clean and chill. The streets of the 19th were empty. I walked us (swaying a little with the fuzz of the booze) to where I'd locked up my bike at the edge of the park. In the fresh air I realised that I was definitely quite drunk.

'What's your name anyway?' I asked, fumbling inelegantly with the D-lock.

'Lal,' he said, taking the keys from my hands. Nicknames that sounded as if they were invented by a five-year-old: definitely posh. We started to walk down the hill towards the Mairie du 19e and the still black water of the canal.

'One sec.' He sat for a moment on the grand steps of the town hall and withdrew a bottle of whisky from the inside pocket of his jacket. 'Drink?'

I half collapsed next to him.

'You didn't have any friends left in there?'

'I did, somewhere,' I said absent-mindedly, failing to add that I was somewhat prone to abandoning my friends when the opportunity of an attractive man presented itself. 'What about you?'

'Just that guy from Manchester. Except he's actually from Leeds. He's my best mate's little brother.'

'Oh,' I said, wiping my mouth with the back of my hand as the whisky burnt down my throat, 'I see.' I swallowed again, 'So you came to Paris for your mate's brother's house-warming?'

Taking a swig himself, he scoffed, 'Obviously not,' and then, with an air of smug, contrived mysteriousness, 'I'm on my way somewhere.'

I rolled my eyes and, ignoring the bait, pulled him up to standing. 'And so are we!' I half sang. '*Viens, vite!*'

We walked back to where I'd begun – the Canal de l'Ourcq, which even at this time was still crowded with sprawling groups, spiralling out in circles from picnic blankets resplendent with endless bottles of wine and hashed-together banquets of cheese, charcuterie, pots of hummus and tabbouleh. It was my favourite place to be on summer evenings. On the sandy strip alongside the quay, *pétanque* players lounged around in a perpetual state of sun-drunk pleasure that lasted well into the night. The air was full of the music of a grizzled troupe of antifa hippies: a violin-ist, a guitarist, and of course the ubiquitous bongos. We watched, grinning, as one of their number attempted to drag innocent female passers-by into sloppy but elated waltzes. '*Mam'zelle!*' he'd cry, rollie hanging limply from his mouth. '*Vous voulez danser?*'

I ended up dragging Lal in, much to his chagrin, and made him dance to a couple of Georges Brassens numbers.

'*Mais qu'est-ce que vous êtes beaux, les jeunes!*' one of the old hippies cried, prompting Lal to spin me round with delight.

Above everything rang the constant refrain of the men selling multipack Heineken from supermarket bags filled with ice. '*Bières fraîches! Bières fraîches! Deux euros, la bière fraîche!*' Clumsily Lal attempted to buy one. He was drunk too now, I noted, relieved that he'd caught up. Open-ing his beer, he pulled me out of the melee to the edge of the concrete embankment. We sat dangling our legs over the water, black but rippled with golden light.

Later, from the canal we careered west towards the steel ribcage of railway bridges that zigzag up from Gare du Nord. Lal had become loud and animated despite his initial attempts to seem cool and aloof.

'I actually quite like Paris!' he declared. 'I never gave it the time of day. I always thought it was all naff accordions and plastic padlocks, but *this*,' he gestured around at the sweaty, garish kebab shops and greasy *tabacs*, 'this is kind of cool!'

As we came onto the bridge, the air seemed to still with relative calm. We walked out to the midpoint, where you're suspended so high that your head reels with vertiginous delight. The dark blue bruise of night was patchily blanching out into pale dawn, flecked with lilac. The metal bones of the bridges, the wire fences and the ropy electrical cables were embossed on the luminous horizon like the black pen strokes of a Japanese engraving. Beneath us, the sweep of miles and miles of wasteland: barbed wire, railway tracks, nodding heads of buddleia jostling between abandoned freight carriages. This was liminal space, the landscape of transit, where you felt as if you were only precariously tethered to the real world. In the distance, the grey tower blocks loomed. The two of us leant against the gridded wire.

'So much space.' Lal whistled. 'I didn't think you got space in Paris. In London and in Berlin everything's all space.'

I agreed. 'It's true – car parks and petrol stations and streets with just houses, gardens . . .'

Our voices sounded hollow and loud, and both of us fell automatically into respectful silence. Then, from underneath us, the chugging rumble of a train.

Lal was half smiling at me. 'You're very beautiful,' he sighed drunkenly, fiddling with the cuffs of his scraggy jumper.

I closed my eyes, expecting him to kiss me, but after a moment, more than a little embarrassed when in fact he hadn't, I opened them to find him looking back down at the railway tracks.

'I can't believe you didn't kiss me!' I cried, outraged. 'I literally just offered you my face!'

He laughed and mumbled something incomprehensible. When at last the rumble of the train had dwindled into nothing, he asked me, bluntly, 'Do you live near here? Can I stay at yours?'

Slightly perplexed, I said he could, but that I *certainly wouldn't* be sleeping with him after such a humiliation.

He let out an exasperated sigh. 'You're *such* a drunk girl.'

We headed home, down the little back streets through Château Rouge. I watched him register the groups of bored prostitutes; teenage girls in platforms and leggings, giggling with each other or scrolling vacantly on their smartphones. The older ones leant on the railings of the Métro, eyes glazed, waiting for 7 a.m. Their pimp lingered in a doorway, lazily smoking a joint. We crossed the boulevard and the neighbourhood perceptibly shifted. Phone shops and bazaars gave way to delicatessens, Italian restaurants and pottery ateliers.

'It looks like Hollywood Paris again now,' Lal said, pulling himself up onto steps that climbed the hill to Montmartre and the Sacré-Coeur. Montmartre: spindly belle époque lamp posts, cobbled streets that once belonged to farmyards – the constant gentle nostalgic hum of the past. 'I mean, look at this, it's like the bloody *Aristocats*.'

An image of Taylor flickered through my mind. 'Don't be such a cynical dick!' I snorted. 'It's gorgeous.'

'Admittedly these steps are pretty cool,' he conceded. He took my bike from me and hung it precariously by the frame on his shoulder. 'I'll take your *vay-lo*, let's climb the stairs!'

He cleared a few steps at once with his long, jaunty stride, clumsily swung around another lamp post and almost smacked into the railings, swiftly abandoning my bicycle. At the top of the stairs, he started to drunkenly wail the opening lines of 'Tonight', of *West Side Story* fame.

'Oh God . . . *Lal*!' I hissed. Bourgeois Parisians didn't take kindly to nocturnal serenading, or any kind of aural disturbance for that matter. He carried on regardless, blowing me a camp pantomime kiss between phrases. Admittedly, his voice wasn't half bad. He'd probably been in the choir at whatever posh Home Counties school he had gone to. It had probably had a *theatre department*.

'Of *course* the boy who wants "gritty Paris" is au fait with musical theatre scores.' I didn't want to let on that I was secretly delighted by his performance.

He ignored me, leaping about in would-be-balletic imitation of one of the Jets (and coming across more as an enthusiastic Monty Python impersonator). He sang the praises of fate, destiny, the stars, my face . . .

'*Lal!*'

His impressive, if slurred, tenor reverberated through the night and he careered back down the steps to grab my hand. I shrieked. The lamplight reflected in his eyes, making them shine like an ecstatic televangelist with a Messiah complex and a drinking problem. He pulled me close to him and spun me away. I narrowly avoided toppling to the ground. 'You should be singing a French song anyway,' I huffed, faux-stroppy, and then slightly alarmed – watched in faint horror as he started to scale the iron railings.

'MARIA!' he bellowed.

Above us, the sound of a window being flung open burst through his big finish.

'*MAIS TU VAS ARRÊTER TON BORDEL LÀ! FILS DE PUTE!*' an elderly woman roared, before hurling a full bucket of water from her fifth-floor window. Squealing, I leapt out of its flight path. Lal, a crazed musical martyr, stood with arms outstretched as if crucified, and was subsequently drenched.

'*Ouais, ferme-la connard, 'ricain!*' the old woman cackled, slamming her window shut.

The two of us stood in shocked, soggy silence for a second, before I began to howl with laughter.

'*Fuck*,' Lal hissed. '*Fuck*,' again through gritted teeth. '*Fuck* that fucking *bitch*, it's *cold*!'

I tried to make my way towards him but couldn't move. He clambered down off the railings and landed in a sorry heap. '*Fucking. Old. Bitch!*' His hair was plastered flat to his face. My wheezing had subsided into a barely suppressed giggle now. 'What did she call me?' he demanded.

'Son of a bitch, idiot, American . . .'

Shaking out his hair, he flounced towards my abandoned bike.

'I was smoking outside a bar once with my friends at four a.m. and one of the crazies who lived above threw a bowl of fish entrails onto the pavement,' I told him.

'You're so dry!' he mewed.

The world was spinning somewhat. 'I'm so *drunk*,' I moaned.

Reaching down to me, he offered his cold, damp hand.

*

I woke up the next morning (merciless sun streaming through the open window and the heat of the day already starting to press down like a paperweight) to find myself curled into Lal's shirtless body. My brain started to creakily churn into action like one of those old-fashioned coin-counting machines. Did I know this man? Check. Was I at home? Check. Was it a positive thing that I was wearing nothing but a pair of skimpy black knickers? Check.

Disentangling myself from him, I rolled lazily out of bed. My reflection was satisfying, I noted, relieved that I had been wearing decent underwear. I staggered over to the kettle, trying to piece together details of what in fact must only have been a few hours before. Had I slept with him? A flash vision of the two of us limping through my front door and me announcing in the voice of an alcoholic school prefect that I would most certainly *not* be sleeping with him after 'that veritable humiliation' before promptly undressing in front of him and semi passing out on the bed.

The kettle boiled. I glanced down at him, feeling for where my body had just been. I remembered the tender moment when, dreaming, he'd reached out and cupped my chin in his hand before pulling me into him with the other and adoringly stroking my thigh. I wondered who he'd been dreaming about.

Tea made, I went and sat cross-legged on the floor by the window. I was due at Gare de Lyon later that afternoon to catch my train to Marseille. There was a text from Anna on my phone – *Jenny will pick you up from the station this evening, darling, pastis awaits!* – and one from Emma: *Are you alive?*

Lal finally lurched back into life as I got out of the shower.

'Oh,' I said. 'Good morning.' I tied my wet hair into a knot on the top of my head.

He blinked and I watched the facts of last night slowly start to register across his face.

'Do you want a cup of tea?' I asked, aware that there was nowhere in the room where I could dress without being completely in his line of vision.

'Tea. Yes,' he grumbled. 'Yes please.'

'I leave in about an hour, by the way,' I said, awkwardly.

'Yeah, of course,' he agreed, earnest and polite. 'Yeah,

me too, to be honest. I need to get back to that flat we were at last night to meet my friend.'

'Milk?'

He eyed me suspiciously. 'You've been in France too long.'

I watched the clouds of white unfurl and slowly turn the liquid opaque. 'Where exactly are you going?'

Sitting down next to him on the bed, I consciously untied my wet hair again, hoping that it would fall around my shoulders like some kind of attractive water nymph.

'Italy,' he said. 'Got a friend with a house in Tuscany.' That made sense; he was exactly the kind of person who would have a friend with a house in Tuscany.

'Nice.'

When he refused my valiant attempt at eye contact, I joined him in staring at the flakes of wallpaper peeling like dead skin around the window.

'So. No more France for you,' I said.

He shrugged, and I got up and stood by the hotplate to put some distance between us. It was time for enforced cheer.

'Well thank you for the spectacular performance, at least.'

He screwed up his face in feigned embarrassment. 'Thank God that old woman hadn't been gutting any *poisson*.'

*

On the Métro to Gare de Lyon, I consoled myself with the fact that, as an Englishman, he would have surely been crap in bed anyway. The misogynist wisdom that I had eagerly swallowed to romanticise my catastrophic love life said that there were two types of girls. There were *girlfriends* – girls

like Emma whom sensitive, insightful men who appreciated conversation and Leonard Bernstein introduced to
their parents. Then there were girls like me who collected,
amongst other dubious swains, drug dealers, ignorant but
noisy political dissidents, sociopaths, stalkers and men who
were into public Japanese bondage. Lal, I told myself, was
far too articulate and sane to want to establish repeated
contact with me.

The station was washed clean with the brilliant light of
the bright white morning, and I felt, as I often did at Gare
de Lyon, that I was already well shot of Paris and coasting
the blue fringes of the Mediterranean. I was for a moment
a spectator in my own life. The crowds milling around me
were blurred smudges of mobile ink on a magic lantern. Pale
blue. White. Hundreds of voices arbitrarily and tentatively
settled in layers in the expanse of space above the platforms.
The familiar notes of the SNCF jingle chimed above the
melee and moved me forward towards the platform. Two
fat pigeons squabbled at the turnstile. I was five hours away
from seagulls.

Two

SAINT-LUC

She might not have been capable of seeing them for what they were, for at that age all people who were not from Northam seemed at first sight equally brilliant, surrounded as they were by a confusing blur of bright, indistinct charm

Margaret Drabble, *Jerusalem the Golden*

8

Michael

'I can already see exactly the sort of thing you're going to write,' I said to the attractive female journalist sitting opposite me. 'All celebrity profiles run along identical templates – especially ones written in hotels.'

Her eyes shimmered with coquettish malice. 'Go on then,' she said. 'If you're so au fait with the formula, profile me.'

I took a sip of the Scotch her paper had paid for, then, given permission by this agreeable little to and fro, replaced the tumbler on the table and openly appraised her.

'*I arrive in the opulent lounge of the iconic Piccadilly establishment to find Joanna Pritchard sitting, legs curled up underneath her and dark hair pulled back into a modest but stylish ponytail. She wears barely a trace of make-up but has that enviable famous-person glow, belied by her simple but elegant choice of a black cashmere polo neck and—*'

'I'm a journalist, not Cindy Crawford,' she scoffed.

'Yes, but you are still a woman, so by default I must discuss your low-key but dazzling appearance and the fact that you miraculously manage to keep your figure despite demolishing a huge club sandwich in my presence.'

She allowed herself an indulgent smirk. 'Well, what am I going to write about you then?'

'Let me see your notes.'

'Oh come *on*.' She folded her arms in faux-stroppy defiance.

'You'll write something about how I look spare and gaunt and how I'm drinking whisky at eleven o'clock in the morning – you all seem to love that *enfant terrible*, rock 'n' roll writer tripe: the prose of Martin Amis, the habits of Michael Hutchence.'

She raised her eyebrows. 'Considering your recent nuptials, our readership will be assuming that *that* incarnation is in the past.'

'How very middle England of them,' I sneered, fishing for a cigarette in my shirt pocket.

'How is Diana anyway?' she asked, gaze fixed.

'Perpetually in dungarees.'

'The pitter-patter of tiny feet?' She smiled sweetly.

'How do you know my wife again?'

'I don't really; she was at school with my older sister. They wouldn't let me play Swallows and Amazons with them. And if they did, I always had to be bloody Roger.'

Diana knew everyone: boys (and they *were* boys – I felt their age difference keenly in those moments) with baggy crew necks and fake accents who edited aggressively cool magazines; flocks of Sloane Rangers with equine profiles in pastel cardigans of whom she pretended to be ashamed; unbearable theatre types who wore berets without a trace of irony, stand-up comedians unforgivably among their number. I'd felt a swell of relief when the film's location was announced. Six weeks on some godawful rocky crag up in the farthest reaches of Scotland. What a wrench that I had a novel to promote.

'Of course if you were still in touch with her, you'd know she was up in Loch Dreadful prancing around with boys in breeches.'

'Oh, I'm aware of that fact,' said Joanna coolly, not breaking eye contact.

I let the silent weight of suggestion balloon for a moment in the air before ostentatiously leaning back in my armchair. I carried on smoking.

'What are you doing for lunch?'

'I can think of other things I'd rather do than eat.'

I could never work out with this type whether the directness was a practised affectation or sincere, but I'd always been grateful for it regardless. Guilt-free fucks. Complicit equals. Brothers in arms. I considered myself a feminist. It was 1987, for Christ's sake; it was general consensus that women were gagging for it too. I was struck with a fleeting, tender memory of Janice Jarman after the sixth-form dance at the girls' grammar. Burtley Common; the grass already damp with dew at half past ten, my feverish adolescent hands desperately hitching up the pale blue satin of her dress only for her to primly push them away. An erection straining uncomfortably against the shiny polyester of the suit I'd borrowed from my older brother. It had been two years since Larkin's 'Annus Mirabilis', but sex had apparently yet to happen to seventeen-year-old grammar school boys in Yorkshire.

'You remind me of myself,' I said.

'I hope you're as shockingly narcissistic as my colleagues tell me then.'

'What are you doing tonight?'

'Research,' she said. 'I'm profiling a novelist at home.'

'No. Not at my house. I want to go out.'

'Fine,' she conceded. 'Freud, ten o'clock, and then we can see where the night takes us.'

*

As toilet stalls went, this one was at least clean. Everything seemed to be moving at double speed as my head reeled with the cocaine, the muffled thud of the music and her snatched breathing. I pulled her shirt off over her head, pinning her slender white arms above her. Her skin glowed bluish white in the ultraviolet light and I could feel her searching for the buttons of my jeans. Pressing myself against her into the damp wall, we kissed. Her eyes were shining as she pulled away, offering me her naked neck. I felt the warmth of her breath as she gasped with delight in my ear. She was so unbelievably sexy. What could possibly be wrong?

'Oh.' Disappointment flashed momentarily across her features as her hands unbuttoned my jeans, but then, unperturbed, she slipped down onto her knees. I closed my eyes and leant back, and melted in the heat of her mouth – *melted* rather excruciatingly being the operative word. Eventually she gave up and, smiling sheepishly, stood and began to kiss me again, moaning softly in what I imagine was supposed to be encouragement. I tried to do it to myself. She took my free hand and pressed the fingers onto the lace edge of her exposed underwear.

At last I cleared my throat. 'Well,' I said, 'this is embarrassing.'

She sighed. Her jaw was clenched and her eyes, lilac and smudged with black kohl, were like saucers. 'You were so hard when we were dancing out there.'

'It's really nothing to do with you.'

'Oh, I know that.'

We stood in silence for a second. She looked determinedly at the floor. Outside the cubicle were shrieks, howls: 'When he wears his hair like that he looks like Tracey Thorn, but with none of her fucking talent!'

'This really doesn't happen to me, you know,' I insisted.

'Oh darling, it happens to the best of us sometimes.'

Joanna's smile was indulgent, almost maternal. She

smoothed down her skirt and ineffectively wiped some of the black from under her eyes.

'Well then,' she said. 'Shall we go back out?'

*

Sunset had turned the water pearlescent and grey, like a gleaming oyster. Grey water, flecked with peels of fading light right up to where it merged with the gauzy lilac and orange of the horizon. I stared out into the dark expanse of sea. I'd walked far enough down the beach so as to no longer be able to hear the noise from the house. Now only the percussive thrum of the cicadas.

Since everyone else had arrived I'd taken to coming here with my notebook under the pretence of working, but my head, of course, was a vacuum.

'Oh Michael, don't be so bloody antisocial. Tom's making spritz, stay for a drink.'

'No, Jenny, leave him!' Anna, in the voice of a benign serpent. 'He's *working*.'

That castrating intonation and suggestion of conspiratorial glee: her long-stunted, stoppered husband was *working* again. I dug my toes deeper into the cool sand. Over the course of an hour I'd managed to write one thing: *1970*, the four spindly figures only rendering the otherwise empty page all the more blank. The second week of March 1970 was the last time I'd seen her. I was horrifyingly close to my seventieth birthday and yet over the last few months, since I'd met Leah, I'd felt like time had been contracting; the decades were all squeezing up against each other like the bellows of an accordion, so that I could almost touch what was on the other side. I swallowed a mouthful of pastis and closed my eyes.

The seventies had been one orgiastic blur of excess. By the end of them, though, I'd started really writing, and after *Richard, Falling* had been such an astronomical success I'd found some sort of stability for a while. There were still a lot of parties, but these were different. This was networking. This was a new breed of hedonism: thrusting, ambitious, goal-oriented. After Lawrence was born, the adroit duplicity with which I coordinated my multiple lives had been thrilling. For those first few years, I'd kept up the appearance of being the model father; I'd churned out (with comparative ease) the two novels now considered to be my most mature, and I'd managed to maintain some sort of life of clandestine freedom beyond the sphere of my wife's consciousness. When it had all fallen apart I'd found myself resigned to it. How else could it have possibly turned out? I'd had a good run, and frankly, I wasn't unhappy when Diana had asked me to leave.

How to explain that first marriage? It was never that I'd not *loved* Diana per se. She was irresistible. She was witty and beautiful and sharp. I'd grown up around a thousand Janice Jarmans; girls who talked about coupons and watched variety shows and thought Marks & Spencer was aspirational; girls who giggled before they were married and grimaced afterwards. At Oxford I'd discovered an entirely new species of female. They listened to Françoise Hardy (and understood the lyrics). They wanted to stay up until four in the morning smoking joints and talking about Artaud.

By the time I'd met Diana, fresh out of drama school and understudying in an adaptation of *Richard*, I was au fait with the type. I was one of them. I'd learnt how to not hold my knife like a pencil, and that tea was a snack taken at half past four and involving, well, *tea*. Later, I'd learnt to unlearn all of this carefully gleaned knowledge and to wear the polite trace of Yorkshire in my accent like a badge, indicative of credibility. My life had been one spent skirting along the fringes of a society of which I was almost a part. To my family I'd been an alien – a haughty, shimmering figment of another world. My distance had allowed me to study them with reciprocal interest, and in Oxford, in London, at every stage of my life, I'd felt an avid spectator of this perpetually shifting play; the cast rotating across the stage, some illuminated with the sudden consuming clarity of the beam of a footlight, others paling meekly into type. It was appropriate, I said to myself at the time, to marry an actress.

The soft patter of footfall, the slap of a sandal against the sand, beating over the hum of the cicadas. Jenny was coming towards me down the silver slope of the beach.

9

'Look, I thought I'd bring you to meet her first, as you're the most generous,' I said to Jenny as we turned on to Wardour Street. 'I want you to vet her before tomorrow night.'

'*Vet* her?' said Jenny, faintly exasperated. 'What, and if I don't approve, you'll leave the poor girl jilted?'

'Oh come on, Jen, don't act like it's not important.'

'I'm here for one reason only. You promised me carbonara, and if I have to sit through one more flaccid steak and kidney pie in the staff canteen, I'll expire. This is a health visit. I'm taking the cure.' She glared at me. 'Plus I want a glimpse of your latest conquest.'

'*Almost* conquest.'

I had met Jenny in my first week at university and had subsequently viewed her from a distance. She was studying modern languages, and was apparently already adept in both French and Italian. I'd heard vague rumblings that her mother had been a wartime refugee from somewhere on the Continent, and other than that had managed to ascertain that her parents were intellectuals, and possibly socialists. She floated around college in fisherman's smocks, black cigarette pants and amber jewellery. I had first plucked up the nerve to go and talk to her properly in the pub at the end of Michaelmas term.

'Jenny, isn't it?' I placed my pint emphatically on the bar.

'It is.' She carried on staring at the bottles of spirits stacked above the flecked mirror.

'We did actually meet,' I ploughed on bravely, 'at Hal Pickford's party at the beginning of term.'

'Yes,' she said. 'You were the one who wrote that nasty little review of Tony Dyer's gig at the JCR, weren't you?'

I flinched. 'You know Tony?'

'Uh huh.'

'I don't think I was entirely critical of him.'

'Hmm,' she said vacantly, 'though you did call him "a parsimonious little toad singing twee three-chord songs about right-on marigolds".' Her chin was propped on the heel of her fist. 'He was most offended by the part about being Tunbridge Wells's finest protest singer.'

I gave a weak mew of protest. 'I did say that the fairer sex tended to fall at his feet.'

'Yes – and somehow made it just seem offensive to the fairer sex.'

Unperturbed, I had pulled up the vacant stool and carried on talking at her until at last she gave in and let herself be charmed. She didn't give much of a damn about Tony, she'd told me later; it was more that she had an innate mistrust of anyone who could 'fling words about like that'. I'd got used to girls like Jenny delighting in acerbic conversation, and what had surprised me the most about her character was that its defining feature seemed to be kindness. By the Christmas vac, she had become my first friend who was a girl. When she'd gone to study in Bologna in her third year, I'd felt her absence keenly. Then, at the end of that year, she had done something so absurdly self-assured (so was the way that Jenny negotiated life) that I, with my dull and conventional upbringing, couldn't believe it. She decided to 'put studying on hold for a while' in favour of 'living a bit'. Apparently, people like Jenny could do that. She'd moved back to London at the end of September and had been working in some dull, clerical position at the BBC.

Vast swathes of our conversation had since been taken up with her complaining about anaemic mashed potato. As I'd wanted to introduce her to Astrid on the latter's turf, the situation hadn't even required the laziest of engineering.

'So she *works* here?' We were approaching the bottle-green awning of Giorgio's. It was a cold, bright day and the little tables on the pavement were jostling with life.

'Yes.'

To Jenny the idea that anyone could have a job as pedestrian as waitressing was absolutely foreign. I pushed the fogged-up door.

'But she's also a model? No . . . A singer? An actress?'

'Something like that,' I muttered, pulling out a speckled putty-coloured chair for her before slotting into one myself. I was all at once on edge. Jenny, unlike me, wasn't used to moderating her voice, and her RP drawl seemed to fill the room. I felt that her company (which had always qualified me as a guaranteed insider) was revealing an aspect of my character I'd yet to expose here.

'What's wrong?' she asked, frowning at me.

'Nothing.'

'Yes there is. You're doing that thing where you sink into your coat collar. I can't even see your chin.'

'I'm doing nothing of the sort.'

'You're nervous! You're actually nervous, aren't you? You really fancy this Swedish siren—'

'Again, she's really not Swedish.'

'*Model*. I can just picture her—'

'*Jenny*.' I'd just caught sight of Astrid weaving through the tables, smiling with genuine warmth at the regular customers. Her cheeks were flushed with the cold. She was wearing the pale blue coat with the fur collar, and strands of her dark hair were escaping from a matching pillbox hat. She caught my eye and gave a small, staccato wave. I saw Jenny return it and was once again swamped with relief that I'd brought her here first. The others would be more of a challenge. I stood up to pull out a chair for Astrid and felt confident now that Jenny would be kind to her. I gripped her by her shoulders and took in the details of her face. Being with her sometimes was like being with an exothermic substance. Happiness came to her with such apparent ease.

*

Jenny gave Astrid the go-ahead (and snarled at me later when I used that expression) and so, quite casually when we'd deposited the former at Portland Place, I turned to the latter and invited her to Julian's party the next evening. She made no attempt to hide her patent glee.

'Yeah, it's nothing huge,' I said. 'Just a small gathering, a few friends; we've got some mates in a band who might play . . .' Seeing her expression stirred the kind of enthusiasm in me that I normally took great pains to hide. 'And Julian's flat is incredible. His mother's a member of the minor aristocracy – her grandmother was an illegitimate child of Edward VII and a great Bloomsbury hostess or something like that. Christ knows—'

She cut me short, reaching up to kiss me, beaming at me in vague disbelief.

'Everything's going so well,' she said. 'Look, it's even sunny. It's like the world doesn't realise that it's November.'

In the pale blue light of the afternoon we walked up to Regent's Park, wandering around hand in hand until the watery autumn sun blanched out into dusk. We got a pint in a pub in St John's Wood and slipped incognito into a cinema to not watch a film. We stayed for the second showing, and later I walked back to Charlotte Street on a cloud and fell asleep imagining Astrid naked.

*

We met the following evening at the entrance to the Royal Court; Julian's flat was just off the King's Road.

It wasn't Julian who answered the door of the flat, but one of his many female satellites. Her face was familiar and I had a horrible feeling she was a friend of Kathy's, confirmed by the loud pantomime sigh she exhaled upon registering my presence, and the daggers that she shot both myself and Astrid immediately afterwards.

'Michael,' she sneered. 'It's been a while.'

'Sarah—'

'*Sara.*'

I grimaced.

She smiled deceitfully at Astrid and offered a hand.

'Astrid.'

'*Sara*,' I said loudly. 'Well, this is nice, isn't it. Julian about?'

No sooner had the words left my mouth than Julian appeared in the hallway. 'Micky!' he cried jovially, coming up behind Sarah-that-was-Sara and slinking an arm around her waist. She wriggled free under the pretence of getting a drink despite already having a beer in her hand. Julian beckoned the two of us in. I watched him give Astrid the once-over. 'He*llo* there,' he drawled, taking her in. '*Pleasure.*'

I tried to see Julian as Astrid must have seen him. Jenny had once described him as slippery but infuriatingly charming. He was tall and pale with a striking square face and the more recent addition of shoulder-length jet hair and a moustache bordering dangerously on Kitchener territory. When I'd first known him, his style had hung somewhere between English eccentric and Beat poet. Since spending the summer in San Francisco, however, he'd acquired a startling number of paisley shirts and skin-tight bell-bottoms. Jenny was convinced that he'd started stuffing his crotch.

'Welcome to *mi casa*,' he purred, leading us into the kitchen to 'fix us up'. He had covered all the lampshades in chiffon scarves and had half-inched a few red light bulbs from somewhere in an attempt to create some sort of mood. He barely needed to. The huge drawing room was an Aladdin's cave of tatty Persian rugs, rich brocade and ridiculous velvet – from the sweeping indigo curtains to the bright crimson pouffes.

'Welcome to Kubla Khan's opium den!' he had crowed when first showing Jenny and me the flat.

'It looks like the changing room at Biba, darling.' Jenny had raised her eyebrows at me, brushing away the fronds of peacock feather from her shirt.

'Let's just hope as many girls will be taking their clothes off here then!' Julian had leered, winking at me.

The kitchen had been decorated by his mother and was brimming: trinkets from the family house in Greece; expensive full-colour recipe books; impressively modern and intimidating gadgets, most of which were gathering dust or being used for totally alien purposes. The kitchen table served as a well-stocked bar. Julian reached for a pair of crystal tumblers, stubbing out his cigarette into the bowl of a pestle and mortar.

'So,' he drawled, measuring out gin. 'Astrid, Astrid, As*trid*. Stockholm?'

'Bow.' Her voice was flat.

Julian cackled and handed us both our drinks. 'And what is it that you do in *Bow*? You must be a model.'

From this entirely new perspective I was starting to understand Jenny's opinions on our friend a little better.

'You're not a secretary, are you?'

'I'm a waitress,' she said.

'And a singer,' I added. 'She just got a regular gig at a club on Denmark Street.'

'Ah. A *chanteuse*. Yes, even the timbre of your speaking voice is . . . *sultry*.'

I watched Astrid half choke on her gin and tonic. Jenny, who was clearly already quite drunk, shimmied into the kitchen. 'Jules, my glass is empty!'

He filled her glass with neat gin, eyes still on Astrid. Jenny went between the two of us, bestowing extravagant kisses, and, having topped up and cadged a cig, was adamant that Astrid *must* come with her at once to meet *absolutely everyone*. 'Come on,' she said in the voice of a stern Girl Guide. 'Swallow that drink and get another whilst you're here. Everyone's dying to meet you.'

Astrid smiled nervously and let herself be led off, squeezing my hand as she left.

'I'll be there in a sec,' I told her.

'No you will *not*.' Julian lit another cigarette, offering me one as he did so. 'This is the hot little waitress from the Italian greasy spoon?'

I nodded. He whistled. 'Crikey. *Bellissima!*' He took a decadent drag of his L&M. 'Does she speak?'

'As much as she needs to,' I said. I felt a slight pang of dissent, but when I was with Julian I couldn't help myself.

'Aha!' he laughed. 'So you've done the deed?'

I shrugged, but with enough of a sly smile to let him know that I most certainly had. I hadn't, of course.

'Phwoar,' he said. 'Well feel free to invite any of her

colleagues. They can come in their pinnies if they've just finished work.'

'Colleagues are all dogs,' I said. 'Facial hair to rival yours, mate.'

He snorted. 'You mock me, but these bugger's grips got me all the birds in California. I am telling you, I cannot *wait* to get back out to the States. Accent like this and you're fucking Casanova.' Julian was studying at the LSE and was in the process of securing PhD funding at Stanford for the following autumn. 'And the chicks are all just gagging for it. Free love,' he sighed. 'The American Dream.' He detached himself from the worktop he'd been leaning on and motioned for us to move. In the doorway he slapped me on the back and, fleetingly slipping back into the Etonian accent he'd put so much effort into shaking, said, 'You'd better watch that one, though, old boy. One slip-up and you'll be spending every Sunday with the in-laws eating fish fingers in Whitechapel.'

Smarting, I followed him into the hallway.

*

When I'd first got into Oxford, my mother had acted much as she'd done when I'd passed my 11-plus. She clasped her pale, thin hands together and dusted them down on the bleeding and faded rose print that in another lifetime had made the valiant attempt to decorate her apron. Then she'd pursed her lips unnaturally – as if finding the correct facial expression was a real struggle – and said, 'Well. You always have been very smart, haven't you?'

I noticed as she'd gone about the automatic motions of boiling water for a pot of tea that her hands were trembling slightly. 'Go and fetch me your dad's baccy, will you?'

Feeling a slow trickle of mildly nauseating guilt that I couldn't quite understand, I shuffled over to the dresser and rifled through his drawer. Mum was sneerily disapproving about Dad's smoking – even more so that he rolled his own cigarettes. There was something vaguely repulsive about watching her smoke, and I was glad that she did it rarely. When women like Lauren Bacall smoked in films, the fine feather of tobacco (floating, gauzy) and the languorous way they held their cigarettes made them look how I'd imagined jazz singers or people who knew what *existentialism* meant would smoke in places like New York and Paris. My mother sucked the limp, yellowing stick (flaccid somehow, like a tapeworm) right into herself. A flash of the old crone in 'Snow White', which wasn't entirely fair, as I suppose Mum must have been quite pretty once, before her personality had got the better of her face. Her stingy exhalations weren't at all ephemeral and hazy. They hung about her in a cloying, jaundiced fuzz. I passed her the ashtray.

'Well, your brother will still be here, at least. It's lucky they give you grants, I suppose, to go to places like Oxford.'

There it was again – the slightest, inexplicable pang of treason, the sense that I was doing something wrong. She stubbed out her cigarette – ineffectively, so that it continued to smoulder.

'You know they let Indians and all sorts go there now, don't you?' She held my gaze with a sort of defiant delight, as if the comment had been a challenge, and I remembered quite clearly how at that moment I'd looked around at the prim little kitchen and felt the same sort of dizzying, vertiginous joy that you get from swimming far out to sea on days when the tide is as rough and jagged as barbed wire.

'I had heard, yes.'

10

Leah

By the time I arrived at the little station, the sun had set and the platform was brushed the iridescent blue of the dusk. I felt as if I'd been travelling for days. Over the course of the afternoon (and the slow evolution of my hangover), I'd watched the fluctuating landscape of France unfold like a film reel: kilometres of flat green and brownish farmland; elegant, slender poplars and church spires; golden stretches of wheat reaching up to the lavender line of the horizon. Sunflower fields. Then, mountains – craggy, sweeping, majestic – and after them a new country: terracotta roofs and bistre walls; dense green olive groves; snaking, dusty roads; geraniums; flat discs of water along the coast and the dainty pink silhouettes of flamingos.

Marseille at the tail end of the afternoon had been a plunge – a shock – exhilarating. The steps at Saint-Charles, where I'd sat to smoke a cigarette between trains, were crawling with people, and beneath them the sweep of the city was unimaginably vast, antique. The voices over the *tannoi* felt incantatory. *Montpelier Saint-Roch, Perpignan, Sète, Barcelone, Genève.* I was a speck of dust. The train from there had been a rickety old local one, full of families and teenagers going back to various satellite towns and villages, and, at this time of year, expatriated clusters of golden Parisians in linen and espadrilles. I'd dozed for a while, and when I'd woken up, the sun was setting into the orange horizon. The train was almost empty.

There were two platforms and both were deserted, so I made my way out of the station and into the car park. The air was thick with the rattle of cicadas. I checked my phone. Another text from Emma, and after it one from an unknown English number with the telltale typos and bad punctuation of an older person, reminiscent of my father's Facebook posts. *Hi leah. anna gave me your number and I am on the way to meet you at the station Jenny.* How the eloquent, articulate and largely literate middle-aged managed to totally lose the ability to write when doing so on a smartphone never ceased to amaze me.

I sat on my suitcase and waited. The car park was empty and only half lit by one lone street light. It was incredible how quickly I'd got used to the constant fullness of the city, despite spending all of my formative years in the sticks. I gazed up at the thousands of stars (the same ones, I suppose, that I'd gazed at every night of my childhood) and shivered involuntarily. For a few minutes there was nothing but the roar of the insects and the whisper of the pines in the breeze, and then, all at once, the spluttering explosion of an engine and a pair of beaming headlights tearing into the night.

Jenny (unnecessarily; I could hardly have missed her) honked the horn, then rolled down the window of the battered old blue Citroën and stuck her head out. '*Coucou!*' Her French accent was convincing.

Waving with reciprocal enthusiasm, I picked up my case. She leant across the seat and pushed open the passenger door, and I clambered inelegantly into the car. On the crackly old tape player she was playing Thelonious Monk.

She turned to look at me. 'Good God, you look just like—' She swallowed, and, regaining composure, said with forced cheer, 'An old friend of mine.' She laughed a little. 'Christ. I feel like I've seen a ghost! Sorry.' She clasped my hand now, warmly. 'Old age, eh? Jenny. Nice to meet you at last.'

'Leah,' I said, smiling. She exuded kindness. I felt immediately and inexplicably at ease in her presence.

Jenny was quite beautiful, with thick straight hair in a messy grey chignon at the nape of her neck. She had a handsome, striking face and was dressed in a tatty old crew-neck sweatshirt, set off with a string of amber beads and trailing silver earrings. Her hands, gripping the steering wheel, were large and elegant – useful hands.

'So how was your journey?' She made the question feel sincere and not remotely like arbitrary small talk.

'Oh, it was good,' I said. 'I always love train journeys anyway. I like watching the country warp and transform. It's so . . . meditative . . . *indulgent* . . .' I caught myself, worried that I sounded pretentious, but saw that she was agreeing effusively, something I'd find she was prone to.

'I like going overland too – and I've been lucky. I got to do the old hippy trail, back when it was still feasible. Went right across Europe and the Middle East, thumbing lifts and catching trains.'

'Wow.'

'Yeah. Bryan – my husband – and I did it right after we got married, in 1976. Missed the hottest summer ever in the UK, mind. Still bitter about that.' She laughed. 'You'll meet Bryan tonight. He's here too, and our son, Tom.'

'How do you all know Michael and Anna?' I asked.

'Mikey and I were at Oxford together back in the Stone Age and I've been unable to shake him ever since, despite my best efforts.' She squinted and leant forward. 'These bloody country roads.'

The faint sign ahead of us was illuminated in the headlights. *Saint-Luc-sur-Mer.*

'Yep, perfect, that's the village – I'm not senile yet!' She jerked the car back into action. 'Soon,' she said, 'you'll be able to hear the sea.'

The village, according to Jenny, consisted of a small square with two cafés (the Café de la Poste and Le Bastringue), a brasserie, a *tabac*, a *boulangerie*, a post office, and, next to the war memorial, a *presse* kiosk. Up at the top end, on the high viewpoint overlooking the sea, was a church, and about five miles out of town was a Carrefour supermarket.

'It's not the most buzzing of places nine months of the year. Well, frankly, it's dead,' she'd said. 'But naturally it just floods with tourists over the summer. We're not too far from Montpelier or Marseille on the train, and there's lots of sweet little towns along the coast that you can cycle to easily.'

The house was outside the village, in a little valley barely accessible by car (Jenny, in keeping with her aura of forthrightness, was an extremely competent driver). It was hidden from the main road by a dense grove of pines. Their sweet perfume, mingled with the saline breeze, was heady as we trundled down the driveway.

'God, it really is a dream, isn't it?'

Jenny hummed in agreement. 'Little slice of heaven,' she muttered, wrenching at the steering wheel to take the sharp bend. At last, the house, silver in the moonlight, came into view. In the dark, I could just about make out the lead-framed gridded windows; the shutters pushed open against the whitewashed stone facade and trailed with ivy. The consumptive engine gave one last valiant breath and petered out into nothing, and in the sudden silence I felt a wave of queasy anxiety. I imagined them all sitting around a kitchen table or on the patio, drinking spritz – Michael,

Anna, and now Bryan and Tom. I imagined the decades of shared history and private jokes; the anecdotes about continents and capital cities that I'd never been to, exhibitions and friends' birthday parties. I'd never been particularly shy but had always been acutely aware of even the tiniest degree of social awkwardness. I squashed down any feelings of nervous anticipation and smiled politely at Jenny. 'Thanks so much for picking me up.'

'Not at all,' she replied cheerily. 'Now let's get you a drink!'

I nodded with what I hoped looked like enthusiasm, and jerked the arthritic handle of the car door open.

Jenny led me around the back of the house ('We never use the front door') and as we came onto the patio, sheltered by an ad hoc wooden canopy and trellised with climbing plants, the sound of a record crackled through the fresh air of the night. I recognised the sweet voice of John Martyn. The table was still littered with the debris of dinner but the stable door was flung open and Anna's voice became audible over the music as we approached. I braced myself.

The back door led directly into the kitchen and my heart broke a little at how perfectly it matched what I'd anticipated: lined with old pots and pans, tiled unevenly with worn terracotta flagstones and charmingly bordering on derelict. There were holes and cracks in the shabby stone walls and it was the kind of ancient room full of alcoves and nooks where shadows are thrown about carelessly across work surfaces and lead casements.

'*Coucou!*' Jenny sang again, tossing the car keys onto the kitchen table.

'You're back!' Anna, appearing seconds later in the doorway.

In the few weeks since we'd seen each other she'd gained an enviable tan and the glow of good health that you forget is even possible when living in a city. She pulled me into one of her characteristic clutches, a cloud of sweet fig and jangling jewellery.

'*Apéro*?' Jenny asked over the chorus of enthusiasm.

'Please!' I replied, a little too eagerly. Hair of the dog, Dutch courage, etc.

Drinks mixed, we went through into the living room, which again was an almost carbon copy of what I'd imagined. It was dominated by one of those big old-fashioned record players, built into a polished wooden stand and surrounded by stacks of LPs. Rough stone walls. Battered mismatched sofas and cavernous armchairs draped with orange and olive-green throws. Shelf after shelf festooned with dog-eared paperbacks.

The three men stopped talking as we came into the room and I felt a pang of self-consciousness until the one I took to be Bryan stood up and clasped my hand warmly as his wife had done before. He was small and stocky, with a grey beard and crow's feet etched into the corners of his friendly blue eyes. He spoke with a slight West Country burr. Next to him was Tom, whom I put in his mid thirties and who had hair cropped closely to his head and a small silver hoop in his right ear. He moved gracefully, like a dancer. He was the kind of person who used the word *interesting* frequently and liberally, and whose hands were an extension of his speech.

Michael was sitting in an armchair in the corner and looked faintly peeved. I went over to greet him and his expression softened. 'Safe trip?' he murmured, kissing my cheek. I felt the sting of the curiosity with which Jenny was surveying us from the opposite end of the room. Feeling judged, I sank down into one of the ancient sofas next to Tom, who, it transpired, was a documentary filmmaker (none of these people were ever accountants or telemarketers). He too would be here until the end of the month, as he was sub-letting his room in Seven Sisters to save money for what he vaguely alluded to as his next project.

'Then Clarissa gets here, and then Lawrence and who-ever he's bringing this year.'

'Maybe he'll bring a girl!' Anna said with conspiratorial pantomime relish.

'I doubt it,' grumbled Michael, who until then had remained largely non-verbal. 'He never brings them home.'

'That's not true,' said Jenny, 'there was Lisa for a long time. And what about that girl who made the fish jewellery?'

Inwardly delighting, I made a mental note to pass this on to Emma.

'Tabby,' sighed Anna. 'She didn't last long.'

'Was she the insanely posh one?' Tom asked.

I suppressed the urge to scoff with total incredulity and at the same time unintentionally caught Michael's eye. For a moment I could have sworn he'd understood, and was doing the same. He shot me a discreet mischievous smile, which I returned before bashfully letting my gaze slide back down to my lap.

'Well, what about Leah?' Anna exclaimed. I laughed politely.

'Oh God, don't try and matchmake the poor girl,' Jenny groaned.

'Especially not with Lawrence,' said Tom, before glanc-ing at Michael and adding a sheepish, 'Well, you know . . . Sorry.'

'Oh don't worry, Mikey's not offended,' Jenny said coolly. 'He was just the same.'

'Whatever that means,' shrugged Michael.

The conversation carried on in much the same way for the rest of the evening – everyone gently taking the piss out of each other but sparing me, as the newcomer; everyone lapsing into private jokes and old stories before being expertly steered back into polite territory by either Anna or Jenny, both of whom had that knack of making you feel as if you too had known everyone in the room forever and that you were absolutely in the loop. Everyone was irresistibly charming. They were frank and funny and clever and all thought that they were completely normal, as if everyone on the planet was as dazzling as they were.

I'd been using my drink as a social crutch and after a few hours I noticed that a filmy haze had settled on my senses. My eyelids felt gluey with it and I remembered just how little sleep I'd had the night before. I was relieved when Jenny, announcing that she was too old to burn the midnight oil, initiated a general shambling stage exit.

'Come and say goodnight to the beach with me.' Tom offered me his hand and pulled me up out of the sofa. I was aware of Michael watching us.

'He's a grumpy old scrote,' Tom whispered by the kitchen door, 'but I think he has a sense of humour buried somewhere under all that misanthropy.'

'You know,' I began as we were walking out onto the patio, 'he's actually pretty sweet to me.'

Tom made a noise of sceptical half-agreement. 'Don't get me wrong. I've known Mick all my life; he's my godfather. I threw up on him at my christening and narrowly avoided it at my twenty-first. Every year he'd buy me a different novel that he'd loved at that age. He never had huge amounts to say to me so he'd take me to the cinema for some peace. I was one of those kids who couldn't stand silence. I was always painfully aware of what I perceived to be social awkwardness, especially around grown-ups.'

'Me too,' I enthused. 'Even now. I talk so much shit around people's parents because I'm determined to show how *articulate* I am. Actually, I do that with everyone.'

He held a tangle of bramble over my head to let me pass. 'Have you met Clarissa and Lawrence yet?'

'Clarissa.'

'Hmm.' He laughed. 'She can be a bit scary, but it's just because she's a bit of a princess. She's really sound when it comes down to it. She just acts the head girl sometimes.'

'What about Lawrence?'

'He's funny. Super-charming. Bless him, though, he's a bit of a shambles. His life's a total clusterfuck of disasters and questionable choices.'

'Hmm,' I grunted. 'That sounds familiar.'

We came into the thicket and I inhaled the woody smell of the air. Tom was using his phone as a torch, casting a little bluish bruise of light around his right hand. When we emerged from the trees, the wind brushed my face. His was pale in the moonlight, and below us I could see the moving marble expanse of the sea hitting the silver curve of sand. I squealed with delight.

'Well you've woken up,' he said.

I ignored him. I took off my shoes and ran.

Michael

I was lurking in the kitchen, thinking that everyone had gone up to bed, when I heard Jenny's voice.

'Michael? What are you doing here all by yourself in the dark?' She flicked on the switch of the small clip lamp on the bookshelf, throwing a beam of theatrical light onto my corner of the room.

'Smoking,' I said.

She was either kind enough not to mention the lack of any kind of cigarette paraphernalia, or just too indifferent to the lie to bother commenting. She looked at me for a moment, searching my face, and then perched on the armchair opposite me. It wasn't the sort of armchair you perched on, but the kind you sank into; we called it the death chair. Her determined resistance to it made me think she wasn't planning on staying put for long, but then she leant back, put her feet up on the stove and let out an audible sigh.

'What are you playing at, Michael?'

I pretended not to know what she meant and wished now that I had a cigarette as a prop. She was twisting her wedding band around and around her finger, a tic she'd had for the best part of half a century.

Neither of us spoke for a moment, and then at last I said, 'I've been writing again, you know.'

Her face remained impassive, half obscured in shadow, and I thought about all her different faces that I'd known, superimposed on top of each other. Imperceptible layers of time, completely unique from one another and yet identical, and woven from the same fibre. When I dreamt of her, the stages were fluid, and I could retrieve the older, buried layers again. I tried to remember her skin when it had been firm like unripe fruit.

'I almost had a fit when she got into the car at the station,' she whispered, putting her fingers to her lips nervously as if she were smoking. Maybe she was craving one too. Her muscles automatically remembered the once-habitual movement. 'How many years has it even been?' she mused. She let her hand fall to her lap and looked at me directly, unflinchingly. 'Oh come on, Mikey, don't pretend you don't know what I'm talking about.'

I matched her look and said again, firmly, 'I've started writing since I met her.'

She shook her head in disbelief, and when Tom and Leah's voices coming up from the garden (tipsy, careering) ripped through the blanket of silence, she stood up and went to leave the room.

'Switch the light off, will you?' I said as she left.

11

Leah

I'd always been an early riser, a habit exacerbated by years of 7 a.m. café shifts. I felt a sense of ownership over the morning, and of the way those pale, rich and silent hours unfolded – hollow and full of potential. Their rhythms and cadences were mine. I woke up on that first Sunday in Saint-Luc at half six, and already jagged shafts of sunlight were sketched across the whitewashed walls and the wooden floor of my bedroom. The window was wide open and the air was full of the crickets, the murmur of the sea hitting the shore, and above it all the reeling cries of the gulls.

My eyes felt too heavy to open fully and I squinted in the brightness of the room, slowly taking it all in. Registering where I was, I felt a little ripple of excitement through my body. I remembered the cool sand under my bare feet last night – scooping up handfuls of salt water and holding it to my mouth to taste. I padded over to the window. There it was, rolling out below: the sea.

I sloped downstairs to the kitchen in search of a kettle. No one else was awake. That was another privilege of my body clock – houses in the morning. Every home assumes a totally different and unique character at the immaculate beginnings of a day. The smell is different; the way light is filtered in through windows and open doors; the way spaces and objects interact with each other; the way dust settles on surfaces. I made myself a pot of tea, and went out onto the patio to read. No one else would surface for hours.

Just before eight o'clock, though, I heard the unmistakable clatter of life from the kitchen, followed by the distinct smell of coffee wafting out. Then Michael appeared in the doorway – a silhouette at first, becoming a tangible human being as he stepped out into the sunlight pooling on the flagstones.

'Bugger,' he muttered under his breath.

'Sorry,' I said automatically.

'No, no, it's not you, don't worry. It's just,' he held up a cigarette, '*this*. Normally no one else is awake at this time. Anna thinks I quit years ago.'

He slumped into the deckchair next to me and leant down to strike a match on the tiles. 'You can't tell anyone.'

'I'll take it to my grave,' I said with faux-solemnity.

Sighing, he leant back into the chair and dragged deeply from the cigarette, holding up an arm to shield his eyes from the sun. It was the most unwound I'd ever seen him. He let his arms fall limply to his sides and closed his eyes. Neither of us said anything. It didn't seem appropriate. When he'd finished smoking, he stubbed out the end on the patio and meticulously cleaned away the ash before hiding it all in an empty crisp packet plucked from the table. He turned and looked me squarely in the face in his unnerving way, then shook his head and glanced away.

'So,' he began briskly, 'what do you think?'

'Of?'

'Well, of all this.' He made a vague gesture that I presumed pertained to our surroundings. I made the appropriate gushing noises.

'It's certainly a long way from Yorkshire,' he said.

'Geographically speaking?' I mumbled awkwardly.

He smirked. 'I didn't grow up like my kids, you know.'

I had the vaguest impression that he was playing up his

accent and wondered what he was trying to prove. We talked for a while and I thought more about what Tom had said about him last night. It was true that he was different with me. I'd seen him fall into sulky silence in the presence of his daughter; I'd seen him speak to his ever-demonstrative wife with indifference bordering on contempt. I'd heard him taking cold calls on the telephone and managing to wring wrath out of even his stiff, limited French. Yet with me he was almost indulgent. He treated me like an ally.

*

After breakfast it was decided that Tom and I would make an expedition into town to buy bread and vegetables. 'Isn't everything closed on Sunday?' I asked hopefully.

'Not the *boulangerie*,' said Jenny. 'And there's a man who sells fruit and veg out of the boot of his Renault in a lay-by. I want to make a big ratatouille this evening and we're all out of courgettes.'

They were so unanimously enthused at the prospect of me seeing the little village that I didn't have the heart to tell them that all I wanted to do was lie nude on the beach until all the residual traces of Paris were bleached out of me by the Mediterranean sun.

We arrived just as the old people were leaving Mass, and all at once the little square was flooded with chatter and activity. Other than one family of earnest, limby Belgians in multi-pocketed shorts and sensible hiking sandals, the seasonal inhabitants had yet to make it out. In the daylight, the village was gorgeous, and in the bakery queue, the feeling of my dark hair trapping the slow drop of warm sunlight was a pleasant one. As Tom talked, I watched the brown, leathery faces of the elderly population wheeze and crack in delight. They spoke in accents I could only just understand,

and when there was a lull in the conversation, they eyed us with unashamed curiosity.

Bread bought, we decided to get a coffee on the terrace of Le Bastringue. The moment I sat down on the cane chair, I was struck with a long-forgotten feeling, one that had characterised my rural adolescence: the weird, jolting shock of seeing other young people you didn't already know; the thrilling, miraculous potential of a stranger. There were three of them, lounging around the brasserie table with louche and confident ease. Legs splayed, arms akimbo behind lolling heads and cigarettes hanging limply from mouths. I tried not to watch them watching me. Tom was oblivious to their presence.

'The thing is,' he was saying, 'I just can't believe she's a Tory. I mean, she used to be so cool. Now she's probably fucking Boris Johnson. Oh – *un allongé, s'il vous plaît*,' he added as the waiter brushed past us.

'*Pareil*,' I muttered. Opposite me, one of the boys took off his sunglasses and flashed me a winning smile.

'*Ça va?*'

'*Ça va*,' I replied, smiling back. Tom turned quickly and gave a curt (and unsolicited) nod of acknowledgement. 'Huh,' he said, 'Frenchmen.'

'She never actually expressly *said* she was a Conservative in the interview . . .' My sentence trailed off as I watched the stranger who was still smiling frankly in my direction. On the table, Tom's phone began to vibrate frenetically. 'Oh bloody hell, it's my sound engineer. One sec.'

I took the opportunity to re-establish eye contact with my attractive neighbour.

'Dylan, I can barely hear a word you're saying,' Tom boomed loudly, like my father on the phone. 'The signal's crap here . . . Yeah, I'm still in that little town . . . Here, wait a minute.' He looked up at me apologetically, putting his hand to the mouthpiece of his mobile.

'This is quite important. I'm going to have to wander around to try and find signal – I won't be long. Sorry.' He hopped inelegantly over the chairs, narrowly avoiding taking one with him, onto the pavement proper. He was barely out of earshot when my new friend called over.

'*Alors, c'est ton mec?*'

I made a show of mock-outrage and replied that Tom was not my boyfriend, an answer that prompted him to clamber over the clutch of tables (a feat he performed with infinitely more aplomb than Tom), and take his seat.

'*Americaine?*' he asked.

'*Anglaise,*' I replied automatically.

'Jérôme,' he said, and, pointing at his friends, 'Camille, Nico.'

'Leah.'

'Are you staying in Saint-Luc?'

'Just outside,' I said. 'I'm working for an English family.'

'Ah, yeah – the writer. But you speak French.'

'I live in Paris.'

He nodded enthusiastically. '*Ça s'entend,*' he said. 'I live in Marseille now but I grew up here. That's how I know your writer. He comes here every summer and everyone knows everyone in this town.'

I nodded in sympathy. 'I come from a small town too.'

'And what do you do in Paris?'

'Avoid adult life.'

He laughed. '*Moi aussi un peu.*' He lit a cigarette. 'I'm a musician but I work in a bar.'

Boys always did that. They always audaciously labelled themselves as artists rather than amateurs.

'*Je peux te piquer un clope, s'il te plaît?*' I asked.

He flicked a cigarette out of his shirt pocket and lit it for me as I held it to my lips. His eyes were so dark they were almost black, and his nose was straight from a Roman coin.

'I'm in Saint-Luc for another few days,' he said. 'We should hang out. I can show you the sights.'

'I hear there's a very impressive Carrefour.'

'*Ah, merde*, so you've already been to the tourist board?' I laughed.

'No, really, though. We're having an *apéro* tomorrow night at my parents' place. You should come.'

Next to the *presse* kiosk I could see Tom gesticulating wildly.

'I'd like to,' I said.

Jérôme flashed me another smile – a line of straight white teeth and one of those squared-off bottom lips that used to melt me when I first moved to France. 'What are you doing this afternoon?'

*

I got back to the house around 5 p.m., having spent the afternoon with the three boys. Tom stayed with us for lunch on the terrace, made slightly awkward by his very limited French and the boys' very limited English, although he had a remarkable talent for narrative hand gestures. When he left, he was absolutely insistent that I stay. 'No one will think you're being rude,' he said. 'Christ knows you'll be here the entire month after all.'

We idled away a couple of hours at the same spot until at last it was decided that we should walk down to the beach, where we lay on the dunes smoking cigarettes and listening to house music on the tinny speakers of somebody's phone. 'This is one of my mixes,' Jérôme told me, patently flushed with pride, but affecting a swaggy nonchalance.

Although I sometimes felt as if I'd spent the past five years congratulating boys on their mixes, I replied with genuine enthusiasm, 'I like this part. Is it Arabic?' only realising how desperately basic I sounded when the words had left my mouth.

He was apparently unaware of my embarrassment. 'My mum is Algerian,' he said. 'This is a sample from a record my grandparents used to play when I was a kid.'

Throughout the afternoon he kept trying to engineer situations whereby the two of us would be alone, and each time his friends thwarted him. Taking pity, I eventually asked him to walk me back to the house. He left me on the crest of the hill at the top of the drive, and for the rest of the evening I held an image of his handsome, tanned face superimposed on the yellowish-blue of the sky, and the green and yellow brushstrokes of the pines and the tall, dry grass. When he gave me the *bises*, his hand lingered for a while on the small of my back.

On the patio, I found Jenny with her hair piled on top of her head, wearing industrial-looking gardening gloves and brandishing a pair of pruning shears.

'*Guten Tag!*' she sang, and then, looking up from her pile of dead weeds, 'I hear you've been chasing trouser.'

I made a mental note to recycle that expression and told her blithely that I had indeed met a very beautiful boy.

'Oh *good*,' she said with relish.

'Do you want any help?' I asked, gesturing at the stacks of brittle brown vegetation.

'Are you a gardener?'

'I'm a country girl!' I said, hoping the pride would deflect from the question.

'We've only got one pair of gloves. Unsurprisingly, neither Anna nor Michael is very big on weeding.'

Instead I was sent into the garden to retrieve rosemary, thyme and bay leaves. The afternoon was thick with the clatter of insects, and the scent of the marjoram infused the air as I crushed it underfoot – the ground was covered in it, growing wildly, crawling across the lawn. Delicate webs of wild fennel invaded the vast terracotta pots of geraniums and the zesty lemon thyme. I returned to Jenny, who by now was chopping vegetables at the table, with fistfuls of herbs. She set me to work dicing aubergine.

'Hmm, I think you'll make a nice sous chef this month,' she said, plucking a slice of gleaming red pepper from the board.

'Do you end up doing all the cooking?'

'Well – it is sort of what I do.'

'You're a chef?'

'A food writer.'

'That's *so* cool,' I enthused. Her evolution as my absolute idol was now complete. 'How did you end up doing that?'

'Well, I was sort of the black sheep of my very high achieving family. I dropped out of Oxford before I finished because I couldn't really be bothered going back, and then, I didn't really have any idea what I wanted to do with my life. One of my older brothers worked at the BBC, so I ended up writing a letter to them and working there for a while.'

More nuggets of gold to transmit to Emma, I thought.

'Anyway, after much purgatory spent filing things, I predictably got put on *Woman's Hour*, and we always used to do little cookery features, and food sort of became my area of expertise – especially Italian food, which was just starting to be all the rage in those days.'

I nodded enthusiastically.

'So that was probably where it all started. My parents were horribly disappointed, even if I was the indulged youngest. They were both such *serious* people. Mamá was Spanish and they met when Dad went out to Spain with the International Brigade. My eldest brother ended up becoming a war correspondent; the other went into politics. My sister moved to the States and ended up in academia.' She shrugged. 'And then there was me, little Jenny, editing a radio slot about tomatoes.'

'My brother and sister are blissfully normal,' I said. 'My parents see living abroad as a legitimate achievement.'

'Well, for me it improved marginally. I met Bryan and he was a total hippy. Fresh out of art school – a ceramicist. My Hampstead-red parents loved it. They were convinced that he'd rejected a life in fine art to pursue one as a craftsperson. We ended up absolute clichés of our generation. I dropped out of the whole career ladder thing altogether for a while. We travelled a lot and we ate a lot and the whole time I was writing about it. Then when I was pregnant I got it all together and made it into something coherent.' She wiped her hands on a tea towel. 'And that coherent thing became my first book.'

It was only then that her identity became apparent and I realised that as a chronically bored teenager I'd read her newspaper column every Saturday. My brain started to involuntarily access all the images I'd invented and stored, lying on the living room floor on infinitely empty afternoons. Faceless woman (was she even faceless? Surely I'd created a face for her, as I'd done for the thousands of characters in every novel I'd ever read) grilling fish on a beach on a remote Greek island, or meeting guerrilla beekeepers in abandoned car parks in Hackney Wick.

I feigned ignorance and carried on slicing the firm, fat flesh of the aubergine.

*

The following morning after breakfast, Michael took me down to the shed at the bottom of the garden, which he had colonised as his study. To me, sheds smelt of petrol, sawdust and sweat, and were emblazoned with pneumatic babes bursting out of ripped plaid shirts and straddling motorbikes or wielding chainsaws (my formative beauty ideal had been consequently questionable). This was emphatically not a shed. Someone at some point had painted it racing green, and the windows had a greenish tint too. Inside, it was cool and musty, and with the wine-bottle hue it gave me a weird, wavy feeling, as if I was literally stepping into someone's memory. The desk, a long trestle table, spanned an entire wall and was chaotic: piles of papers and notebooks; newspaper clippings and Post-its stuffed in rusty old tea caddies and sun-bleached chocolate tins; trinkets; postcards and photographs with curling edges. I inwardly delighted at the sight of an ancient Woolworths carrier bag transported directly from my childhood.

'I'm a hoarder,' said Michael. He had his back to me now and was pottering around with a stubborn lighter, a camping stove and a tin kettle. 'Tea?'

'Please.'

When at last he'd managed to ignite the hob, he turned a couple of old wine crates upside down and motioned for me to sit on one of them. Sighing, he clasped his hands together. He'd started to bite his cuticles. 'I write in here, so I'm alone for most of the day. If you really need me, you can come in and interrupt.'

'OK,' I said.

He sat down on the other crate. 'So alongside what you've already been doing – the admin stuff, the reading, emails – I think we've developed a good enough relationship by now for you to start the next project. Frankly, Leah, you're going to think I'm mad. My editor thinks I'm mad. My wife thinks I'm mad. My children think I'm mad . . . Not mad in a creative genius sort of way, but mad in the old-man-losing-it sense. I hardly know you at all and I'm going on a lot of trust here. Trust and . . . feeling.' He perceptibly shuddered at the word, which seemed too big for his mouth. 'Trust and feeling. Things I normally avoid.'

In the far corner of the room was a stack of cardboard boxes. He pointed at them. 'Those boxes are my life between 1968 and 1970. It's stuff that's never seen the light of day. Most of it's very private – excruciatingly so; a lot of it's probably total dross. I want you to sort it into chronological order, then read it and type it all up.'

'OK,' I said again.

'You're going to know me – or what was me – quite well by the end of the month. I hope you won't judge me, and needless to say, I'm taking your discretion as a given.'

'Of course.'

He sighed. 'See what you read as you'd see a piece of fiction. That's what a diary is, after all.'

The shrill whistle of the boiling kettle pierced the air and he got up to make the tea.

*

I decided to lug the boxes up to my little bedroom. It was only when I put them down that I felt the full weight of them occupying my borrowed, intimate space. There were three of them altogether, and for about five minutes I couldn't even bring myself to open them, I just sat on the floor looking at them, as if awaiting spontaneous combustion. I texted Emma.

He has literally employed me to read his diaries.

I don't get this man, she replied. *Has he not heard of*

digitalisation? More importantly, are you even qualified to do that?

And then:

And by 'that', I mean qualified to be his shrink.

It does kind of feel like he's exposing himself to me – like this is the literary equivalent of one of those pervy old men who gets his dick out on the Métro.

OMG, he's a cerebral flasher!!!! she replied, sending a stream of aubergine emojis.

Bracing myself, I tore at the masking tape on the first box and inhaled the smell of age. Each one was full of identical navy-blue notebooks, each notebook in turn full of his elegant black hand. I opened one at random and read a few lines.

> . . . *crashing bloody hangover in Senate House not helped by J turning up and dragging me out to lunch with his mother, who had apparently requested the presence of his 'lanky northern friend'. Proving that alcoholism is hereditary, Mrs Gresford polished off about two bottles of gin and encouraged us to do the same. Serious old lush in the country-house mode: horse-faced, lots of name-dropping, talent for making G&Ts miraculously disappear . . . Filthy sense of humour . . . Unsettlingly attractive by the time we were on to pudding . . .*

*

Jérôme's parents' house was about a forty-five-minute walk from the Youngs'. I'd spent the rest of the day sprawled on my bedroom floor, opening each notebook, checking the dates of the first entries and putting them into piles depending on their year, all the while determinedly trying not to read anything, which was difficult when sentences such as 'Kathy put the little tab of acid under my tongue like a priest giving holy communion' proliferated every other page. I was grateful when Michael didn't join us for lunch on the patio. If he was the flasher in a beige trench coat, I was more eager voyeur than disturbed victim.

I stopped when I heard Jenny's voice from the garden, demanding hydration.

'It's six o'clock somewhere in the world, Bryan!'

According to my watch it was half past five. I went down to the beach for a swim and joined them all for a fleeting pastis. There was still no sign of Michael. At seven, I set off for the *apéro*.

The house was one of several squat bistre bungalows about a mile out of Saint-Luc, each one with a sloping terracotta roof and a dense green ring of vegetation to give an impression of isolation. Jérôme's was at the top of a long drive, dusty and scattered with brown pine needles. At the end was a clapped-out red Renault with a fat ginger cat sprawled across the rusting bonnet, baking in the evening sun. I reached out to scratch its vast marmalade belly. From the garden I heard peals of laughter, and the cyclical snicker of a bass line. The cat deigned to open one reptilian eye, briefly appeared to consider some kind of movement and then thought better of it. I felt a profound swell of affinity with the creature.

There were five of them altogether: Jérôme, Camille, Nico, and two girls who were introduced as Alice and Elisa and who seemed so warm and friendly after years of *parisiennes* that for a good moment I took their enthusiastic greetings and apparent interest in me to be some kind of bizarre and sadistic joke.

'Your French is *so* good!' Elisa gasped.

Since the age of eighteen I'd been surrounded by people to whom speaking a second language adeptly was taken for granted. When I'd first moved to London, I was in total awe of all the kids who slipped so seamlessly between multiple languages. I remembered masking a grimace when a self-proclaimed 'Citizen of the World' international-schooled friend had said, 'God, I find it so patronising when English people compliment me on my English. Like, what, do they think we're all so dumb that we can't learn their language or something?'

'I've lived in France for a while now,' I said sheepishly.

The five of them were positioned artfully around the pool, and the colours of the scene – the David Hockney turquoise of the water, the rich terracotta of the tiles, the violent bloom of the bougainvillea and the luminous light-bulb glow of the bottle of pastis on the low table – seemed saturated with extra pigment. Jérôme handed me a small tumbler of the Ricard.

'You know your writer is a bit of a legend in Saint-Luc?' Alice began.

'He is?'

'Yeah, but it's not hard to be a legend here,' snorted Camille.

They'd all left Saint-Luc for bigger towns – Lyon, Montpelier, Nîmes. They'd known each other since childhood, but rather than lapsing into old anecdotes and private jokes, they focused their attention on me. They talked about school exchanges in Manchester and Folkestone (the latter was noted particularly for one barbaric family who seemed to subsist entirely on *sandwichs aux frites*). They asked about London and delighted in complaining about Paris, and above all they wanted to know about the Youngs.

'Are the kids there?' Elisa asked eagerly.

'Not yet,' I said, 'but they're both showing up at some point.'

'When we were teenagers, they seemed so chic and sophisticated. They'd come here every summer with friends from London and we'd spend the first week sort of dancing around them. Then someone—'

'Always me,' Camille interrupted.

'*C'est clair* – Camille would invite them to a party at someone's house in the bigger town where we all went to school. Didn't you really fancy the sister, Nico?'

'She was my first great love,' he sighed, 'but all I could say to her was "I like to play football in the park and my favourite band is the Kooks."'

'And then there was this one summer when we were like fifteen, sixteen,' Alice said, taking up the tale, 'when she – what's her name again? Claire?'

'Clarissa,' I supplemented.

'Clarissa, that's it. Well, she and her friend came to this party with us, and Nico was trying so hard—'

'By that point my linguistic capabilities extended to discussing substance abuse, films and the comparative merits of various renewable energies. Thank you, high school education.'

'So Nico was really giving it his best,' Alice continued, 'when this absolute arsehole from the year above us who had just spent a year living in Idaho, or some shithole in the real *trou du cul*, nowhere end of America—'

'Swooped in and charmed her from right under my nose! All on the basis of him being able to communicate with her competently. Twat.'

'And we never really saw them after that,' Elisa concluded. 'They probably had better things to do than hang out in some small town with their parents, I guess.'

'Though of course Nico spent the next summer fuming over all these wild fantasies that Clarissa was down the road with the Idaho guy performing sex acts beyond the power of even his filthy teenage imagination,' Jérôme said.

'Fuck you!' Nico jeered in joke-outrage. 'I learnt the past tense for that girl.'

We hung around for a couple of hours by the side of the pool, drinking quite solidly. I'd forgotten how dangerously easily the feather-light aniseed delight of pastis slips down your throat until the moment you decide to stand up and realise that you are, in fact, smashed. It was the best kind of drunken revelry, however; the kind where you feel totally accepted by this new, shimmering group of people and find yourself talking loudly and freely and commandeering the speakers to play 'La Isla Bonita' multiple times, all the while declaring that it's the *best pop song ever written* and dancing with joyful abandon. When at last everyone started to get a little less exuberant and began making vague noises about going to respective homes, I went with Alice, whose mother's house was in the same general direction as Michael and Anna's. As we parted, she said to me:

'Jérôme is a really good guy, you know.'

'*Ça se voit*,' I said, attempting to sound both friendly and non-committal in equal measure, and, giving her the *bises*, disappeared into the dense wall of pine trees.

*

The following morning, I established what fast became my daily routine. I woke up early and revelled in the total absence of social obligation. I brewed a pot of tea, lay out on the patio reading and then walked down to the beach for a swim before breakfast. In my absence, Jenny had been to the village and bought piles of croissants and bread still warm from the baker's oven. I slotted in at the table next to Tom, my hair dreadlocked by the sea and leaving a trail of salty water around me that dried in seconds in the hot morning sun. I poured myself a thick black coffee from the silver moka pot. It was gritty, treacly and bitter. It tasted like the Mediterranean. Yawning, Tom handed me a slice of watermelon.

'Thanks,' I muttered.

'Good night?' He grinned.

Jenny smirked at us from across the table. Bryan was immersed in his sketchbook. Anna was yet to surface and Michael had apparently already slunk off to the shed.

After breakfast, I retreated to the ascetic cell of my room to work – this was, after all, my bourgeois summer by proxy. Although the volume of emails had dwindled since the beginning of August, I still had proofs to plough through; turgid experimental novels, mind-numbing spy thrillers and debuts that literary agents were pushing as 'state of the nation' and 'necessary'. I'd finished sorting the diaries into chronological order the previous afternoon, and on the Tuesday morning, I began to read and type. They started, as Michael had told me, in the summer of '68. He'd just moved to London to start a master's, but in all honesty he didn't seem particularly enthralled with academia. I got the impression that he'd taken up postgraduate studies because he'd always been clever enough to coast along, and this was the most straightforward way of getting enough money thrown at him to achieve his lifelong ambition of moving to London (despite having no idea what he was destined for other than 'greatness').

For all his laissez-faire attitude towards academia, when it came to his diaries, he was certainly diligent. By the end of the day I was au fait with the main characters of his life, all of whom, other than Jenny, were painted with the poisonous precision of a satirist's pen. There was an irresistible cast of louche Soho moochers, middle-class aspiring hippies, and 'limp', 'insipid' or even 'incontinent' members of the university faculty. The entries were sneering, funny, repulsive and absorbing all at once.

Content-wise, it was mostly an uninterrupted narrative of picaresque, hedonistic West End loafing. The occasional nod was given to current events, such as what he rather pretentiously referred to as *les événements* in Paris, or the war in Vietnam. Although he pointedly made fun of his erstwhile undergraduate ambitions to write, the entries were peppered with scraps of poetry (atrocious), ideas for stories (illuminating) and genuinely amusing limericks (deeply off-brand). Above all – and rather disturbingly, given what Emma had deemed the *infrastructural perviness* of the job itself – younger Michael was permanently gagging for it. He was the archetypal 1960s cerebral love rat. Some of it was worryingly erotic. Some of it was just a bit nauseating; I'd really have preferred to eat my own eyes rather than have them endure reading the words *the fragrant perfume of her cunt*. I kept reminding myself that this was a job, and that I couldn't be squeamish.

Jenny tended to summon us all to eat at around two o'clock, so at half past one I'd allow myself a dip in the sea to pull me back into the real world. The atmosphere at lunch varied depending on whether Michael elected to turn up. When he did appear, he was agitated and terse, and poisoned the mood accordingly. He was even more misanthropic when Anna joined us, which was a mercifully rare occurrence. She'd been unusually solitary since my arrival and spent most days elsewhere, catching up with old friends in Montpelier, or in Marseille, where she was involved in what she mysteriously alluded to as her latest collaboration. The blade of tension between them that I'd got used to in Paris seemed to have escalated to full-blown hostility since they'd migrated south. Tom expressed open joy when neither pitched up at lunch, and a week in, he even broached the topic with me – the outsider – as we were walking into town one evening for a drink at Le Bastringue.

'He wasn't always like this,' he began as we made our way along the dust road, carved out of the green stubble of the *garrigue*. 'I mean, yes, he was always grumpy, but he used to be funny and charismatic as well. And he never used to be so . . . well . . . *petulant*. I mean, I didn't come last year so I didn't see him then, but I know Mum's been worried about him for a while. If you ask her, he hasn't been right since before they moved to Paris.'

'Do you think it's something with him and Anna?'

He raised his eyebrows. 'Oh it goes way deeper than that, I think. I mean – you know all about writer's block? The artist who, well, can't get it up, for want of a better analogy.'

I nodded, not wanting to probe but hoping he would stick to what appeared to be type and tell me more.

'He hasn't written anything big since the millennium. Yeah, I think it was around then because I remember watching it on TV on a Sunday night.'

'On *TV*?'

'Yeah,' Tom mused. 'It was his first and only script – and it was super-fucking-well received. After that, everything went mad for a while. It was just a little BBC feature-length drama, but he was getting calls from people in Hollywood and, like, *really* famous actors. It was crazy.'

'And then?'

'Well, he went out to California for a bit. And then he came back. And then just,' he shrugged, 'nothing.'

'Hmm,' I said, stooping to pick some stray celandines. 'What was the film about?'

'Oh, textbook TV hit really: London, the sixties, attractive young posh people and some adorable fittie from the East End thrown in to shake things up a bit. Maybe it *was* kind of trash actually . . . televisual soma for middle England and self-congratulatory exposure for the already over-represented chattering classes. Mum thought it was rubbish. I was a kid; my critical faculties were hardly at their sharpest.'

When we returned later on, Anna's handbag was on the kitchen counter, and the following morning she was her former effusive self, once again acting the attentive hostess and not even letting me pour my own coffee.

'I won't be about as much as usual this week,' she announced as Jenny did a vague head count for a shopping list. 'I've got some work to do in Marseille. Oh, and of course Friday night I definitely won't be in for dinner, and actually, I'll probably go before lunch to make the most of the trip.'

'What *trip*?' Michael demanded.

'To Marseille,' sighed Anna curtly, letting the mask of jollity slip somewhat. 'To pick up your *daughter*, who gets in that evening.'

'Ah yes,' he muttered, apparently without interest. 'Very good.'

*

One significant thing happened in those first few days. I was walking up the coastal path, where I'd taken a little detour after my early-evening swim, when I heard footfall behind me. Below me was the dramatic plunge of the sapphire Mediterranean, the almost-setting sun glinting off little white sails in the distance; wheeling gulls; little capillaries of sea foam as waves crested and fell. I stopped and turned around.

'*Salut*,' I said. Jérôme was standing behind me.

'Walk with me?'

I nodded and followed him as he turned off the path.

'You were in the sea,' he said blandly as we scrabbled up a rocky slope. He offered me his hand. 'Your hair's wet.'

'Where are we going?'

'To my favourite place.'

'How did you know I'd be here?'

'I didn't,' he said. 'I was walking and fate smiled fondly upon me.' (Or something along those lines; I'm probably taking great poetic licence with some of the translation.)

We wound up and up until we came to a small spinney, where the air that had smelt of salt water and driftwood was all at once dense, green and tenebrous. Jérôme was mostly mute, leaving me to talk myself into a frenzy reminiscent of Tom. I was telling him about Michael and Anna, and Michael's behaviour.

'Do you think he wants to fuck you?' he said.

'I'm sorry?' I asked, flustered.

'I think he wants to fuck you,' he repeated, not looking at me. 'It's this way.'

We emerged from the trees and back into the spectacular chalky light.

'Wow,' I breathed.

We'd come to a hidden viewpoint. Across the bay I could see the twin peak on which the church was nestled, its modest white spire pressed onto the endless blue of the sky, beneath it the lapis water. Blue on blue on blue and edged with the full spectrum of green – from jade to olive – of the scrub.

'It's incredible,' I breathed.

Jérôme sat down and lit a cigarette. I went and sat next to him, hugging my knees to my chest.

The sun seemed to perpetually fall on his face – he radiated sunlight. His skin was that absolute unblemished olive, and pulled tautly over the angles and sinews of his lithe body. As he inhaled the cigarette, his dark hair fell over his dark eyes. He offered it to me and I took it gladly, hoping the nicotine would slow my heart, which at some unknown juncture had started racing. As I passed it back to him, he held my gaze and smirked as if in on some joke I wasn't. He took the cigarette from me and stubbed it out, then, taking both my hands in his, pinned me to the ground. His irresistible weight pressed onto me and he started to laugh, face inches from mine, revealing a row of straight white teeth. I bit my lip.

'I've been wanting to do this for days,' he said, and kissed me, the kind of kiss you feel in your whole body, and that makes your limbs somehow feel rigid and liquid at the same time.

12

Michael

I'd woken up badly, let's just put it like that. My sleep had
been all torn up with these miserable dreams of Astrid, and
God, they were so vivid I could have touched her. I could
smell that boxy suede swing jacket she'd bought from the
Oxfam on Upper Street that still clung on to the cigar smoke
of its previous owner. Sometimes, when she'd helped Giorgio
and Rosa in the kitchen after a shift, her fingernails would
taste like garlic – a taste still new and foreign to me, but then
evocative somehow, inexplicably, of something from my
childhood. (Years later, I was blindsided on the Old Moor
Road on the way from my parents' house to the church
where my niece was to be married. *Allium oleraceum*. It was
spring, and resplendent with the untainted pigment of the
season, and above all the scent of wild garlic. I sat in my
suit on a damp tree stump – luminous and squirming with
life – and stared at my shaking hands, waiting for them to
morph into hers.)

In the dream, I'd been with her on the 38 towards Hackney Central. She was preserved and crystallised and young,
and she said we were going to a party. I kept looking down
in horror at those same hands of mine, which looked withered and prehistoric, bulbous with knotted purple veins.
When we got off the bus, surrounded by betting shops
and crackheads and chichi florists', I found myself pumped
through with a kind of social anxiety I hadn't experienced
for decades. She was dressed like Clarissa and her friends, in
Doc Marten's patent creepers, and a little cropped top with

one of my old denim jackets. She was glued to her phone. 'What are you doing?' I'd asked her.

'I'm texting Julian for directions,' she'd replied in a monotone, eyes fixed to the screen.

When we'd arrived at some hideous warren of ex-council blocks with misguidedly optimistic and sugary names (Cornflower Terrace, Begonia Walk), she'd abandoned me at the door almost immediately and left me wandering, in a sort of shimmering, unreal purgatory, through the unnaturally proportioned flat. Corridors warped and stretched; poky rooms overflowed with nubile teenaged bodies and then emptied in seconds. In the kitchen, Lawrence was leaning against the scuzzy fridge, smoking a joint and drinking from a can of Red Stripe, talking to a girl who must have been her. I kept trying to speak to them, but they both ignored me with studied contempt.

At last I came to a locked room, and from within I could hear the marching drum, the stirring jangle of the strings and the voice of Grigoris Bithikotsis urging the people onwards. 'When they clench their fists,' he sang in Greek. I reached for the handle but it was completely unmovable, and no matter what I did, no matter how much force and determination I used, it couldn't be shifted. The noise was getting louder and the metal of the handle was starting to cut into my palms like rope in the school gymnasium. The more I struggled, the stiffer it became. The racket from inside the room was deafening.

Then I felt a palm on my shoulder. It was Leah. She motioned for me to move aside, and wordlessly she opened the door. It swung out slowly and daylight flooded into the dark corridor from within. I charged in. The room was empty and silent, and the little window flung open, looking out onto the vast expanse of the Aegean in August.

You don't need a bloody psychoanalyst to work that one out.

*

Every morning she goes down to the beach at about quarter to eight and comes back with her hair wound up on her head in a salty, knotty rope that tumbles down as she sits on the patio, squeezing oranges for Jenny or mopping glistening little diamonds of melon juice off her chin (she's a messy eater, I've noticed). This morning I wanted to intercept her – to talk to her, to explain myself; but when I got to the crest of the dune that slopes down to the cove, I couldn't quite bring myself to disturb her. I watched her swim the length of the bay and thought what a cliché I was – an old man watching a girl weave through the water, her long brown legs kicking out ripples laced with the glint of the morning sun.

She pulled herself up onto the rocks and was startlingly, maddeningly naked save for a pair of black bikini bottoms. I knew that this was the moment at which I should have turned away, but instead I found myself sitting cross-legged on the dune, oblivious to the sand flies and the barbs of dry grass, feeling some of the pleasure she must have felt as she closed her eyes under the warm stroke of the new sun.

I felt the most glorious sensation when I half closed my own eyes and a whole collage of images was fixed onto the scene: Astrid, nude on the balcony in Athens (how was it that even their bodies were identical? I realised with a flash of guilty excitement that I knew exactly how Leah's breasts would feel), her tanned skin against the green of the fig tree, layered on top of the scene before me. The effect was similar to when they paste up adverts on the walls of the tunnels in the Underground; a small tear in the poster for the Cézanne exhibition reveals a flash of the flawless white teeth of a comedian playing the Apollo – gleaming canines reverse-consumed by modest sunset-coloured apples.

*

'I wonder where Leah could be.' Jenny glanced at her battered wristwatch and tossed the salad for what felt like the hundredth time that minute.

'Mum, I'm pretty certain she hasn't drowned. The sea's like a millpond this evening – she's probably very much alive.'

Jenny was terrified of drowning, and had been for as long as I'd known her. It was so utterly at odds with her character, but the only time I'd ever seen her truly angry – really explode, incandescent with rage – was when Julian pushed her into the Cherwell. It had been me who'd taught Tom to swim, a miraculous testament to my love for his mother considering my famed and chronic lack of patience. We were in Cornwall. Tom was about six, I'd guess, so it must have been the late eighties. Yes, it was '88 – Diana was pregnant with Lawrence, which was probably why I'd been roped into marine instruction, in an attempt to stir some sort of paternal instinct.

Bryan placed his hand on his wife's. He was largely non-verbal compared to the rest of us. He spoke rarely, but when he did, what he said was measured and considered. When he and I had first met as young men, I couldn't help but think that he didn't like me – I was all posturing, swaggering snarl and he was just this tower of terrifying silence. I called him the Monk. I'd used words as both my defence and my armoury for as long as I could remember. His lack of inclination to speak had wrong-footed me for a sizeable chunk of time.

'Let's just start, Mum,' said Tom. 'As soon as we start, she's guaranteed to appear – like when you're waiting for ages in a restaurant and the second you get up to piss, your food comes.'

As if on cue, Leah came scurrying up from the direction of the beach, a ball of nervous energy.

'I'm so sorry,' she puffed. 'I totally lost track of time. Please say you started without me?'

Her face was flushed, her eyes were dewy and her hair was already dry.

13

I was late, of course; she'd told me seven and by the time I'd come out of the Central Line it was already half past and I found myself tearing down Charing Cross Road in an attempt to be even remotely on time. The club was a subterranean drinking hole on Denmark Street, run by a Harlem-transplant jazz fiend called Jeremy, who was apparently wont to regularly fire his pianists and valiantly step in himself to replace them, leaving the bar dangerously unmanned for great chunks of the evening. It was the kind of business model, I gathered, that ran mostly on charm, luck and charisma.

After a fair deal of frantic toing and froing, I found the unremarkable entrance, and after it a dank stairwell. I flung myself down it to the basement, to a dubious black door from behind which came the muffled thud of music and conversation, and intermittent bursts of laughter. I pushed it open. Everything was suddenly in spectacular stereo. Billowing plumes of blue smoke threaded through with luminous chinks of halogen and the burning ends of cigarettes. Pale, delighted faces gleaming in the crepuscular glow. The languid yawn of a brushed drum, and the tonic heartbeat of the keys.

She was sitting up on the little makeshift stage, on a high bar stool, with her legs crossed elegantly. She was wearing a pair of cropped navy cigarette pants and a man's white shirt, and she was smoking and laughing with the double bass player. She'd had a fringe cut and her hair was up, save the strands falling across her illuminated face. The milky light framed her; its soft beams fixed her like a pinned butterfly.

I bought myself a gin from the man who must have been Jeremy and positioned myself against the bar, my back turned with studied hostility to anyone who might so much as try and strike up conversation with me. Astrid took the microphone and started to sing. I felt my head swim. The double bass player closed his eyes and nodded in smiling approval to the drummer, who grinned back. Behind me, Jeremy whistled.

'Not bad at all, mate,' wheezed a hoarse regular.

'Hmm,' he replied. 'Not so sure how I feel about the new keys guy, though.'

I was untethered from their reality. The song finished and the bar erupted into applause, and she beamed with gauche delight. When she clocked me, her childish smile tripled in size. I raised my glass to her and felt all at once that the two of us were alone in the crowded room, like lovers meeting in the kind of old Hollywood film my sister used to take me to on Saturday afternoons. There was a projector beam anchoring us together, with everyone else fading into mundane obscurity offstage.

*

It was naïve to have expected her to be a virgin, I suppose. Two weeks previously, in the pub, Julian had made some passing snipe dressed up as an almost-compliment. 'Best thing about girls like that,' he'd gloated, 'is they always know exactly what they're doing. I bet she's a minx, eh, Micky?' Jenny, noticing my squeak of discomfort (she always seemed to be aware of even the slightest tremor of feeling), had said, as she lit a cigarette and stared at the ghastly crystal ashtray, 'Well, I suppose that's a good thing. You hardly want a blushing virgin, do you?'

I'd imagined the moment so many times before it actually happened; idle moments on the 68 or in the library, or kicking through the crisp piles of dead, parchment-confetti leaves in Cartwright Gardens. I fantasised about her pretty mouth; lips parted, eyes wide with fear and desire in equal measure and her breath shallow and quick. My tongue would brush her earlobe and I'd whisper something obvious that she'd find irresistible, something like *I could never hurt you* or *you can trust me* – the kind of crap that never worked on frigid teases (a flash of Sarah-that-was-Sara's face) but would undoubtedly work on Astrid. I knew she wanted it as much as I did. Her kisses lingered that little bit longer. When she pressed herself against me it was done urgently – greedily.

That night, we'd been walking down Rathbone Place, Astrid gliding on a current of euphoria after the gig. We'd stopped to kiss in a doorway under a greasy electric-blue street light and she'd whispered in my ear, hands clutching at my tense shoulder blades, 'I want it to be tonight.' We'd raced up the staircase to my flat, giddy and careering. She'd pulled me down on top of her, onto my hard single mattress, and unbuttoned my shirt with easy, unexpected dexterity.

After the act, she lay with her head on my chest and her thick hair tickling my nostrils. We shared a cigarette.

'You've done it before,' I said.

'Haven't you?' she asked ironically.

'I'd like to think that was apparent.'

'Hmm.' She giggled and turned over, her chin pressed to my collarbone. 'It's not normally like *that*, though, is it?'

'No,' I agreed, 'it's not.'

*

'A clairvoyant!' I announced triumphantly.

'Why on earth would a clairvoyant have worn such a dull jacket?' Jenny said. 'No offence, darling.' She turned to Astrid. 'I mean, it's not *dull* at all, of course, but you'd somehow expect a clairvoyant to be decked out in sequin-spangled paisley – you know, more like Julian.'

'Ho ho ho! Great arbiter of style and a comedian to boot! What fortune we have to be your mates, Jen,' Julian said, taking a swig of his pint. 'But she's right, a clairvoyant would never have worn that jacket. If it had been a clairvoyant's, it wouldn't smell like cigars; it'd smell like sage and sandalwood.'

'Oh Jules, you're so irredeemably Anglican, aren't you? Those smells smack of High Church, not lair-of-a-seedy-charlatan—'

'You see!' I cried. 'That's the vibe I'm going for. Madame Sosostris style. Some gloomy corner of a red-light district just after the First World War. Wizened old medium – former hooker,' I added. 'Smokes Cubans and sleeps with corrupt bobbies and vicars to keep the law on her side.'

'No one in the twenties wore swing jackets, darling,' Jenny sighed.

'That's the point – she's a *clairvoyant*,' I insisted desperately. 'She can see the future of fashion!'

The four of us were in a pub just by King's Cross. It was the day before Christmas Eve and the whole of London seemed to have fallen into a drunken festive stupor. My train to Leeds was leaving in forty-five minutes and I'd been steadily draining pints since lunchtime in order to muffle the panicked hiss of anxiety that inevitably accompanied trips up north. I hated them all madly – even Jenny, whose devoutly secular parents (of Jewish and Catholic stock) banned all mention of 'that capitalist holiday' and lived in denial of Dean Martin, satsumas and the Immaculate Conception. She'd still be here, at least, at the centre of the universe, attending dazzling parties and throwing coins at carollers on the Tube. Julian was off to the country pile (I pictured Noël Coward, vast drawing rooms and legions of drunk chinless relatives) and Astrid to the Dickensian home of Christmas itself (as Julian hadn't failed to point out: 'Is Tiny Tim a cousin of yours, sweetheart?' I'd kicked him under the table).

The closer I got to King's Cross, the more I felt I'd be torn forever from the life I'd painstakingly constructed here. More pressing still – though I didn't dare admit it to anyone – was the nauseating prospect of being without Astrid for five days. Since that first Wednesday spot at the club, I could probably count on one hand the nights we'd slept apart. She'd essentially moved into my flat on Charlotte Street. We'd got to that point I'd until now only ever read about and scoffed at: entire days spent in bed. Not even necessarily making love, just being together, *Summer with Monika* style. I glanced at her across the table, swirling the ice cubes in her Scotch, and felt a jarring swell of uncertainty push at my chest. What would they all do when I'd got on my train? Maybe Jenny would go and meet a friend in Bloomsbury, or her sister for dinner somewhere near the student union. Maybe Julian would offer to take Astrid home in his stupid soft-top car . . .

'A lady private investigator,' said Jenny smugly. 'I am in no doubt that that jacket once belonged to a lady private investigator.'

We thought we were being clever. Astrid had turned up glowing with pride at her new jacket and we were trying to decide *from whose dead hands Oxfam had prised it*.

'She's got a sweet little flat off Marylebone High Street

and she smokes cigars whenever she has male clients over, to impress them, but is generally more inclined to Sobranies. She was born in India, of course, but her parents were—'

'Eaten by tigers!' Julian supplemented.

Jenny grimaced a little. 'OK, her parents were eaten by tigers,' she conceded, as if humouring an overexcitable child. 'Anyway, she got shipped off to some dire boarding school after the – ahem – tiger incident, and during the school holidays she had to live with a monstrous maiden aunt in Scotland . . .' Her eyes flicked up to meet mine. 'No,' she said, 'worse still – Yorkshire . . .'

Julian started to bray, as he often did when caught off guard.

Astrid's eyes met mine and I managed to filter out everything my friends were saying. Under the table, I ran my foot along her calf.

'I'll miss you,' I mouthed, and her face split into a toothy grin.

'Oh you two are just vile!' Jenny said, interrupting herself. 'Come on, Jules, let's go get the next round.'

On the jukebox, the first notes of 'White Christmas' oozed into the throng of the pub.

'Do you reckon this song is about cocaine?' Julian said to Jenny, pushing his chair back.

'Oh Julian, you're an absolute tosser sometimes, you know.'

'Well,' he sniffed, 'guess my Christmas is going to be more exciting than yours then.'

*

A blisteringly cold night in January, about a week after I'd got back to London. She'd put on a record – Dusty Springfield. Ice pearled at the hinges of the window frame. Our breath stood out for a second, like frosted glass, when we spoke.

'I like these nights,' she whispered. I felt the round of each syllable on my neck as they formed, lived for a moment and then buried themselves there. She pressed her nose into my skin. I reached for her hand and stretched it up with mine, pulling her body up with it until our mouths were level and our lips touched as we spoke.

'Me too.'

I liked having no heating. I liked having zero inclination to leave the flat. The metallic light of outside, grazing the misted surface of the window, looked hostile and foreign. I felt like everything I'd ever wanted was right here, sealed in with the peeling skirting boards.

'Do your parents know about me?' she'd asked earlier, body pasted to mine for warmth as we'd walked down Gower Street towards the chippy.

'My parents don't know about anything,' I'd said, surprised at the calmness of my voice as it acknowledged their existence.

A quiet little *oh*, barely audible – maybe I didn't even hear it, maybe I just saw it make its imprint on the stark night air. The bell jingled as I pushed at the door. Searing acetone light. The radio playing the racing report. Fat and salt.

'You want fish too?'

She'd nodded, apparently fixated on the speckled linoleum of the floor. I made determined small talk with the boy at the counter, feeling acutely that I'd upset her somehow and wanting to get out of there. The racing report had stopped and some man with an excruciating public school accent was talking about the Five Nations match that France had just lost to Scotland.

'We've been dead calm tonight,' said the boy.

'It's the cold, isn't it?' Something banal like that. I was looking at Astrid, drumming my fingers on the steamy counter. 'Sounds like Jules, doesn't he?' I chuckled limply, pointing up at the ceiling to the disembodied voice. She shrugged.

'Salt and vinegar?'

'Here, let me do it,' I said. They never put enough.

Back at the flat, with her fingers smeared in newspaper ink and grease, she asked me if I was ashamed of her.

'Where did that come from?' I asked, stunned.

She screwed the pages of the *Evening Standard* into a tight little ball and walked over to the basin to wash her hands.

'Why don't your parents know about me?' she asked.

'*That*'s what you're upset about?'

'What do they think of all your posh friends? Do they like Jenny?'

I held my hands up, palms flat. 'My parents don't even know Jenny exists. She'd eat them alive. They'd probably think she was a communist. Or they'd look at her hair and think she was into free love or something.'

She looked directly at the light, as if trying not to cry.

'What would they think of me?'

'Christ. I don't know. Fuck knows. I'm sure they'd like you. Or my dad would . . . I don't know. The last time my mother liked someone, butter was probably still rationed.'

I wiped my hands down my jeans and stood up. Crossed the room to where she was and placed my hands on her shoulders.

'Hopefully we'll never have to find out. Hopefully you'll never have to meet them.'

'I *want* to meet them,' she insisted.

I looked at her then – at her eyes with their liquid irises – and I felt absolutely certain that she was the only person I counted as family. I pulled her in close to me and spoke into the crown of her head.

'You're my family. I don't give a shit about my parents.'

I held her very close to me like that for a long time and realised quite acutely how much it terrified me that she was a separate entity to me; that we weren't entirely joined – bound – even if it felt that way. I wondered how tightly I'd have to hold her until we were. Still speaking into her hair I said:

'My parents have treated me like a fucking changeling all my life.' I wanted to smoke but I also didn't want to let her go. 'I grew up thinking I was an alien, and then I went to university and I thought I'd find people like me, and I was just surrounded by people like Julian.'

She conceded a little laugh.

'I love Jules and Jenny, but they don't know anything about me. They don't know anything about anyone. They live on Mars . . . Do you hear the way they speak sometimes?'

I held her about an inch away from me, took in her eyes again, the slope of her nose.

'You're my family,' I said again, more firmly this time.

She grinned at me, and for the first time I felt responsible for her. It wasn't entirely unpleasant.

14

Leah

Clarissa hadn't been exaggerating: it was apparent from the moment we heard the slam of the car door from the drive that something had happened between them in Marseille. It was ten o'clock on Saturday morning. They'd been due back the previous evening, but Anna had called at the last minute to say she was too tired to drive and a friend had offered to put them up.

'Too tired to drive?' Tom had said sceptically. Jenny gave him a stern look. Evidently some discretion about personal matters was still required in my presence. Tom was characteristically oblivious. 'And who are all these *friends* in the south of France anyway?'

'Well you know Anna,' Jenny said firmly. 'She always knows people everywhere.'

'Hmm.' Tom shrugged, and then, indifferently, 'Have you got thirteen down yet?' He'd spent the afternoon devising a crossword and had given it to me to complete, saying as he did, 'Fuck money, I need to leave now. This holiday has aged me thirty years.'

'Thirteen down is impossible. It feels like a cryptic clue,' I said.

'Ah,' he mused, 'that would be because it is. That's the one about Destiny's Child and Alfred the Great, right? Think about getting rid of the vowels and it might make more sense.'

Jenny let out a harassed sigh and went to go and find Michael. Tom pushed his phone across the table towards me.

'Look at what Clarissa just sent me.' His voice was brimming with conspiratorial delight.

What the fuck is going on with Anna? She was like an hour late to pick me up and then when she finally did turn up she was acting like she was on Prozac. Then she says we're staying at this guy's house and it's like this artists' commune . . . Seriously – can't even. Apparently we're coming back to the house tomorrow morning. So much to tell you it's not even real. How is Dad being? Is he still being weird? How have you not warned me about any of this?

I snorted.

Tom smirked. 'Mum thinks Anna's having an affair.'

'What do *you* think?'

'If she is, it's both overdue and deserved.'

'What about Michael?'

'Fuck, Michael's had so many affairs he may as well just throw in the towel now and admit that he's polyamorous.'

'And what about now?'

'Fuck knows. But if Clarissa's not coming home tonight, can we please go into Saint-Luc with your new friends to avoid the atmosphere here? And they say *we're* emotionally needy.'

*

'Make it stop,' Tom groaned when Clarissa slammed the door. He put his head in his hands. 'My mouth tastes like a thousand ashtrays.'

I felt surprisingly sprightly. Tom and Camille had conveniently bonded over the most anorak particulars of camera operation the night before, leaving Jérôme and me free to sneak off to the beach for the vast majority of the evening. Everything had felt deliciously teenage: the silverish tint of his skin under the starlight, the keen thrill of the risk of being caught – his hand over my mouth as I came.

'I envy you your youth,' Tom spat. 'Just wait till you hit thirty.'

It was then that we heard their voices from the drive; Anna's first, in a tone that sounded totally alien to her usual honeyed placidity.

'I just don't understand why you're being such a stroppy cow about this, Clarissa!'

Tom shot me a look.

'A stroppy cow?' Clarissa, incredulous. 'Did you actually just call me a *stroppy cow*?'

'Well I can't believe you're being such a prude. Who kidnapped my groovy stepdaughter and replaced her with Mary-fucking-Whitehouse?'

'*Groovy stepdaughter!*' Tom mouthed at me in horror.

'Anna, this isn't a case of being a prude. It's a case of realising that this guy is an absolute creep.'

'You're just like your father,' Anna cried.

With that we heard footsteps ascending the staircase, and shortly afterwards the gurgle of the shower bursting into life.

When Clarissa emerged, she acted as if nothing had happened. She pulled Tom into a giddy hug and then rather unexpectedly did the same to me. I felt as if blessed by her benign radiance.

'You both look *brilliant*,' she enthused. 'I'm still Brockley Beige. I've got a lot of catching-up to do.'

'How long are you staying?' Tom asked.

'Probably until the end of the month. I've technically only got two weeks' holiday, so I'll need to start working remotely after that, but the gallery's closed – all the clients are in Sardinia on their yachts or whatever – and as long as I've got a Wi-Fi connection, I'm good. It all depends on how long I can put up with these mid-life crises, I suppose.' She looked at Tom with an expression that attempted to be gracefully discreet but was in fact blindingly obvious. 'So what have I missed? You know, besides the adolescent behaviour of my so-called parents?'

'Leah got a boyfriend,' Tom hummed.

'I did *not* get a boyfriend.'

'Whatever. Constant re-creation of the video for "Wicked Game" would suggest otherwise. He's so attractive it burns my eyes.'

'Jesus, you move fast,' Clarissa said with some admiration. 'Who is he anyway? Maybe I know him.'

I cringed. 'You do, kind of,' I said, and recounted the story they'd told me about Nico the first night at Jérôme's.

'Oh my God, *that* guy. Nico was hot. My fourteen-year-old self was madly in love with him, but he just had nothing to say so I assumed he wasn't interested and snogged the one who kept talking about his life in America instead. It's like he thought I *was* an American. He kept asking me if I missed corn dogs and I had no idea what the fuck they even were.'

'I still don't know what they are,' I said.

'Yeah, he was actually such a dickhead. He tried to sleep with me, and when I said no, he was outraged and was just, like, *but English girls always do*,' she put on a ridiculous accent, 'and then he never invited me anywhere ever again. I was so mortified that when I got back to the UK in September, I slept with the first guy who pretended to be nice to me, after a couple of glasses of Blossom Hill at the Year Ten disco.'

I grimaced in sympathy.

'And now after all these years I discover that the nice one did fancy me after all! So much teenage drama and lowering of self-esteem that could have been avoided. We should actually hang out with them,' she said, pushing her hair back from her face. She'd had it cut since I'd last seen her and it made her look like a nineties supermodel, or the lead singer of an art school Britpop band. There again, in the acetone sun, was that look of Michael – terrifying, impatient and completely magnetic.

*

It had been a while since I'd had a friend I was mildly afraid of, and with Clarissa I couldn't quite put my finger on what was wrong, as from the moment she arrived, she treated me like I was one of them.

'I'm so excited you're here this year!' she said that morning, without even the slightest trace of insincerity. 'I haven't been here for longer than a week since I was about seventeen, and now all my friends are in chronically boring relationships, I came *this* close to having the dullest summer ever.'

'Think how I feel,' Tom moaned. 'I'm in my thirties and I'm on holiday with my bloody parents *sin amante*, all to get a bit of cash from the room I rent in a warehouse in Seven Sisters that'll probably get bulldozed and turned into some kind of perverted Bourneville development for bankers by the time I'm back in September. It's all so desperately millennial.'

'At least you're not at the beck and call of some coked-up former YBA hanger-on with kids called Scarlett and Monk. She literally tried to send me to their primary school in Stoke Newington the other day because she'd forgotten to put za'atar on their hummus pots.' She sighed. 'All I can hope for is that the local kids bully them.'

No, I think what put me on edge with Clarissa was her relationship with her family. Anna went out again and didn't come back that Saturday, and once again, her absence was left unmentioned. When Michael emerged from his shed for lunch, blinking in the afternoon sunlight like a vexed mole, Clarissa's greeting was cool.

'Hi, Dad,' she yawned, staying resolutely put in her deckchair. He wandered over without much enthusiasm and kissed her mechanically on the crown of her head.

'Hello, darling,' he murmured, and then, 'What are we eating? Has anyone cooked anything?'

'I think Mum's on strike,' Tom said. Eager for the excuse to escape, I volunteered to go and put together some sort of salad.

In the cool shade of the kitchen I had a moment to consider their frankly alien behaviour. I thought of my own father smiling at the ticket turnstile with shining eyes every time he dropped me off at the train station. My personal brand of pop psychology had made me faintly suspicious of anyone whose parents could be so austere.

From the fridge I took a punnet of plump cherry tomatoes and another of rocket. I started to chop garlic, chillies and red onion to roast with cumin seeds, coriander and chickpeas. In an old Moroccan bowl I crumbled cubes of milky-white feta, slicked over with olive oil and the juice of a knobbly, sun-coloured lemon. Outside, Tom and Clarissa were talking in hushed voices. Michael's wasn't among them. I lazily picked a nectarine from the fruit bowl on the kitchen table and pushed a knife into its soft white flesh. I sank my teeth into the stone-less half and the intense flavour of fragrant sunlight burst onto my palate. Leaning towards the open window, I could hear snatches of what they were saying.

'I'm not going to resent her because Dad's a . . .'

'It's not her fault that he's an old . . .'

'You really think it's that?'

'You really think she doesn't . . .'

'He's just a relic really, isn't he? A total antique.'

'Anna, on the other hand . . .'

'I'm not going to tell him exactly . . .'

'More just . . .'

'Plant the seed?'

'But why do you resent . . .'

'Acting like a . . .'

I was straining to hear what kind of seed Tom was insinuating Clarissa would plant when I heard a distinctly human rustle behind me. I started, letting the knife clatter noisily onto the tiled floor.

'Jesus Christ,' I breathed.

'Sorry,' mumbled Michael, looking thoroughly unapologetic. He was staring at me and I felt fixed – pinned to the kitchen counter.

'I'm just roasting some chickpeas for the salad,' I said inanely, going to pick up the knife so as to occupy my hands.

All at once he was crouched next to me, his hand on mine as I reached for it. Our faces were inches from each other and I felt the thundering drum of blood pulsing at my temples. Slowly he raised his hand to my face and, fixing me again with his gaze, ran his thumb along my bottom lip. I held my breath. Then he smiled at me, as if his behaviour was the most natural thing in the world and said:

'You had nectarine juice all over your mouth.'

His smile was patronising – indulgent. It seemed to imply that my apparent unease was gauche and childish, so I forced a little laugh and stood up as if nothing had happened. I leant casually against the work surface. Still holding the knife, he took a seat at the kitchen table.

'It's funny,' he said at last. 'It sometimes seems as if you're from a totally different planet to Clarissa and Tom.'

Being singled out from the other younger ones made me feel inexplicably uncomfortable.

'Don't let them make you feel nervous,' he said.

'I don't,' I replied through gritted teeth.

He was tracing the outline of his hand with the knife. 'You're adorable,' he said, not looking at me but rather at his hand, and the blackish silver of the blade.

Any response I could have mustered got caught up in my throat and felt hollow and futile anyway. I stared at the floor.

'And that's a good thing.' I could feel him looking at me again. I dared to raise my gaze to meet his, only for it to be caught by his hand on the table. A stream of red bloomed at his palm and was running in a bright channel onto the scuffed wood underneath.

'Michael,' I gasped.

He looked down indifferently as the blood pooled and retraced the lines on his palm.

'Hmm,' he mused, raising his hand to his mouth and licking a little of it away.

I watched him in disbelief. 'What did you do?' I whispered.

'Oh don't be so wet,' he chuckled. 'It's not like I've been crucified.'

I tried to speak but found myself making dumb, goldfish shapes with my mouth where I wanted to form words.

'I wanted to see what it felt like,' he said. 'You know, when you're there, talking to someone and they're boring you, and you suddenly wonder what would happen if you pulled their hair or slapped them? Or when you're standing on the platform waiting for the Tube and you just dare yourself to hurl your stupid, cumbersome body right in front of the train as it hurtles towards you down the tunnel? All that blinding white light and the symphonic *bellow* of the train . . . The mad forward momentum; forwards, forwards, *forwards*!'

My own palms felt all at once cold and damp as I balled them into nervous fists.

Calmly, he stood up. 'Well,' he said, 'I'll go and clean this up in the bathroom if you're going to be so squeamish about it.'

With that he left the room, leaving me feeling foolish, small and hysterical.

15

Michael

It took her a while to notice I was there. I watched as she bit into the firm flesh of the fruit, her pretty white teeth disappearing under the pinkish stain of her mouth and sticky streams of juice running down her chin. She ran her tongue over her top lip (the bow of her lip; have I mentioned the bow of her lip?) and then licked the bottom one too, and it was like my heart was in a vice.

Afterwards, I went to pick up the knife for her; I just wanted to help her, I didn't want to unsettle her. God, what a slap in the face when she went so hard and rigid under my touch! I was so close I could see the liquid glisten on her lips. I couldn't help but reach out and touch her. It felt so right. It was how we'd always been. We'd never had to ask each other's permission because it was so unclear where I ended and she began. She'd loved it when I tugged at her bottom lip with my teeth when we were making love. I'd feel her limbs stiffen underneath me and she'd hold me tighter and I'd know that the moment I slid my fingers inside her she'd be wet.

I wanted to feel the juice of the nectarine on my thumb. That was all. It was a totally natural reaction.

*

That first weekend was excruciating. They spent every second together. She and Tom had taken to each other instantly, of course, but now that Clarissa was here they had solidified into a single unit, and I felt even more cut adrift and liminal than before. They spoke quickly, in a language I couldn't understand and felt little desire to engage with. At lunch on the patio that day, the air was thick with this *din* – this proliferation of voices. I said little, and was faintly aware that when I did speak it came out in caustic bursts. Each time, Jenny would look at me with that concerned, thin-lipped sympathy that used to make my heart swell and that now just left me feeling irked. *What?* I wanted to say. *You're surely used to it with your monosyllabic husband, aren't you?* I was tired of my life being measured out in language.

The atmosphere at the table had been one of barbed, opaque tension, though Tom and Clarissa seemed totally oblivious to it. Jenny had found me in the bathroom just before we'd gone out to eat, winding toilet roll around and around my palm.

'Michael!' she'd gasped – so much bloody gasping, I felt as if I were in the school play. 'What on earth have you done to your hand?'

Then there she was, scrabbling for the ancient first aid kit in the cabinet under the sink and kneeling at my feet as I sat on the edge of the bath, bandaging me up like some kind of Girl Guide. She was always so very capable. No-Nonsense Jenny.

'I cut myself in the shed,' I said limply.

She knew I was lying and she looked at me with searching, pleading eyes. 'You have to talk to me,' she said quietly.

No. No more words.

In the evening, they went to the beach together, and I could hear their soaring peals of laughter carried on the wind. On Monday they had a veritable fucking party there. Leah had emerged from her room at around half past five and come down to the shed to check in with me.

'I've written up the synopses of the two manuscripts from last week that I thought you might want to read,' she said, standing tentatively in the doorway, framed in the virgin sunlight of the outside world. 'And also I forwarded an email from the features guy at the *LRB* to your personal account so you can take a look. It's about the piece on Max Frisch.'

'Well come in then,' I huffed, standing up to usher her in. 'And close the door behind you.' I pulled an old wine crate out from under the desk so she could take a seat.

She had a beach towel slung around her shoulders, and her hair was all piled up on top of her head.

'And how are you going with the diaries?' I asked, not looking at her.

'Very well,' she said, too enthusiastically. 'I just passed the point where you've met that girl, Astrid.'

I felt a definite stab of alarm when she said her name. Forcing myself to look at her (though all I wanted to do was fix my gaze to the floor – I could feel my hands trembling a little) I made myself say – in a voice that I aimed at firm, kindly condescension – 'I think it's better if we don't talk about the diaries so directly. Words like *you*, that kind of thing. It makes it hard to . . .' I hesitated, 'keep things professional. Do you see why that's important?'

She'd turned bright red and I felt comfortable that I'd reiterated our dynamic. I patted her knee to underline that it was a small slip-up – I wasn't really angry. I gestured towards the beach towel. 'Going for a swim?' It struck me how jolly my voice sounded. It wasn't remotely affected. I felt more myself today, more like a whole, coherent entity. Then, as she nodded, something quite spectacular happened; for the duration of a blink, or a heartbeat, or an exhalation, the matter around her seemed to warp and re-form. The particles of light settled on her face differently and I knew all at once that I was right. Warmth spread through my body as if administered with an intravenous drip. In less than a second she was gone again, but it didn't matter. For a moment she'd come back to me. I'd slipped seamlessly through decades, and if I'd been ready for it I could have reached out and touched my past. She was within my reach. She was the spine of the anchor lodged right into the heart of the years that had made me.

*

'You're very sprightly this evening,' Jenny said to me at supper, her voice vaguely suspicious.

I smiled broadly at her. 'Where are the kids?'

'They're having a barbecue on the beach tonight with the French boys.' She poured me a glass of wine.

'Oh to be young and beautiful,' I hummed, and I meant it without a trace of bitterness, because I knew now for certain that time was as elastic as the springy flesh of a teenager. You pinch it, and it relaxes instantly, straight back into its correct form.

After Jenny and Bryan had gone to bed, I strolled along the coastal path under the luminous disc of the moon. It was full, and so potent that the whole indigo dust sheet of night was washed clean with its viscous, milky light. The crickets chattered in the undergrowth, and on the stave beneath them, the tide washed the shoreline in perfect 2/4 time. Everything felt purposefully and sublimely orchestrated. For the first time in weeks, the universe was benign again.

As I came around the bend, I saw them – all limbs and glowing cigarette ends, moving on a pagan axis around their campfire. The rattle of tinny music and her body carried by it, like the rhythmic ebb and flow of the water, dancing with somebody else. The two of *us* dancing in the flat on Charlotte Street; Astrid emerging from the bath, dripping water across the floorboards, and coming into the kitchen. She was naked and her hair was hanging in Medusa coils at her breast, but she absolutely *had* to come and dance, because I'd put on the record of Nina Simone singing 'Suzanne' live, and she couldn't not, could she? And how could I be angry with her, when the counterpoint beat of the music played across her features and illuminated them with the very same delight it gave such an otherwise melancholic song? She put her hands to mine and we danced as a barefoot pair; and as she pressed her body into me, she left her damp silhouette as an Astrid-shaped stain on my clothes. Then all at once, Nina Simone's voice gave way to Grigoris Bithikotsis's and the saline perfume of the air was too much; too evocative – too overwhelming. Astrid on the balcony in the fig-pressed light. Astrid fixed under the beam of the spotlight at Jeremy's. Light, light, too much light. Head streaming with it. Too much light. The water all electrified with it.

A wave of debilitating nausea, and I stumbled forward, on to my knees, and threw up into the cricket-loud scrub.

*

After breakfast on the Tuesday morning, Clarissa came down to the shed. Leah had already disappeared up to her room to work and Tom had gone into town. She knocked, as she'd been trained to do since she'd first discovered power over her own limbs, waddling around our first flat in Highbury.

'Hi, Dad,' she trilled, lingering in the doorway, looking uncharacteristically uncomfortable.

I motioned for her to come in, and as she sat down on

the crate in front of my desk, I felt quite keenly how awkward the whole set-up was – me behind the table and her in front, as if it were a job interview or the headmaster's office. She pushed her hair off her face and sighed.

'Do you want a cup of tea?' I said at last, shifting uneasily in my chair.

'Please,' she said, and I got up, grateful to have something to do, and to have the opportunity to turn my back on her unsettling eye contact. The hiss of the kettle on the camping stove defused the oppressive silence somewhat and – my back still turned to her – she finally began to speak.

'Dad, I don't really know how to tell you this – and to be honest, I'm kind of reluctant to say anything because I don't really even fully know what's going on . . .' There was something false about her voice, a bum note, that you'd only have recognised if you knew her well; she'd inherited her mother's thespian talent after all.

'Go on,' I said, mildly intrigued as to where this was going.

She sighed a little too dramatically and folded her arms. 'Dad,' she said, 'aren't you, like, a little bit concerned about Anna?'

'Anna?' I exclaimed, rather stunned. 'Why on earth would I be concerned about Anna?'

She gave me the same look of strained sympathy that I'd resented Jenny for the day before, and I wondered if she'd learnt it from her, by osmosis, as a child.

'Dad, she's never here.'

I racked my brains as to when I'd last seen my wife. Friday? The sweltering remains of Friday morning, drinking a coffee on the patio and talking about the airport. Yes, that was it. Friday.

'No,' I replied, 'I suppose she's not.'

Clarissa got up to decant the boiling water into the teapot, now that the kettle was whistling hysterically.

'And that doesn't worry you at all?'

'Well, not particularly,' I said. 'Should it?' I was still vaguely perplexed by Clarissa's sudden interest in her stepmother. 'She's not a teenager, you know.'

My daughter placed the pot and two mugs on my desk and sat back down in front of me again, arranging herself elegantly and folding her beautiful slender hands in her lap.

'Dad,' she said again – how unnerving that she kept addressing me like that, as if trying to constantly reiterate our profound bond.

'Daughter,' I replied, with some affectionate irony.

'Look, I . . . Well I . . . Ah, no, I really shouldn't say . . .' She was really hamming it up.

'Go on,' I said indulgently.

She paused for a second and looked at me directly. My daughter was objectively a very attractive woman now, with her big blue eyes and fine retroussé nose. She carried on with her contrived fidgeting and at last placed her hands on the desk, as if she were at a negotiating table in a boardroom, about to broker a deal.

'When Anna and I were in Marseille, well . . . she wasn't on her own.' She paused, the pause of a politician dealing with a delicate issue.

A glacial wave of unpalatable reality. 'I'm sorry?'

Going for the Oscar, Clarissa bit her lip. 'I . . . I think . . .' She gave me a brave little smile. 'No. No, actually, it's nothing. It's really not my place to say.'

'Clarissa—'

'No, really, Dad. It was wrong of me to say anything. I really don't know if anything's even going on.'

'What are you trying to suggest is going on?'

She was standing up now, her mug in her hands.

'No, Dad, really, I'm almost certain it's nothing. It was wrong of me to come.'

'Clarissa,' I insisted. I was trying to appear calm but I could see from her face that it was futile.

'Really,' she said again, in a patronising tone that smacked sourly of her mother, 'I'm sure it's nothing.' She was edging faux-gingerly towards the door.

'*Clarissa.*'

'Try and put it out of your mind. I'm sure I'm probably overreacting. Anna loves you very much,' she said, as her parting jibe.

'Darling—'

It was too late. The door dragged to an excruciating close behind her.

I sat in silence for a minute or so, and at last reached for my phone. I searched for the last message from my wife. Saturday morning.

I've had an argument with Clarissa. I'm sure she'll take great delight in telling you all about it. Ring me later? I'm going to meet my friend from Marseille xx

I'd replied, two hours after her message: *Don't worry, darling, I'm sure it's nothing. Have fun x*

Gripped by a sudden wave of fury, I hurled the stupid phone across the room. It hit the chest in the corner, clanging harmonically off the combination lock. I stared for a moment at the contemptible object. When I finally went to pick it up, the screen had smashed, splitting and fragmenting the image of Anna's face. Cheap piece of shit, I thought: the phone and my wife.

16

Leah

Jérôme lying next to me, naked, flat on his back on the tiles, both of us leaving dark, human-shaped stains on the terracotta. His tanned skin glistens with little beads of water. He's staring at the pinkish dusk sky and lazily tracing the outline of my breasts. My breath comes in flutters; he knows he can make me come just from doing that. I close my eyes. He rolls over so he's half on top of me, his long limbs a cage between me and the endless sky. I smell his breath – tobacco, beer – as he leans down to kiss me. He opens my mouth gently with his tongue and his hands move from my breasts, down in spirals to my navel and then between my wet thighs. I dig my fingers into the twin hollows between his shoulder blades and his spine as he runs his finger along my clit, and bite his bottom lip, desperate to have any part of him in me.

After teasing me for what feels like an excruciating eternity, he slides his fingers inside me and I gasp with delight and open my eyes to see the lines of his face – the thick black eyebrows, the cheekbones, the angle of his jaw dusted with dark stubble and the bridge of his nose. He laughs at me adoringly and pulls away. I look at him – plead with him – and he laughs again and brings his fingers (calloused, useful) to my mouth, still open in a round O of pleasure and anticipation. He drags his fingers along my lips and pushes them into my mouth, and with his free hand he makes me come. I can feel him, hard against me, and as I orgasm, he pushes himself inside me.

We've spent the whole afternoon this way. The house, the jade disc of the pool and the little spinney of pines are ours entirely. The day has been a sun-drunk stupor. He's leaving for Marseille tomorrow. When we finish, me straddling him, he pulls me down onto him and kisses me violently, his fingers grabbing my hair. He stops at last and sighs in happy disbelief, then holds me close, covering my damp skin in kisses. At last he says, '*J'ai la flemme de rentrer à Marseille lundi*' ('I can't be bothered to go back to Marseille').

I say nothing, but stare at the white-gold glint of the sunset reflecting off the surface of the pool. I don't think he's getting attached – but then I never credit men with the ability to get attached anyway, so maybe I'm being unfair. Yesterday he told me to come and see him in Marseille. 'Bring Clarissa and Tom, if you want,' he said, trying to take the edge off it. 'I'll maybe come back one day next week anyway, if you're around.'

In truth, I've been thinking about Lal. He'd been inevitably flitting in and out of my mind since the day I left Paris, and then last week, out of nowhere, he sent me a photograph taken just off the *autostrada* in Liguria. He was straddling the road sign of a little town we'd talked about, and the caption read, *Thanks for the tip. The locals here appreciated my musical talents*. I hadn't even remembered giving him my number, and reread the message in a state of high agitation about five times over before, embarrassed at my own excitement, flinging my phone onto my bed, and affecting total disinterest. I spent the next hour concocting a perfectly pitched, pithy response, but of course when I finally did bite the bullet and reply, I was greeted by radio silence. I kept telling myself I didn't care, but of course I did.

At my side, Jérôme lights a cigarette and gazes at the wispy plumes of smoke, threaded through with dusky light.

'Be careful with that writer of yours,' he says, feigning nonchalance. I'd told him about the nectarine juice and a look of carefully suppressed concern had briefly managed to surface on his features.

'He's absolutely harmless,' I insist. 'Just a bit eccentric.'

He closes his eyes, reaches for my hand, and takes it, in a moment of touching tenderness.

*

In reality, the nectarine thing had left me deeply unsettled, which in a way was why I'd told Jérôme about it in the first place. I was trying to neutralise it by turning it into a funny anecdote. I'd wanted him to make a joke about it, so that instead of feeling belittled and destabilised, I could feel buoyant. I prided myself on being a collector of unbeliev-able stories and eccentric weirdos. I'd built my self-image around the accumulation of adventure. I'd always wanted to be Dora Maar, sitting at a table at Les Deux Magots and staring at Picasso, clasping a knife. I wanted to be Martha Gellhorn, or Janis Joplin – living everything to the point where you necessarily get burnt sometimes. I was hungry above all to live. I wanted to feel everything there was to possibly feel.

The problem was that all of this depended on me seeing myself as towering and unfazed. After Michael had got up from the table, though, and I'd turned back to the oven, checking the chickpeas on automatic pilot, willing them to be done so that I had something else to do with my hands, I just felt small. I felt singled out. I felt like when I went back outside, Tom and Clarissa would see it on my face and they'd think, God, she's so naïve. I remembered Alex's jokes about me being Michael's mistress, and instead of it feeling glamorous, it just felt seedy. I hated the idea that any of them might see me as out of my depth, or worse still, as a victim. I didn't want to be the victim kind.

The further I got into his diaries, though, the harder my spin was to swallow. If I let myself think honestly about it, there was something more than a little creepy about asking someone forty or so years your junior and within the sphere of your power to read them. They were . . . how to put this delicately? Of their time? It wasn't that he was a total misogynist – his friendship with Jenny, patently the most valuable of all his relationships, was testament to that. No, his apparent contempt for women was inextricably linked to sex. It was then that erstwhile human beings became *birds*. They slotted conveniently into textbook virgin/whore dichotomy and any kind of character they'd once had was pasted over with his own projected version. It didn't take long for me to start to view our own relationship through the prism of his diaries. Had that been his intention?

Then a day or two after the nectarine incident, the whole register of his diaries shifted. Michael met a girl and the bawdy *Carry On* vibe became something more sinister. There was something claustrophobic in the way he wrote about Astrid. All the other people who had cropped up so far had felt real. When he'd written about Julian's mother or about Hector, his supervisor at UCL, you could see the first traces of the novelist he was going to become. When he wrote about Astrid, his own response to her was so all-consuming that I couldn't imagine her at all; his own strength of feeling had somehow erased her altogether.

Some of the excruciating pornographic passages, on the other hand, were disturbingly erotic. I'd read them and I'd feel myself *feeling* them – and afterwards I'd have to lie flat on my back on the hard parquet, staring at the ceiling until my head stopped swimming.

*

Thursday evening. Clarissa, Tom and I were loafing on the terrace at Le Bastringue, having fled there after another fraught scene at dinner. Clarissa ran her tongue along the sticky edge of a Rizla and rolled her cigarette into a perfect white stick. 'It's not the first time he's been like this,' she said.

Tom snorted. He was still looking a bit peaky after Michael's outburst. 'Here, give us one,' he said, reaching for the packet of American Spirit.

Clarissa lit hers. 'I remember there was this one summer when he spent every evening lying on the floor of his shed listening to "If You See Her, Say Hello", smoking. It was when we were really little. Lawrence and I used to sneak down and climb the chestnut tree and watch him. It was the summer Mum left him. Well, she left in September – the first week back at school. Then there was the Christmas after the TV film, just before he went out to California, when he was running around like a frisky cat, pinging off the walls like you do when you take 2C-B, before the hallucinations kick in . . .' After a minute or so, she stubbed out her cigarette in the old Pernod ashtray. She was a fast smoker. I eked out each cigarette for at least a long pop song's worth of contemplation, but Clarissa seemed to inhale them all in one go.

There had indeed been a marked development in Michael's behaviour towards us since Clarissa's arrival. His lofty personal-tutor guise of yore had become more indulgent mentor, and the pleasure he took in my company increased in a parallel trajectory to his growing misanthropy with the others. At meals (he'd appear from the shed a little wild-eyed and generally dishevelled), he'd sit scrutinising the cutlery and skimming the surface of our conversation only enough to make the occasional barbed comment to his daughter, who took them with bored indifference as if they were arrows bouncing off the shell of a tank. Sometimes she'd throw a weary pellet back in his direction: 'Yes, Dad, you're right, all my generation cares about is status and material goods, unlike yours. I'm sure that huge collection of art you've accumulated in that house you own in north London has nothing to do with demonstrating your exquisite taste and education to all who pass through.' Jenny would start to valiantly pilot the conversation away, but by then Michael would have inevitably zoned out again anyway.

Anna had now been gone for five days. We knew that she was at least alive, as Clarissa had spoken to her on the telephone.

'I'll come back when I want to,' she'd said firmly, an adverb chosen by Clarissa that had caused much mirth with Tom, who'd said, 'She spoke to *you* firmly? Well, there's a first for everything.'

That evening's particular fracas had begun over something trivial, as they tended to. Tom had expressed a political opinion that had spurred Michael into a hissing, venomous assessment of Tom's privilege. We'd all sat in horrified silence, until, from nowhere, Bryan had spoken. 'What is *wrong* with you?'

Michael had blinked like a favourite child at the novel sensation of punishment.

'What?' he'd said blankly. 'Why are you defending Julian, for Christ's sake?'

A moment's confused silence. 'Julian?' Clarissa had said, perplexed. Jenny, blanching, had left the table.

'Well if she's going to leave, I'm leaving too,' Michael had spat.

The four of us left had sat for a long, wordless moment, before Bryan had given a throaty baritone laugh, put his fingers to his temples and screwed his eyes shut.

'Of course,' he'd said.

'They've definitely talked about Julian before,' Tom insisted now, between drags of the badly rolled cigarette. He rolled enthusiastically tight ones that strangled the tobacco and required constant relighting and Olympian levels of breath control.

'I probably zoned out like I always do,' Clarissa said. 'I'm not like you lot. I find everyone's weird self-mythologising in this family kind of dull. We're like a family made up entirely of anecdotes and dead people. I was always more interested in their living friends. Like that one who used to sneak off at the New Year party and take a shitload of coke and then come back and dance like Mick Jagger with everyone else's wives.'

'Lechy Andrew?' Tom said.

'That's the one!'

'You know he had a thing with your mum after the divorce, don't you?'

'Ugh, no, stop, this is *exactly* what I mean,' she groaned. 'You don't know how lucky you are,' she added to me, and I nodded with faux-sympathy – secretly, passionately jealous that they came from the kind of family who had New Year parties and anecdotes.

'Anyway, you absolutely know who Julian is. I've even met him.' Tom paused and looked vaguely smug. 'Your dad fell out with him long before the pre-internet age, which I think made it a bit awkward for Mum, but she kept in vague touch. He came to London when I was a kid. He brought me a Tamagotchi.' He poured more wine into our glasses, and from across the table I felt the burn of Clarissa's gaze.

'What?'

'Well,' she said, looking pleased with herself, 'if anyone knows about this Julian guy, surely it'll be you, right?'

'Uh . . .'

'I mean, you're basically being employed to coordinate the omnishambles that is Dad's diary, right?'

'I am,' I offered gingerly. I was naturally hesitant talking to Clarissa and Tom about the work I was doing for Michael. Although we mentioned it rarely, I still couldn't shake the idea that if I were in Clarissa's position, I would find my very presence in the nest suspect.

'So who's Julian?' she insisted.

'Julian was their old mate from uni who went off to America and never came back,' Tom said, evidently aware of my discomfort – as was Clarissa, I suppose, though it was obvious she derived a grain of pleasure from it.

'Come *on*!' she begged, needling me. 'Dish the dirt!'

I swallowed a mouthful of wine and wondered how best to diminish her interest. 'To be honest, I don't know that much about Julian. Your dad takes it for granted that the reader is already acquainted with him. I mean, you do that in a diary, don't you? You just write about all these ready-made characters. It's not a novel.'

'Stop avoiding the question.'

I sighed. 'Well from what I can gather from my very limited knowledge . . .'

'Pertinent disclaimer!' Tom interrupted, only to be hushed by Clarissa.

'. . . Julian, Jenny and Michael were a happy little trio, and I feel like maybe your dad put him on a pedestal a bit. He was like this fabulous glamorous posh kid with a Mitford-sister mother and a house in South Ken with William Morris wallpaper.'

'Eww,' said Clarissa.

'Yeah, so far so very un-Tom.'

'I felt a definite kinship with him aged eleven, to be honest. I mean, I mentioned the Tamagotchi?'

'I feel like he was a bit of a creep, to be honest.'

'Sounds right up Dad's street,' Clarissa sniped, and I felt a swell of gratitude that she'd said it rather than me.

*

Coming up along the dirt track that night, through the fragrant coppice of pines, the house pale in the calcium glow of the moon, I thought to myself how different it had looked on that first night. Clarissa and I, drunk, were swaying arm in arm, intermittently doubled over, wheezing with fits of giggly laughter about almost nothing. We were mates. We were connected, bonded, on the same page, perhaps. We were at that stage of new friendship where the links that joined us felt unlike any links ever forged before: unique and elastic and natural. I felt a sting of guilt at my erstwhile *mauvaise foi*; my original misogynist assumption that Lawrence would be the easier sibling to crack.

As we came onto the drive, she ground to a sudden halt. 'Well,' she said huffily. 'She's back then.'

Anna's car was parked up next to the house.

'She can deal with Dad. Perfect,' Clarissa said, and flounced inside.

17

The Anna who appeared at breakfast the following morning was more herself than ever. She shimmied across the patio in a gauzy saffron kaftan, already wearing jewellery and a slick of mascara. She was radiating – no, *oozing* (such an Anna word after all) – health, charm and confidence. She floated over to the dining table and pulled out the chair next to mine. '*Darling*,' she sighed. 'How have you *been*?'

Mouth full of melon, I emitted some enthusiastic consonants and awkward thumbs-up gestures. Clarissa interrupted me from the other end of the table. 'How have *you* been, Anna?'

Unmoved, Anna put on her warmest, most professional smile. 'Marvellous, thanks. The project's going so well.' Clarissa snorted. Anna ignored her, gracefully. 'Pass me the coffee, will you?' she said to Tom, and then, as she poured it, 'I was thinking that tonight we should have a little gathering.'

Clarissa rolled her eyes and Anna carried on stoically.

'Lawrence and his friend are arriving and it would be nice to really welcome them properly, you know? Plus I've been so busy with the project I've barely seen any of you for a week.'

It was the second time in as many minutes that she'd referred to this project, and each time she did, it provoked the most Michael-esque of reactions in her stepdaughter. As I appeared to be the only one in the dark about it, I thought it better to just go on pretending that I was as au fait as the rest of them and to grill Tom as soon as I could get him on his own.

'I thought you guys could invite the French boys if you liked. We won't go mad – just an olives and drinks kind of thing.'

'Oh, I can cook something,' offered Jenny with a knowing smile.

Anna contrived to light up her face. 'Really? Well, I can make cocktails! What do you think?' she asked Michael, who was pouring coffee and studying the paper.

He took off his sunglasses and rubbed the lenses on his shirtsleeve, then examined them in the light. 'Yeah. I don't see why not.'

A collective wave of relief rippled across the table. Even Clarissa seemed impressed.

'Brilliant,' Jenny said. 'All right then, I'm going to need a head count for food. The French boys?'

'Jérôme would probably come back for a little *fête*,' I said.

'Maybe Nico?' said Clarissa. I shot her a conspiratorial smile.

Anna beamed. 'Perfect. So that's the seven of us, plus Larry and Luke . . . Do we know what time they're getting in?'

Clarissa shrugged. 'I think Lal said around six in his text.'

I felt my jaw go slack despite myself. My insides seemed to contract.

Anna smiled serenely. 'So us, Luke, Larry . . .'

A *posh-person nickname*; I suppose it should have been obvious really.

*

I lost almost a morning's work to frenetic panic. When I finally gave up even trying and went down to the beach to swim, I found Clarissa. I laid my towel down next to her and tried to discreetly probe.

'So what's he like then, your brother?'

She sighed. 'He's a boy. He's pretty cool – he's funny, charming, I guess . . . Girls love him; it's kind of sickening actually. Oh my God, if you fall in love with him, I'll actually have to leave.'

I tittered nervously and made a limp joke about employment ethics. Lal had certainly been infuriatingly lovable. I tried to get a picture of his face in my mind, standing on the railway bridge in the dusky light. Had he looked like Michael? Or even like Clarissa? All I could picture was long gangly legs, his right foot hanging out of the bed. Hairy toes.

Clarissa gave a little feline yawn and asked me to put sun cream on her back.

'His friend's kind of up himself too,' she murmured into her beach towel. 'Like – he's cool, he's super-clever, but I think he's got a bit of a chip on his shoulder. He's northern so he thinks I'm a silly posh girl, but of course he doesn't think Lal's a silly posh *boy* because boys just can't be silly, right?'

She moved a little, adjusting to get comfortable, and I watched her slender ribs ripple underneath my hands.

'They both think they're super-fucking-bohemian just because they've never had real jobs. Luke's like setting up an artists' squat in Lewisham or something and he works in a bar and sleeps with lots of posh girls slumming it in SE-whatever.'

I detected a note of bitterness in her voice and nastily assumed it was a telling one.

'They're fun, though. It'll be fun when they're here. Dad might become vaguely human again in the presence of darling angel Larry too, which is always good.'

'Darling angel Larry?' I asked.

'Lal's Dad's favourite,' she said matter-of-factly. 'I mean, it's fine. I prefer Mum anyway.'

*

Jenny had set me to work egg-glazing and breadcrumbing an endless procession of sliced aubergine. I'd got no work done all day and the position of sous chef was a welcome distraction. She'd mixed us both a spritz and had put on a Serge Gainsbourg record. As always, her very presence was soothing. She'd been pottering around, making small talk and singing along (fairly tunelessly) in her perfect French to 'Couleur Café' when at last she sat on one of the high stools, looked at me frankly and said:

'Michael's not being too much of a bore with you, is he?'

'I'm sorry?' I said, managing to flick a great viscous trail of whisked egg into the bowl of breadcrumbs.

She sighed and asked for a cigarette. 'We're in France. It doesn't count.'

She smoked like a real, dedicated smoker, or a gourmet who'd been living off cornflakes for decades.

'Phew!' she whistled. 'This fag's going straight to my head. Christ knows what would happen if I smoked pot.'

I thought of the Jenny of Michael's diaries, dropping acid at parties in Hampstead and staying up until seven in the morning.

'All right then, I'll cut the bullshit, shall I?' she said, exhaling loudly. 'And this is coming from a place of concern because I really am very fond of you, Leah – we all are.' She put her hand on my shoulder to reiterate her words and said, 'Michael's not being . . . well . . . a creep with you, is he?'

I shuffled awkwardly and laughed. 'No. Well . . . not *really*. I mean, not as the scale of creepiness goes.'

'Of course we're all worried about him too – patently,' she said, apparently feeling like a bit of a Judas. 'But I did want to check with you. I'm just a little concerned that he's got some sort of idea about you.'

'What kind of idea?' I asked defensively.

'Oh . . . oh, well, nothing really, it's just . . . What exactly is he getting you to do?'

I began to reel off my daily tasks, attempting to make them sound as pedestrian and unthreatening as possible. 'I deal with his correspondence, I read a lot of the manuscripts he gets sent . . . At the moment I'm transcribing his diaries.'

'All of them?' She gasped. 'How much is he paying you?'

'No, not all of them. Just from the end of the sixties, when you guys had graduated.'

'The end of the sixties?' Jenny repeated. She leant back on the stool and pinched her eyebrows. 'Jesus, Michael,' she hissed.

I was about to ask her to reciprocate my candour when the voices of Clarissa and Tom drifted in from the drive. Jenny began furiously to stub out her cigarette in the sink and gave me a look of clownish guilt that quickly vanished from her face as the others entered the room, hot, sweaty and laden down with shopping bags full of alcohol.

'Phew!' Clarissa cried. 'Town was scorching!' She flopped down into the armchair, the clang of bottles bouncing off the stone walls. 'I'm actually really looking forward to tonight.'

'Yeah, I wonder why?' Tom scoffed bitchily, mopping the sheen of sweat from his forehead.

Clarissa smiled faux-sweetly and turned to me. 'We saw Nico in town,' she explained. 'He's definitely coming.'

'*Voilà!*' crowed Tom.

She scowled at him. 'And he says Jérôme will come too,

obviously. I told him your text probably just didn't send because of the crap signal in this wilderness.'

I managed a neat little smile and a *brilliant*. Jérôme's text hadn't arrived because naturally I'd never written it. Me, Jérôme and Lawrence: what a happy threesome. What a fun evening ahead.

*

Clarissa heard them first, and despite her disparaging assessment of them earlier on the beach, her delight was obvious. She sat bolt upright in her deckchair, almost upending a vast chalice of spritz.

'Can you hear that? It's a car. It *must* be them!'

Sure enough, the rumble of the engine came in a crescendo as it rounded with a wheeze onto the driveway. Real posh people always had crap cars. The tin shed on wheels that trundled onto the driveway was true to type, and even with the glint of the low evening sun, coming off in a brilliant shaft from the windscreen, the boy behind it was unmistakably Lal. I wondered if he'd clocked me yet.

Clarissa raced over to them, and I felt grateful that Tom stayed put and lit a cigarette, giving me an excuse to do the same. I watched them both unfold out of the little car, as tall men tend to do. I say *them*, but of course my gaze was focused almost entirely on Lawrence, who doubled in height as he stood up. He shook out his hair, stretching. Clarissa danced around him until at last he scooped her up into a hug, and then time sort of slowed right down as the three of them, the magnetic, attractive siblings made a trio by Luke, came towards us. I tried to decide once and for all how I would react. Did I openly recognise him and thus risk humiliation if he denied our meeting? Should I feign ignorance and instead look like a total sociopath if he did the opposite? The three of them were close enough for facial expressions to be read, but his remained impassive. He concentrated quite determinedly on his sister, who was in the middle of an animated monologue.

'Mate!' cried Tom, standing up as they approached and pulling Lawrence into one of those distinctly masculine embraces before doing the same with Luke. I realised that suddenly everyone was standing except me, and felt it acutely in a wave of painful awkwardness. I was about to get up too, already dreading that peripheral hover you're subjected to as the token outsider when a group of old friends are greeting each other, when Clarissa came and dragged me out of my deckchair (how could I be so gauche as to still be sitting?) and pushed me in the general direction of her brother.

'And this is Leah!' she said triumphantly.

I beamed at him with a sort of blank neutrality that I hoped would encourage him to decide which path of action we were going to take. He pulled me into a friendly hug and I remembered how his arms and torso had felt, naked and pressed into my own body. Sensing the lie of the land, I was about to say something like *Well, how ridiculously small is the world?* when from another reality I heard him say, with apparent warmth and sincerity, 'Leah. It's so good to finally meet you.'

My heart jerked. The embrace ended and we were back facing each other again, the smile still fixed on my face.

'Yes,' I heard my own voice reply, and then, clumsily, 'Overdue.'

Before I had time to even register his reaction, I was being introduced to Luke, and as that was happening, the grown-ups were suddenly flooding onto the patio. Dazed, I went through the motions of conversation with Luke and felt rather like I'd been dropped into a play in the third act and swept up in an unanticipated and totally inexplicable musical number; everyone else was au fait with the steps and I was obliged to act as though I was too. The other members of the cast rotated around while I smiled dumbly at the centre, waiting for the moment when everyone had taken their position for the next scene and I could politely slip off to the loo and breathe, and manically assess everything that had just not happened.

The shadowy cool of the bathroom was pleasant. I sat on the edge of the bath and stared at my reflection in the speckled mirror, attempting to hinge myself on the steady drip of the tap. He was evidently insane. A megalomaniac. Either that, I thought, or, grasping at the straws of charity, he had that thing where you can't remember people's faces – I'd read about it once; a journalist had gone and interviewed small children and lonely adults in places like Wigan and Peterborough who couldn't even identify their own father. It was likely that he had that, right? I laughed at my reflection bitterly. Of course I had knotted myself into this sticky web, all in the pursuit of bloody *trouser*. True to form.

The French boys were due to arrive in about an hour, and in the meantime I occupied myself as much as possible, eagerly volunteering to do things like lay tables and slice fruit. Clarissa sidled up behind me at the patio table and surveyed the vastly growing brilliant swells of lime, lemon and orange.

'Are you OK?'

'Yeah, yeah – all good!' I sang. 'What can I say, Pavlovian throwback to dinner parties at my nan's. She trained me young!'

'You seem very . . . jolly?'

'I'm always jolly!'

She raised a cynical eyebrow at me. 'Come sit,' she insisted. Fully aware that my smile didn't extend much beyond a pained tension around my mouth, I followed obediently.

They had all formed an unconscious ring around Luke and Lawrence, who were lounging, smoking and rolling out tales from their adventures like a well-versed comedy duo.

'Nah, but the best part,' Lawrence was crowing, 'was that he was absolutely convinced that Luke was Italian, literally for *no* reason, and he kept translating stuff for him. So he'd be there to me like, *Hey, your friend, very beautiful!* and then he'd shoot Luke this conspiratorial smile and be like, *Una bella donna, é?*'

'And I was just like *Si, si. Andiamo. Molto baci.*' Luke finished Lawrence's sentence, exaggerating his monotone northern lilt for effect. Everyone laughed and I attempted to twitch my mouth into a similar expression of appreciation.

'Oh darling,' Jenny said, noticing me lingering. 'Have we run out of deckchairs?'

'Here, you can sit on me if you want. This one's super-sturdy and I'm nothing if not gallant,' said Lawrence, beckoning with matey enthusiasm.

'No, here, take mine,' Luke said, standing up before I could protest and ushering me into his spot. Now of course I was next to Larry, and I felt his gaze graze my profile.

'So,' he said, 'it's not been too nightmarish bunking in with this mad clan?'

His total ease with this game was staggering. I turned to him and searched his face for even a trace of the truth, and found nothing. I was stirred, at last, by a latent sense of competition.

'*Mad* certainly being the operative word,' I said pointedly, and returned his banal grin. A flicker of surprise played out on his features and was gone in a second.

'Well you've got me as a buffer for the weekend, Leah,' said Luke. 'Before I go back to the Costa del Deptford on Monday.'

'Oh, you're not staying?' Clarissa said, trying not to sound too wounded.

'No rest for the wicked. We're putting on a bunch of nights at the space, so it's off to work I go.'

'*Work*,' snorted Lawrence.

Luke looked almost offended.

'Tell us all about your space, Luke,' Anna purred. 'We want to know *everything*.'

'You definitely don't want to know *everything*, Anna.' Lawrence smirked.

'I wouldn't be so sure about that,' chuckled Michael.

Jenny, as always, swept in. 'Larry, be a doll and come and help me bring out the food from the kitchen. People will start arriving soon.'

He stood to attention. 'At your beck and call. I am your devoted sous chef.'

'No,' said Jenny, 'that's Leah. You can be my *plonge*.'

I knew the hierarchical reference would probably be lost on him, but it made me feel warm inside regardless.

*

'This is brilliant!' Clarissa trilled. 'It's just like old times.'

I'd rarely seen her so enthusiastic. She was leaning in the crook of Nico's arm, both of them sandwiched into the hammock in the garden, smoking and drinking some dubious murky cocktail that Luke had claimed was his speciality. The rest of us were arranged around them on the low stone wall. I was half aware of Jérôme idly trailing his fingers through my hair. He'd said little all night, being well out of his depth when the conversation had inevitably jerked back into English. I'd felt a physical twinge of tenderness for him as he'd awkwardly introduced himself to the boys, his mouth apparently unable to chew through the cadences of the shared mother tongue that had bonded me so effortlessly to Larry. I'd only ever known him in French – cocky, flirtatious, easily intelligent and open. In the way that *his* language when I was first learning it had tended to soften my character, reducing me to something compliant and naïve, my own had the opposite effect on him. English made him shy and sullen.

I remembered the first night we'd spent together; he'd played me the old Algerian Raï song that he'd sampled, and he'd held me close and whispered the translation of the Arabic lyrics in my ear, his voice a delicious extra bass line against the soaring vocal track. He delighted in that language. He'd told me that he'd made a conscious effort to improve the childish familial Arabic that he'd spoken with his maternal grandparents and that his mother had so consciously shed in school as a child. I remembered the confident depth of his voice on my earlobe and I felt the unpleasant press of guilt around my clavicle again.

His reticence wasn't just because of the linguistic shift. By the time he'd arrived, I'd already been drunk, having necked Luke's cocktails fast in search of a feeble social crutch. Then Michael, still unsettlingly cheerful, had inexplicably reserved all of his usual frostiness for Jérôme, greeting him with suspicious *froideur*. Admittedly, the latter had hardly made any enthusiastic overtures towards his host. He'd been civil and polite. I should never have told him about the nectarine thing.

The new arrivals didn't help, of course. Larry and I had somehow managed to become entangled in some jarring game of one-upmanship as to who could make the other feel the most uncomfortable.

'You know I was actually in Paris a couple of weeks back,' had been his first jibe.

'Oh really?' I'd said, feigning disinterest.

'Yeah,' he said. 'I was at a party full of English people near that park in the 19th. Wouldn't it have been crazy if we'd crossed paths?' He looked revoltingly pleased with himself.

Everyone else had been blissfully oblivious to this tension between us, except, apparently, Jérôme. As soon as he'd arrived, he'd put his arm around me in an uncharacteristically proprietorial way that had instantly put my back up. Rendered even less discreet than usual, courtesy of Luke's mystery mixes, I'd gracelessly wriggled out of his grip. I couldn't help but feel that Lawrence had surveyed the whole gaffe with a look of cool amusement, and for a moment I really did despise him. I'd leant back on Jérôme (a twinge of guilt at seeing how visibly hurt he was) and made some limp excuse about the heat. My drunken inner monologue, inclined to dramatic hyperbole anyway, concluded that I was in fact a monster.

Everyone other than the two of us appeared to be dusted in that shimmery golden glow of a successful *soirée*. A few of the neighbours (mostly antique) had pitched up, and with their blessing the speakers had been brought out onto the patio, which Anna had lit up beautifully with candles and little garlands of lights, throwing moody, theatrical beams about, and making everyone look sublime. Couples were dancing barefoot and explosive peals of laughter drifted on the cool evening breeze, over the chatter of the records.

'*Viens danser*,' Jérôme said softly, his bottom lip brushing my earlobe.

'Gladly,' I said, trying not to look at Lawrence.

'*Ah, les lovers!*' Nico crowed in his ever-endearing Franglais, making me cringe down to the quick.

Jérôme pulled me towards the music. One of the marginally younger neighbours had put on 'Do You Really Want to Hurt Me?' by Culture Club. The sentiment wasn't lost on me.

'I don't understand you,' he said, holding me very close so that his voice was barely above a whisper.

'I don't really understand me either,' I said, wasted and self-indulgent.

'One minute you seem to be so into this, and then the next you're distant and cold and I feel like an idiot for letting myself feel anything for you at all.'

'You shouldn't feel anything for me,' I slurred. 'I'm really not that kind of girl.'

'Oh come on,' he hissed. 'Cut that bullshit, no one believes it. You need to stop trying to narrate your life and just live it. *Not that kind of girl?* You sound like a fucking pop song.'

I wasn't used to this directness and it stung. The bridge of my nose burned. He looked down at me, and what was evidently genuine pain flashed across his features. The dark shadows cast by the amber candlelight made him quite heart-stoppingly beautiful, and his smell – a faint tang of sweat, pine needles and salt – was so right that I wanted to bury my idiot face in his chest and retreat there forever. Neither of us said anything for a moment, until at last:

'His son seems like a jerk too.'

'Huh?' I murmured.

'The writer – his son. He's totally conceited.'

'Why are you being so defensive?' I demanded, knowing of course that he had every reason to be.

'*Oh là, putain Léa!* You're so impressed by them, aren't you? You're so desperate to be part of their world . . .'

Smarting, I jerked away from the warm envelope of his body. I felt unsteady on my feet and vaguely nauseous. 'That's not fair,' I spat. It was totally fair.

'*Léa* . . .'

'I'm going to get a cigarette.'

'Don't.'

'Don't tell me what to do.' I hated myself for being so petulant.

'Have one of mine,' he offered as an olive branch.

'I have a pack in my room, thanks.'

He winced, and I turned on my heel and left. As I crossed the patio, I glimpsed Michael from the corner of my eye, leaning on the support of the canopy, framed by trailing leaves so that he looked like a figure in a fresco. He was alone – entirely – coolly watching the scene.

Inside, my head spun and I sat on the staircase up to my room for a second to steady myself. I closed my eyes and leant my head on the banister and a few seconds later felt someone distinctly male sit down next to me. Assuming it was Jérôme, I put my hand on his comfortingly solid knee.

'I don't think your boyfriend would like that.' It was Lawrence's voice, of course. I snatched my hand away.

'You're a sociopath,' I said.

'I try.'

I opened my eyes lazily and looked up at him. He was smiling at me. 'Isn't the world small?' he said inanely.

'Did you know who I was? When we met in Paris?'

'I had a vague inkling, confirmed by social media sleuthing.'

'You're unbelievable.'

'Lighten up! It's a bit of joke – come on, admit that this lengthy charade has added a bit of spice to an otherwise dull evening.'

'It's been so fucking awkward,' I groaned.

He laughed and I felt an involuntary and unwelcome softening towards him.

'Anyway,' he said, biting his thumb around the cuticle just as his father did, 'it's been kind of fun, being in on this secret and everyone else being totally oblivious. Plus your face. Priceless. Points for acting, though.'

I said nothing, and at last he said, 'Yeah, I'm sorry about that morning – at your place. It was a bit weird, wasn't it?'

'Hmm. Just a bit.'

'You know I did want to kiss you – I mean obviously . . .'

Again that involuntary feeling, a jolt, a frisson.

'But I knew who you were. I knew you'd been working for my dad all summer – that you'd be here. Now *that* would have been fucking awkward.'

Proud and infinitely more animated, I said, 'Who said I was harbouring a grudge about that?'

He ignored me. 'Well it all worked out for the best anyway, didn't it? Now you've hooked up with Gallic-charm-incarnate himself and you can fix me up with one of his sexy French mates.'

I smiled amicably and felt my poor heart recoil and curl up like a woodlouse.

*

By the time we returned to the hum of the party, Jérôme had left. He'd texted me saying we'd speak tomorrow, but that he was feeling tired and misanthropic and wanted to be alone. Of course he'd been kind enough to text and hadn't just stormed off into the night. Typical.

'Come on!' Luke cried jubilantly as we approached them, sandwiching himself between us. 'We're going to the beach!'

Now that some kind of peace had been made with Larry, I was my usual brand of exuberant inebriated again. Tom grabbed my hand.

'Good,' he enthused, 'you're back. These three have been doing a ton of coke and I've had to put up with them for an hour.'

I'd really been gone for an hour?

'You were offered some!' Clarissa whined.

'My mum and dad are *right there*. I'm thirty-four years old, for Christ's sake!'

Walking to the beach, I ended up in a pair with Luke. He was high and chronically verbal. 'So you're a normal person, are you?' His jaw was clenched.

'I'm sorry?'

'You're like me. A normal person?'

'What . . .' I was hesitant, wondering how indiscreet I could be. 'You mean not . . .'

'Fucking posh,' he said. I laughed. 'You feel it when you get to uni. Larry and I met in freshers' week and I was like half impressed by him, half repulsed by him.'

I looked around nervously. 'Oh don't worry,' Luke insisted. 'He knows. Pretty much everyone I met there had been to private school, or to one of those *state grammars*' – he appeared to reserve a particular distaste for those – 'and they all had parents with these polysyllabic jobs.'

'Oh my God – yes,' I agreed enthusiastically. 'Everyone I grew up with was . . . er . . . bi-syllabic? Teach*er*, farm*er*, butch*er*, build*er* . . . Even the poshest ones at school were doct*ors*.'

'Precisely,' he agreed. 'No one you meet at uni is normal. So in short,' he offered me his hand, 'pleased to meet you, fellow normal person.'

I shook it feeling vindicated and – admittedly – a little smug. 'The worst thing,' I said quietly, 'is that I still can't shake this adolescent desire to *impress* them.' He was nodding. 'You know, to infiltrate them.'

'Don't worry,' he said. 'That doesn't last. The age of social mobility is dead, so you soon realise that infiltration is a mug's game. You just have to console yourself by listening to "Common People" again and again and again and thinking, would I really want to be that chick from Greece?'

'We should swim!' Clarissa cried, just ahead of us. 'I mean, look at that *sea*!'

It was true that the water looked ultimately tempting. It was flat and calm and rippled with the silver spray of moonlight. The sky was cloudless and so crammed with stars that we were all illuminated, and I had that swell of pre-emptive knowledge that this would be one of those moments I wouldn't forget – a film still that would flit back into my head every time the tail end of a night was iridescent like that. Next to me, pupils flooding her irises, Clarissa started to lift her dress over her head.

'Leah, you're not staying clothed! Absolutely not!' She stood before me, nude, and washed in the moonlight; I was struck all over again at how radiant she was. 'Your turn!' she said, smiling.

I obediently followed suit.

'I love tonight,' I heard Luke snicker behind us.

'You guys too!' Clarissa insisted. 'We're all going to swim!'

She took my hand and we went first. The water was cool and clear and for a moment I felt infinite, floating along with the ebb and flow of the tide. I closed my eyes for a second.

This was exactly how I'd imagined my life would be.

18

Michael

Jenny was drunk, and I told her as much when she strutted over and rounded on me like some kind of aggressive pigeon.

'You're making her read your diary?' she spat, thrusting her hands into the air. 'What the hell, Michael?'

I drained the dregs of my Scotch. 'Why are we having this conversation?'

'Because it's necessary and overdue.'

I sighed. 'She's transcribing them so I don't have to,' I told her matter-of-factly. 'That's the luxury of success. I don't want to have to cringe at my twenty-something self; it'd just be too ghastly.'

'No,' she said. 'No, you're not giving me that.'

The kids were all down at the beach, the neighbours had departed and Anna and Bryan were elsewhere (maybe she was trying it on with the Monk now; that'd be just about theatrical enough for her). Jenny and I had been the last drifters at parties – the dregs at the bottom of every ashy glass – since 1965.

She slumped into the deckchair next to me and pulled her baggy cardigan around her. It was that chill part of the night just before dawn, and the sea breeze had teeth.

'You really don't think there's anything remotely odd about that?' she demanded.

'You're exasperating.'

We sat in silence for a while until at last I said, 'The kids are down at the beach.'

'You were off with Jérôme too,' she said.

'Which one's Jérôme?' (Images of him holding her close to his lithe tanned body as they danced.)

'Oh come on.'

I sighed. 'Jenny, you're over-thinking this. You're being neurotic.'

'Neurotic? Oh Mikey. Why couldn't you have just bought a stupid car or grown your hair and gone to India or something?'

'It's not *like* that, Jenny.' I paused. 'She's inspiring me.'

'*Inspiring* you?' She shook her head. 'Oh that's just so *you*, isn't it. So what, she's your muse, is she?' She stood up. 'She's neither your muse nor Astrid – she's a tangible, bodily, bloody human being . . . And so was Astrid.'

'Don't try and tell me *anything* about her, Jenny,' I hissed.

She gave me one of her long, searching looks, and finding nothing, I suppose, she took my face in her hands and kissed me on the forehead.

'None of it was your fault, you know,' she whispered.

But it was of course – it was all my fault.

Three

SAINT-LUC

En une piece de samit
A or brusdé e tut escrit
Ad l'oiselet envolupé;
Un son valet ad apelé,
Sun message li ad chargié,
A sun ami l'ad enveié.
Cil est al chevalier venuz;
De sa dame li dist saluz,
Tut sun message li cunta,
Le laüstic li presenta

Marie de France, *Laüstic*

19

Michael

It was the beginning of our second year and Julian was living some kind of comically contrived life of belle époque decadence in an old Arts and Crafts cottage in Summertown. He'd decided he couldn't possibly carry on living in college, as the head porter was apparently a fascist. Naturally, there was a convenient property-owning cousin to pitch in (or a maiden aunt, or maybe a third wife of some long-dead illegitimate uncle). The sheer number of family members that Julian seemed able to pluck out of thin air never failed to stagger me. I'd had my brother and sister, and a couple of insipid cousins. My mother had always thought it was faintly shameful to have lots of children. Suspicious. Foreign. Possibly Roman Catholic.

The sun that came through the window of Julian's study (slanted, refracted through the gridded window panes) was softened by the beginning of autumn. It was late September. Everything had that end-of-an-afternoon feeling. The light was just starting to shift. Julian stubbed out his cigarette and cleared his throat.

"'Marion was a war baby and she always liked to claim it made her tougher than the rest of us, though of course she could barely remember any of it, and even I could remember the very end of rationing – one of my earliest memories was my mother gloating about the first Christmas cake she'd made with real sultanas, and real oranges. My brain was still plasticine then. When I try to remember the precise taste of the cake, I remember candles, 'In the Bleak

Midwinter', mint-green paper crowns, and the musty feathers of the stuffed robins that she'd bought in T. J. Hughes and had put up in nests of tinsel on the mantelpiece."'

'You can cut the Brontë accent, Jules,' I sighed. 'And you know, you really don't have to read it aloud.'

Julian shrugged and reached for another cigarette. It took him about ten minutes to read the whole thing, during which I tried not to visibly squirm in the armchair. I pretended to flick through a magazine and ignored his occasional verbal annotation: 'Ooh, 'tis grim up north, eh?' Every once in a while he'd pick out a sentence and smirk. '"Marion was incandescent",' he'd repeat, or '"Little white stars of wood anemone"? Bit much . . .'

'It's all very English,' he'd concluded before even getting to the second page. 'A little bit Laurie Lee.' Two pages later, he'd crowed: '"She took a shine to me . . . Her benevolence protected me . . . thuggish older brother and his sadistic friends . . . monosyllabic father . . ." There, there, Micky!'

By the time he finally finished, though, he looked almost moved. He folded the pages neatly and handed them back to me. Lit another cigarette.

'So she drowns,' he said in an unusually small voice. 'The sister gets pissed by the lake because of Alan the nasty boyfriend and the mean mother and she drowns?'

'It's for the writing group.' I grimaced. 'It's memoir writing.'

Julian exhaled a long needle of smoke and raised his eyebrows. 'I see,' he said. 'Have you shown it to Jenny?'

20

It was spring by the time Astrid moved into the flat on Charlotte Street. By that point we were spending every night together anyway, she loathed her landlord and we both had this vague idea about saving money, though neither of us particularly knew what for. She was moving in on a Sunday morning and I'd gone out the night before and got absolutely rat-arsed with Julian. We'd pitched up at Jeremy's bar, where Astrid was picking up a shift, sometime after one in the morning. We must have been all kinds of obnoxious, because I remembered quite clearly that Jeremy himself had told us to clear out.

'Michael!' he'd roared. 'Get your coat, settle up, take Dorian Gray and get lost – the both of you!' I liked him immensely for that – his ability to be astronomically rude to you one night and to have apparently forgotten it entirely the next. He was a good sort.

I tried to telephone her flat to apologise but was told by her evidently gleeful landlord that 'Madam has already left and is on her way over to you presently.' Less than ten minutes later, I heard her call up to me from street level. I went and swung out the open window, and wolf-whistled down at her like a docker.

'All right, gorgeous!'

She was standing on the corner in a little pool of morning sunlight and she had to shield her eyes with her free arm when she squinted back up at me. It was gloriously sunny out – certainly a good omen, I thought to myself merrily. She had a little carry suitcase and a frighteningly of-the-moment olive-green carpetbag. Her pastel coat with the fur collar was slung over her shoulder and she was wearing multiple jumpers and the Oxfam swing jacket.

'You could come down and help. I'm wearing almost all of my clothes at once. I'm boiling.'

'Let's get some of them off then, shall we?' I leered, feeling like Julian.

Amongst her small collection of possessions were copies of skirts and dresses from Biba and Chelsea Girl that she'd run up herself (was her mother a seamstress? Or did I invent that later on a romantic whim?), a few jazz records and, bizarrely, a fairly hideous print of a bird in the style of Arthur Rackham or Edmund Dulac (had either of those men been the editor of *Jackie*, or even just blind).

'What on earth is *that*?' I asked as she produced the offending object from the bottom of the case.

'It's a nightingale,' she said.

Oh sweet child of the urban sprawl. I didn't quite have the heart to tell her that the bird was most certainly *not* a nightingale; that nightingales were small, brownish and unassuming and that *that* looked more like some kind of acid pheasant.

'It's ghastly.'

'I've had it since I was little,' she said, undeterred.

'You are *not* putting that up on the wall.'

'Yes I am.'

'You can put it in the bathroom,' I sighed, praying for the effects of mildew.

What surprised me the most, however, as I watched her unpack the modest material element of her life onto the floor of my flat, was a stack of A5 exercise books.

'What are those?' I asked, reaching for one.

She snatched it away from me and said rather defensively, 'It's my diary.'

'Your *diary*?'

'I'm not illiterate, you know, Michael,' she huffed, stuffing the books back into her bag.

'Well, what do you write about?'

'Things,' she said.

'What sort of things?'

'I don't know – just things, I suppose.'

'What do you say about me?'

She rolled her eyes at me and stopped what she was doing. She undid the top button of her blouse, and with more than a little irony, in her best come-hither drawl said, 'I write about when you unbutton my blouse.' She tugged at the next few buttons and slipped the gauzy fabric off her shoulders, then knelt down next to me on the sofa and reached for my hand. 'I write about when you touch me here, and here . . .'

*

'. . . and *here*,' I told Julian triumphantly, later that afternoon in the pub.

He swallowed a mouthful of his pint. 'Blimey. Dream bloody flatmate right there, old boy. She is a minx, isn't she?'

'Quite.'

'And now apparently a little scribe. How sweet. You should start doing some writing again, Micky. You two could be the Shelleys of the 1960s – the Bedsit Brownings.'

'Oh come off it, mate.'

'I'm being deadly serious.'

We ordered another round. The sting of my hangover was lessening slightly.

'God, I wonder what she *does* write about, though,'

he mused. 'Bodice-rippers, Mills & Boon, swashbuckling pirates . . .'

'She said it was a diary.'

'. . . ponies . . .'

'She's from bloody Mile End, for Christ's sake, not Malory Towers.'

'God, I hope it's sexy,' he carried on.

Again, that jerk of panic that I'd felt this morning. 'It *won't* be sexy,' I grumbled.

He shot me an incredulous look, patently delighted that I'd set myself up quite so spectacularly. 'Oh it won't?' he sneered.

I sighed. 'Come on, Jules. Do you really think she's writing erotica? Some kind of cockney Henry Miller?'

'Hmm. Cockney-Kinky: Lady Chatterley fucking a barrow boy. I *like* it.'

'Not a chance,' I said decisively. 'It'll be "Dear Diary,"' I put on my best pantomime dame, '"today it was sunny, but not too sunny, which was lucky because I had to get the Tube and it does get awfully hot down there."'

'"That tall, gangly fella came back into the caff again this morning."' Julian now, taking up the baton with predictable zeal. '"He's quite funny-looking but there is something unsettlingly handsome about him."'

'Unsettlingly?'

'You're right – more likely *very*. "Very Handsome." Handsome with a capital H. Yes, that sounds about right.'

'"Dear Diary,"' I began again, '"saw a fabulous picture with Julie Christie in it yesterday evening. She did look ever so pretty."'

'"And that Alan Bates, oh he does make me feel all tingly."'

'You've got such a one-track mind, Julian!'

He looked at me, mildly amused. 'How could you *not* with a girl like that?'

*

Walking home later, I felt a ripple of guilt about the whole conversation. Astrid wasn't necessarily erudite and I didn't hold out hope for much literary talent; but at the same time she wasn't dense, and she wasn't shallow. It was unfair to see her as some dreamy, nebulous waif – a cloud of pink ribbon and vanilla – staring out of her window, writing about Hollywood and flowers and practising her signature as *Mrs Michael Young*.

I got home before her. I stuck on a record and lay on the bed with my shoes still on, feet dangling off the edge. I lit a cigarette and stared at the ceiling. Guitar strings plucked like falling water. Leonard Cohen's voice: 'Suzanne'. I thought of how kind she was, how accommodating. I thought of her laughter and of how transparent she was when we listened to a song she loved. There was one night when we were walking home from Regent's Park just at the beginning of spring – one of those cold, pale evenings – and there'd been a busker playing off Woburn Place. She'd stood there watching him, transfixed. He was playing some old Irish song about a maiden's lover going off to sea – a real hackneyed dirge. She'd made us watch the whole thing, and afterwards she'd talked to him for what felt like an eternity; she wanted to buy him a drink in the bloody pub next door.

I was asleep by the time she got home. I vaguely heard her keys jangle in the door but only felt a snatched burst of sound breaking through in my dreams. In the same dream I felt her body press against mine – her face cool from the street, her breath and the caress of her lips warm; her palms too, reaching under my shirt and putting the slightest bit of pressure on my chest.

'You fell asleep in your shoes,' she whispered, somewhere in what·I took to be reality. The heartbeat of the finished record pulsed and throbbed through the room.

I rolled over to face her and pulled her mouth to mine – her perfect Astrid smell was somehow all at once both in my dream and in this realm of potential reality.

'I love you,' I mumbled – awake or asleep, I wasn't really sure.

*

'So in short, you've made no progress whatsoever?'

'I wouldn't say no progress . . . I admit there's not a lot of *tangible* development, but this past month has been more of a sort of . . . well, a period of . . . gestation.'

Hector, my thesis supervisor, shot me one of his driest looks from across the desk (intimidating, mahogany, cluttered and chaotic – a chaos unfortunately not indicative of his mind, which was as sharp as a bloody razor and evidently immune to my spin). He sighed, picked up a magazine and began to leaf inattentively through its pages. For about half a minute I sat somewhere in between the folds of uncomfortable silence, until at last I managed a weak 'What are you reading?'

'Hmm. Nothing too interesting. It's some kind of groovy literary journal that I should apparently be reading. Too many adjectives, not enough substance.'

'I see.'

His gaze slid back down to the pages in his hands and I looked determinedly at my knees. He let his hands fall to the desk and, still not deigning to make eye contact with me, said, 'You can go now, if you want. I'm sure you have lots of pressing matters to attend to and several novel ways of frittering away your bursary.'

I cleared my throat. 'These past few weeks have just been a bit . . .'

'Oh yes. I can only imagine. Do write to me when you have something of interest to discuss, won't you?'

*

'I don't even know why I bloody started a master's in the first place,' I grumbled, between forkfuls of rigatoni.

'Money,' said Jenny. 'And of course a passion for early modern poetry, let's not forget that.'

'Oh sod off, Jen.'

She smiled sweetly.

'No, but in all seriousness,' I carried on, 'how did I manage to even remotely con them that I was a viable candidate for academia?'

'Because you're a horribly talented con artist,' she said. 'Or at least you were. Maybe love is softening your edges.'

It was the first time Jenny had teased me with that word and I hadn't objected – a lack of denial that she digested smugly but without comment, instead asking, 'How is conjugal bliss anyway?'

'Blissful,' I said, truthfully, though I didn't really want to talk about Astrid here, at Giorgio's, even if it was her day off. I jiggled in my seat. I had other things on my mind anyway. I was having one of those days where you can see all the precariously knotted threads of your life going lax and starting to unravel.

'What am I *doing*, Jen? Really, what am I doing?'

'Oh Mikey, what are any of us doing? I spend my days filing for Auntie – I can assure you it's less than thrilling.'

I glanced up out of the steamy window feeling tragic and self-indulgent. Outside, a light rain was streaking the glass.

'What am I doing *here*? Why are we in London, Jenny? When did our lives get so predictable? I'm getting itchy feet; I think that's it. I think I need to go somewhere.'

'Michael, you just had a bad meeting with Hector. You don't need to go anywhere; you just need to pull your finger out.'

'Maybe Jules'd let me hide out at their house in Greece. I could write again, and fish, and live like some kind of ancient mystic hermit.'

She snorted; my inclination to whimsy tended to be lost on Jenny. 'Sure – you, the fish and the colonels. Anyway, hold on, Lawrence Durrell, what about Astrid?'

'What about her?'

'Well what are you going to do with her when you sod off to find your muse in the Cyclades?'

I shrugged. 'To be honest, I hadn't even thought about her. I suppose she could come with me.'

'Come with you? What about *her* life, Michael? What about her singing?'

'She could sing in Greece.'

Jenny raised her eyebrows at me.

'What? Or she could wait for me here. Or we could just see what happens. We're not engaged, you know, Jenny. You sound like my mother.'

She gave me a tight little smile. 'You're right. It's nothing to do with me. It's your life.'

For a few seconds we ate in silence, the gurgle of the water as I poured it from the jug into our little canteen glasses suddenly overbearingly loud in the resulting void. She sipped a little and then said:

'If you really want to feel terrible about yourself, you should come and gatecrash my college reunion drinks thing on Friday night – we'll be in desperate need of some blokes to avoid it being completely tedious. We've been encouraged to bring eligible bachelors. Jules is predictably eager.'

I grimaced. 'Gosh, I'd love to, but I actually have to pull out my own teeth that evening.'

'You could bring Astrid,' she suggested.

I couldn't think of anything worse – Astrid in some pub in Chelsea with the thrusting, burning bright young things of my alma mater.

'Oh come *on*,' she insisted. 'We can mock people quietly together and bask in the glow of unmerited superiority.'

I wiped my finger around the plate to get the last stains of garlic, salt and tomato.

'We'll see.'

*

It was packed that night at Jeremy's. Over the months she'd been doing her Wednesday-night slot, Astrid had gathered quite a dedicated following. They perched at the bar and leant on ceiling supports and their faces blurred into one – pale discs to be picked out in silvery billows of blue and milky beams of electric light. They requested their favourites and bought her drinks, and the fact that she picked up shifts there made her more *theirs* than ever. I was a regular now too. I took friends who hadn't met her so they could see how fine she was, and when the crowd bellowed with adoring rapture I sat there smiling in smug silence, my heart and my head swelling.

I was alone that Wednesday and I'd got there about half-way through, so I stood backed up against the greasy exit and flicked through that morning's paper. She was singing a new one – one I'd heard her singing in fragments in the bath. I didn't know until much later that it was her own.

'She's bloody talented,' said a disembodied voice from the left-hand side. I snuck a glance and saw a man: thirties, soigné, in a stylish open-necked shirt with one jarring concession to youth culture: a pair of garish suede winkle-pickers. 'Listen to that phrasing,' he said in a low voice to his friend. 'It's effortless – and you think it's perfect and classical but it's actually kind of freaky. It's original. How did she think to dip that note there at the end of the verse?'

The friend, a squat bullfrog of a man, necked a bit of Scotch and nodded earnestly.

'Yeah,' he said, in the raspy, affected voice of someone who likes jazz. 'She looks a bit fresh, though – a bit green . . . bright-eyed.'

The first man shrugged and stubbed out his Silk Cut on the wall.

'That's not a problem,' he said. 'That's not a problem at all. I'm going to talk to her. Good old Geoff – this was a great tip.'

I felt an iron clamp on my gut – an iron clamp with teeth. I eyed them from behind my newspaper as the slimy one closed his eyes in delight, nodding along on the wave of her *freaky phrasing*. The dapper one was writing something down on a napkin. I knew that at all costs I had to stop this; I had to at least delay it until I could come up with a better strategy.

Peeling myself away from the wall, giving the pair a gratuitous smirk as I did so, I wove through the mass of bodies towards the stage. Astrid clocked me and grinned at me in her adorably unprofessional way. I replied with a pained frown and gripped the edge of the stage. I could tell from the wave of concern that passed over her features that I'd successfully struck the balance between melodrama and measured agony. I could convince even myself of a whole range of sensations to elicit sympathy – despair, stomach pains, bereavement, hangover, ambiguous childhood trauma . . . By the time she'd finished her set, I was grey.

'What's wrong?' She'd made a beeline for me.

I winced and felt a few expertly controlled beads of sweat pool on my hairline. 'Oh – nothing serious. I just . . . I feel *dreadful*,' I breathed. 'I don't even know how I got here. I felt a bit funny this morning and didn't notice it get worse in the library – I was in such a pit of books. I practically sleepwalked here from Bloomsbury.'

I could tell from her face that it was working.

'I'll probably just go home.'

She held my arm. 'I'll come with you. Really, don't worry. I'm done here. We can escape through the back. It's packed; no one will even notice that I've gone.'

'No, darling, don't leave on my account. There'll be people here wanting to buy you drinks and tell you how lovely you are.'

She smiled up at me. 'I don't care about them, I care about you.'

I spotted the scouts combing the crowd as we slipped out unseen. By the time we got back to the flat, I'd managed to inhabit my illness so thoroughly I was capable of nothing more than bed, and as I drifted off into fretful sleep I watched a hideous procession of record sleeves, ticket stubs and grainy newspaper photographs: her face multiplied and ready for consumption.

21

Clara epitomised the feminine type that had haunted my first term up at Oxford; she was the classic model of the species – all at once scaring me shitless and leaving me mad with resentful adolescent frustration. She was the daughter of a famous West End theatre critic, and she herself had been a bit of a would-be thesp. My first encounter with her was bathed in the pale glow of the limelight, up on stage playing Phèdre, and no matter how many times I'd seen her since, drunk and face collapsing at the tail end of a party, or the following morning at a lecture, hair all askew and eyes ringed and grey, I could never disassociate her with that initial lustrous aura, and above all applause. In my internal narration of scenes into which she flitted, applause followed her like an operatic theme. It was her personal soundtrack.

I don't know how it had come about that she, her flatmate, Julian and I were the last ones standing at that sweet-intentioned college reunion. It had been organised by some earnest, nameless little erstwhile secretary of something like the Women's History Society, or the Amateur Watercolours Club – a real mouse with NHS specs and orthopaedic shoes. A *Cecily* – yes, let's just call her Cecily for the sake of this story. Anyway, poor witless Cecily had organised this little *soirée*, and against all odds *everyone* had shown up (I suppose we were all at that stage of our lives where we were feeling a little adrift and were seeking some sort of anchor in nostalgia and familiarity). It hadn't been in a pub as I'd thought but in fact in Cecily's twee drawing room in Highgate, in an all-female flat she was sharing with some other hopeless spinster (Millicent?). By nine o'clock

you couldn't move for people, and Jenny had been right –
there was some thrill to be gleaned from seeing all those old
faces again and quietly mocking the ones who'd ended up
in the civil service.

Julian had been putting the moves on with Clara's friend
for a sizeable chunk of the evening, and that's how I'd ended
up thrown together with her at the end of the night. The
two of them had gone into the garden for a cigarette (Cessy
and Milly did not appwove of smoking!), and Clara had
come and sat down next to me on the sofa, her bare knees
touching mine.

'God, I can't believe she's falling for Julian Gresford,' she
sighed, smoothing down the brown suede of her miniskirt
with flat palms.

'You must admit he has a certain charm,' I said.

'Julian? Perhaps . . . I always fancied you much more,
though. I had some romantic idea that you were a sort of
tortured artist, and I always had this chip on my shoulder,
expecting that you probably thought I was very posh and
frivolous and liked making a spectacle of myself.'

I laughed. 'Christ. Could not have been further from the
truth. A hick like me? You always impressed me horribly. I
still remember seeing you as Phèdre in that first Michaelmas
term and my eyes coming out on stalks.'

She gave me a look of self-deprecating disbelief, but I
could see the faint burn of bashful pride beneath it.

'God, I must have been awful,' she said.

'You were spectacular.'

She smirked. 'I doubt it. Thank God all board-treading
aspirations were – well – *trod* out of me in the real world.'

'You don't act any more?'

'Christ, no – I've predictably joined the family trade and
I write about it instead.'

'Well, don't worry, I've gone and joined the family trade of drinking myself to a slow death, so it could be worse.'

She looked at me over the rim of her wine glass and I suddenly realised with a jolt of incredulous excitement that I was absolutely in with a chance. I'd not slept with anyone else since I'd first met Astrid. I hadn't needed to. All at once, though, it no longer felt like a question of need . . .

'What are you doing really?' she asked.

'Ah, nothing much – ostensibly a master's.' The face of the talent scout flashed through my mind again and I felt inexplicably inadequate. 'I'm thinking of moving to Greece for a while,' I added. She looked encouragingly impressed. 'You know, I think the political situation out there is just so fascinating, and it's such a unique experience to be able, as a foreigner, to go and live under that kind of regime . . . As a writer, it's unmissable.' I didn't tell her of course that I was planning on sequestering myself on a tiny island in the Cyclades almost immediately upon arrival, staying well away from any risky Athenian political dissidents.

She nodded approvingly at my maverick bravery and then, feigning indifference, said, 'And what about that gorgeous girlfriend Jenny told me about? What are you going to do with her?'

There it was – the fleeting, but all the same quite nauseating, wave of guilt. 'Oh, you know; we're only young, aren't we? It's not really anything serious. The Russians might bomb us into oblivion tomorrow.'

Again: that implicit look.

At that moment, Julian and Clara's friend clattered back into the room through the French windows, smashing a plant pot as they did so and collapsing into fits of wheezy laughter. Cecily stormed into the room, her dressing gown already pulled tightly around her matronly bosom.

'Really!' she lisped like a middle-aged schoolmistress. 'Really, chaps, this just won't do. What were you even smoking out there? Were you taking marijuana?'

That of course set us all off dreadfully. Jules could barely speak and instead just swayed from side to side, gasping hysterically. The flatmate hung from his shoulder, doubled over. Only Clara attempted to maintain a straight face. 'I'm so sorry, Cecily,' she said. 'It is horribly late, isn't it. We really should be going.'

'I'm going home with Julian,' the flatmate declared. Cecily looked on in horrified disapproval.

'To Julian's flat?' said Clara, herself clearly a little put out. 'That's a bit of a pull, isn't it?'

'Don't worry about it, Clarabelle,' Julian slurred. 'Mick'll accompany you back to your quarters; he's very chivalrous.' He gave me a knowing smile and clumsily draped his arm around the flatmate's shoulder.

Clara looked over at me. 'Would you mind?' she asked.

'Course not,' I said, inwardly grinning at my luck.

'Well would you *all* mind terribly just getting a bit of a wriggle on, please?' Cecily huffed. 'It's one o'clock in the morning and I've got a *lot* of things to do tomorrow.' She glared in the general direction of the garden, as if anticipating a veritable opium den to have to be dealt with.

Outside, we walked together to the Tube at Archway, where Julian managed to hail a lone taxi.

'Do you live very far from here?' I asked, hands thrust into my pockets as the headlights streamed away.

'Oh no – not very far at all,' Clara said. 'I can't begin to imagine why she got the idea to go all the way to his place. We're just around the corner.'

'Julian's very house-proud. He likes to show off his lair.'

For a moment we walked on in silence, until at last she

said, 'So it's not very serious with this girlfriend then, all things considered?'

'Oh no,' I said blithely, and then, affecting the disposition of the tortured-artist type I knew she so much wanted me to be, 'Why degrade something so beautiful with a label, or with meaningless, futile promises? No, I don't hold much truck with *girlfriends* or *boyfriends* at all.' I put just enough derision into the terminology she'd used to make her feel a squeak of pliable insecurity. She looked down at the pavement. 'I mean, if two people are attracted to each other, why shouldn't they fuck?'

I said the last word for effect. She managed to laugh. As she unlocked her front door five minutes later, I pressed her up against it from behind and whispered in her ear, 'Do you think I could come in?' I felt her squirm with delight.

After the act, she looked at me differently.

'God,' she said, half impressed, half unnerved. 'You're a real sadist, aren't you?'

I shrugged, rolled over and went to sleep.

22

Leah

The weekend that Luke spent with us was one defined by heat. We barely slept after the party, and what sleep we did grasp at was sticky and fretful. When I think about it now, I see snatches of blue light in a hazy, blurred line between the horizon and the sea; I see the pale curves of Clarissa's limbs kicking out silver trails in the water; I see Lawrence's white teeth, starkly lit against his shadowy face, grinning as he leant forward to grab me and pull me into the cool pleats of the sea. I see us all afterwards, lying naked on the sand, and I hear the lap of the tide, the chatter of the cicadas, the shallow wisps of our breathing and fragments of our conversation.

Later we limped back through the spinney to the garden, where we collapsed in a tangled heap of legs and salty hair on the grass. Lawrence rolled a joint. Talk turned surreal and hilarious. Clarissa and Nico sloped off somewhere à deux; Tom went to bed with the excuse of misanthropic age and the two boys and I lay on the lawn crushing knots of marjoram between our fingers, smoking, giggling. Sometime after sunrise, the membrane of difference between sleep and waking reality grew slack and translucent. I remember my head on Larry's chest and my legs sprawled across Luke's, and the rhythm of Larry's fingers absent-mindedly trailing caresses along my arm. When they thought I was asleep, they talked about relationships and people they knew.

'Man, by the end he told me that everything about her annoyed him – even the way she took off her jeans.'

When I finally did wake up properly, around ten o'clock, they were both fast asleep. The patio table was littered with coffee-making paraphernalia, so I knew Michael must have been down and seen us. I pictured him coolly sipping his drink in one of the deckchairs, surveying us in passive silence. Disentangling myself from the boys, I got up and made my way through the cool silence of the house – through the bric-à-brac of empty glasses and crumby plates and the diminished corpses of burnt-out candles. In the bathroom, I stood under the shower and tried to piece together the vignettes of the evening. I felt a pang of guilt over Jérôme and then another as it was effortlessly swamped by that same still of Larry's teeth and eyes shining in the moonlight. At last I felt something close to clean.

We were right in the midst of the *canicule* that weekend. It was what would have been four-showers-a-day kind of weather had we been in the city. The most pressing obligation any of us had was to make vague attempts at cleaning, and after that we were free to mooch around as some single, unproductive, hung-over/still-drunk entity. There were few things finer, I thought to myself, than entire handfuls of days where you stayed in a fused pack like that; becoming blissfully interdependent and insular – one happy cog in a pluralistic, composite person.

In the evening, the boys and I trudged up along the coastal path to Nico's, where he and Clarissa had apparently been holed up since their stealthy exit around dawn. We loafed in the garden in varying degrees of nudity in the balmy heat of the evening. Clarissa and I had somehow managed the unprecedented feat of wresting control of the music from the boys. I put on 'No Chill' by Abra. About halfway through the song, Larry, who'd been sitting quietly rolling cigarettes, said:

'I mean, it's an all-right song, but she's a bit psycho, isn't she?'

'She's a bunny-boiler,' Luke agreed over the top of my head.

'She is *not* a bunny-boiler, she just has *feelings*!'

Nico nodded along enthusiastically, not sure who he should have been agreeing with. '*Mais c'est quoi un* bonnie bala?' he asked me innocently.

'Lal, *you're* the bunny-boiler,' Clarissa jeered at her brother. 'Remember that Tinder girl last summer?'

'Well I mean that was different, seeing as she was like a ten out of ten *babe*.'

'Ugh, you make me hate men more than life itself,' I groaned.

'Yeah, right, because you're treating Jérôme with such conscientious compassion after all.'

Nico's vague attempts at comprehension intensified at the mention of his friend's name. I gave Larry the daggers. 'I just don't do relationships,' I said. 'And neither would you if your love life was even half the omnishambles that mine is.'

'Man, you know *nothing*. My love life is a total fucking disaster.'

'He's not lying,' Clarissa agreed enthusiastically.

'I'm like a magnet for the deranged. I must have dated every fucking harpy in Hackney.'

'*Harpy*, nice.'

'Oh stop being such a social justice warrior, Clarissa. You remember Vanessa?'

'I mean, dude, that's what will happen when you date a girl who makes performance art out of her menstrual blood,' Luke sighed.

'She was really cool,' said Clarissa, in an aside to me.

'This is why I try and avoid socialising with most of the

girls I sleep with,' Luke said. (Clarissa rolled her eyes.) 'It's a disturbing thing to witness.'

*

'Leah. *Leah.*'

I was somewhere between sleep and reality again, but that was definitely Lawrence's voice coming through my bedroom door in a hissed stage whisper. I pulled the sheet around me like some kind of makeshift toga and hobbled over to the door. I poked my head around it. Sure enough, there he was, standing in the corridor, eyes wild.

'What time is it?' I yawned.

'It's half-five-ish. I'm taking Lukey boy to the airport. Come with us.'

'Five *a.m.*? Is it Monday?'

'Come on. Don't be boring. We're going to have an adventure.'

I gave a resigned little sigh and in return he offered me one of his brazen boyish grins. 'Come on, Princess Leia – we can't pilot the *Millennium Falcon* without you.' He could see I was weakening. 'Luke's Chewy, obviously.'

I smirked. 'Obviously.'

'If you don't come, what are you going to do today?'

'Work. For your dad.'

He reached for my hand. 'Dad won't even notice you're gone. He's strayed way too far into Jack Torrance territory for that now.'

His apparent disregard for the state of his father's mental health was revolting and maddeningly appealing all at once, and just as I'd realised with his sister that first night in Paris, I felt that I was incapable of doing anything other than obeying him blindly. I watched the glee play across his face as he registered my wordless assent. He started to whisper-sing, '*Marseille, Marseille, Marseille. Soleil, soleil, soleil. Un petit holiday . . .*'

I clamped my hand over his mouth. His eyes gleamed.

Luke was sprawled across the back seat, lips parted and eyes fluttering in grainy, almost-sleep. 'He's been there for about an hour,' Lawrence said. 'He didn't trust himself to get out of bed, so he never went.'

'Did you sleep?' I asked, and cringed as he caught my gaze caressing the tired lines of his face.

'Meh.' He tugged at the stiff door on the driver's side. 'I napped a little bit.'

I followed his lead and slid into the passenger side, attempting to do so without even the slightest thrum of clumsy sound. The burred synthetic fabric of the seat chafed against my bare legs. Luke started as the car dipped under our weight.

'Is he . . .' I began in a hoarse whisper.

'Oh, don't worry about him!' Larry chuckled, grabbing Luke's exposed ankle affectionately. 'Once he's out, he's out. He could sleep through nuclear war. It's a talent.' His eyes flicked across to meet mine. 'Just you and me to the airport.'

I hadn't anticipated the singular pressure of being in the front seat. As I'd grabbed clothes and splashed cold water on my face, I'd imagined slinking subserviently into the back as I'd spent my adolescence doing – rolling cigarettes for my older sister and her friends in souped-up Nissan Micras, all at once irked and relieved that I was only ever observed through the rear-view mirror. Now we were unavoidably next to each other, with barely enough space between us to contain what I suspected was a mutual feeling. I tried not to watch the sinews jump in his taut arm as he jerked the key in the ignition. As he pulled the car out of the drive, he sang again, under his breath, '*Marseille, Marseille, Marseille. Soleil, soleil, soleil . . .*' He sucked his cheeks in as he dragged at the steering wheel, looking out of the window, not at me.

'Shall we put some music on?' he asked once we were on the road. The country here was flat and rinsed with the indigo tones of end-of-summer dawn, with the faintest promise of mist. Blue olive groves, the inky blue ribbon of the road, violet stamps of cypress trees. Shadows played across his profile and his eyes stayed fixed on the road.

'Won't we wake up Chewy?'

He smirked and started fiddling with the dials on the dashboard, lurching through gasps of radio stations. Syrupy pop songs with hideous, algorithmically generated English lyrics (the kind they play in French supermarkets that leach into your brain and leave you stranded in sonic purgatory, inexplicably singing *girl I love you, I give you my keys and my CDs. Summer party, whoa whoa whoa* for hours on end). Adverts for Decathlon. He stayed a while in the swell of a soaring jazz trumpet and I felt for a moment like Jeanne Moreau walking around and around Paris in futile circles in *Ascenseur pour l'echafaud.* I closed my eyes for a second – one of those phrases where the music is so exquisite, even over a tinny car radio, that you have to close your eyes just to try and contain all the beauty.

'You like jazz?' he asked, his eyes still fastened ahead.

'Of course.'

'*Of course,*' he mimicked, switch flicking in his jaw. 'I can't stand it.'

I looked at him incredulously, playfully – a look that said, *you're a contrary philistine but I'd still like you to take my clothes off.*

'But . . . *Miles*?' I said.

'Roll me a cigarette, would you?' He started to tinker moodily with the dial again. In chastened silence, I did as he asked. When at last he was smoking his cigarette (torn from my hand without so much as a thank you), he said, 'Jazz is what my dad listened to every time he was fucking someone who wasn't my mum.'

The stutter of the tuner again – hopscotching over Téléphone and Celine Dion and lingering at last on the opening snicker of 'Weird Fishes', a jagged fragment of nostalgia for both of us, apparently.

'Ah, *wicked*!' Larry exclaimed, drumming his fingers on the steering wheel. 'The French like Radiohead.' The flush of anger had dissipated from his face almost as quickly as it had appeared, and as the melody began to cascade along down the ribcage of the drumbeat, he dropped his hand carelessly to my knee. I felt the impact of it ricochet through me, his fingerprints tinting the web of nerves right up along my limbs. Conscious of every atom of my physicality, I tried to minimise the sound of my breathing. Oblivious, he kept his eyes trained on the road. The faintest increase of pressure as the song ballooned, and then, as it shed all that growth and was swallowed by the obnoxious shriek of a jingle, he let his fingers trail and fall to the gearstick. The absence of them on my thigh stung.

'I fucking hate jingles,' he said.

'Me too.'

He looked at me, and some more confident strand of my personality forced me to match his gaze. He smiled and shook his head.

'What?' I demanded.

'Nothing.'

'*What*?'

An endless pause, and then, 'So what's the deal with you and Jérôme then?'

(The sting again, spreading along my cheekbones now.)

'Distinct lack of deal,' I muttered. 'He lives in Marseille, I live in Paris . . . Sex is fucking incredible. He's a DJ. He smokes too much weed. I've done the DJ-pothead thing like ten thousand times before and it never works out. I'm attempting to be a grown-up.'

He smirked. 'So you don't fancy paying him a little visit then?'

Now it was my turn to fix my eyes ahead.

Outside, yellowish sunrise flickered out across the horizon, glinting silver lakes into violet. About a stone's throw from the airport, Luke let out a strangled groan.

'You see: Chewy,' Lawrence said.

'Why am I mobile?' he groaned.

'You're going to the airport, boyo!'

He sat up and blinked. 'Fuck. I feel like fucking shit.' He rubbed his eyes and, registering my presence, shot Lawrence a sceptical look. 'Nice of you to come, Leah,' he said to his friend rather than me.

Farewells were dispensed with little ceremony ('Sorry, mate, no way am I paying for parking. See you in a fortnight, yeah?'), though I at least got out of the car to stand up and give him a hug. He crushed me in an affectionate fug of sweet fermented alcohol.

'You get yourself to London soon, mate? It's been nice to meet you. Watch your back with these posh twats.'

'Fuck you,' Lawrence crowed, then, to me, 'Come on, pal, we've got places to be.'

*

Marseille. Car abandoned at some miserable underground warren near the station and the two of us standing at the crest of the steps at Saint-Charles where about three weeks previously I'd snouted a solitary hung-over cigarette. Larry lit one now and whistled at the ancient sprawl of the city beneath our feet – the vast sweep of terracotta, the urban climax of the Mediterranean. 'Wow.'

Down the steps, two at a time, the city still asleep but already everything bleached with white sunlight. Down Boulevard d'Athènes – appropriately named because it really did feel like we were in the cradle of the Mediterranean here – and on to La Canebière, where the air started to smell of the sea. Les Noailles; the chatter of the market being born, and seagulls. '*J'ai faim*,' Larry said, pronouncing it with a thumbing English M. We skirted up into the weave of market stalls and bought nectarines as they showered down from the traders' crates. A lithe teenager in a greying wife-beater strung up huge, glistening watermelons and, grinning at us, set to them with a machete, as dextrous as an acrobat. He presented me with a gleaming crescent whilst his father scowled and ashed his cigarette into the first figs of the season.

We swerved back onto the gaudy main drag towards the saline pull of the harbour. Soon white masts like skyscrapers reached up to tease the skyline. Beyond the Métro, the super-markets, the red and white chain stores, all at once was the old port, washed in lye morning light. We found our way to a freshly unstacked terrace and perched on a pair of old cane chairs, damp with dewy sea mist, to order *petits crèmes*. Screeching, garrulous gulls. The stained-glass Mediterranean lapping the old stone ramparts of the port. The waiter telling his colleague about some Parisian *connasse* he'd slept with last night.

Lawrence unfolded his long concertina limbs and sighed, swinging back on the hind legs of his chair, arms crossed behind his head.

'Go on then. Dish the dirt. What is it that Dad is getting you to do anyway? What does being "his assistant" involve?' His eyes were closed against the sun and there was something about the way he dressed up the question that was totally removed from Clarissa's menacing needling; or maybe it was just that I was incapable of seeing anything remotely menacing about him anyway, the morning light brushing the angles of his face. I stretched my legs out across his. He smirked. 'All right – get comfy then.'

'I get to read his diaries. Squat in the ashtray of his twenties chasing down an old girlfriend.'

'Astrid,' he said.

'Oh. You know about her?'

'Barely. Dad's not one to talk much about his conquests, but there was this one time when I was about fourteen and he was taking me to the orthodontist. We weren't seeing much of him at that point – I think it was when he was working on the script – and he was in this weird sentimental mood. Very not like him. You know, looking back on it now, I guess he was shit-faced. Huh. I remember the nurse kept giving me these strained smiles and all I could do was try *so* hard not to look down her top as she leant over to check my molars. You can't imagine how hard it is being a teenage boy.

'Anyway, we went to the pub together afterwards and he bought me my first pint. I couldn't eat the salt and vinegar crisps because I'd just had my braces tightened. He kept calling me *son* and he wanted to talk about girls . . . Fucking mortifying obviously.' He was tracing circles with the edge of his thumb around my ankle now. 'He asked me if I had a girlfriend. I was too embarrassed to tell him that I was madly in love with Polly Hobbs from drama but that she barely registered my existence as a virile entity and just saw me as – fuck's sake – *so nice, like a brother*! Here – get your sandal off.' He pushed at the leather strap, and when the offending sandal flopped to the ground, he started to massage the arch of my foot.

'So Dad keeps telling me that love should be everyone's priority, and that he's sorry he was always such a crappy example to me . . . And at this point I'm starting to shuffle on the bar stool and pray for a quick death, and I say to him, "That's not true, Dad, we all know you love Anna," and he just gives me this look, this misty-eyed *look*, and he says, "Oh no, Larry. No – I only ever loved Astrid and I fucked that one, didn't I?"'

He nodded at my raised eyebrows.

'The next thing I know, he's picking a fight with the land-lady about something, and then he stubs out his cigarette on the bar and just gets up, tells her she's a dried-up old narc – and I quote – and leaves . . . without me. I had to scamper off after him. It was awful.'

'What did your mum say?'

'Ah man, she was *livid*. She wouldn't let me get in a car with him for ages afterwards and it always made me feel so guilty about the whole thing. Like I'd ratted him out. But I never told anyone about the Astrid bit – the not-loving-Anna thing; even if it would have *made* Clarissa's adolescence.'

'Yeah, they really don't get on, do they?'

'Mm. Clarissa never forgave her for the affair. She sees her as some kind of wicked home-wrecker or something. To be fair, Anna *is* just so bait, you know? Even when we first met her when we were kids you could see right through her.'

'I think she's kind.'

'She is kind. She's also a wanker, though, isn't she?'

'A wanker?'

'Well – she's up herself.'

I snorted.

'What?' he asked.

'Polly Hobbs from drama?'

He held his hands up and laughed. 'You sound like Luke.' He caught the attention of the misogynist waiter and ordered two more coffees and a Ricard.

'It's not even nine a.m.!'

He shrugged. 'Evidently I learnt from the master. Anyway, poor Anna got it in the neck from Mum at home too. She'd call her things like *decorative* and *fashionable* and I guess Clarissa just picked it up by osmosis.'

The coffees arrived. 'You're all very hard, aren't you?' I said.

He smiled. 'Hey, I don't have a problem with her. Good for her if she's sleeping with this creepy sculptor. Dad deserves it.'

Not wanting to let on that I was completely in the dark about what had been going on, I arranged my features into a non-committal *indeed* and shrugged.

'You know what, we should actually go to his bar and investigate.'

'We should,' I said, gleefully affecting comprehension.

'And what else shall we do today?' he said, stirring his pastis into his *allongé*. I winced.

'Rent bicycles. Loaf on terraces. Sun ourselves.'

'I want to eat sardines and *panisse*,' he said.

'Doable.'

From nowhere, he pulled my foot to his mouth and bit

my big toe. I squealed, drawing daggers from Misogynist Waiter.

'Huh,' he said. 'You taste like pastis.'

*

The day unfurled in front of us like a new bird testing out its wings. We wound up to the old town, Le Panier, because we thought we ought to – it was all suitably picturesque and lavender-filled – then tumbled back down to the port and ate deep-fried *beignets de sardine*, tangy with lemon. Larry impersonated all the various seagulls, each of whom we gave a different character, backstory, hubristic secret. He was already drunk, I think – I was on the way. I flirted outrageously with the waiter to see how he would react. He was, of course, unmoved.

We rented bicycles; crawled along the curve of the coastline towards the Vallon des Auffes. Shingle beaches packed with leathery geriatrics and frolicking, peacocking locals. Neon lifeguards. Almost art deco, would-be Riviera, seafront terraces with faded waiters, faded sunloungers and luminous cocktails. The sea – all churned up, lapis and brilliant – slamming into the frayed, rough-hewn shoreline. The old fishing village, with its winding apricot streets and passages dropping off straight into the sea. We scrabbled down to the rocks and perched there for a while, battered by the tide but pleasantly so. On a pocket of relative flatness, we unravelled under the hot afternoon sun. We stayed there for a few hours – a slow, heartbeat rhythm of eyes-closed, unmoving sun-worship and slow, lazy conversations; dipping into the water intermittently in a half-arsed sort of way. When the afternoon was all budding and fat with pollen, we clutched our way back up and onto the majestic sweep of the coastal road.

'All downhill from here,' Larry said, unlocking his bike.

Blue, blue and more blue. Soigné villas nestled up in the scrub.

To the port again and up La Canebière, then veering north-east-ish, through the Senegalese and Tunisian shops (huge hessian sacks of spice; maize, woven baskets and pottery) and up to La Plaine, where Jérôme had told me once that all the young people hung out. There was the first golden note of evening. We crested the hill onto a square lined with palm trees and packed with bars, and found a spot on a packed, jostling terrace. The crowd was a mixture of hip and beautiful people and hapless *baba cool* types in baggy shorts with marijuana-leaf transfers and white-people dreadlocks. Someone was playing the Pharcyde on a rattle-box radio.

The bar squatted on the *rez-de-chaussée* of a grubby Parisian-style building – all shutters and elegant Haussmannian balconies, but with chipped paint, leprous, peeling windowsills and scrawls of graffiti. Clusters of red plastic chairs and tacky brasserie tables emblazoned with adverts for gossip magazines spilled and sprawled out onto the square, just about hemmed in by stubby palm trees in scruffy technicolour pots. A lone Scouse accent floated, incongruous and lost somewhere in the choir of French voices.

Another round of pastis. My head felt light and giddy.

'What are you reading?' Larry asked. His hands were empty; he was watching me.

'Eimear McBride.'

'Hmm. It's very . . . *pink*.'

'I'm sorry, should I be reading Kurt Vonnegut?'

He shrugged and then gave me an indulgent smile. 'Calm down. No need to burn your bra.'

'I don't wear a bra,' I said through gritted teeth.

'I've noticed.' A comedy dirty-uncle wink. I kicked him under the table and he started to lazily rub his foot along my calf. 'Jesus Christ, you could light a match on these!'

'Hilarious.'

'I try my best.'

I started trying to read again but couldn't ignore his fixed gaze or the indiscreet footsying under the table. I put my book down.

'Are you flirting with me?'

'Of course.'

I sighed. 'You're horribly confusing, you know that, don't you?'

'I can't help it – you're beautiful and I'm drunk.'

'Oh for fuck's sake. How are we supposed to get home?'

'We could stay at Jérôme's?'

'Oh great – you, me and Jérôme, the happy threesome.'

'It's fine,' he said. 'We'll go to Anna's bloke's bar, I'll have one glass of wine then a very strong coffee, then we can nap in the car a bit *et voilà* – home in one piece!' He tugged on the sleeve of his fisherman's smock (Jenny's; stolen, of course) and I felt the pressure of his foot on mine.

*

The bar was at the end of one of the little side streets up on the hill, off the Boulevard de la Libération. 'So when did you find out about this Anna thing?' I asked, attempting nonchalance.

'Clarissa told me. And don't worry, you can stop pretending you know what's going on. I know you don't, she'd never tell you. She's weird about our parents.'

'Oh you *twat*, you let me squirm all day. Tell me now!' I said.

'Here we are!' he said breezily. 'Right, don't mention Anna. We're undercover, all right?'

It was an unassuming little place with a blacked-out vitrine. 'You go first, you speak French,' he said, pulling at the door and pushing me in.

It was quiet enough inside for my entrance to draw the stares of every single person in the room. Five people were propped up at the bar – three of them laughably beautiful girls – and behind it were a pair of barmen apparently extracted directly from Hackney Wick or Williamsburg. The lighting was minimal – candles mostly – and Mac Demarco's first album oozed out of the speakers. I felt judged. At last, a faintly ironic *bonsoir* was offered, not by either of the barmen but rather by the man holding court with the women.

'*Venez boire quelquechose.*' He somehow made the invitation seem more like a threat. If it hadn't been for his evident, unwavering self-assurance he would have been jarringly anachronistic. He was dressed more like an Australian backpacker in Thailand than a hipster. At first glance he was actually pretty good-looking, but upon closer inspection there was something wrong with his face; he looked like a very handsome man drawn by someone who couldn't draw. He was a big guy, and the hulking Viking look was topped off in every sense with a thick mane of golden hair that was more Middle Earth than Bushwick. It looked artificially brushed and shiny, like the crowning glory of a clean-cut seventies pop star. It made me think of Charles I. Or a spaniel.

I slunk onto the empty bar stool next to him and felt his shining, globular eyes size me up. Finally he smiled. He had the kind of mouth that has perpetually damp lips. '*Bienvenue*,' he purred.

'Hi,' said Larry loudly, apparently feeling neglected. He spoke over our heads to the barmen. '*Un pichet de rouge*, please?'

'You said one *glass*,' I hissed.

'Oh come on, let your boyfriend have a bit of fun,' Charles insisted in a Peter Sellers accent.

'She's not my girlfriend,' Larry said directly to the girls. 'She's my sister.'

I felt the brief but expected mallet blow somewhere around my heart and Charles's eyes visibly lit up. 'How sweet,' he said. 'A family vacation.'

'Sort of,' Larry hummed. 'What red should we drink?'

'*Anthony, tu peux sortir le Jura qu'Olivier a ramené, s'il te plaît?*'

Remaining non-verbal, the barman produced a bottle and poured three glasses of wine. Charles took the first of them and held it up to the dim light. 'Ah,' he sighed. 'You see the way the *reflets* filter through that perfect colour? Look at the silt settle at the bottom of the glass – like stardust. It is so *beautiful*.'

I suppressed a derisory snort. He fixed his glazed blowfish eyes on me. 'And beautiful things have to be tasted, *non*?'

Embracing the role I decided it would be the most amusing to play, I gave him a prim but all the same low-key-come-hither smile. Larry leant over me gracelessly and made a grab for a glass.

'First and last one, sis – promise!'

I hated him with every fibre of my being.

*

Three hours later, I was brimming with drunken abundance and still utterly in the dark about Anna's role in this dubious hipster set. Charles was a sculptor by trade, and, I gathered, had decided to try his hand at opening a louche nocturnal hangout as a vehicle to sleep with girls, drink good wine and take vast amounts of cocaine with relative impunity. When eventually the bar started to fill up, he remained fixed to his stool whilst his staff darted about like harassed ants, drowning under an avalanche of dockets. He was blissfully oblivious, leaving his seat only to smoke and, at one point (excruciatingly), to waltz behind the bar to make me some food after I expressed the slightest pang of hunger. He crouched next to the little fridge.

'You like cheese?' he asked.

'I love cheese.'

'Here, I make you *planche*.' He was insisting on speaking to me in English to great comic effect. The language barrier rendered him only more absurd. ('What do I live for? Good wine, *l'art*, beautiful women . . . I live for beauty.' At one point he even leant over the bar and fed me half of a fig. A *fig*.)

'*Bon, du Morbier, un bleu d'Auvergne, un domaine de Bresse, un Saint-Félicien, un tout petit peu de confiture aux Reines-Claudes . . .*' He recited the composite parts of his cheeseboard with holy reverence. In his defence, in spite of his cringingly contrived personality (he was a painstakingly curated *bon vivant libertin* type), he did evidently know what he was talking about. Much to the patent relief of his colleagues, he worked fairly swiftly and slotted back in next to me on the less obtrusive side of the bar. Since Larry had swooped in on his intended victims, I now had the fortune of being the sole object of Charles's attention.

'Oh!' I exclaimed through a mouthful of tangy, yolky Morbier. 'This is *delicious*!'

'You like food?' he said, placing a faintly clammy hand on my knee. 'You are very *sensual*, I see this.'

I looked over at Larry, who was in the full throes of an Italy anecdote, arms flung wide and eyes even more so as the girls giggled appreciatively. I did the same to Charles.

'*Putain*, you have such a sexy little laugh!' he leered.

I necked the dregs of my glass and watched him refill it instantly. Oozing Saint-Félicien. Too late to turn back now.

'So. A sculptor,' I began, searching for something to discuss other than my apparently carnal nature.

'*Ouais*,' he said. 'All that work behind the bar and over there in the back – all me.' He gestured at what was undeniably seriously impressive decorative stone masonry: a head of Christ, a pair of bodiless hands, sprigs of laurel, a nude in fragments. I noticed for the first time the naked curve of a woman's spine disappear and reappear in the thrown shadows of the candlelight. Now that he was talking about his art and wanted to be taken seriously, he'd slipped seamlessly back into French. 'And the photos too, they're mine – the more *savoury* work that I can exhibit here, that is.' His hand was creeping up my thigh now. 'I would love you to pose for me.'

They were all nudes, of course. A bit naff really, obfuscated and disjointed. They looked as if they'd been taken with a camera obscura. Women in parts. Soft fuzz.

'You want to go take some coke?' he drawled.

Larry was valiantly working his way through the bottle of wine. I sighed. 'Why not?'

He gave my knee a little squeeze.

*

'I do a lot of work down here actually,' he said, crushing the rocks into powder with his credit card. He racked up two generous lines and motioned for me to sit next to him on the stack of pallets.

'Huh,' I said. It didn't look dissimilar to any of the dry stores of restaurants I'd worked at before. 'Like, *art* work?'

He smiled (his mouth again like glistening cod roe). 'You'll see, if you like.'

From his wallet he produced a tiny silver straw. I inwardly recoiled. Was there anything tackier than cocaine paraphernalia? He handed it to me first.

'And they say chivalry's dead.'

He leered, feigning comprehension, and I bent my head to take the line.

'Fuck,' I breathed.

'Yes. It's the good shit,' he said (English again now, to show off all he'd learnt from gangster movies). He took his line and shook his head like a wet dog.

We sat in silence for a second. Upstairs, the muffled hum of music and laughter. Larry had been dancing to Talking Heads with a Spanish girl. Charles's hand had found its way back to my thigh again, and now his breath, steeped in wine, was warm on my cheek. As his mouth brushed my earlobe I closed my eyes and thought that it would be over quickly. He kissed me and pushed my ragdoll body down onto the pallets, crushing it beneath his own.

'You have great tits,' he breathed in a seventies porn star voice. 'I love small tits, they're so much more *elegant*.'

Dewy mouth on my collarbone, hands under my dress, hands everywhere.

'I . . .' He pressed a pale finger to my lips and started to unzip his jeans. His free hand on my arm, the pressure so hard I thought it'd probably bruise.

'*Suce-moi*,' he whispered.

A wave of nausea. I tried to sit up. 'I really don't want to do that.'

'Come on,' he murmured. 'Put it in your mouth. You've got such blow-job lips . . .'

I managed to sit then, and felt his hand slam onto the nape of my neck.

'Come *on*,' he insisted. 'You're a fucking tease.'

All at once a surge of revulsion and resistance. 'Fuck you.'

As I pushed him away, I heard the sound of light footfall on the staircase.

'What the fuck are you doing with my sister?'

Charles turned around. Larry told me later that he wanted to laugh when he saw him standing there – ridiculous Hawaiian shirt framing a raging priapic erection.

'*Mais t'es sérieux, mec?* Fuck off!'

I willed myself to disappear.

'You fuck off, mate. That's my sister.'

'*Mais putain*, she's a grown-up. She chose to be here.'

'Leah, come here,' Larry insisted, ignoring him. Half mortified and half immeasurably grateful, I started to pull at the straps of my dress and scrambled towards him.

'You're not obliged to your fucking *prude* brother, you know.'

Larry put an arm around me. 'Yes she is.' He pulled me in close to him and I attempted to hide in the crook of his arm, wanting to die of shame.

'*Mais* – it's 2016. Have you not heard of female liberation?' said Charles, outraged.

'No. Now fuck off,' Larry spat and began to turn away.

'Your sister's a fucking prick-tease! *Salope!*'

'What did you just say?' A sudden halt. I felt his body go rigid.

'Larry,' I hissed. He'd left my side now and was squaring up to Charles. '*Larry!*'

An agonising swell of tension, and then, 'I'm not going to hit him. I'm not a fucking caveman.'

He came back towards me then and held my face in his hands; searched my eyes with uncharacteristic tenderness. I could feel my nose burn. Charles was still fuming. '*Connard . . . putain . . . fils de pute.*'

A glint of wicked humour in Larry's eye as from nowhere, he kissed me.

Charles combusted. '*Mais non. C'est pas vrai. Putain.* Fuck. Do you know where that bitch's mouth just was?'

I smarted and Larry laughed. 'She's my sister. I love her. Unconditionally.'

'Fucking *deviants*!' Charles cried. '*Perverts!* You two get the *fuck* out of here. Now.'

Lawrence took my hand and we scaled the stairs, two steps at a time. I could feel his body convulsing with smug delight at his coup. Outside on the street, he fell apart, doubled over and wheezing.

I closed my eyes and leant against the cold wall, all at once wishing I were sober.

*

'You have to admit it was funny. Did you see his face?'

'Of course it was funny,' I sighed. 'I'm just not in a very funny mood.'

Lawrence pulled me into him and kissed the crown of my head. 'Come on, pal, cheer up. It was a good kiss too, right?'

I let his body take the weight of mine. It had been a good kiss, I supposed. The memory of it was misted over with the acidic residue of shame and fear and the vague feeling that I was going to throw up. We were driving very slowly out of the city and all at once I felt very not-drunk. We'd decided to get out and off the *autoroute*, and to try and find a little country lay-by to pull up in and sleep off the booze.

'Stop looking at me and look at the road.'

'I can't help it, you're gorgeous,' he slurred.

The comment, which hours ago would have made my heart flip, now just irked me. We were leaving behind the glittering neon web of motorway around Marseille.

'Well it certainly had all the makings of a great adventure,' he said. 'The south of France, good soundtrack, handsome couple, drugs, sex . . .'

If you count sexual assault, I thought, but nodded along silently.

Down, down, down the little black ribbon of a country road. Cicadas again, emptiness, and at last – a lay-by. The car shuddered to a silent stop.

'I'm sorry,' he said. 'I'm probably being a dick, aren't I?'

'It's fine. Really. It was my own fault.'

He looked out the window. 'Don't say that,' he said quietly. And then, 'Leah . . .'

'What?'

'Look outside . . . no, actually, *come* outside.'

The whistle of the cold night air. The sky indigo and everything bruised with night. Endless spray of stars. We'd parked next to a field of huge nodding sunflowers.

'Fuck,' I laughed.

He held my hand and the two of us stood, half laughing at how majestic they were, bathed in moonlight. His face was white with it. He wrapped his arms around me, his chin on the crown of my head. I wanted to forget everything that had happened and crystallise this *now* – this exquisite moment.

I lifted my face to his and closed my eyes.

'I would have fucking killed him, you know.'

*

We set off sometime after dawn. I dozed as he drove, head nodding on his shoulder, and only started to surface as the car lurched to a stop at the bottom of the drive.

'Well,' he said.

'Well,' I repeated.

'That was fun.'

'It was.' A nervous, approval-seeking smile.

He sighed. 'We probably shouldn't do this.'

'This?' I said.

'This. You and me – well, you know it's not a good idea. With Dad, with you working for him . . .'

'Right. Yes. Of course.'

'You know I really like you. You're cool. You're chill – and it's probably a bad idea if we just hook up sometimes and—'

'Absolutely,' I affirmed, cutting across him so I didn't have to hear any more.

He eyed me nervously, and then, when convinced of my laboriously constructed nonchalance, scraped a smile in my direction. He looked relieved.

'That was jokes, though, wasn't it?'

'Yes,' I said, smiling inanely.

'That guy's *face*, I swear to God . . .'

*

It was as I pushed at my bedroom door that I felt a jolt, the vaguest wash of unease. Somebody was in there.

Michael was standing with his back to me by the window, hands thrust into his pockets. He must have heard me at the door but didn't move an inch.

'Hello?' I whispered, trying to make my voice sound sunny but unable to mask the nervous tremor.

He didn't bother to turn to face me. I closed the door silently behind me and knew that something awful was about to happen. I stood awkwardly, feeling the trepidation prick my skin.

At last he shook his head. 'You haven't forgotten, have you, Leah, that you're being paid to be here?' His voice was unsettlingly calm – disappointed rather than angry. I felt the slow drip of certain humiliation, the anticipation of it pooling in my limbs, and the familiar contraction in my chest and the back of my throat.

'Of course not,' I said quietly.

I noticed now, in the shafts of dawn light, that he was shaking.

'I don't think I'm being unreasonable to expect you to take this seriously.'

I tried to speak, but the words were strangled by the pressure on my throat.

He carried on. 'Instead of going out and spending all your time getting pissed with my children.'

'I—'

'Don't bother.' He turned to me now but wouldn't look me in the eye. 'You could have at least had the courtesy to ask for the day off.'

My voice came out all jittery. 'I didn't know . . . We didn't plan anything . . . Lawrence just asked me spontaneously in the morning and I thought it'd be OK because it was just one day and . . . I thought you wouldn't mind if I maybe worked the weekend instead and—'

'It's just not really professional, is it?' He smiled condescendingly.

I looked very hard at a knot in the floorboard. 'No,' I muttered, 'it's not.'

He shook his head again, smiling to himself. 'This is what happens when you employ people who don't have any real experience, I suppose.'

I felt that like a wasp's barb and blinked to try and stop the tears I could feel collecting beneath my eyelids.

'I'm so sorry,' I murmured.

'Just try a little bit harder to be responsible, will you? It's not a big ask, is it?'

I wanted to melt into the floor.

'Sleep it off. I don't want to talk about this now,' he sneered, and with that he left the room, leaving me paralysed with guilt and shame.

I climbed into bed and all at once felt very small and very lost.

23

Michael

I'd known of course that when I managed to get Astrid out of Jeremy's that night, I'd been putting a sticking plaster over a gaping wound. I was like one of those robust Edwardian lunatics you see in old sepia photographs – staring down the camera with all the imperial fortitude they can muster, knowing they're about to go and scale a Himalayan peak on a jar of Marmite and a working knowledge of Milton and ancient Greek. In short, I was comically doomed. My performance had bought me time and little else. Astrid was one of the most talented performers I'd ever seen. Now that the ball was set in motion, nothing could stop it. She was going to make it. She was going to make it and I was going to be a washed-up hanger-on, propped up at Jeremy's bar insisting that I'd lived with her before she broke America. When I thought about my future – which all at once I was forced to do – I saw a cavernous vacuum of wasted opportunity. Then I saw hers: soaring, golden, thrilling.

*

A Friday. I was in the flat, lying on my back on the floor; smoking a joint, drinking a cup of cold tea and listening to a scratchy Melina Mercouri '45 whilst reading a battered paperback edition of *The Greek Myths for Children*, both of which I'd found in a charity shop the day before. The front cover of the book had been valiantly vandalised by its previous owner, who, in a fit of prudish horror, had scribbled out Zeus's flaccid little penis and covered his shame in some sort

243

of biro toga. It was mid afternoon when I was jolted into reality by the jangle of Astrid's keys in the door. I scrabbled around for some more erudite reading material as she burst into my little bubble of tranquillity. Her face was flushed and her eyes dazzled with enthusiasm.

'You won't *believe* what happened to me today,' she said, all in a stream – no spaces between the words.

I blinked dopily. 'What happened to you today?' I yawned, stretching, and padded over to kiss her – because she looked so adorable with all that childish vim that I decided I needed to touch her immediately. She returned my kiss and threw her arms around my neck. I liked it when she did that. It made me feel like Cary Grant.

'A man came into the caff after the lunch rush and marched straight up to the counter and asked if a young lady called Astrid worked there. And Giorgio said yes – a bit suspicious – and the bloke said it was nothing untoward at all and that he'd been told to come to the café by Jeremy Carson, and that it was to do with my *career*!'

I felt my flesh grip the bones underneath it in an attempt to hold on to its form and substance. Astrid was oblivious. I was aware of the hurtling monologue of her story, and splinters of it managed to pierce my consciousness: '. . . he'd been there that night you were so poorly . . . was so smartly dressed, I think his shirt alone must have cost about a month's wages; not that posh though . . . he was so nice – so normal . . . compared me to . . . said I had the potential to . . .'

My skeleton strained against the taut muscles. I was vaguely aware that she'd stopped talking and was looking at me, still all illuminated, waiting for me to respond. I held her close and kissed her again so that she would close her eyes and wouldn't be able to see my collapsing face. I pressed her head into my chest and spoke into her hair so as to muffle the tone of my voice. I threw out words like *incredible* and *of course* and a couple of empty *I love you*s. She kicked off her shoes and flung her handbag onto the one armchair we owned, and started pirouetting around the room. Finally she came to a breathless standstill. I watched the delight slide off her face like a melting Cornetto. 'Why are you all grey?'

I pointed at the ashtray on the floor. She ate up the excuse and creased into her lovely infectious laughter. 'I don't even care!' she sang. 'Go to bed. In fact, I'll come with you! We can celebrate later.' She launched herself at me and I felt my legs go unsteady, which only made her giddier. 'Let's go somewhere *nice* tonight,' she whispered in my ear. 'I can pay – Stephen said he's going to make me wildly rich and famous.'

She found her own feet again and began to hop around, pulling at her dress. 'Come *on*!' she insisted, and triumphantly she hurled it at me: a flash of gingham; tomatoes, oil, basil, the tang of her sweat. I watched her in an impotent daze as she disappeared behind our bedroom door; I gripped the dress, balling up the fabric into a tight, contained fist.

*

The days that followed spooled into a single liquefied entity. Time warped and spilt out from its apparently enduring frame – enduring because I knew that in the morning, Astrid still woke up and left for work; Jenny still popped over with fish and chips at what I suppose must have been the hour designated for eating them. Outside, at what I took to be half past eight, suited men with umbrellas and polished shoes moved together in a synchronised, purposeful motion.

One night, I was taking a nocturnal walk (it was a Wednesday, I suppose, as Astrid was at Jeremy's and I was supposed to be there too). It was the kind of stroll you take with your hands thrust deep into your pockets and your head bent down against the horizon. I walked past a pub off Lincoln's Inn and heard the metallic clang of the bell for last orders. The jeering cadences of the landlord's voice – *las'oarders, las'oarders* – were like a channel into the realm of the living, a temporal pin spiked into a corkboard. 'Last orders': a tangible marker of time that still existed in everyone else's reality.

I'd been moderately drunk since around the moment Astrid had told me about Stephen. (Stephen. What an irredeemably ugly name. I bet he'd been a Steve growing up – he was just the kind of oleaginous geezer who'd be called Steve and would be good at pool and would get some girl knocked up and think he was half decent for taking care of it.) That night we'd gone to Jeremy's and had got completely rat-arsed, even Astrid, who was usually pretty good at being restrained. Jeremy was positively effervescing with glee at the idea of what this could all mean for the bar, and consequently the cup ran shamefully full.

Fragments of the night: Julian lurching onto the stage and commandeering the piano, which we all tended to forget he played, and well. He pulled Astrid onto his knee as he did so, and they sang 'Dream a Little Dream of Me' in clumsy, charming harmonies. He asked her to take a cigarette from his breast pocket and light it for him. I watched her giggling, holding the filter towards his parted lips. Jenny placed a steadying hand on the crook of my elbow. 'Shall we go out for some air?' said her disembodied voice from somewhere between the folds of nebulous lilac light. I remember gritting my teeth – the stabilising sensation of a clenched jaw.

I remember slow-dancing with Jenny and my heart swelling with love for her. Her hair, tickling my nostrils, had the faintest tang of patchouli. I remember Jeremy knocking about words like *industry* and *manager* and *tour*. Astrid seemed to retreat into the ether, the curves of her features obscured by distance. When we got home, we made the kind of love where I pinned her down against the mattress, fixing her under the weight of my body. The next morning, little grey blushes – thumbtack bruises – fluttered over the surface of her slender biceps.

When she was at work, I fucked Clara. I invited her over in some sort of attempt to recolonise the flat as entirely my own. Afterwards, she got up to make a cup of tea. She padded around the room hesitantly, on her tiptoes, like a tourist unsure of the local customs and not wanting to offend. Whilst the kettle boiled, she flipped through the records. The dreaded 'nightingale' fell out of the sleeve of *Sketches of Spain* (in the end I hadn't even conceded the bathroom). She bent down to pick it up and I watched her face crumple in a moment of unguarded laughter. She thrust the offending sheet in my direction.

'What on earth is this?' she called. 'It's *hideous*!'

I ignored her, and saw her visibly recoil when she realised she'd said something wrong. She carried on in silence, and when she came back to bed, she lay next to me but distinctly apart, too cautious to even risk brushing my skin with hers. She trod discreetly through a roll call of neutral topics until, when her tea was at last drunk (it felt like an eternity), she began to dart around the room collecting clothes, all of a sudden in some sort of rush to get back to work. As she was leaving, she said to me (she did look so beautiful, framed in the doorway, lit from behind by the light from the skylight in the hall), 'What are you going to do with all your stuff when you go to Greece?'

'Excuse me?' I said.

'Greece,' she said. 'You told me at that party that you wanted to move to Greece.'

Greece. I laughed. Of *course*. In Greece I'd be a wayfaring Byronic-fucking-*hero*. A moment of brilliant illumination – white light, the colour of an Ionian wave cresting as it rears up to die; the colour of snowy cottages with cyan windowsills . . .

I took Clara's face in my hands and kissed her, slowly, adoringly, sincerely even. She looked up at me, perplexed and elated. Attempting to recover her usual studied disinterest, she said:

'I'll see you soon then, I suppose.'

'Absolutely,' I replied, kissing her again and knowing that she probably never would.

*

When Clara had left, I made a strong pot of coffee, ran a bath and shaved. I rehearsed my speech in front of the greenish bathroom mirror, the one Astrid liked because it flattered your reflection.

'I'd been going to tell you about it that day you came home with the news about Stephen,' I told myself with an air of tragedy. 'But you'd been so thrilled I just didn't know where to begin.'

I shook my head and started again, this time with a tone that suggested more reluctant resignation.

'I just can't imagine not waking up to you every morning,' I sighed. I allowed my reflected self a little grin at that last touch and splashed my face with cold water. I felt like a functioning human being for the first time in days. She'd be home by five o'clock.

When finally, at gone nine, she walked through the front door, I was drunk again.

'Where the fuck were you?' I grunted.

She looked startled. 'I had a meeting with Stephen after work.'

'A *meeting*?'

'Well, yeah. We ran over a bit so he took me to get egg and chips at the café near his office.'

I snorted and stood up, kicking my chair back under the table as I did so. She followed me into the bedroom.

'What on earth's got into you?' She put her hand up to touch my arm. I jerked it away.

'It's not important,' I snarled.

'Why are you so angry?'

'You said you'd be home at five,' I said, my voice quaking. A small, sober part of me knew how hysterical I sounded.

'No I didn't.' Her voice was diminished but firm, like a child who's been dealt some sort of banal injustice and has no power to understand or to right it.

'You're always home at five.'

She sat on the edge of the bed and fixed her gaze on her hands, folded with solemn dignity on her lap. I'd expected her to carry on needling me, but she was borderline catatonic. She was making a concerted effort not to cry, but her eyelashes were brimming. I realised we'd never argued before, and that this was the first time I'd seen how she would react.

'He gives me the creeps.'

'Who?' Her voice was hollow.

'*Stephen*,' I spat.

'Right. Of course. That's what this is about.' She sighed.

'What the fuck is that supposed to mean?'

'You think he wants to sleep with me.'

249

'Do bears shit in the woods?'

A few trailing, globular tears were running down her cheeks now. 'I knew you'd been acting funny since I told you,' she whispered.

'Oh don't cry,' I sneered – something about her crying made me angrier; it was like she was trying to elicit sympathy.

She shook her head. 'Why are you being so mean?'

I ignored her and lay back on the bed. 'There's no point talking about this now – not when you're all emotional.' She flinched. 'Let's discuss it in the morning.' I closed my eyes emphatically, although I was wide awake. Next to me she gave a pitiful little sniff. 'Oh for God's sake, try and sleep.'

*

When I woke up the following morning, I knew I'd fucked up but couldn't quite remember why. Then it all started to come back in shards – a rough jigsaw of how events had panned out. I felt for Astrid's body but she'd already left. I suppose I should apologise, I thought, but then maybe if I didn't, if I stayed indignant and unmovable, she might just think it was her fault anyway – she was the one having dinner with some slimy old predator, after all. Dozy cow. She'd put the words in my mouth, but how they hadn't crossed my mind earlier was incredible. Of course he wanted to sleep with her. How could she possibly be so naïve?

I shuffled out of bed to put the kettle on and groaned. Even the action of being vertical was a pain. There was an empty bottle of gin on the table; just the idea of it, of the sterilising, medicinal tang, made my nostrils sting. Hazily my eyes registered a scrap of paper propped up against it – an old pools coupon. There was her sweet, girlish hand.

I love you, it said. She played the pools every week, and when we'd moved in together, she'd stopped using her father's birthday for the numbers and had started using mine instead.

'You know it's called the idiot's tax, don't you?' I'd said to her.

'We always played it at mine,' she'd replied, as if that were reason enough.

From the library, I telephoned Giorgio's. 'Will you tell her to come and meet me after her shift? Tell her to come to Cartwright Gardens, I'll be there.' I was playing tennis with Julian that afternoon. He liked to go to the court at Cartwright Gardens to watch the first-years from UCL preen themselves 'like dainty birds' for their boyfriends in the halls next door. I heard Rosa relay the message to her and I heard snatches of Astrid's flustered response.

'She says you know she's busy this afternoon,' Rosa snickered.

'Tell her it's urgent,' I said, and hung up.

I made sure to change out of my tennis whites before she arrived, deciding that there was something so intrinsically jaunty about them that they'd detract from the gravity of the mood I wanted to create. Smoking a cigarette with Julian after the match (he'd lost, gracefully, as always), I'd told him about my plan.

'I'd probably only move there for a couple of months – scope it out, you know.'

'Micky boy, it sounds like a plan,' he said. 'Bit hairy in Athens, mind, but you're a foreigner, so they wouldn't touch you. And you know I'll be there a bit this summer at Mum's. Oh God, when I tell the indomitable Mrs Gresford, she'll be in raptures – you know how much she adores you. Don't know how she'll feel about your missus, though.'

I shrugged. 'Hmm. Do you really think it's a good idea to take Astrid?'

He raised his eyebrows. 'Were you thinking of not?'

I leant back on the statue of John Cartwright, his plinth pockmarked with pigeon shit and lichen. 'I don't know, mate. I'm worried she's getting too involved, you know. Maybe moving in together wasn't such a good idea.'

Julian slung his racquet over his shoulder. 'I tried to warn you,' he sighed. 'But look, if you're just going for a spell, then keep her on the back burner. Write her the odd gushing, superlative-riddled letter. Make it a little blue now and then to give her something to think about when she can't get to sleep at night,' he added with a salacious wink. 'Anyway. Talk of the devil, thar she blows; a veritable vision in gingham. Cue me clearing off to avoid the painful third act.' He clapped me on the shoulder. 'Best of luck, old boy. I'll be in the pub should you need me.'

Before I could encourage him to make a discreet exit at the Euston Road end, he was striding towards her, arms flung open and racquet swinging elegantly from his shoulder.

'By Jove, if it isn't the sexiest tablecloth I've ever laid eyes on!' he hollered before pulling her into an extravagant embrace. I looked on as she shuffled awkwardly, staring at the ground and pushing a sheaf of hair behind her ear. I saw Julian point me out with his racquet and laugh uproariously. Twat. Wondering how long he'd see fit to hold her captive, I shambled back onto the crescent of the lawn. Next to me, a pretty little undergraduate was furiously underlining her copy of *Ulysses*. I decided categorically that I didn't want her to overhear what was going to be said. There was something almost indecent about it.

'You were playing *tennis*?' said Astrid in a low voice, glowering at me when she reached me.

'Let's go to a café,' I insisted.

'I thought you said this was urgent.'

'I didn't realise tennis and urgency were mutually exclusive.'

The would-be Joyce scholar had stopped annotating and was looking at us shyly. I shot her a bland smile and took Astrid's hand. 'Come *on*,' I hissed. 'This is not the place.'

We started walking, aimlessly, but in the general direction of Euston. 'Where are we going?' she demanded.

'I don't know,' I said, truthfully, although my feet now seemed to be carrying themselves towards the station.

'Did you get my note?' she asked, apparently relenting a little.

'Yes.'

'I don't really understand what happened last night.'

'I had a lot on my mind.'

We'd reached the point where a few years before the Euston arch had reared up from the pavement. The new station squatted ominously in its place, a smug, sterile temple to functionality.

'It *is* ugly, isn't it?' she said. 'I'm not wrong?'

I shrugged. The sudden proliferation of northern accents smacked jarringly of my past – anachronistic amongst the streamlined pillars and panes of gleaming glass. Yes, here was a good place to have this conversation, in the echoing hall, right in the thick of an orchestra pit of transient voices. Still not daring to meet her eyes, I sat down on one of the benches under the lurching fresco of the departure board. She flopped down next to me. Birmingham New Street. Manchester Piccadilly. Holyhead . . .

'My old man was born in Crewe,' I said, absent-mindedly.

'Not me,' she said, with a glint of pride. 'We're East End through and through.'

'I bet you're not,' I said. 'I bet somewhere down the line you're Polish or Scottish or even from some dull little village in Kent, refugees from the Industrial Revolution. People move, you know.'

'I know.' I could tell from the tone of her voice that I'd come across as spiteful and petty.

I put my hand on her knee. 'Though judging by that deathly urban pallor, I'd say you're probably cockney right back to the Norman Conquest.'

She slapped me playfully, and gingerly managed a smile – one of the timid ones that used to flit across her features right at the beginning, when we were still strangers. She was testing the waters. I felt a ripple of guilt for what I was about to do.

She was talking now. I was studying the departure board. Liverpool Lime Street, calling at Stafford and Chester ('I'm not totally naïve, Michael, I can look after myself'); Newcastle-under-Lyme ('Anyway, Giorgio reckons Stephen's queer, you know'); Glasgow Central ('How could you ever even think I might do that?')

'Astrid.'

She blinked as if the word had slapped her smartly across the face.

'Yes?'

I kept my eyes fixed on the stark white letters in their comfortingly familiar font.

'I'm leaving London.'

Out of the corner of my eye I could see her frowning. 'What do you mean?' she said. 'Why would you leave London? What are you talking about?'

Watford Junction. Hemel Hempstead. Tring.

'I wanted to tell you when you found out about Stephen, but you seemed so excited I couldn't bring myself to.'

A moment of excruciating silence. 'I don't understand. Where are you going? Where did this come from?'

It was at that point I think that a total vacuum of feeling neutered any real sense of the interaction for me. I was struck by my total lack of compassion. It felt like killing an ant on a picnic blanket on one of those dense, debilitating afternoons in August.

'I'm sorry,' I lied. 'This isn't about us. I'm just . . . I'm stagnating here.' I knew she was looking at me; I could feel the burn of her gaze.

'No you're not.' Her voice thronged with panic. 'You're not. You're studying; I know you're writing. Your friends are here – *I'm* here. Where would you even go?'

'I'm going to Athens,' I said, ignoring her use of the conditional tense. 'Probably in about a month. That way you can find somewhere to live.'

'Athens?'

'In Greece.'

I heard her laugh then. 'Thanks, thanks for that.'

'Look, you know how I feel about you.'

'I don't know *anything* now.' I still wasn't looking at her, but her voice was clotted with tears. 'Why on earth would you go to Athens? You've never even talked about Greece before.'

'Yes I have,' I protested. I turned to face her and placed my palms on her lap, engaging with her, trying to convince her. 'I'm doing nothing here. I want to go and *see* something – live something! You're right – I have been writing . . .' I paused for effect. 'But how am I supposed to write anything meaningful when I haven't *seen* anything? The situation in Greece right now, the dictatorship, the student activity . . . I need to start *experiencing* things. My life is so trivial.'

'And what do you think you'll be doing in Greece, Mick? You don't know anything about Greece. You don't even speak Greek. You'll just be another rich foreigner. You'll just be Julian's mum.' She shuddered.

I stood up, hands thrust deep into my pockets. 'I think maybe you need to be alone to digest this,' I said into the air in front of me.

'Michael . . .'

But the hoarse beginning of her sentence trailed off into oblivion as, head down in my collar, I slunk off towards the entrance to the Underground.

*

For the first hour after I'd told her I was leaving, I felt sprightly – light – a pleasant swell of relief. I got off the Tube at Embankment and wandered along the river with no particular aim, zigzagging, veering: Temple, then along to Blackfriars and up to St Paul's. I felt inconceivably cheerful. On the steps of the cathedral I sat smoking, writing, people-watching, the sweep of Ludgate Hill below me and Wren's dome and all those columns lurching above. London felt like my domain again. I watched dowdy tourists flitter around me and felt so adamantly that I wasn't one of them. Chancery Lane. Lincoln's Inn. Dark brown brick, lawyers in vampire gowns and Sir John Soane's lead window panes. On High Holborn, though, the idea of it caught suddenly at my throat: that she might not be waiting for me in the flat. A glacial drip, but then warmth at the memory of the press of her body. Of course she'd be there. The evening sky was all Turner yellow as I dipped into a pub off Russell Square for a steadying drink – just to be sure.

She went back to her parents' house that night, I suppose. She wasn't in bed when I shambled in. I put on a record and sat on the kitchen floor. All at once, I felt everything.

24

Leah

Just from pure exhaustion, I suppose, I managed to sleep for a few hours after Michael had left my room. It was a clotted, swampish sort of sleep, though, all churned up with claustrophobic dreams: the brush of Charles's moist mouth and his right hand cupping the nape of my neck; Michael's face. I kept dreaming that I'd somehow upset Clarissa and that he'd asked me to leave, and my brain had managed to process and petrify the exact angle of disappointment glancing off his features from the half-lit room that morning. I was almost grateful to wake up. I sloped over to the age-spotted mirror. My features were soft, malleable. I looked knackered. Little smudged bruises collected on my arm.

I wanted badly to go downstairs and make a cup of tea, but the idea of running into anyone – of having to communicate with anyone from the house – was too excruciating to even contemplate. Instead I went into the little bathroom next to my room – the one no one else ever used, where I'd once seen a centipede the size of my palm and where the deeply unfashionable pink suite hadn't been changed since about 1973 – and ran a bath.

I sat naked on the cold floor tiles, listening to the water tumble down from the arthritic tap, and attempted to shut my eyes against everything that had happened in the past twenty-four hours. Charles, Michael – Michael's face. I'd really fucked it. Lawrence too – stupid, gormless sunflowers. I ran the bath to scald and it was only as I lowered myself into the clouds of steam that I felt the first wave of indignant dissent. *Not really professional.* His behaviour had hardly been professional since my arrival in Saint-Luc. He'd encouraged me to feel part of the family; it was only under their aegis that I'd start to dismantle my guard. Yes, there it was – the welcome sting of stubborn anger, of injustice. I watched my thighs turn pink in the heat. Fuck him. Fuck all of them.

Back in my bedroom, I checked my phone. Clarissa: *Are you alive?* Tom: *Is everything OK?*

I turned it to flight mode and dragged the bolt across my bedroom door. He wanted to see more dedication? I'm Paul fucking Simon, I thought – a rock, an island.

I shrugged off my towel and sat cross-legged on the floor next to the pile of diaries.

11th May 1969
Anyway it seemed right that I should do it in the station. Symbolic – transience, moving on, etc.; it pleased me as a motif. It really wasn't planned, though, as contrived as it seems. Until the moment the words started coming out of my mouth, I still had the vague idea that I'd ask her to come with me. Then she looked at me and she had that look in her eyes – that terrifying look, dependence. I knew then that I was doing the right thing. She'd got that way girls get when they get attached . . .

12th May 1969
She's taken them, even though she left behind so many other things. I suppose she packed in a hurry. A couple of blouses trailing the bathroom door, stockings that smell so much of her it kills me . . . the fucking 'nightingale' . . . But not the diaries. Not even one. I looked everywhere. I just need to know what she was writing about.

Outside, a soft rain had started to fall. The first bad day I'd seen in Saint-Luc. It occurred to me that he wrote a lot about Astrid writing a diary. From the moment she'd first moved in, he'd seen it as some sort of personal affront. I made my way over to the window and lit a cigarette. The chill spray of the rain was welcome against my cheek. My head was too full of Michael; I felt the pressure of his personality, his voice straining against my own. What I would give, I thought, to hear *her* voice for once.

14th May 1969

Well this is a pretty picture. It's five o'clock and I've been sitting on this bloody park bench for the best part of two hours. Smoked cigarette after cigarette. Tried to read, couldn't. I know she's there. She finishes her shift in half an hour and I know she'll walk out this way to catch the 25. It's been three days now and nothing. Fucking heartless cow. I tried every Parker in Mile End in the directory and none of them knew an Astrid, and of course I couldn't remember her actual stupid bloody Christian name, could I? Today then: I got so desperate I gave in and went to Giorgio's. He clocked me as soon as I rounded the counter, though, and told me to clear off. The look he gave me.

I tried to reason with him – explained I couldn't clear off (the idea of it!). Explained that I needed to speak to her. He told me she wasn't working, but I know she works Fridays. I swear I caught a glimpse of her hands at the pass – slender fingers, fingers that I knew so well, that knew every part of me . . .

'I know she's in the kitchen,' I said, my hands balled into fists on the counter, trying to make sure the old man didn't see how fucking unbalanced I felt.

'She's not here,' Rosa insisted drily. Then, with a nasty
little smile, 'She's with Stephen today.'

I put the diary aside and opened up the Word document
on my laptop. For all of Michael's sins, even his pretentious
twenty-year-old self (*it pleased me as a motif*) could spin a
pretty gripping narrative. The more questionable his actions
became, the more invested I became in the diary, not only
in the hope that after everything – Clara, Stephen, this weird
new self-aggrandising obsession with Greece – he would do
something to redeem himself, but above all with trying to
muddle through what was true or not. I couldn't help but
start to notice some subtle inconsistencies in his version of
events – flaws that became all the more glaring the deeper he
wound down into his paranoid belief that Astrid would out-
grow him. Similarly, the boundary between the fragments of
his writing practice (the paragraphs of short stories, the lines
of overwrought poetry) started to blur, and what was apparently fiction began to bleed into what seemed to be fact.

He started to write about his dreams. He wrote about a
telephone call with his favourite sister – the one whose death
had supposedly been the most traumatic event of his adolescence. In one entry he'd write about meeting Clara again
for the first time since university at a party in Highgate,
but a week later he'd remember a day trip to Brighton with
her just weeks before he met Astrid. In all these layers of
untruths and half-truths, the one person I wanted so much
to hold on to seemed to become less and less substantial. I
needed to find out what had happened to Astrid. Attempting to trace her was becoming more and more fraught, and
I found myself stupidly attached to her and to this futile
effort to establish her identity. I propped open his notebook
to where I'd left off, and began to type.

25

Michael

'Astrid.'

She visibly recoiled when she saw me, and mouthed a predictable expletive. She looked as if she wanted to flee but couldn't quite make her legs work, and instead shrank into herself. I leapt up from the bench before she could get a chance to master her limbs.

'*Astrid.*'

I stood right in front of her but didn't have the nerve to touch her. It was only when she looked as if she was about to bolt that I managed to place my hands on her shoulders.

'I can't talk to you, Michael.'

'Hear me out – please.' Involuntarily I gripped her a little harder and felt her squirm.

'You're hurting me,' she insisted quietly, and I noticed my knuckles were turning white.

'Please, just come and have a drink with me. I need to talk to you.'

*

The day after I'd told her about Greece at the station, I didn't dare leave the house in case she rang or dropped in. In the end, it was Jenny who turned up.

'What's wrong with you?' she'd asked. 'Where's Astrid?'

'She's having dinner at her parents',' I'd lied. 'And you'd best go really. I'm supposed to be meeting Clara for a drink.'

An unimpressed twitch at her temple. 'Clara Stanton?'

'And?' I'd asked, propelling her towards the door.

'Why are you having a drink with Clara Stanton?'

'To talk about Oliver Goldsmith, and I'm late – *allez*!'

'I'll come with you, I like Clara.'

'*Jen.*'

*

Three days. Three crystallising, pickling days. It was agony. Hemmed in at the horrible flat – supernaturally vast without her and yet all at once perpetually shrinking. Now she was here in front of me, her shoulders contained in the width between my palms, all of her in my gravitational pull, and yet – her face. The idea that she had the agency to leave me again.

'Please,' I insisted. 'Come for a drink.'

I watched the turmoil play out across her features – better judgement versus what we both knew was what she wanted. At last, a quiet mew of concession. Still I couldn't quite let her go. I cradled her in my arms as we sloped down Greek Street, heads turned to the pavement as if ashamed, into the murky womb of the pub. It was still early enough to slide comfortably into a little booth, and as I talked to her I kept cadging glimpses of my refracted reflection in the stained glass. She said almost nothing for a while, but her eyes were glassy with tears.

'I just don't understand where it came from, Michael.'

'I was scared,' I said, gripping her hands. 'I was scared that life was sort of dwindling right in front of me, shrinking to *us*, to our flat, to some dull job . . . I went to that college reunion and everyone there was so unimaginably dull, so stagnant, so . . . *resigned*.'

'But *we're* not like that.'

'I know. I know – I know that *now*. But there was just

something about it – about being a two, about conjugal bliss – that's what Julian kept calling it.' She laughed bitterly. 'I had a stupid, *idiot* bloody crisis. I freaked out, Astrid.'

She tried her best to affect an unmoved expression, but I knew that half the battle was won. She was in love with me. It was agony for her too – this being apart. I knew it was just within reach.

'I'm going to get another drink,' she said, refusing me eye contact again. 'Pint?'

'Please.'

I watched her glide off through the shuffling drunks and grey ghost people to the bar. She probably shuffled too, all things considered, but I could only ever see her float, really. She felt, I think, like she'd lost a round. Like she needed me more than I needed her and that being with me anew was a risk. I had to make her think it was mutual. She needed to see me as damaged, a shambles, to realise that I needed her more than anything else. I had to tell the Marion story. That would ignite the feeling within her, I thought – that was the kind of truth that bound people inexorably together. You couldn't know that about someone and think it was as simple as just severing everything. I had to tell her.

She slipped back down onto the swell of cracked bottle-green leather, pushed the hair off her face and let her head fall into her hands. Smoothed her eyebrows, renewed her refusal to meet my gaze, focused instead on somewhere beyond the dingy door to the Gents'. Neither of us spoke for a moment and I knew then that it was time.

'I have a tendency to fuck things up, Astrid,' I began. She smiled ironically. 'I have problems letting myself feel things for people.'

'Oh here we go.'

I paused. 'I had an older sister called Marion. She was

so wonderful. She was my . . .' I paused to take a dramatic glug of my pint, 'she was my *world*.'

There it was, the first ripple of curious sympathy, the softening of her gaze, which at last she let settle on mine, where both of us knew it belonged.

I cleared my throat. 'I don't really talk a lot about my family, because there's nothing much to say. I have a brother. I had a sister. My dad's an unremarkable, reliable sort – probably hasn't expressed an emotion since VE Day. My mother is . . . *hard* – the less said about her the better. They're shadow people. They're shadow people out of choice. They choose to live small, minimal, safe lives.

'Then there was Marion. Marion was . . . *electric*. She wasn't like other people we knew. She was naughty and funny and sharp and we were made for each other. We were thick as thieves from the moment I could talk. She took me under her wing. She'd take me to the library, and to the milk bar in town on a Friday. She took me to the cinema and she'd let me sit with her in her bedroom, which was like this extraterrestrial universe. I shared a room with Phil, my brother, and it was all old gym socks and football boots. Marion's was this sort of feminine proto-teenage paradise. She had posters of Paul Newman and Julie London that she'd torn out of magazines. She had her own record player that she'd saved up for for years. We'd lie on her bed and we'd read together and listen to music. She'd tell me about what she was going to do when she was grown up. She was like this flash of colour in my life. A kingfisher in a row of up-down terraces. I adored her.

'Then when she was about seventeen, she fell in love, with this man who . . . At the time, I idolised him, but *now* . . . well, now, as an adult, I can see he was a total prick. He wasn't particularly bright, but he was charming and good-looking, all swaggering adventure and everything that most of the boys we knew weren't. And by this point, life at home was so miserable; Mum had got so *misanthropic*. One night she had a real blow-out with Marion over Alan, and the next day Marion just left. Well, you can imagine – rural Yorkshire, a seventeen-year-old taking up with a man out of wedlock . . . It was *awful*. For a few months we didn't even see her and I can't tell you how much it dragged – how desperate I got. It was Dad I think who finally arranged something with her and Mum. Marion came over for tea, with Alan. She was wearing an engagement ring and that pleased Mum a little, but she was all stiff and formal, not like herself, and I *knew* something was wrong . . .'

Astrid took my hand.

'This is the condensed version, of course – the potted, woeful tale.' I laughed nervously. 'Anyway, from that point onwards she'd come to tea about once a fortnight, Sunday lunch once a month – to which Alan was always obliged. I remember the last Sunday lunch, when he hadn't turned up and there were some goings-on I wasn't privy to. I was too young. Everyone loved telling me that I was too young to know any of it . . .'

At that point I knew I'd hooked her in and I started really spinning it – everything, colouring in all the little details. I chose one excruciating bit as the opportune moment to get up and get us another round. I made all the characters flesh and bone. Then: the final act.

The lake. Ripples of late-spring sunlight as the warp and weft of the water, dazzling its surface. Marion drunk and giddy, little snatches of pop songs and nursery rhymes spilling from her too-fast mouth as she waltzed me around the grassy bank. Me so happy just to be with her, collecting up fistfuls of celandine and daisies to make her bracelets.

Then at last the feeling dying; how she'd flopped down in the grass and drawn up her knees to her forehead, let the brimming tears tumble down her cheeks . . .

'She started talking then about things I didn't understand but that seared themselves onto my brain all the same. She said she had a friend who knew a man who'd do it. She'd gone with him to his little flat in Leeds, but she'd got there and it was just so sordid, everything smelling of bleach, and a white kitchen tablecloth, and him with such cold hands. He was a sadist, she'd said. She just couldn't.

'She sat there and she wept and I tried to curl into the crook of her arm, and she said that she remembered me being born, and how I'd gripped her finger with my little purple hands. And how could she do that? she asked me – and I said, "I don't know," as if I'd understood. She made me promise not to tell Mum, and I solemnly agreed. Then eventually she stopped crying. She took the little flask from her handbag and swilled a bit of what was in there, and she asked me to go back into the woods and get her some of the bluebells that we'd seen growing on the way. I didn't want to leave her, so, scrabbling for something, I reminded her that it was bad luck to pick bluebells. She laughed and said that it would make her so happy – and that it wasn't bad luck if you picked them for someone else anyway . . .

'I didn't want to leave her, but I was so torn because she was so insistent that it would make her happy . . .'

Astrid. Astrid's real, physical hands caressing my own. She held them as if she could protect me from everything just by enveloping my fingers in hers.

'Of course she wasn't there when I got back. Her handbag was open on the patch of grass where we'd been sitting. The flask was being washed about by the ebb of the water down on the bank. But she wasn't anywhere – just this vast stretch of glassy water. Not even a ripple.

'I ran as fast as I could to the nearest house. Blind panic. I've never felt anything so terrifying. The police were called – my parents; people from the village started to appear as the gossip sifted through from house to house. It was only because everyone was in such a state that I wasn't sent home, I suppose – that I saw her when they found her . . .'

'Michael . . . You don't have to go on if you don't want to.'

But I did, of course. I was in my element then, found phrases like *shadows around her eyes* and *purple stains as lips* tumbling from my mouth and watched as Astrid's eyes widened just to take in the horror of it, and have space enough to accommodate it. Tonight she would come back to the flat. It would be tender, half-lit oblivion and afterwards, when she was drunk on my dependence, I would ask her to come with me – because I realised now. I'd wanted to go alone, but how could I go without her?

26

Leah

At the end of the day there was a sharp knock on my door. For about four and a half seconds I sat at my desk trying not to breathe too loudly, until at last Clarissa's muffled voice insisted that she knew I was in there and that I had to let her in. Gathering my towel around me (I hadn't dressed all day), I limped piteously to the door.

'Well fuck me, you are alive then.'

'Apparently.'

'Look, whatever happened with my brother, I'm sure it's not that bad.'

I pulled a face. 'Ugh – it's not just your brother, it's so many things.'

'None of which are that bad. Here, I brought you tea.'

She pushed her way into my room and I suppose I was mostly grateful.

'I'm too embarrassed to ever go downstairs,' I said.

'All you did was go to Marseille.'

'Your dad hates me.'

'He categorically *doesn't* hate you. Did he read you the riot act over your little adventure?'

'It was awful.'

She gave me a winsome smile. 'That's just what he's like,' she said. 'I'm honestly surprised that's the first time you've ever incurred his wrath.'

I sat down next to her and, before I realised what I was doing, instinctively nuzzled into her.

'I feel like shit,' I said.

'That's what happens when you go out on the razz with Lal.' She handed me the tea.

'What did I miss anyway?' I sniffed.

'I escaped most of the day with Nico,' she began, moon-eyed, 'but according to Tom, it wasn't fun. Dad and Anna had some huge domestic and Tom ended up going to the Calanques with his parents. Said he felt about twelve again. He was very grumpy with me when I got home last night.'

'Poor Tom.'

'Poor Tom . . . He should have joined you two on what I hear was quite an adventure.'

I pulled a face.

'My arsehole brother is proper into you. Please don't be taken in by him.'

I attempted my best cynical eyebrow raise and insisted that I was not the sort to be taken in by any kind of man (ignoring the flutter at her phrasing; *he* was into *me*). Clarissa looked unconvinced.

'Don't get tangled up with Lal,' she said. 'He's not a good idea. Stick with Jérôme . . . Or maybe swear off men altogether for a while – extricate yourself from all your self-inflicted romantic drama and get your own shit sorted first.' She delivered this eviscerating judgement with a shrug that signalled that her advice had closed the conversation. She looked over at the pile of diaries. 'You working?'

Smarting, I followed her cue. 'I've almost finished,' I said. 'Let me finish this last one, then I promise I'll come and tell you everything about Marseille.'

Again that sceptical look. 'How much do you have left?'

'Like twenty minutes reading max.'

She stood up. 'If you're not in my room in half an hour, I'm coming back.'

'Twenty-five minutes, I swear!'

When she was safely out of the room and I'd heard the dull thud of her bedroom door close behind her, I picked up the last diary Michael had given me. It ended on 24 July 1969 and I'd finished it about half an hour ago. They'd gone off to Athens, but just before that, a whole handful of pages had been torn out. My head was full of it; I was totally stunned. It made so little sense that she would have given up everything to go on this bizarre, whimsical trip to Greece with him. Why had he conveniently cut off the diaries at that moment – and what was more, why had a month of entries been removed?

It had been a thick, oppressive afternoon. The sky had been a churned-up vortex of grey, turning the fractured sea violet and the pines denser than ever. In the cage of my little room I'd got a prickly sort of cabin fever. The more I read, the more I felt a slow twist of unease. Where was she? Where was Astrid? I thought again of the diary she'd apparently kept that had driven Michael so mad. How typical of him to want to be in total control of the narrative. He was so preoccupied with her voice: Astrid the singer, Astrid with her much-fetishised East End lilt. Where it had mattered, though, her voice had all but disappeared under the din of his own.

27

Michael

I only bothered going to dinner to see her face, but God knows it was an effort. I'd spent the whole day pinned to the concrete floor of the shed, listening to the rain pelt the corrugated iron roof and watching the light warp around me.

The migraine had come on the day before, just after I'd seen her leave with Lawrence and Luke. I'd not slept and had sat on the headland for the best part of the night, watching the black void of the sea. I'd found a little bag of cocaine in Lawrence's room after the party, and I was in such a state that I'd gone to my desk and racked up a few lines. It had been years since I'd done it, of course, and the ripple of well-being it had given me was quite astonishing. I'd felt maddeningly agitated though, too. It was probably cut with something speedy – kids know fuck all about how to take drugs these days. Still, I felt this immense grip of self-belief that I hadn't experienced for years; and when the feeling started to twist its way out of my body again, leaving me paranoid and insignificant, I took one more line, and then another. By the time I'd seen that rust-bucket car of theirs pull out of the drive (and was his hand on her thigh? I didn't imagine that, did I?), I was bloody soaring.

Then all of it – horribly – at once. The excruciating kick in the stomach as I realised that the only bit of high left was in the screwdriver force at my jaw, and no matter how hard I clenched, I couldn't keep it in. All those zinging atoms of relief were working their way out of me and I couldn't stop it – the merciless exodus of feeling. Soon the oil-slick heat of the day bore down on me. I was paralysed, immobile. I hadn't come down like this for a lifetime.

I remember Anna's face as she'd torn her way into the little cocoon I'd made myself in the shed.

'Michael? Are you . . .? Look at your eyes . . . your jaw . . . You *are*, aren't you?'

I'd told her to sod off, and the cracked vulgarity of it against the dulcet timbre of her voice was like piss shot through a glass of milk. All at once, though, I'd wanted her; that acute ache of being alone . . . But no, it wasn't her I wanted at all. I just needed to sleep. The heat, though – Christ, it was so fucking hot. If I could just *sleep*. I managed to that night – in a manner of speaking – and as soon as I'd woken up I'd gone outside and looked for the car. It was still gone. I knew that they'd left to take Luke to the airport, so how was it possible that now, twenty-four hours later, the car was still gone?

Her bedroom was dark and cool. I could just lie here and wait for her; she'd be back soon. My diaries were stacked up by her desk, and the sight of them, and the image of her reading them, made me feel like little bits of me were being made whole and substantial again. The pillow smelt like Astrid. I went and picked up one of the old notebooks; how uniquely evocative the sight of it was – even my handwriting exactly the same and yet unknowably different from now. I flipped through it looking for the right kind of passage; buried my face in the smell of her, felt for her soft, downy hair – the little golden bit at the top of her thigh. God, it was intense. It was Technicolor, surround sound, virtual reality. She was here all over again.

After I'd laid into her when she'd finally got home (she'd

looked so pretty as her face had gone all pinkish and her eyes had filled up), I'd spent the whole day nailed to the floor. Crucified. It was the first real rain of the month. It had been brewing for days and now it struck violet right across the sky. Under the sky, the sea was violet too, and the dense green of the pines turned all onyx and matt. I felt alive again. The idea of her made me feel alive again.

Seven of us cramped around the little kitchen table, and my vision all speckled. She was next to Clarissa (who was all at once Diana – God, I felt dreadful) and Tom. Larry ate in silence. He looked grey and he hunched over the flaky *tielle* on his plate like a hungry troglodyte, pausing only to greedily neck his beer. She risked meeting my eyes a couple of times and I beamed back at her to let her know it was all forgotten, that this morning had been an aberration – that I loved her. I watched her flit seamlessly between herself and my Astrid. Jenny would turn to me, face unlined and hair black again, before turning back to talk to her grown-up son. I had to stop myself from laughing out loud. Huh. And so everything goes on, *ad infinitum*.

*

The following morning it was Leah, not Astrid, sitting on the deckchair with her legs stretched out in front of her, writing something in one of her notebooks. I sat down next to her and lit a cigarette, and I'm sure she looked at me as I flicked the ash, looked at my hands, the 'masculine join at the wrists' (that's what I'd heard her say once, gossiping with my daughter). I felt that electrical surge, that kick you get when you know someone's fair game. Astrid again; the underside of her breasts, the backs of her knees . . .

'I finished typing up the diaries, so I'll bring them back

down to you today,' said Leah, in reality more brusque than I would have liked.

'Oh?' I said.

'I wanted to show you that I take this seriously,' she said, with that same acidic tang on her tongue.

I cleared my throat. 'Leah,' I said softly, 'I was in a vile mood when you and Larry got back yesterday. I didn't mean to be quite so curt with you.'

In a monotone, eyes on the flagstones: 'I'm sure I deserved it. I should have told you instead of just taking off.'

Without thinking, I put my palm on her naked thigh. I felt the breath still in her lungs and was about to snatch my hand away when she turned and looked at me. Exactly the same eyes. I dared myself and my burning fingers to make their way towards the hem of her simple summer dress. She'd yet to draw breath. A millimetre, drag, an inch . . .

'I'm going to go and swim now,' she blurted out. A part of me wanted to stay immobile and test her, but then both of us heard the rumble of Anna's car in the driveway and I tore my hand away. She stood up in an attempt to flee to the beach before social obligation could intervene, but it was too late. Anna had already seen her.

'Hello, darling!' she called from the car as she clocked me. She pursed her lips. 'I've brought a visitor for you.'

A visitor? A tall, grey-haired man in a pale linen suit got out of the car, and after what felt like an eternity, he turned to face me. But no – now I really was going mad, wasn't I? It couldn't possibly be.

'Micky, old boy!' he cried in a jovial mid-Atlantic burr. 'It's been a bloody lifetime.'

I felt my blood plummet and my legs lose substance. As he made his way closer to us, his features solidified unmis-takably into slightly altered versions of the ones I'd once known so well. He wasn't even looking at me now, though; his eyes were fixed on her.

Julian took one look at Leah and started to laugh. 'Jesus Christ, Mick,' he whistled, 'you haven't changed at all.'

Four

SAINT-LUC

Tu caresses la rondeur de ton ventre en pensant: ce n'est pas seulement une forme humaine, c'est aussi des idées, une intelligence qui se développe. C'est miracle l'enfant, il découvre le langage. Le secret des mots est dans un ventre de femme

Emma Santos, *La Malcastrée*

28

Michael

I'd been deeply sceptical when Jenny and the Monk had first announced that they were moving out of London, but then as someone who'd actually endured the drag of growing up in the countryside, I was always suspicious of any Londoner who chose to abandon civilisation for Norfolk or Sussex or, God forbid, west Wales. They were about a year or so into what I still kept calling their little Ted Hughes experiment in Devon. Things must have been going well, I'd joke to Jenny on the phone – after all, no one had gassed themselves yet. I could almost hear her rolling her eyes on the other end of the line. *Still tasteless, Mick – it's not getting funnier.*

I arrived on the morning of Good Friday. It was the end of March. We'd had a real dog of a winter, Jenny and Bryan more than most. She'd miscarried for the second time just before Christmas. I hadn't been about. Honestly, their rural migration had been convenient for me; I'd found it difficult to be around her when she was pregnant. After New Year, they'd gone out to the States for a month, and now they were back and full of it. She'd been her usual upbeat self in postcards, acting as if Christmas hadn't even happened, and ploughing on determinedly, as if the way the sun came through the giant redwoods in Oregon was really moving enough to efface everything they'd gone through before they left. She'd insisted I come down for the Easter weekend. We hadn't seen each other since the book deal, and to be honest, a weekend of R&R in the wilds of Devon was genuinely appealing.

'You can come and dry out after all your celebrating,' she'd said on the phone. 'I can smell the booze from here.'

I'd rented an Austin Allegro (piece of shite) and had miraculously made it to the West Country in one piece, stopping at some kind of genteel bed and breakfast in Dorset on the way. Antimacassars. Chintz. Interior stained-glass windows and an ancient landlady in curlers sipping sherry out of a Jubilee mug. It was the kind of place aspiring divorcees would spend a night with a prostitute in 1912 to try and get legal separation from their wives. There was a stuffed golliwog slumped drunkenly over a Royal Legion collection box at the reception desk. 'That's my little Gurkha!' the old lady had chuckled ominously as I'd eyed the flaccid doll.

In Devon, even the air smelt of spring. The hedgerows were studded with early dog violet, and along the coast, red campion bloomed. Jenny and Bryan's track almost wiped out the Allegro. She was waiting for me at the front door, waving madly. She looked good: virtuous, healthy. Her skin was tanned and she was wearing paint-splattered dungarees. Bourgeois quasi-hippies in the countryside were always decorating something. My skin looked sallow in the rear-view mirror.

It had only been a couple of months since we'd last seen each other, and yet I felt strangely overwhelmed by the sight of her. I'd been thinking too much about things that had happened recently. It was the book deal. It was hitting my thirties. It was exhaustion. I didn't like myself that morning. I held Jen very close and inhaled the familiar smell of her hair.

'All right, Mick?' she said when I finally let her go, twisting her wedding band around on her ring finger like she always did when she was nervous or concerned. 'You OK?'

'I'm just tired,' I said dismissively. 'I spent last night

at the Unity Mitford Bed and Breakfast. Didn't sleep that much. Life's been a bit mad recently.'

'Well you can sleep all afternoon,' she said. 'I'll show you your room if you want to dump your bags. Come on.'

Afterwards, she sat me down at the kitchen table and started toasting hot cross buns and making tea. She wanted to hear all about the deal and about me quitting my job at the magazine. When we'd been through all of that, I asked her about America. By the time she'd got to the East Coast, the hands of the grandfather clock by the door were grazing midday.

'Micky, there is one other thing I have to tell you about New York,' she said, twisting her wedding ring again. I'd half guessed what she was going to say. 'We stayed with Jules on the last night.'

'Great,' I said blandly.

'He's doing really well out there. He says he's not coming back – in a couple of years he'll be able to get citizenship.'

'That's nice.'

'I told him about your book deal.'

I nodded.

She pursed her lips. 'Every time I tried to speak about you, he got so defensive. I don't know what went down between the two of you, but was it really that bad?'

I felt my jaw clench despite myself. Jenny stood up to go and refill the kettle. She always had to keep herself busy during these kinds of conversations. When she spoke again, her tone was terse.

'Maybe you just have to respect that she didn't want to be found.'

For a moment I felt a swell of anger, before the habitual self-preservation kicked in. Jenny and Julian had exchanged letters at first, and then, about five years in, the letters had dwindled down to Christmas cards. They'd seen each other maybe three times since he'd moved there permanently. He evidently still hadn't told her. He wasn't a threat to me, but if I let my emotions get the better of me, she might start to suspect that she didn't know the whole truth.

'Jen,' I said, hoping that I sounded placating, 'if Julian ever decides to come back to the Old World – to return to one of his ancestral piles or whatever – I'll toe the line, OK? It's not even that big a deal.' I dug with my thumbnail at a large knot on the kitchen table. 'Sometimes people just drift apart.'

29

I was liquid by the time this new version of Julian pulled me into a would-be brotherly embrace, and all I could think, as he boorishly clapped my back, was how damp my shirt would be, and how he would know then how in control of the situation he was. I tried to anchor myself in the reality of his features. Looking at him was like looking at warped heat rising off tarmac in August; the space around him was deformed, as if he was the burning end of a candle wick. I heard his voice introduce himself to Leah (though again, not quite his voice any more, cadences of American polluting the RP). I watched her curtail her astonishment (because of course she knew who he was). I was fast-forwarding a cassette, and the translucent ribbon of tape was derailing.

'Nice surprise?' whispered Anna, whose lips were now brushing my earlobe, her body pressing into mine, arms snaking around my hips. Was I being paranoid, or was her sweet voice laced with malice?

I'd forgotten how Julian smelt. When he'd embraced me, my brain was flooded with him – and with all these automatic feelings that had been uniquely tailored for him: of love and of complicity, and then of some other unnameable thing, where the polar extremes of superiority and inferiority met. Yes, so much of my relationship with him had been defined by the struggle between the two.

'Oh my *God*.' Then his name, in Jenny's voice. She was barefoot and in the T-shirt Bryan had been wearing at dinner last night. Her hair was black again, but it was new Julian grasping her by the shoulders and laughing at the absurdity of it all. I saw her put her head in her hands and shake it.

'I can't believe you're here,' she whispered. She reached out for me. Almost unable to speak, she said, 'Michael, come here,' and pulled me towards them so that the three of us were standing together. She seemed to be radiating light. There was too much light; both of them were wreathed in it. Their veins were filled with light-bulb filament and it was burning my retinas. I blinked, and squinted, and as I closed my eyes, the outlines of their bodies pressed red onto my eyelids, I felt my nostrils reel with a cloying, familiar odour.

It was the smell of the Piccadilly Line.

'Jenny,' I managed hoarsely, and directly afterwards, I fainted.

*

I was only out for a few seconds, but when I came to, I was struck by a clarity that had evaded me for weeks. They'd managed to prop me against a sunlounger, and when I scraped my eyes open, Jenny and Julian were crouching at my side.

'Oh ho ho!' Julian laughed as I flickered back into consciousness. 'Cancel the smelling salts, he's back!'

Jenny held a glass of water in one hand and mine in the other, without any pressure, that drawn look on her face. 'How do you feel?'

I gave her hand a little squeeze and cleared my throat. 'Well, that was embarrassing.'

'Not at all, Micky, I've been known to make both ladies and gentlemen swoon in my time.'

It was such a Julian line. Now that his features were stable, I took a good look at him. He radiated good health. He had the perpetually olive skin of someone who lives in the kind of place that lemons grow. The lines on his face, the deep crow's feet, were the lines of lightness and joy. There was a warmth in his eyes that hadn't been there when we were younger.

'I'm going to put on a pot of coffee,' Anna sang in a voice that was over-egged with cheer. 'Come and grab some cups, will you, darling?' she said to Leah.

I dusted myself off and slowly hoisted myself up. Jenny looked concerned. 'It's not too hot for you to be out? You're feeling all right?'

'I'll be fine under the shade. Really, I'm OK. Please don't make a fuss.' The small of my back was aching from where I must have knocked the chair, but it was vaguely comforting; the physical sensation pinned me to reality.

Under the shade of the patio. 'How many years has it even been?' Jenny's voice was softened with disbelief. 'The last time I saw you was with Tom in – what? – '96? But Mick . . .'

'Getting on for fifty,' said Julian drily, not taking his eyes off me.

'God,' she sighed. 'A lifetime.'

'Two lifetimes.' Did the corner of his mouth curl up into an amused little smile when he said that?

'I just can't believe you didn't let slip in your last email!' Jenny was still glowing, totally oblivious. 'You and Anna have a lot of explaining to do.'

They emailed? This was an alarming new development.

'Well I won't ruin Anna's fun. I'll leave that story to her.'

Jenny reached for his hand. 'You look fabulous.'

'That's what half a century in California does to you. *You* look fabulous.'

'Oh, I look old.'

'We *are* old. You look happy.'

She was visibly dazzled. 'I am.' The hot morning swelled

with the dense chorus of the cicadas. 'You're still in California then?'

'Most of the time, with stints in New York. We used to have an apartment on the Upper West Side, but we sold it a few years back. David's got a little pied-à-terre in Williamsburg because he thinks he's a thirty-year-old, of course . . .' He paused and smiled at me. 'David. My husband. You don't have to pretend it's not shocking.' He flattened his palms on the table. 'You just never know who you'll fall in love with, do you?'

Jenny looked at me too. She was in raptures. 'Oh Jules, I'm so happy for you.'

I stifled a derisive laugh. How could she be buying this? *My husband?* Julian – gay? If anything, that part was believable – he'd had the odd fling way back when, but I'd just put it down to free love or boarding school. It was the *you just never know who you'll fall in love with* that I was struggling with. Please. Julian the shirt-lifter I could get my head around; but Julian *married*?

'I'd love for you both to meet him one day,' he was saying now. 'I just . . . God, I don't even know where to begin. It's overwhelming, seeing you both like this. I feel so terrible that it's been this long, that we let life get in the way.'

He fixed his eyes on the broken butter dish that the kids used as an ashtray, as if he didn't dare meet Jenny's gaze.

'I feel like there was this traumatic rupture in my life somehow—'

'*Traumatic?*' I sneered. 'Oh come on, Jules, we're not in the Valley now.'

Their reactions and the sound of my own voice made me realise how silent I'd been since we'd sat down at the table. Jenny glared at me. Anna, always the queen of perfect timing, chose that precise moment to glide out onto the patio, followed by Leah, who appeared to be carrying all of the breakfast accoutrements at once. A flash of Astrid balancing stacks of plates at Giorgio's: I felt calmer.

'So did I strike gold or *what*?' said my wife smugly as she flopped elegantly onto a chair.

'It's certainly a coup,' said Jenny. 'Will you please both put us out of our misery and tell us how on earth any of this happened.'

Leah slotted in next to her and I couldn't take my eyes off her. She had her hair all piled up on her head and her neck exposed. I remembered kissing that neck, pressed against the bathroom wall on Charlotte Street – how her breath would quicken, and how she'd twist her head up, offering herself to me. I noticed then that Julian was looking at her too. I clenched my fists under the table and made myself watch Anna instead. David, my arse.

'Julian and I have a friend in common,' my wife purred. 'An artist friend, Osei.'

Julian simpered. 'When I made the connection, I just had to get in touch. David and I were coming to Europe this summer and I knew it was the right time.'

'He wanted to surprise you! Isn't that sweet?'

Anna's version of events would be uninformed at best. She'd not have even the slightest inkling of how much Julian must have been using her as a pawn to bring this about. Involuntarily, my balled-up fists tightened.

'At first I was a little sceptical,' she said.

'You didn't even reply to my first email. You left me hanging!'

'Well I wasn't going to reply at all. But then you sent me some very . . .' she paused, letting her gaze rest on me, 'illuminating photos.'

Julian defused the tension before anyone else could pick

up on it. 'Anna is too young to remember the fashion crimes of our youth.'

My wife let the ominous weight of our eye contact bloom for just a second longer. She pursed her lips. 'It was the sideburns that swung it,' she said. Anna was a bad liar.

'So you mean you and Michael haven't spoken for, what . . . forty-five years or something?' said Leah. I couldn't work out whether she was attempting to get a foothold in the conversation out of politeness or – rather frighteningly – if she was actually trying to dig. 'That's crazy,' she breathed.

'Oh, the naïvety of youth!' Julian scoffed. 'It was a lot easier to lose touch before Facebook, you know. The US used to actually be far away.'

She gave a little shrug of assent, but it was evident that she wasn't buying it.

Most of what he said, however – over the spooling, excruciating hours that followed – was happily swallowed by my family. In a staggered parade, the others began to join us. Bryan first, followed by Clarissa and Tom in quick succession, and then at last my son, around the time that 'breakfast' spilled into 'lunch' (it seems futile to try and give that first day any solid markers of time – it was one of those cricket-loud summer days that oozed and stalled like sap making its slow progression down the rough bark of a tree). Neither Clarissa nor Tom could hide their voyeuristic excitement at this potential insight into our past. Clarissa audibly italicised his name when introduced, and Tom even prefaced it with a scandalised *the*. The pair of them went into mutual raptures about their last meeting, when Tom had been twelve.

'Good to see my legend's been kept alive and kicking,' Julian drawled, before once again trotting out the excuse that pre-internet America was so far away.

It was a spectacle that was painful to watch. He'd evidently lost none of his schmoozy public school charm, but he'd managed to take apart the very fabric of it and refit it into a garment infinitely more appealing to the modern temperament. First came the subtle and stoical plea for their sympathy:

'I mean, one of the reasons I didn't come back for so long was because it was so difficult with my family. My mother came *this* close to disinheriting me when she found out about David . . .'

Not a chance in hell. His mother had been of the chain-smoking theatre hag variety. She collected old queens.

Next came the artfully dropped insights into his groovy LA lifestyle, tailored to impress my children. He finally cemented their blind adoration when, asked what he fancied for lunch, he announced with a self-deprecating wince that he was a vegetarian. Watching them all scramble to denounce the over-consumption of flesh was almost too much. He even curried favour with Bryan. He made the Monk *laugh*. When, at last, a picnic at the beach was unanimously agreed on, I made an excuse to go down to the shed. I needed to be on my own – to gather myself together and work out what the fuck I was going to do.

'You should take Julian with you!' Anna cooed. 'He's such a big fan of your novels.'

'What a compliment,' I said inanely.

Julian looked back at me over his sunglasses with an expression of cool amusement. 'I'd be honoured.'

It dawned on me then that it was safer to keep an eye on him. 'Come along then, *mate*,' I grumbled, turning my back on the table.

Across the lawn, down the patio and skirting the thicket of pines, I let the silence bud between us, and it was only as I jerked at the rusty door handle, flakes of green paint speckling my hand, that I spoke at last.

'What the fuck are you doing here?'

Julian put his still hand over my shaking one and in a swift, easy motion pulled open the door. 'Let's talk inside, shall we?'

We sat opposite each other on the two overturned wine crates like pugilists. I let the cool green mustiness settle on me like particles of dust, and in turn settled into the pleasant, shadowy envelope of the room.

'So: this is where the magic happens . . . ahem, happened.'

'Cut the bullshit, Jules.'

He grinned. 'God, Anna did warn me that you'd been grumpy lately, but I thought you would have lightened up a little at least for the return of such an old friend.'

'What did she mean? Illuminating photos?'

Julian shrugged. 'Anna's a visual artist. When she didn't reply to my first couple of emails, I thought I'd soften her with some examples of her medium.'

Watching him in all his smugness, I felt an uncharacteristic primal urge to jump him. He inspired a kind of physical volition in me. Somewhere in the mist of my conscience, though, a whisper of rationality reminded me to be calm – that he was the one with the upper hand, after all. I tried to modulate the tone of my voice.

'How exactly did you really end up emailing my wife?'

He smirked. 'Anna's a very successful photographer. I've been aware of her work for a considerable number of years.'

'Jules . . .'

'Your new assistant seems like a nice girl.'

'She is,' I said through gritted teeth.

'Jenny wasn't wrong.'

'What's that supposed to mean?'

'She doesn't remind you of anyone?' he said. When I didn't reply, he carried on. 'David and I were in Europe for the summer, and when Jen sent me a rather concerned email a few weeks back, I thought maybe I ought to try and drop by, just to check in on you all.'

'Concerned?' I repeated.

'She was trying to make a joke of it. I think she felt a bit nervous and she wanted someone to tell her it was all fine – someone who'd been there. I found it kind of alarming, though. You'd managed to find some kind of *lookalike*? Ugh.' He shuddered. 'The more I thought about it, the more I thought that maybe it wasn't right that you'd just gotten away with everything for all this time. That there are only a handful of us who know what really happened.'

I made to protest and he cut me down after a single syllable.

'I knew that if I suggested to Jenny that I come, she'd tell you. She seems to have this strange idea that we're all still best friends and that you and I just drifted apart . . . Bloody likely. Then I remembered the Anna connection. Our little friend in common. When she was so bloody loyal to you at first, ignoring all my messages, I wondered exactly how much she even knew herself.'

'What did you show my wife?'

'She must be very patient,' he said. 'To a duplicitous point, to be honest. I'm surprised she hasn't already shown you. I'm intrigued to know what her plan is.'

He stood up, exhaled calmly and began to stroll around the room, humming jauntily, picking up objects, turning them over, smiling fondly at my bric-à-brac. I watched him in fascinated horror. I'd been waiting for this moment for the best part of fifty years, and now he was here, in front of me, limbs and skin and a depressingly agile skeleton. Tangible, undeniable flesh; hands picking up an old CD of *Blue* by Joni Mitchell, and his crooked mouth saying, 'Christ, this takes me back. Remember Kathy?' There was something almost grotesque about it – this impossible and yet evidently concrete apparition; for a moment, I felt a stab of genuine panic.

'What did you send Anna?' The idea of my wife knowing something and withholding it made me feel even more paranoid.

'Ah. You've even got a little whistling kettle! You're so bloody English, aren't you? Here, should we brew up? For old times' sake?'

'Julian!'

He stopped, replaced the kettle on the camping stove and dropped the dumb delight act.

'It's not fair that you got away with it, Michael. I was happy to just forget about you like she wanted. To be honest, I always thought you'd been let off lightly, but . . .'

He was still talking, but the idea of *her* submerged me: The idea that she had *wanted* things. That she had asked him to act in a certain way. That she hadn't just ceased to exist.

'. . . after Jenny telling me about your new girl, I decided that this mutual silence had gone on for too long. And you know what, when I saw her, I was glad that I'd come here. I don't know what you're doing, but it's fucked up.'

'Julian. If we could just . . .'

He started for the door. 'I don't know if you're looking for some kind of twisted cosmic redemption through her, but if you are, it's not going to happen. You're probably not even doing that, though. Everyone credits you with this nuanced emotional intelligence because you're an *artist*, but you probably just want to get laid.'

He paused. Inhaled. Exhaled decadently. Once again the picture of serenity, he let his hands drop to his sides, his right knuckles pale from gripping the door handle, and beamed at me. His face was utterly sinister.

'I could just tell you to leave.'

'You could. But I suspect you're not going to. Not when I could still tell you what really happened to Astrid.'

The evocation of her name, the two flat syllables of it, blindsided me.

'And what's more, I guess you're not going to want to piss me off either. What would Jen say if she knew the whole truth? Or your wife? Or your kids?'

There it was again – the dull thud at my temple, the sensation that my brain was lurching away from my skull. Standing in the doorway, Julian was all at once speckled; the light and shadows around him dappled and mutable. He reached out his hand, as smooth as it had been in 1969, and in a benign, paternalistic voice said, 'Come on, let's go down to the beach.'

*

Tumbling down the sand dunes, I couldn't seem to fix a single image clearly before me. Everything was moving too quickly – the fast-forwarding cassette again, all the sounds – the garrulous seagulls, the chime of Anna's cut-glass laugh – obscured by the whirr of a football rattle. The scenery jerked about in front of me as if I were watching it in stop motion. Jenny paddling in the shallows at Brancaster beach two summers before she got married, tunelessly singing 'The "In" Crowd' by Bryan Ferry (they'd played it on the radio five times on the way down from London. I hated Bryan Ferry). The waves lapping the shore, water whipped up into lily of the valley: Whitby, 1959. There was Clarissa, though, pouring wine into plastic flutes and handing them to Bryan, Tom, and now Julian . . .

Julian.

'Go on, you two, get together! Act like you actually like each other!'

He'd bought a Leica – because that was the sort of thing Julian could do on a whim. He'd said he was going to use it to document his great American odyssey and he'd started talking about things like aperture and exposure *all the fucking time.*

'Kiss her!' he crowed.

'Jules, your taste is so questionable. I'm not kissing her; it's tacky.'

'Oh *go on*, don't be a snob!'

And then I'd looked at her, at her hair all bleached with sun and salt water; at her brown skin flecked with freckles – galaxies of them, right across the bridge of her nose – her white teeth spreading into a smile against her tan. And you know I think that despite everything – despite everything that would happen – I loved her more in that moment than ever.

'Julian!' she squealed.

I held her body close to me, barely perceptible rays of sunlight glinting off the sea spray on her limbs, calves caked in sand, and thrust my other hand up in mock-threat towards the camera's invasive lens.

'Yeah, piss off, Jules,' I grumbled affectionately between salty kisses.

'Your kids will thank me one day!' he insisted. 'Ugh, God, you're both so photogenic, it's sickening.'

But it wasn't her; it was almost her?

Julian had his plastic cup in one hand and an iPhone in the other.

'Jesus Christ, Jenny, look at them. It's uncanny. Here, kids, smile – I'm gonna take a photo!'

Larry's hand on her waist. She shrieks as he pulls her down into the folds of cyan water.

That is my son, I tell myself. That's my son. It's 2016. That is my son.

She emerges, spluttering, pushes at his chest; he loses his balance a little . . . 'Oh Jesus, don't give Lal any more vino,' my daughter cackles. Her mother used to cackle like that.

You're both so photogenic, it's sickening.

I stumble, float; let my legs give way to gravity. Jenny passes me my own acrylic glass and I swallow its contents whole.

Your kids will thank me one day!

The colossal juggernaut of time hurls itself away from me. Everything dissolves.

30

Leah

Four nights after Julian arrived – a Sunday – we were sitting on the terrace of Le Bastringue, drinking Suze, our new favourite drink on the merit of its beneficent cheapness.

'It's frightening,' Tom said. 'Yesterday morning I caught him leading Mum in a meditation session. *Meditation*. She came back from the beach all serene and dopey as if he'd slipped her a couple of diazepam in her coffee. Mum doesn't do spirituality. I just don't buy it. I don't trust white men in collarless shirts. He's either a sex fiend or a misguided repentant super-capitalist.'

Clarissa raised her eyebrows. 'You're being unfair. If he's a sex fiend, he's a monogamous one. Yesterday he spent like ten minutes showing me his Instagram feed – it's almost exclusively pictures of him and his husband being super-cute and making you feel like an emotional failure. They have a Shiba Inu that's better dressed than Leah. It has a tiny tartan jacket.'

Since Marseille and Julian's arrival, I'd felt like an outsider. He had slipped seamlessly into the household, and furthermore had triggered a perceptible shift in the atmosphere. Everyone was utterly charmed by his bright, uniquely West Coast blend of languor and sincere enthusiasm, its usual queasy earnestness tempered by the last residual traces of *Withnail & I*-style Englishness. He'd exorcised the house of its moribund energy: no more of Jenny's tight-lipped smiles or Michael's barbed comments. Anna's laboured crusade for harmony had become redundant, and the new guest diffused infectious, irresistible lightness. I, on the other hand, couldn't shake the sense that I was being surveyed.

For the past two mornings, Julian had come and joined me on my pre-breakfast swim. 'Good *mor*ning!' he'd sung cheerily as he'd bounded onto the patio.

'Oh. Hi!' I'd said, aping said cheer in order to hide the fact that I was deeply nettled by this invasion of my daily solitude.

'Going for a dip?' he'd asked. His tendency towards quaint *Blue Peter* presenter expressions kept dragging the newer incarnation – Julian 2.0 – straight back to the version I'd become so used to in Michael's diaries. The ease with which he coordinated this duality disturbed me, and as much as I had a pressing desire to be near him (out of masochistic curiosity; the way you want to run into an ex's current at a party), I wanted to do it on my own terms. I still wasn't sure quite where I stood with him, or even where Michael stood with him (something had definitely gone on there, even if everyone was playing at happy families). Anxiety aside, I couldn't deny that the surveillance was mutual. Having become so well acquainted with him over the summer, I was totally fascinated by Julian; above all, I suspected that if I played my cards right, he could be the one to enlighten me about what had happened to Astrid and Michael after they'd left for Greece. I'd felt utterly bereft since finishing the diaries, a feeling underlined with more than a squeak of concern.

'Uh huh,' I'd croaked.

'Splendid,' he'd beamed. 'Let's bounce!'

'They're all hiding something anyway,' Clarissa said, and I felt a stab of relief that she felt it too.

'You reckon?' I said, a little too enthusiastically.

'Yes. It's weird that they were estranged for, like, fifty

years,' she said. 'Don't give me that no-Facebook bullshit. We may have Facebook but they had fucking Concorde.'

'You know they actually took Concorde a couple of times too?' Tom added.

Of course they did. Of course they had the kind of parents who'd been on Concorde. Images of Jerry Hall, clinking champagne glasses and swaggering Halston-clad abundance.

Throughout this exchange, Larry had been demonstratively non-verbal, as he always was whenever we started to speculate on the lives of their parents – as if he was above it all. He'd caught my foot under the table and pulled it up onto his lap, and had now apparently decided to silently torture me, running his thumb along its arch just as he had at the café on the Vieux Port in Marseille. Every so often he'd catch my eye and offer me a conspiratorial smile. Mostly he just scrolled, mutely, through something evidently more thrilling on his phone.

'The thing is, I can't help but really like him,' Clarissa continued.

'I *know*. He should be insufferable, but he's actually endearing.'

'So unlike Mum and Michael,' Tom chimed in, before looking at me wickedly and asking, 'When did it all change?'

I pursed my lips. 'I told you. The diaries end when they're all still best mates and Julian's an aggressively heterosexual 1960s perv with a Brian Sewell accent. I know nothing.'

Clarissa was right that there was something irresistible about Julian. He was so open, easy-going and personable. He inspired effortless confidence. In a few lengths of the cove that morning, I'd found myself willingly discussing my thoughts on Michael's diaries that I'd refused to divulge to

Tom and Clarissa, and it was only afterwards, as we were all sitting together at breakfast, Julian sandwiched between his old friends, the three of them laughing and dazzled with liquid Mediterranean sunlight like something out of an Olivio advert, that I'd started to feel the gnaw of anxiety at the pit of my stomach. I realised with an excruciating twist that *I'd* somehow ended up being the one who'd been interrogated. I watched them all eat breakfast together through a dulling film of paralysing distance. Had I just really fucked up?

'And there haven't been any hints so far as to why Dad and Julian had their little bust-up?' Clarissa asked.

'Nothing,' I insisted. 'As far as I can gather, your dad's behaviour in the late sixties veered way off-brand. He went to live in Greece under a military dictatorship, which I admit I had to look up on Wikipedia. I'd had no idea he was so . . .' I hesitated, 'engaged.'

Tom scoffed. 'Hardly. Mick wasn't going off to Athens with some kind of *Homage to Catalonia* fascist-fighting impulse. He went for the ouzo and the Med. He was off on some freewheeling Leonard Cohen personal development odyssey.'

Clarissa nodded. 'It's true. The politics didn't even touch him. He was a privileged foreigner. The authorities loved the West because the colonels were all in bed with Nixon. I did a school project on it once out of some weird, misplaced proxy guilt on Dad's behalf. The security guys who administered the torturing guidelines were pretty much trained by the CIA.'

'Guys, why do we care so much about this?' Apparently immune to words like 'torturing guidelines', Larry jerked his legs apart, letting my heel drop unceremoniously to the floor. 'Julian's cool because he didn't have life-sucking children. He's different to before because "before" was a lifetime and an ocean away. Can we please change the record now? Can we instead talk about this night in Marseille that Jérôme has invited us all to?'

'Excuse me?' Jérôme's name in his mouth was unpleasant.

'Check your phone *de temps en temps, s'il vous plaît.*'

'You and Jérôme *chat*?'

'Should we not?' he said, over-egging the innocence for my benefit.

I gave him a gritted smile in return. The idea of Jérôme, whom I hadn't seen since the party but with whom I had been exchanging depressingly stilted texts, made the organ I took to be my heart contract to the size of an acorn. I swallowed. 'That's not what I meant.'

'Apparently he and his mates are organising a party on Thursday night. We should all go as a sort of final blow-out. A little farewell to this strange but pleasant' – he decided to shoot me an insufferable knowing look at this juncture – 'summer.'

'Yeah, I saw the invite. I'm down,' Clarissa agreed.

'Yeah, fuck it, me too. I need to see some other faces that were born post-decimalisation before I start a process of accelerated ageing by osmosis.' (Tom, obviously.)

'All right then, wicked,' Larry declared, unlit rollie wilting on his bottom lip. 'One final bender and then back to London for us, and back to Gay Paree *pour toi, ma petite.*' He hoisted up my acquiescing ankle again.

'Oh stop it, Lal. I've got attached to her. Let's not talk about the end.'

I necked the tart, sticky dregs of Suze in my glass. Since I was a kid, I'd been a habitual marker of time; a compulsive noter of anniversaries; a human stopwatch. The inevitable – and now very much nigh – end of this summer was a temporal landmark that I'd been denying with an uncharacteristic fastidiousness. Return to Paris meant return to washing dishes and asking people if they wanted the gluten-free option; return to thankless, trailing hours *not* teaching English and to that vertiginous feeling of having no idea what I was doing with my life, and of suspecting that I might be drifting passively towards failure. The idea that I'd ever thought that taking this job might have altered that reality seemed embarrassingly naïve now.

I had realised that when we all left Saint-Luc, it would be necessary to extricate myself from working for Michael. I thought again about the morning Julian had arrived; about Michael's fingertips glancing off the seam of my dress, and about how I'd felt so repulsed and perturbed by him that tears had stung my eyes when I'd thought about it afterwards. Still, though – that perverse thrill. It had reminded me of watching *Belle de Jour* as a teenager, and of the way shame had pricked at the edges of my conscience as I'd found myself turned on by Catherine Deneuve's most odious client. The disparity between excitement and nausea had set self-loathing creeping over my skin like a rash. I'd felt like a victim of my own social conditioning. I wasn't a teenager any more, though, and I knew that the gap between imagined fantasy and endured reality was too immense to risk dealing with it.

Tilting back on his chair, Larry pressed a thumb into the ball of my foot. I looked up at him and saw that he wasn't even looking at me, or at anyone; he was just totally within himself. He'd probably never questioned any of his desires or impulses at all. I jerked my foot out of his grasp.

*

'Let's go to the beach,' he whispered in my ear, bottom lip grazing my skin, hand catching mine against my better judgement. Clarissa and Tom had just gone up to their rooms and we were alone on the little slate step by the front-door-that-no-one-ever-used. The sky was blurred with luminous milky stars and his face was flecked with moonlight. The heavy press of silence. The distant lap of the tide; the clean, dewy scent of the night.

'No,' I sighed, 'I'm tired, I'm going to bed.'

'Come *on*. It's the end of summer, let's go swimming.' He pushed a strand of hair behind my ear. Why did men always do that? Was it a sort of instinctive expression of tenderness, or was it something they'd learnt from watching a thousand cinematic heroes do the same thing, as the camera pinned the face of their love interest? Often, in those swelling seconds before a man went to kiss me, I found myself experiencing it as if from without; a clear picture in my mind of how my eyes (limpid, pooling – I hoped) looked, or how the shadows glanced off the bridge of my nose or the upward (placating, inviting) tilt of my chin. How could I best compose my features to look like Nastassja Kinski or Helena Christensen?

If I was honest with myself, when Larry had kissed me, it wasn't like when Jérôme and I had kissed. There wasn't that same transcendental feeling; that feeling that I was no longer consciously acting but that my body knew exactly what to do. His eyes didn't swim when he looked at me. Most of the time he didn't look at me at all. Wasn't that why I wanted him so much, though? I had told myself that our spark didn't hinge on what I looked like. Larry and I shared a mother tongue. Consequently, I had decided that he knew the real me.

When I spoke and conversed and interacted with the

world in my second language, I was so often a more vulnerable version of myself. It was something I'd thought about a lot. In some ways, being denied the armour of my mother tongue could make relationships more direct and more honest. Distanced from the weight of words, I could be uncharacteristically open and truthful, and couldn't benefit from the potential for artifice that English afforded me. On the other hand, when, in university, a friend had asked me why I always hooked up with French boys and I'd made some flip comment about English ones not liking me, a grain of that blithe comment had lodged itself like a splinter somewhere in my self-esteem. Larry laughed at my jokes and understood my references. He'd told me I was funny. If he thought I was funny, why didn't he want me? My spiralling narcissism craved more than anything the validation of someone like Lawrence wanting me.

'I thought you didn't want to do this?' I said under my breath.

'I said I didn't think we *should* do this.' He snaked an arm around my waist and pulled my body towards his. I felt my back arch despite myself and he smiled down at my easy compliance. It was only as he closed his eyes – as our faces were so close that I could taste the Suze on his breath – that we heard their voices, coming up towards the house from the pine grove.

'God, I have to admit I nearly laid an egg when I first saw her at the station . . .'

Our respective pairs of eyes flashed open in mutual alarm, an amusingly alien expression on Larry's face. The voice was unmistakably Jenny's.

'Think how I felt!' Julian replied. 'I've already got the dual Richter Scale shock of seeing you two for the first time for years, and then suddenly there *she* is – fucking Astrid in a bathing suit. Thank God I have impeccable cholesterol or I'd have probably keeled over right there in the driveway!'

Jenny sighed. 'Jesus. You know when she first arrived I was seriously creeped out by it all . . . Well, that's why I emailed you; I wanted you to reassure me that—'

'Reassure you? Come on, Jen; what the hell is he doing? I talked to Leah on the beach the other day about the work she does for him.' The particular derision he reserved for the word 'work' was almost too much. 'Correspondence, reading . . . But *typing up his diaries*? I mean, really!'

The resonant silence spoke volumes. I felt Larry's eyes give me the laser treatment and kept mine determinedly lowered.

'Jesus,' Jenny whispered again, and then, I gathered from the creak of a bench, sat down. 'Give me a cigarette, would you?'

'I only smoke blunts now, and you can't even buy weed on this goddam backwards continent.'

A pause, and then, 'It's chilling, isn't it? I mean, obviously it's been years since I last saw Astrid. But you don't really forget someone, do you?'

'No.'

'I don't know if it's the mannerisms, or the way they hold themselves or something. I mean, I know they can't be that similar . . .'

'Jenny,' Julian said softly, 'they're the spit of each other.'

Lawrence's arms dropped to his sides like a wordless accusation, and he was staring at me now. I felt an inexplicable twinge of shame wash over my body.

'It's just mad, though, isn't it? I mean, I know you get people who look like each other sometimes, but with Leah and Astrid it's like . . . It was like seeing a ghost. It just all came back to me. How Mick was when he got back to

London. And the not knowing . . . We never knew . . . Oh God, I'm a silly old cow, I'm tearing up . . .'

We heard Jenny blow her nose and I imagined the two of them sitting on the damp old bench by the spinney, Julian handing her a tissue. Larry wasn't even looking at me now. I couldn't help but think that he looked disgusted as he processed the fact of what they were saying. I felt the pages of my life here start to fold in on themselves, smaller and smaller and smaller, until I was being suffocated in a little square of solid, unbendable paper. Torn phrases from Michael's diaries started to layer in thick, insulating snow-drifts of words, trapping all the air between myself and reality:

When my fingers grazed the seam of her knickers . . .

I should have guessed she wasn't a bloody virgin . . .

Bending her over the arm of the sofa, I pushed up the tight little suede skirt (God bless Mary Quant!) . . .

I closed my eyes as tightly as I possibly could and tried to steady myself against the rough surface of the wall.

'I don't know, Jules. I feel like he thinks he can find some sort of redemption through her. Or like she's going to cure him or something.'

The soft downy part at the top of her thigh . . .

'Oh Jen. I don't think it's as noble as that, darling.'

Lawrence looked at me then; swallowed and smiled and at last gave a bitter little shake of his head. Did he think I was implicated in all of this?

'What happened between you two, Julian? I know you saw him. I know he went out to California. I'm not totally clueless.'

'Don't you ever wonder,' he said at last, 'why on *earth* she agreed to go to Athens with him?'

'Because they loved each other.' Jenny's voice was firm, quiet, almost childish.

Julian gave a disparaging snort. '*Jenny*.'

'You weren't there afterwards. You don't know how it felt to pick up the pieces.'

'Trust me, I know more than you think.'

'What's that supposed to mean?'

For a moment, neither of them spoke; then at last Julian's voice, calm and measured again, cut through the night. 'Astrid had her whole future ahead of her. She had that agent, she was going to leave the café; everything was happening for her . . . It doesn't make any *sense*, Jenny. Think about it rationally.'

For the first time in weeks I felt the cold lick of the night. The whirling bellow of the crickets was debilitating. I became vaguely aware now of Lawrence, of him raising his palm to my cheek.

'Leah . . .'

I pushed his hand away.

'You *know* there's something he's not telling you, Jenny.'

'*Leah*.'

I didn't let him finish. I had to be as far away as humanly possible from it all: away from what everything they were saying meant – about Michael, about me, about this whole stupid charade of a summer.

*

The first thing I did when I woke up the following morning (which was punishingly early; I couldn't sleep) was to get my laptop to go through Michael's new emails. Anything to occupy me would do, and the most I was expecting was an email from an editor chasing up an expired deadline. I did it whilst the kettle was boiling, down at the kitchen table. It was still early enough for the flagstones to feel cool under the soles of my feet, and I knew I had a couple of hours of solitude before the others started to surface. For now there was just the ratchet snicker of the cicadas. No breeze at all; the leaves were still.

He had two accounts; the one to which I had full access was his professional, public one, and I'd been instructed to forward messages of interest to his AOL address (even his email server was in keeping with his personal brand of dinosaur). The network was punishingly slow. I could see from the little bracketed number at the top of the tab that he had three unread messages, but they were taking forever to load. Then all at once they appeared, popping into the rows of bland subject matter. The first was the expected nag from Digby at the *LRB*. The second was from his agent, tentatively titled *Checking in*. The third one, sent at eleven minutes past three in the morning, was from an unknown account. As I hovered over it with the cursor, the browser urged me to *Add to contacts*. The letters of the new address throbbed on the screen: *j.f.gresford*. I braced myself and opened the email.

Mick,
Despite appearances, I'm really not into this whole
protracted torture routine (although Anna evidently is –
looks like you've finally found your Machiavellian match
there, mate). In the spirit of being a good guest, then,
I thought I'd share the photo that so effectively spurred
her into responding to my efforts to reach out.
You seemed so anxious to see it after all,
Best,
J

When I initially scrolled down, the black-and-white photo beneath the text was blown up to the point of abstraction – apples of cheeks exploded beyond comprehension into sand dunes, or bed sheets swollen with wind on a washing line. I double-clicked on it and waited as the new window loaded, and then when it finally did, and had snapped into a size that allowed you to make out what the image really was, I felt the breath catch in my chest as the facts of what I was looking at registered one by one.

31

Michael

I'd never woken up before Astrid in London, but there was
something about the air here, about the quality of the light
– and, I suppose, the slow fug of heat – that made me wake
almost with the sunrise. I'd leave her sleeping, the thin sheet
thrown off her tanned, sand-coloured body in the night (one
of the first markers of delightful foreignness when we'd
arrived a month before had been the sheets. No more suffo-
cating northern eiderdowns; bedcovers here were paper-thin
parachutes of cotton). I'd slip into the kitchen and put on a
pot of coffee and let the plumes of rich, bitter vapour fill my
nostrils. Even now, the smell of stovetop coffee makes me
think of Athens: dense, opaque and antique after a lifetime
of thin, pale Nescafé.

On the mornings when the billows of coffee didn't wake
her up, I'd take my cup out onto the tiny balcony off the
kitchenette, crowded with great parasols of fig leaves that
blocked out the lacerating morning sun. It was a squalid
little apartment in Gazi – the skeleton of the towering gas-
works stencilled on the skyline – and we adored it. It was
on the first floor with a shower in the corridor, and it gave
on to a courtyard, meaning (along with the former tenant's
apparent passion for dense foliage) that we got little light –
but what light we did get was of the pure, Grecian variety.
The light there was greenish, as if filtered through a web of
pine needles, and the whole of Athens was washed with it
– with that ancient aquatic green. We'd get it in fragments,
splicing up the shadows in the flat, granite-cutter shards of

it projecting flashes of colour: the worn terracotta floor, the cloudy rose-pink walls with their lustrous blue tiles around the gas hob, the underside of Astrid's left knee.

I sat on one of the spindly iron chairs and lit a cigarette. It was August now and the city had started to empty out; in two days' time, Julian would arrive from London and we'd join the annual Cycladic diaspora, taking the boat out to his mother's house on Syros. It had been planned for weeks, but now I was loath to go at all. I liked the slow spiral of my days here, and the way the particles of dust settled on the abandoned streets. Those of us that were left felt liminal – bonded in our removal from mainstream society. Dustmen, widowers, bachelors, Monday-to-Friday types. The crowd at the taverna we'd taken to frequenting were transient foreigners like ourselves, immigrants, dedicated drinkers, bouzouki players who made their money playing for the tourists on the ferries from Piraeus, and who at night played for the rest of us for free.

Sometimes, on Saturdays, we took the boat to Aegina. Astrid had never been on a boat before, and we'd sit up on the top deck, looking out onto the endless blue of the Saronic Gulf, broken only by the rocky green islands and the roaring trail of white breakers left in our wake. The sky was always brimming with seagulls, flocking around the boat, less aggressive in flight than when strutting and terrestrial. Airborne, they were perfectly streamlined flying boats. When the deck was empty, she would sing to me; gibberish renditions of the Greek songs she was learning at the bar – a scrambled, nonsense mash of consonants and syllables, floating into the air in her beautiful, rusty voice.

We'd hitch a lift to the beach from the little port. We'd swim and flirt and bake under the sun, and in one of the villages nearby we'd eat coarse taramasalata and char-grilled squid on a terrace grown over with fat red geraniums: Martian plants compared to the prim little runts that my mother used to grow in the conservatory at home (the same conservatory that had apparently marked us out as posh; the pride and joy of her small, inward-looking life). We'd get back into Piraeus late. On Saturday nights it was especially squabbling and chaotic. After the standing heat of the day, the cool, maritime whistle of the night air was cleansing. The *ilektrikos* train to Piraeus in August felt like the *Mary Celeste*.

The idea of loud, boorish Julian was repugnant. I liked having Astrid – and Greece – all to myself. Not that I *did* have her entirely to myself. She had taken to expatriation with a zeal I had definitely not anticipated. I've said before that she was exothermic, and it was a quality that evidently transcended language.

The mornings then, with the fig-pressed light sketched across the curves of her body. Her features all soft with languid happiness. Sometimes I used to have to press the flat of my palm into her chest – that little plane beneath the collarbone – to make something so sublime feel tangible. To steady myself in the solid realness of her body. Latch onto her gaze with mine, like a little hook-and-eye fastening. What a thing to be looked at like that – to have a look like that reciprocated. Dust her shoulder with kisses, and the blade of her cheekbone – her eyelids. What a thing. When her eyes were open, they gleamed, and I suppose mine must have too.

Afterwards, though, after those reaching, luminous hours, she'd leave. All at once terrestrial, she'd knock back a coffee, slip into a light cotton dress (embroidered at the hem with indigo anemones – clusters of them, supplicating faces turned up towards the sun), pannier slung over her shoulder, and she'd flitter off into the shadowy hollow of the building

– the cool, dark stairwell with its church hall acoustics, and its clean liquid air.

'Where are you going?'

'*You're* going to write,' she'd say with indulgent pragmatism, 'and I'm going out.' Flat leather soles slapped the staircase.

For the first week or so, what she did with that blank, open stretch in between the unlacing of our limbs and the laden heat of noon was a mystery to me, but it didn't surprise me that she'd apparently acclimatised so seamlessly. Astrid was a creature with a great capacity for delight. We'd arrived in Athens about a fortnight after Neil Armstrong had set foot on the moon; we'd watched it back in London, holed up with Jenny and Julian in the latter's flat, him rolling joints and smoking them alone because I wanted to be completely lucid. For a second I'd managed to drag my eyes away from the crepuscular, milky glow of the screen – floating on the oscillating waves of Pink Floyd's 'Moonhead' – and my gaze had landed right on her pale face. The look of total, ecclesiastical awe had been so touching that I'd wanted to memorise it with the detail of an Old Master. Weeks later, I'd seen it again, this time thrown out into the pure light of morning when I watched her take in the Mediterranean for the first time. It didn't trouble me then to wonder what she did on those abundant mornings, swollen with potential; and as much as I was a little peeved (although of course I'd never have admitted it), it all felt quite inevitable when I began to work it out.

*

'*Gia sou, Christinaki.*'

'Ah! *Gia sas kyrie, Pano!*' she'd trilled brightly, looking up from the little ramekin of briny fish.

The old man beamed at her with genuine affection, made a jolly remark that to me was just a jumble of consonants and facial expressions, and shot a brief and yet unashamedly arbitrating glance in my direction before sloping off back to the bar.

'Was he talking to you?' I asked, quietly incredulous.

'Uh huh,' she affirmed, gracelessly pulling the plump body of a sardine from the delicate web of its tail.

'What did he call you?'

'It's their nickname for me,' she said plainly, and proceeded to carry on with the more important task at hand.

'How do you know him?' I needled, stemming my outrage.

She shrugged. 'I dunno. Just from around, I guess. I see him sometimes in the morning when I come here for a coffee.'

A grunt. 'Well . . . what do you talk about?'

She laughed, swallowing her mouthful to gently mock me. 'Not a lot,' she said, 'though we have developed a pretty efficient language of hand gestures.'

It was then that I noticed that Panos and his friends were smiling fondly at us from the bar. When our glances crossed, the leathery old men raised their little tumblers affably, and I heard one of them say the word that I knew to mean *husband*.

Later that week, I'd gone with her to the market and had been bowled over by the veritable proliferation of enthusiastic greetings: small children in the doorway of our building; heavy-footed gorgons, the kind with faces drawn into perpetual grimaces who normally wouldn't so much as deign to spit at a youth; apparently all of the market traders. The épicier (an Adonis in the D. H. Lawrence mode that a music hall stage direction or a tawdry Victorian novelist would have deemed a *dastardly scoundrel*) gave her a salacious wink as he sloshed an extra ladleful of glistening mauve olives into the jam jar she'd handed him. '*Oriste, Christinaki!*'

'The *olive man*?' I'd hissed.

She popped one of them into her mouth and turned around to grin at him. 'He's one of Panos's friends,' she explained, waving her hand dismissively.

'Naturally.'

Yes, evidently, in spite of her somewhat restricted communicative means, within a week Astrid had become part of the community – certainly not *one* of them, but still a cherished and fascinating curio; a sort of indulged animal. Had we been in England, I imagine I would have felt more chronically misanthropic than ever. There, her indiscriminately bushy-tailed appreciation of everyone used to grate somewhat. Here, under the press of a different sun, proximity to it was like proximity to Jenny in those first terms up at Oxford – a passport.

We trailed then through the teeming kaleidoscope of the market. Lapis-black flies dipping into the vats of phosphorescent cheese, wallowing in their cloudy liquid; honeycomb; headscarved old women in socks and sandals embroidering billowing sheets of white cotton; fragrant mounds of oregano, thyme and rosemary; terracotta bowls of yoghurt – my favourite discovery thus far – and then stacks of painted ikons, the same bold, primary colours of a Matisse canvas. Antique men who had once been refugees from what had been Smyrna, staving off the mounting heat of the morning. I followed Astrid's deft and light-footed route, and at the end of it flopped down next to her on a sagging wicker café chair, dazed and overstimulated.

'Hi! Christina!'

She was being addressed again with this name they all had for her, but this time in the sharp, charming angles of a Greek speaking English.

'Dimitri!' she cried, standing up clumsily to kiss him. 'Sit down with us – are you busy? This is my boyfriend, Michael.'

He proffered a friendly hand – large, elegant, the back of it dusted with the same coarse black hair that covered his face. 'A pleasure,' he said, pulling a third chair over from the neighbouring table. 'I've heard a lot about you.'

How odd, I thought, when I hadn't heard a crumb about him. I composed my features into benign curiosity and asked him how they had met.

'I'm a guitarist,' he explained bashfully. 'Christina heard me and my friends playing at the taverna and she came and sang with us a couple of mornings this week. We're trying to teach her Greek songs and we've been doing some American ones too.'

I had noticed her singing – snatched notes in the morning; melodies without lyrics pervading the ripe blue hours after the siesta. Foreign notes I'd assumed she'd picked up in the bar, with me, in the evening.

'Why do you practise in the morning?' I asked, trying not to sound like I was picking holes in the story. He looked at me a little disbelievingly.

'Because of the Asfaleia,' he said in a low voice, as if it was the most obvious thing in the world. 'It's dangerous to practise at night.'

'Of course,' I mumbled, feeling stupid and chastened for not having thought of the civilian police. It was the second summer of the military junta and most Athenians lived diminished, discreet existences under the sinister gaze of the Asfaleia and the ESA, the secret police. The insidious fact of the regime bounced off the surface of my reality, and that first burnished Sunday morning, I wasn't yet aware of how dangerously implicated Dimitri and his friends were. We exchanged small, digestible pleasantries. It didn't occur to me then that it was strange for someone like him (multilingual, educated – he was studying maths at the university) to be spending the summer in Gazi, and not out on some cyan island paradise.

We ate with him and his friends later that evening – gallons of sweet white wine, zingy tzatziki, creamy fava, piles and piles of grilled pork, salad crumbled with feta and drizzled in citrusy olive oil. It seemed that they all lived with urgent abandon: cigarettes clutched, legs crossed or knees drawn up to jutting chins, arms thrown about, thrust forward in their chairs to speak as if launching each word like a missile. I lived much as I always had and always would – on a lulling crescent of apathy.

*

The Acropolis at night: white, stoical, solid and understated. Superimposed on the violet sky. Crisp pine needles and the little white cottages of Anafiotika. Jade-eyed cats. Uniquely empty in August. I went there on my own in the first glow of dusk. In Athens – at that time at least, though I haven't been back for decades – you could still see little clutches of stars, constellations with Greek names. I sat and smoked, and took great comfort in being a tiny stitch in the cosmos.

32

Leah

They weren't wrong. She did look like me, but only to a point. We were undoubtedly a similar type, and when you don't know someone that well, it's easy for your eyes to exaggerate that sort of thing. The resemblance was strong enough for me to know that it was Astrid straight away, but she was far from my double, as they'd all been trying to make out. We looked as similar as this younger Michael (standing next to her in the photo, laughing with her, body twisted towards her and hand just grazing hers on the desk that they were both leaning on) and Larry did, or like a well-cast actor in the Hollywood version of someone's life, where you do a double-take before realising that the nose is a little wrong, or the eyes aren't the same colour. In the end, though, it wasn't our resemblance that made the breath still in my throat: her face was hardly the first thing you noticed, after all.

After the initial, visceral shock of the image, I closed the tab. I got up and made the tea, the very idea of the photo existing on my computer making me feel slightly panicked. I sat down on the floor with my knees tucked up under my chin and tried to process what this new information meant. Now at least everything made a bit more sense. I couldn't be certain, but I felt pretty sure that the photo had been taken in Greece – you could see that from the clothes they were wearing, and from the sun-dazzled vista in the window behind them. Endless kilometres of sea; a world away from Frith Street.

I was about halfway through the mug of tea when the unease started to morph into something entirely different. Dawn was just whiting out into morning and the house was still silent. I found myself feeling buoyed, and with a purpose and a sense of vindication that I hadn't felt in weeks, I went back to the table and forced myself to look at the photograph again. Before I could get cold feet, I forwarded myself the email and – feeling my fingertips fizz – erased any trace of it from Michael's account. I snapped my laptop closed. Afterwards, when I walked down to the beach, I felt giddy with the sense of my own agency.

*

Michael lit a cigarette. Since Julian had come back, he was openly smoking – in the house, in front of Anna, lighting one from the last, scrounging them off Larry – and relishing it. He drew the wine crate closer to mine and leant forward so I could taste the tang of second-hand smoke as if on the tongue of a lover. He inhaled deeply, and ashed directly onto the floor.

'I suppose you're wondering what the point of all this has been,' he said to a stack of yellowing newspapers somewhere to the left of my feet. I wasn't afraid of him any more, or of any of the feelings he triggered in me. For the first time, I felt like I had the upper hand.

He stood up and walked over to the old portable cassette player. 'It's very easy for your life to become unthreaded, you know. Maybe you don't, actually – you're so young.' There was something about his tone that smacked of the confessional drunk at the tail end of a party. I wondered how honest he was going to be.

He began to root through the chaos of the desk – hands moving frenetically, and yet the rest of him slouched into a sort of brittle resignation. Since the last time I'd been in there – before Marseille, I suppose; certainly before the arrival of our latest guest – his shed had assumed the fly-paper-yellow disarray of the lair of an ageing hoarder. The light that had once been greenish was now the colour of curling sellotape, or nicotine-stained cuticles. The pains-takingly arranged towers of paper gathered and tumbled, and he seemed to be shedding paper himself, like an old snake sloughing off its coarse, redundant skin. He let the cigarette butt fall (float) into a squalid bowl greased with tomato sauce, and he brushed a whole stack of cuttings onto the floor in a sweeping, stroppy ejaculation of disgust. The comforting arboreal damp of the shed had shifted into something fungal and claustrophobic.

'It's so easy,' he continued. 'You make one choice and it's like you pick at one stitch in the bloody seam and suddenly the whole fucking tapestry is unravelling, and every time you try and move it – just an inch – another row just pulls and bites the dust.' He began to furiously rub his thumbnail against his mouth, tearing at the ragged, long-suffering cuti-cle with his teeth. 'Oh for fuck's sake, where did I put it?'

A needle of red bloomed at the corner of the nail. 'Of course my life was small – minimal. I can't pretend to be part of anything really. Everything was so much bigger than me, but if I'm honest I really didn't even give a shit.'

He picked up a battered old Pan paperback and sent it spinning, like a discus, across the room. I closed my eyes as it whistled past my head.

'Have you ever read those diaries of people during the Second World War, or the Cuban Missile Crisis? What's it called – *The Mass Observation Project*, or something equally Newspeaky?' He put on an unmistakably feminine, vapid voice. 'Sixteenth of October 1962. It really is all heating up with the communists in Cuba. Ron's convinced we'll all be blitzed into nuclear oblivion by the end of the week. Today has been really awful. I missed the bus and spilt blackcurrant jelly all down my new shirt. It'll never come out – and dry cleaning's so expensive . . .'

Losing the thread of his soliloquy altogether, he launched himself across the desk and grabbed a small cassette tape. 'Yes! Remember these?'

I felt a spike of patronised resentment. How young did he think I was?

'Of course.'

'Do you remember how you used to be able to buy blank ones and record things off the radio – and off other tapes if you had one of those double decks?'

(Electric-blue woodchip and white skirting boards: memories of lying on the fitted acrylic carpet of my childhood bedroom, eyes fixed to the buttons of the tape player I shared with my sister, poised to record the Corrs on *The Chart Show*.)

'And do you remember how you had to find the exact right moment on the tape reel? Because if not, you could record over what was already on there?'

(Her outrage when I'd accidentally done exactly that to 'Save Tonight' by Eagle-Eyed Cherry.)

'I've been thinking about that a lot recently – that layering of sounds. Pasting them on top of each other – Proustian superposition. Fragmentation. A sort of audio collage. I had a friend once who used to make collages. He had a colossal sort of life – not one measured out in coffee spoons.'

He began to prise the little rectangle of plastic with its inky blue film from the case, then opened the slot for it on the stereo. The familiar hissing sound of it sliding out – an injection of the past.

'Here it is then!' he said triumphantly, reeling as if drunk. 'Here's my tribute to my friend – but mostly to *her*, of course.'

A second more of that hissing, the tape winding backwards, and then the first notes: a plucked, quivering guitar, followed by the deep, elegant timbre of a voice I recognised as Leonard Cohen's, with its expectant, European T's. It was the first line of one of the poems he'd written on Hydra, talking about looking at the moon in Greece. Michael's eyes swam a little, and he gripped the edge of the desk until his knuckles blanched.

Then another guitar, fuller again, all six strings caressed with acquiescence. It was the opening bars of 'If You See Her, Say Hello'. He sank onto the paper-brushed floor and latched onto the swell of the song. I didn't dare to speak, and the shed brimmed with the hoarseness of Dylan's nasal voice until that too was swamped by a new sound – a triumphant, marching, patently Hellenic one. A language that was all just sounds to me, but sounds that urged me forward regardless. Michael hummed along vacantly and whispered, 'This one's called "Otan Sfiggoun To Xeri"; "When They Clench Their Fists".'

Then a new layer: a voice – a woman's voice, which I knew instantly belonged to her, even though I'd never heard it before. A floating, disembodied laugh. 'You're recording me, aren't you? I won't sing if you're recording me!'

It felt like the voice of a ghost. There was something sinister about hearing her speak. He slumped then, lay flat on the floor, his head under the shadow of the desk.

His voice now, but younger. Less guarded, more BBC and more significantly still, all webbed with light. 'I want him to hear you sing it just once. Go on . . .'

An exasperated giggle, and then – faltering at first and afterwards heartbreakingly robust – Astrid sang the first line of 'You Don't Know What Love Is'.

Michael's legs stiffened right down to his right foot, which made little arcs in the air to the rhythm. I could hear his breath, wheezing gasps of it, from under the canopy of the desk. He had his palm pressed firm against his mouth to stifle any sound, and his closed eyes were screwed up into little raisins.

She stopped singing then, and there was an aching, pregnant pause before the chimes of a thudding 2/4-time piano lurched mournfully into the air above us. Greek again. I didn't know what it was at the time but I'd find out later:

> *Xilia myria kymata makria t'Aivali*
> (Aivali is thousands of waves away)
> *Meres tis armiras ke o ilios panta ekei*
> (Days as saline as the sea and the sun always out)

A briny, imploring voice. A mouthful of seawater. A jilted lover looking out onto a stretch of violet water, out of step with the sunset glinting off its rippled surface.

He lay flat on the cool, damp floor, staring at the ceiling, and carried on the ebb and flow of the music. His breath gradually regained its slow, tidal constancy, and as the piano faded out, Leonard Cohen began to speak again, about overthrowing the ones he'd loved for an education in the world. Michael passed his palms over each cheek.

Later, when I remembered his half-coherent, hollow speech – enchanting and laboured all at once – I thought about the detail he'd omitted with regard to this mania for collage:

Erasure. The layering of stories – the layering of new truths over old ones.

*

The tape reel finished its final orbit with a curt little *click*, and Michael opened his eyes, his gaze fixing mine. Neither of us spoke. The absence of words should have pulled awkwardly between us, but the rush of power I'd been feeling since the morning still hadn't waned, and I felt comfortable in the silence, waiting for his confession. In the cool light, his face looked younger, more open than it had before – it was the face of the voice on the tape.

He emerged from under the desk, dusted himself off and cleared his throat. He eyeballed the floor and shook another cigarette out of the packet on the table. Finally he sat down, folded his hands on his lap, and with a sigh began to speak.

33

Michael

I remember the end in fragments now, but I'll try and be as coherent as possible. I can feel everything splintering.

It was after we got back from Syros in September, I suppose, that things started to fall apart; that the predictable and inevitable rot set in. Syros: the woody scent of the eucalyptus in Julian's mother's garden, and the cedar trees fringing the beach. The marine blue of the water wagons, and the jingle of the beaded bridles of the donkeys that pulled them. The trestle table with a gingham cloth where an ugly girl sold roasted pistachios on the harbour. The jetty and the metallic clang of the bells in the ancient church. Endless, febrile adolescent fantasies about doing things to Astrid in that church, in the clean, sacred light.

There was the beach, and Julian with his camera, talking about America all the time. There were parties with Mrs Gresford's coterie of rich northern European bohemians (self-ascribed), posing for photos barefoot in kaftans, clutching Spanish guitars and Gauloises. There was the costume party where I slipped up with that Danish girl . . . How did no one ever find out? I was dressed as a Berber, in swathes of blue and saffron linen plundered from Mrs G's closet. She was Circe and had thick corn-coloured hair and bracelets made from old copper piping that left little green smudges on her soft arms. People were always openly discussing the Junta over long blue-smoke dinners. They chewed it over with all the cool, non-committal impunity of wealthy foreigners, as if it were a game of cards. Astrid fixed her gaze on her lap as they did so. I assumed she was embarrassed about how little she understood.

Then later, a balmy evening at the end of September; Julian had left after two nights with us in Athens on his way back to London. He'd gone just before the siesta, and we were so exhausted after hosting him in our tiny little flat (all that zingy, clumsy-pawed enthusiasm) that we'd fallen asleep straight away. I was woken up by the sound of Astrid getting dressed – sitting on the edge of the unmade bed, putting on her sandals.

'Where are you going?' The effort to speak was colossal through the gauzy shade of sleep.

'I have to go and see Dimitri – it's important. I've got to go now.'

'No. Come here now.'

I wanted her so much – it had been two days. I tried to pull her towards me, but I was slow and lumbering and my fingers just grazed the cotton of her dress.

'Why do you have to see fucking Zorba?'

'Don't call him that, Michael.'

'Don't call him anything . . . Come here.'

'Michael.' Her face was drawn into hard, gritted lines. She was usually so pliable.

We never fought, but we really rowed then. I snatched her pannier from her arm to exorcise the sudden impulse to grab something else (her, I suppose). The 12-inch that was inside went flying across the room, shattering spectacularly as it hit the latch of the window. Her face drained of colour. I scrabbled on the floor for the sleeve. Try-hard psychedelics, a mop of Rossetti hair.

'Donovan? Really? Honestly, babe, I think I did you a favour.'

Astrid's eyelashes were pearled with tears and she clasped her hands to her face. 'Fuck,' she muttered, 'fuck, fuck, fuck.'

'Why are you carrying a Donovan record around with you anyway? What, were you and Dimitri going to have a groovy little folk jam or something?'

'Stop talking, Michael, please.'

That stung – this whole new alien firmness in her voice.

'God, I'm sorry. I didn't realise you were such a fan of the Hurdy Gurdy Man,' I spat.

She let her arms fall to her sides and shook her head at me; walking towards the window, she stooped and picked up the jagged pieces of vinyl, and hurled one onto the bed. It was a middle piece of the record, the bit with the adhesive label and the track listing. It didn't look much like a Donovan record, mainly because the script was in Greek.

*

What it took me a long time to admit, or even identify, was that the first thing I felt wasn't jealousy of this new depth to her relationship with Dimitri, but jealousy of the fact that she of all people was involved.

'You realise how much danger you're putting us in, don't you?'

She let her gaze slide to the floor. Outside, the tonic shudder of grates being pulled up over vitrines, the city waking up for the night.

'All of us – you, me, all three of us.' I drew my hands up to my temples. 'I just can't believe he'd even ask you to do this.'

'He didn't. I offered.' Her voice was low and pinched.

'You *offered*? Are you serious?'

'It's nothing, Michael. It's nothing compared to what they're doing. I just pick up the records at the guy's flat in Kaisariani and take them to Dimitri. They're already in the fake sleeves.'

'Astrid, this isn't *nothing* . . . You're smuggling records that have been banned by the military state. The *mi-li-tary state*.' I pronounced each syllable separately, with its own flat weight, as if talking to a moron or a foreigner. 'This isn't like shoplifting from the fucking corner shop, you know! Do you know what they do to people who protest the regime here?'

She groaned. 'They're not going to catch us, Michael.'

'Can you hear yourself? This city is infested with secret police and you're crossing it with banned records by guys who are having their – fuck knows – their fucking finger-nails pulled out on Bouboulinas Street. For Christ's sake. How can you possibly be so naïve?'

But already, as the words tumbled from my mouth, it wasn't images of Astrid's punishment that needled at me, but rather ones of her legacy. Snatches of her impending legend proliferated grimly within me. She was part of something – a stitch in history, striking like a bright blue vein in a pale, thin wrist or a column of gleaming marble. I could already hear the hushed whispers of admiration at the cosy dinner parties of our future: *when she lived in Greece . . . part of the resistance!* I could read the human-interest footnotes in history books; the gushing asides in newspaper articles, the thoughts of every reader, that they'd do the same thing, of course.

'I'm going to go upstairs to use Mrs Petraki's phone,' she said quietly.

'You cannot implicate her in this. They tap telephones, you know!' I spluttered pompously.

She replied with a withering look – the kind I didn't know she was capable of.

*

Later, as we were edging our way along Thessalonikis towards Monastiraki to meet the modern-day Edelweiss-fucking-Pirates themselves. I felt more misanthropic than ever.

'Are you doing this through some kind of melomania?'

'I don't know what that means,' she said tersely, to her shoes.

'It means "love of music". It comes from the language of this country to which you've apparently developed such a burning devotion.'

She flinched a little.

'Or is it because you fancy Dimitri? I admit he's pretty dashing, in a Greek sort of way.'

'Michael, could we please not talk about this on the street?'

I scoffed. 'Oh. That's rich, isn't it? Now you're worried about taking risks.'

'I don't know why I did it, OK?' she hissed. 'It just felt like the right thing to do.'

Wasn't that so like her, I thought, to act entirely on an impulse because something felt right? Of course.

'Do you not feel bad about any of it, Michael?' she asked me, voice still lowered to a whisper. 'Do you not feel bad that we're living this normal life and this is all happening right around us? You can even see it. It's not like it's just in the news.'

I suppose I did feel bad about it – in passing. I felt bad when I was routinely ignored by the military police (malleable country boys, plucked from ignorance and poverty

and moulded through brutality into brutes themselves).
I'd felt bad when one of Dimitri's friends had come out
of a two-month stint at the ESA headquarters last week.
He had been caught feeding information to the resistance
radio run from Germany by Deutsche Welle. The beatings,
the isolation and the vermin-infested cells aside, I would
always remember him talking about how the guards had
turned his own medium against him. They had tortured
him with sound: electric bells, motorbike engines, colossal
gongs, and pop songs played on an endless, excruciating
loop. His ears, he told me, still buzzed with the treacly
lyrics. The other prisoners had said they'd played the
music to drown out the sounds of screaming; he'd said
the songs themselves were worse. When he came out, he
bought fifteen copies of the same LP and systematically
smashed each one up on his knees. The prison where he'd
been detained wasn't far from Piraeus and the port where
we used to get the ferry to the islands. It was surprisingly
easy to tune these things out.

Astrid's friends, all students at the university, were
crowded around a table on the pavement outside a dingy
little taverna.

'I'm sorry about the record,' Astrid whispered to Dimitri
as he stood up to kiss her cheek.

'Couldn't be helped,' I heard him reply, and I resented
him for his calm, kind acceptance of what had happened.
Well it could have been, couldn't it, I almost found myself
snapping at him, but I didn't, of course. I didn't want to
look small-minded in front of them. I suppose I even wanted
– in some abstract way – to be involved.

The two of us sat down and I watched Astrid perform
Astrid, as if the past few hours hadn't even happened.
They talked about trivial things, which made me resent

them even more now that I knew what they were actually involved in, and I didn't feel the slightest inclination to engage. I sipped my *tsipouro* coolly and chain-smoked, and after a while, a predictable, adolescent idea started to form in my head.

Opposite me, through plumes of lilac smoke, sat Ioulia, framed quite prettily, with the trails of jasmine climbing up the wall behind her. Dimitri was midway through some gushing lecture on an obscure stringed instrument from the Nile Delta. I caught her eye and smirked.

What's the point in even dwelling on it? Another sordid, dull little tryst – a limp self-esteem boost. Automatic. Furtive – but only on her part, not on mine. By that stage I wasn't even that bothered about trying to be discreet.

*

About a week later; early – the streets still glistening with what a romantic part of me remembers as morning dew but was probably, I suppose, just sterilising water from the street cleaners. We were on our way out to Piraeus to get the first boat to Aegina when Astrid stopped, apropos of nothing, and inhaled so sharply it was as if the air had burnt the roof of her mouth.

'Oh my God,' she whispered, and went to grab my hand as the colour drained from her face.

The bistre wall of the building just ahead of us (thirsty, neglected, peeling leprously) had been covered with posters, evidently freshly minted just before dawn. Richard Nixon's jowly potato head; the unmistakable peaked cap of a Greek military officer pulled low over his famous widow's peak and a stethoscope slung over his tie. In his grasping little hands a scalpel, and beneath him row upon row of faceless bodies, bruised and swollen like rotting fruit. Spindly

Greek characters (red, sanguine) stood starkly to attention at the top of each collage. At my side, Astrid seemed to reel somewhere between nausea and elation. Looking around feverishly to check that no one had seen us, she pulled me along to the other side of the street. We walked on in silence to the train.

'What was that?' I asked her at last, trying to steady my voice.

She stood up on her tiptoes to kiss me, and as her lips brushed my earlobe, she whispered his name.

34

Leah

At about seven o'clock that evening, the sea was cool and flat, threaded through with the glint of the setting sun. I floated along with my eyes closed, feeling the whisper of the current tease strands of my hair and brush the outline of my body. I thought about everything Michael had chosen to disclose, and about everything he hadn't. Afterwards, I hiked up to the little viewpoint where Jérôme had first kissed me – almost a month ago now, but it felt like infinitely longer – and I lay on the scorched earth, the bristles of sun-bleached *garrigue* biting into my back. The Greek song that Michael had played that morning, 'Xilia Myria Kymata', was thudding around my brain. My head was still brimming with it.

It had been creepily fascinating to watch him build up the layers of the story and all the while wilfully conceal the most important detail. With the grace of an actor soliloquising, his performed confession had tumbled out smoothly into the dank half-light of the shed. There'd been just enough tactical self-abasement to diminish the suspicion that he might be withholding information to make himself look better. He had claimed that Astrid's political engagement had left him feeling impotent, and that the resulting affair with one of their Greek friends had spelt the sordid end of the relationship. He didn't know that I was aware of what he was omitting.

As I rounded the edge of the spinney back towards the house, I heard their voices carried on the air (dusky, fragrant with the smoky smell of grilling meat). Everyone was there, and once again, everyone was unnervingly festive, as they had been since Julian's arrival. Someone had dragged the speakers out and put on a Stan Getz record, and Jenny was shimmying across the patio, barefoot, with a bottle of Grolsch. I wondered if *she* knew what I knew.

'I've been demoted!' she giggled as she clocked me, nodding to the barbecue, where Julian was turning over kebab skewers and apparently effervescing with signature cheer. Julian knew – and now he was threatening Michael with the evidence.

'I thought you were a vegetarian,' I said to him, surveying the rows of glistening pork and flopping down on the bench next to Larry.

He shrugged. 'Everything in moderation, eh? Jenny and I went into Marseille today and found a really good Turkish supermarket. We got Greek yoghurt, halloumi, labneh . . . I can indulge in the pleasures of the flesh for one night!'

The pleasures of the flesh – very Julian *c.*1969. Did he even deliver the line with a little leer?

Lawrence opened a bottle of Grolsch with a lighter and handed it to me. I decided to play him at his own game and leant back into the hollow of his body. He let his chin settle on my forehead.

'What are you cooking anyway?' I asked Julian.

'Souvlaki!' he announced. 'To take Mick right back to Athens in the old days.'

Michael looked up from the novel he was reading with an anaesthetised smile. 'What a treat.'

My eyes caught on his fingertips, pressing the spine of the book against his thumb. The image of them as they were in the photograph flitted through my mind again – one hand grazing hers on the desk, the other just underneath the enormous swell of her belly. He was making comedy eyes at its size. Their child must have been just about to come to full term.

35

Michael

The last Thursday in August. We were planning on leaving on the Sunday morning and everything felt on the cusp of something – like it was all winding down. The kids had gone off to Marseille and there was something artificial in the atmosphere at dinner. I sat down at the table on the patio, my nerve endings dulled and bruised. This waiting game with Julian was starting to deplete me. Over the past few days I'd had the impression that he'd been trying to scare me: the Greek food, the loaded comments, and even some kind of conspiratorial feeling between him and my wife. Little smirks exchanged over breakfast. A trip into town à deux . . . It was becoming a question of *when* now rather than *if*.

In the shadow-sieved light of the candles, his face – or at least the angles of it anyway – looked almost as it had done then. Dark circles under his eyes, though, washed with the flickering glow. Bryan poured the wine and Jenny piled salad on the stacks of chipped old Moroccan plates. It was all so gruesomely habitual: the material of our pleasant middle-class summers and the exchanges of our pleasant middle-class lives. Anna watched me like a bored and beautiful cat, her gaze flitting between Jenny and myself. I could read her well enough by now to know that she'd elected this evening for the big confrontation. I'd become so fatalistic about it all that I almost felt relieved.

'Pass me the mosquito spray, will you, darling? These stupid candles never work.'

'This is the olive oil from Simon's place in Spain, isn't it?'

'I feel like their generation just has a different understanding of race to ours.'

'It's no wonder the majority of British people feel deracinated from Europe. It's actively encouraged – Blighty the maverick uncle knocking back a Scotch in the morning whilst everyone else drives on the right, cheats on their wife or goose-steps to gaudy pop songs . . .'

I felt elevated from said gruesome normality. The air crackled with anticipation. We'd finished eating and the plates had been cleared. I was starting to like the idea that everything would be tied up neatly tonight, like a change of scenery at the theatre.

'Of course if anyone could enlighten us what it was really like to live under a right-wing regime,' Julian began, 'it would be Mick, wouldn't it? You could tell us a thing or two, couldn't you?'

Over the decades, Jenny had become adept at diverting any kind of allusion to my time spent in Athens. 'Oh Jules, not now,' she groaned. 'Not here.'

'Why not?' said Anna coolly. 'He's always been so cagey about it; I want to know more. What's the point in marrying an old man if he doesn't even tell you his stories?' She barely even bothered to dress up the little dig as a joke.

'There's really nothing to know, Anna.' Jenny was forcing brusque cheer into her voice now. 'He lived there for less than a year. He wasn't even involved with the politics.'

Julian scratched his nose theatrically to mask the smirk playing across his face.

'Hmm.' My wife grimaced and took a swig of her wine. 'And I suppose you would know. As you never fail to remind us, you know Michael best, don't you?'

'Jesus, Anna. Ouch.'

Bryan muttered the first consonant of some would-be neutralising platitude, but Anna carried on speaking before he had the chance to grow the syllable into a word.

'The two of you have always made me feel so inferior, so out of the fucking loop.' Her voice had become shrill. She sounded faintly hysterical, which gave me a misplaced sense of reassurance. 'I don't think you realise that Michael is a pathological liar.'

'*Anna!*'

'And that there's a lot you don't know either, Jenny.'

Jenny rolled her eyes. 'How about you stop being so bloody obtuse and just tell us what you're getting at then?'

Anna simpered smugly. She looked at Julian again as if taking a cue, and I watched her pale, elegant hands float up from her lap and reach for the phone next to her wine glass.

'When Jules first got in touch with me' – *Jules*; I watched Jenny wince – 'he had some lovely old photos of Mick that he wanted me to see . . . You know, despite his nice emails, at first I was so resistant to replying. I wanted to protect Michael. Can you imagine? You all like to go on about how much I missed, but I'm not a total idiot. I listen when you all speak, you know. I wouldn't want to miss any pearls of wisdom. After nearly two decades together, I knew that "Julian Gresford" was a strictly taboo subject. I assumed he was some kind of monster. I was hardly going to invite him over for dinner. Poor Michael, I thought – poor emotionally stunted Michael – whatever could have happened to him?'

Her hands fluttered gracefully across the screen of her phone. 'And then, when his kindness went unanswered, "monstrous Julian" decided it was time for me to know the truth. He sent me some photos. Here, would you like to look at them?'

'Anna.' I heard the urgency – despite myself – in my voice as I went to try and grab the phone. My sudden surge of action surprised even me. I had no idea what was on the screen, but I knew that I didn't want Jenny to see it.

'*Oh*.' Jenny covered her mouth with her hand. 'Oh my God.' She closed her eyes and pressed the phone into Bryan's hands.

'Will someone please show me this photo?' I said.

My wife gently prised the phone from Bryan and placed it, faux-benevolently, on the table in front of me. I felt my heart contract.

'Where was this taken?'

Julian sighed. 'My mother's house in Syros. She took it when you went there that last spring, to send to me in the States.'

Of course. It was Mrs Gresford's study. Suddenly all the details of the room came back to me. The bric-à-brac on the desk, the bobbled upholstery of the armchair in the corner, the musty smell of it, the pinkish hue of the light. I couldn't wrench my eyes from the photo: Astrid, eight months in; and me, leaning against the edge of the desk, caught mid laughter, making huge eyes at her enormous belly.

'She was . . . But I don't understand. I don't understand how I didn't . . .' Jenny was speaking in half-sentences. Her voice was dimmed down to nothing. Anna, who had evidently had more time to digest the betrayal, was somewhat more eloquent.

'He got the poor girl pregnant, convinced her to go to Greece with him, and then kindly abandoned her when he lost his nerve at the last minute. That's pretty accurate, isn't it, Michael?'

'That's not how it went.' My voice sounded new, foreign and disembodied. 'That's not how it was at all.'

Voyeur

The look that Julian gave me then was a challenge. He wanted to know how much of the truth I'd really be willing to tell.

36

Leah

Pale violet fuzz where the calm sea, grey now with dusk, blurs into the white evening sky. Tangerine spilling onto the stacks of buildings bunched along the coastline. The pulse of the car radio. Tom rolling cigarettes for Lawrence, and Clarissa trailing a hand out of the open window to feel the saline lick of the mistral.

'Has he sent you the exact address yet?' Lawrence shouted over the thrum of the engine, the wind rattling through the car and the bad nineties techno-pop. His long, bony fingers drummed the steering wheel.

I glanced down at my phone and felt a twinge of excitement at the idea of Jérôme – of his brown wrists and the hollows of his cheeks, dusted with sandpaper stubble.

'Forty-two Allée Léon Gambetta,' I called. My phone shuddered in my palm again. *J'ai hâte de te voir.*

I replied: *Moi aussi.*

I had a train ticket back to Paris on Saturday afternoon and the idea of it made me feel featherweight and relieved. Anna had insisted on me getting a lift with them on the Sunday morning, but after the events of the past week, I wanted more than anything to be able to move about independently again. When Larry and I had got back from Marseille and Michael had made it so achingly clear that I wasn't part of the fold, I'd felt bereft and minimised. Now it made my head reel with freedom. The cinematic duplicity of their behaviour – the poison emails, the sliding panels of untruths and now this calculated withholding – had been staggering. It was miraculous that Clarissa and Tom (and in all fairness even Larry, to some extent) were apparently so well adjusted.

Jérôme lived a stone's throw from the station, in one of those wonderful old buildings you get all over the Midi: a huge, wooden door leading into a vast hallway – cool and shadowy after the liquid Mediterranean radiance of the street – all cold patterned tiles and cobalt light and generations and generations of footfall echoing within the gloomy, beautiful walls. So much space after Paris: big, airy rooms with high ceilings and windows right up to them from the worn terracotta-tiled floors. Shutters painted cream or pale blue or green. Coving, curlicues, and in the daytime, light – so much light. The palette: the walls in the big kitchen were saffron, red and lime green, and the apartment was full of clutter – books, records, art and above all plants. The two balconies were bursting with green – every variety of basil; parsley; the flash of a gleaming red tomato.

The living room was already crowded with people when we arrived, all of them luminous, the premonition of the night ahead glittering on the surface of their skin. Jérôme clocked me from across the room and flashed me a row of beautiful white teeth. I felt the force of it press my collar-bone and grinned back shyly.

'*J'suis trop content que tu sois venue,*' he said, having pushed through the tangle of limbs and feather-light plumes of smoke to get to me. He kissed me and told me that he'd missed me, and for a moment I wondered if maybe it wasn't a better idea to just throw it all in in Paris and move here to grow basil on the balcony and sleep in the smell of him. I was hardly particularly ambitious, after all – it didn't look like much else would ever happen with my life as it stood.

Then from the kitchen counter, something unexpected: Larry eyeballing the two of us, and an unmistakable hint of something I'd not yet seen configuring his features: jealousy. I willed myself to stop enjoying it.

About an hour or so later, Jérôme had to leave to go to the venue to set up, and I found myself untethered again in the press of the crowd – all tipsy and maddeningly verbal. I was talking, animatedly, at someone when I felt the print of a palm on the small of my back.

'Nico gave me some Mandy; come and help me make it into bombs?' Larry said.

'No,' I said, faintly irked that he'd cut me off mid flow. 'I'm really bad at it anyway – the Rizlas always get stuck to my fingers.' I was never the one who sorted the drugs; I was always just conveniently around when they were being taken.

'Come on,' he insisted. 'Tom's abandoned me for some guy and Clarissa's with Nico and everyone here speaks really, really bad English. Save me.'

I let myself be dragged off to the bathroom.

'So you do like him really,' Larry said, licking the edge of his Oyster card. I was sitting on the side of the scuzzy avocado bath, sipping acidic white wine from a plastic cup.

'Yes,' I replied defiantly. 'He's a babe. But as you keep reminding us all, it is the end of summer, so that must mean it's doomed.'

'Who do you like more – him, or me?' He wasn't looking at me as he spoke.

'Him.'

'Open your mouth.'

He pressed a finger onto my tongue, and with it the synthetic stab of what I'd always thought tasted like toxic,

342

robot salt. I couldn't help but meet his eyes as I essentially fellated his finger. He smirked. Why did I have to insist on being the architect of my own undoing?

· *

Violet again. Violet and pale blue and flecks of rose, and the gorgeous feeling of the breath filling my lungs. All of my limbs so light I'm convinced I'm made from stardust, like the song – or from the rattle of the percussion and the weightless pulse of the music. Everything feels galactic – incandescent. Snatches of Tom's laughter, his eyes gleaming like freshly pressed coins as he grabs my hands and stretches me up, up, up into forever. The ground is sprung like a gymnasium and we're all filled with gold filament. When I close my eyes I can see long, straight roads cutting through deserts that I've only ever lived in in the fabric of my imagination. Waterfalls tumbling in the vibrant pure pigment of Japanese animation. The aisle of the church in the village where I grew up, bathed in the pink light of the stained-glass windows of St Francis of Assisi. They're playing a Tamil song that the guys from the café used to play at work – 'Urvashi Urvashi' – and I feel suspended in the snicker of its rhythm until the tendrils of a new song grow right over it like vines creeping up a cracked stone wall. I think of Michael's cassette tape collage again, and with enthused, druggy conviction, what I sweetly take to be a profound idea flits into my conscience. Eyes still closed in pleasure, head rolling back on my shoulders, I start to whisper it to Tom.

'It's like there are all these layers of temporality, right? And the layers are like fabric and stitched through all these layers is this thread. The thread is memory – experience – this lovely, cosmic, musical, nostalgic-human . . . sunrise-coloured *feeling* . . .'

'Have a cigarette, babe, you're talking like a high person.' Tom stuffed a Marlboro Red into my mouth and tucked my hair behind my ears. 'Come on, let's go outside and get some air.'

'Yes! Yes – air – I love air. I love you, Tom!'

'I love you too, come on.'

Outside, the cool touch of the night was delicious. Tom and I sat on the kerb and Lawrence and Clarissa tumbled out after us.

'I'm fucking spangled,' Larry mused, radiating bliss.

'Mmm . . . me too.' The words oozed out of Clarissa's mouth. She crouched down next to me and began to paw at my shoulders.

'I love you,' I enthused.

'I love you too! Imagine if we'd never met, man – *imagine*!' She rolled her lips over her teeth and sighed decadently, and I could feel the delightful sensation of the air flickering through her chest and out through her mouth. Tom draped an arm around me. 'You'll have to move back to London with us.'

'Oh no,' I said. 'I'm going to move to Marseille now and grow basil with Jérôme and make babies and live in dungarees.'

'That's the spirit, Leah! That's what Emily Davison threw herself under that horse for!' Chemically buoyed, Lawrence's words bounced off me like hail hitting the pavement.

'Don't kill her little dream, Lal!' said Clarissa, affectionately pushing her thumbs into the space between my shoulder blades. 'What are you going to do this year anyway?'

Lawrence stubbed out his rollie on the concrete floor. 'I thought I'd move in with Lisa.' He shrugged.

The pressure of Clarissa's thumbs at the nape of my neck increased almost imperceptibly.

'Let's go back in,' she said, with an urgency that I assumed was just a consuming narcotic whim. 'I want to dance.'

*

'Who's Lisa?' I asked him the following evening. We were driving home. Tom and Clarissa were dozing in the back seat and I was up front with Larry, yellow sunlight slanting in through the windscreen and illuminating the trails of dust motes hitting the dashboard. He was listening to middle-of-the-road white-man soft rock. 'It's my weakness,' he'd confessed. 'Give me a highway, give me the Eagles.' I wasn't entirely surprised.

'Huh?' He looked fixedly out in front. The empty *autoroute* apparently all at once required serious concentration.

'Lisa?' I repeated.

His face was perfectly still and he spoke flatly, without even the slightest trace of emotion. 'Lisa is my sometime girlfriend,' he said.

If he wasn't going to betray any emotion, I certainly wasn't either. I felt a band of burning embarrassment at my temples and frowned to try and keep it in. I could feel him looking at me. 'The sun is in my eyes,' I said, squinting more theatrically than before.

He let his hand rest on my knee. He gave it a little squeeze.

'You never asked me if I had a girlfriend, Leah,' he said softly.

I laughed and thought how that was a line that I wouldn't be forgetting any time soon. The album track faded out politely.

'You said your love life was a fucking disaster.'

'Yeah. Isn't it just?' he muttered.

We drove on for a few kilometres in silence. The sun was low now, tinting the tarmac and the hazy green fringe of the *garrigue*. Still not deigning to look anywhere other than directly in front of him, he began to speak.

'Look, Leah, things with me and Lisa are complicated. We met when we were at uni but we've been long-distance for most of the time we've known each other. Our relationship's always been open. I'm not the possessive kind – you know that.'

I nodded. Of course he was making this about how progressive and tolerant he was.

'Next year it looks like we might actually be in the same place. We've been talking a lot this summer, and I don't know . . . I don't know what I want to do.' It was his turn to squint now at the burning glare of the sun. I decided that I didn't want to hear any more about it. I smiled brightly at his profile – urging him to make eye contact with me. He kept on looking straight ahead.

'That's exciting,' I said. Even I could hear the hollow ring in my voice. I watched his right hand glide across the steering wheel.

'Oh come on,' he groaned. 'Don't be like that.'

'I'm not like that,' I insisted, and turned up the radio.

37

Michael

It's very easy for your life to become unthreaded, you know, I'd said to Leah, or something along those lines anyway. It had just been a comment – a stupid misplaced comment to a guy in a bar, dropped like a cigarette end onto the pavement. I hadn't meant for any of it to happen. That's what I told myself, but had it really been as careless as that? I'd thought about it so much for such a long time. Part of me at least had wanted to wound him.

She'd started showing in the autumn. We hadn't told anyone when we left London, and when Julian had left Greece in September, it was still early enough that we could get away with keeping it a secret. We didn't want people at home to know because we didn't want reality to dent it, or for them to tell us that we were mad for trying to pull it off. She'd told me about it around a month after we reconciled after that stupid tantrum I'd thrown over Stephen. When she'd said she wanted to keep it, after the initial horror I'd actually felt oddly serene. I didn't have to struggle any more to establish myself as 'something'. I had a purpose. It was a brave enough gesture to give me a feeling of identity, for a while longer at least. It felt like we still had agency in the choice we were making, and that we weren't going to become like our parents. Anna was wrong. I had never wanted to abandon them. If only that *had* been the way things had turned out.

We'd seen through the winter in Athens and the first notions of spring – the longer, pale evenings; the irises pushing through, and that change in the air. The novelty in the breeze. The air smells different in March, doesn't it? We'd gone to visit Julian's mother at her place on Syros the first week. Mrs Gresford was genuinely thrilled. I can remember her taking the photo, actually. She'd thought it was all a hilarious joke. *Julian's just going to die – he'll never believe it!* It was good to have someone like that supporting us. We knew how everyone else would have reacted. Maybe, all things considered, they would have been right.

*

It had taken Astrid longer than I'd expected to clock on to Ioulia, and the stupid thing is that none of it was even worth it. I was just trying to prove some point – trying to exercise my freedom – and that was the way I'd always done it, I suppose. I was more in love with her than ever at that point. I was more excited about our future than I'd ever felt about anything. Sometimes she'd grab my hand and press it onto her belly, and in those last few weeks you could feel the imprint of a heel, thrust out towards the world.

When I try and remember it now, it all seems to have happened so quickly; one event tumbling directly into the next and everything beyond my agency. We got back to the flat in Gazi and the little envelope was waiting with the concierge. As soon as I saw it, I knew that the Roman letters were too clumsily executed to be his, but I'd never have thought that Ioulia could have been capable of such malice. Astrid surveyed the childish script with an air of nervous energy. I suppose by that point she was so far in with Dimitri's activities that any unknown hand could be a potential threat. Five or ten golden minutes – racing up the stairs, dumping our bags, putting on a pot of coffee, kissing in the soft evening light – when we didn't realise how our world was about to be blown apart.

*

'I suppose you think you're like fucking Ted Hughes, don't you?' She held the letter at arm's length and kept staring at it wildly, as if it was a poisonous animal – too scared to drop it or provoke it, but unable to confront it either. 'Tell me it's not true.' Her voice was subdued and collected. '*Tell me it's not true.*' Tightly wound then. I thought about how, in school, we'd wind elastic bands around our fingers until they turned blue. That's how I'd describe it, I thought, when I wrote about it.

She saw it on my face then. The thing is, everyone thinks I'm so duplicitous – and I am, to a degree; but there was something about her expression – plaintive, placating, headlights from the cars on the street below grazing the soft outlines of her face – that made me unable to lie.

She went to stay at Dimitri's that night. The idea of him being her white fucking knight made the blood drain out of my limbs. I offered to leave instead.

'Where would *you* go?'

'A hotel?' I offered, weakly, as she threw things into a little drawstring bag.

'Stop talking now. Please.'

It was like dropping a glass and watching it slip in slow motion from your grasp – you somehow have time to register that it's falling and that it's going to smash. You have time to formulate that thought – to synthesise that impression into language – but you somehow don't have time to *act*, and to save it from shattering.

*

There are words that you wish you could scoop back into your mouth, that you let fall carelessly, gracelessly.

Aristotle was an off-season barfly, so we didn't meet him until September, but at that point he became a fixture in our lives – part of the scenery of the taverna. I liked him for his name (I still wasn't used to the proliferation of Socrates, Archimedes, Adonises) and for his English, which was smug and idiosyncratic, having been learnt (purportedly) from English spies in Crete in the forties (although any tales of his past smacked more than a little of the fantasist, I'll admit). The first time I'd met him, he'd introduced himself as 'Aristo – like Onassis,' proffered a too-firm handshake, and leered at Astrid between puffs of his little ivory pipe, the bowl of it stained the colour of mucus, much like his teeth and his clipped, pointy fingernails. Astrid didn't like him for that: he was the kind of man who leered at women, and I noticed when he spoke to her that he had a habit of licking his top lip, his flecked tongue grazing the bristles of his damp moustache.

'He's repulsive,' she'd said to me once, 'and so much worse than that.'

He was also acerbic and amusing and perennially generous. Never could a man go dry with Aristo as a drinking partner. I tended to avoid him out of consideration for her aversion to him, so naturally, that night I made a spiteful beeline for him.

'Michael, old fruit!' He clapped me on the back. 'What will be your tipple of this night?'

'Elephant tranquilliser if it's available,' I replied, pitching it at *drily* rather than *tragic*.

He ordered us a pair of double gins, delivered with one of the most painful puns I've ever endured ('Chin chin up, old man!'), and he set himself up valiantly to talk me into a coma in lieu of my requested sedative. He was a good sort really, I thought, necking the first glass, one of those men that women couldn't possibly understand, because they were too intolerant of his outward misfortunes.

Over the course of the long night, he delicately layered tales of his more thrilling past (he did something horribly dull now – either a clerk in an office or the kind of job involving endlessly taking other men out to lunch) until I felt comfortably buried in a sort of snowdrift of his various invented histories. Do I remember much about anything I said at all? I was talking on automatic pilot – speaking from a pressing, petty, drunken need to confide in someone. As the following few weeks unfolded in a monstrous Faustian procession, bits of it splintered my carefully deadened conscience. I remember feeling triumphantly vindicated at the look of perfectly composed horror on his face when I'd said the word *pregnant*. 'Imagine putting a pregnant woman in that kind of danger.'

I remember dragging myself up by the banister to the flat, and I remember finding the key I'd left for her under the mat, should she change her mind. I remember lighting a cigarette and standing out on the balcony and breathing in the sweet floral tones of the first blooms of honeysuckle. Everything bathed in moonlight. The brush of the leaves in the wind sounded a little like the brush of the sea. The first whisper of anxiety crept in then. I shrugged it off and told myself that Aristo was too much of an oddball to possibly be connected to the state. He was a drinking partner, I insisted through drags of the cigarette. No one else would ever hear what I'd told him, and besides, if *I'd* been indiscreet, Dimitri had been far worse – and he'd had no right to involve her like that (and not to involve me? Is that what I'd really thought?).

Astrid came back the following afternoon, and when I saw her standing in the courtyard, I thought of the spring before, and of her standing in the flood of warm morning sun on the pavement on Charlotte Street. She didn't want to just leave like that, she said. She wanted to try and understand, and forgive. We were going to have a child together. We were going to make a life together. The next few days burned. I lived a sort of half-life made entirely of feeling on the one part, and denial that I might have slipped up on the other. I'd been drunk and looking for a sympathetic ear, but I'd never *meant* any of it. I kept trying to tell myself that I was just being paranoid. We loved so fiercely in that little smattering of days, and every day that it didn't happen, I told myself again that maybe it never would. But of course it did; it was only a matter of time.

I'd arranged to meet her at quarter past six at our spot at the viewpoint at Anafiotika. It was a cool and unusually quiet evening, sun glinting off the worn whitewashed staircases that wound up to the clearing, where we'd sit together and survey the antique sweep of Athens below us – the Acropolis, wreathed in its halo of sunset, fixed like a postage stamp above it all. There it was again; that greenish light that stage-lights all my memories of it now. When she wasn't there by half past, I knew something was wrong. At quarter to seven, I felt the anaesthetic drip of fear.

Through the winding knot of passages – that anachronistic Cycladic village in the centre of Athens. Street lamps popping on one by one, lighting my path down, down, down – the earth shuddering under my feet and the paving stones slick beneath me. Through the chaos of the streets, all of them shrugging off the soporific hum of the siesta to crack out into night. The grind of engines. The bird-call lilt of rising and falling voices.

Voyeur

At the taverna, the old men sat in silence. Panos shot me a rheumy, pitying look.

'Christinaki?' I gasped, clutching at the last bit of air in my lungs.

He motioned for me to come closer, and whispered a scramble of words that I didn't understand. I could only make out two: *Dimitri. Asfaleia.* After it, a deafening absence of sound.

*

When I got back to the flat, everything was normal, in order, utterly undisturbed, and yet I couldn't shake the unsettling impression that someone had been in there. I wandered around with the slow, sluggish movements of someone coming down off drugs, surveying everything with numb precision. I found it at last on the bedside table, a little note written on smooth manila paper:

> *Your services for the country were greatly appreciated, my chum. You are infinitely welcomed in Greece.*
>
> *Cordialement.*

What else do I need to remember?

38

Leah

Tom and Clarissa finally woke up as we approached the village. Larry and I had barely exchanged another word, and I'd kept my eyes closed out of politeness, or maybe even pride, so that it looked like I was asleep, rather than just angry at him. Tom's voice had been a signal to feign waking up.

'That's weird,' he said.

'We're home?' Clarissa mewed in the sweet, childish voice of someone still half asleep.

'Did my mum text you?'

'Huh?' She blearily reached for her phone, and I watched in the rear-view mirror as she adjusted to being awake.

'"Hi, darling",' Tom began to read. 'Jesus, I'll have to edit. Woman can't type to save her life.' He blinked. '"Remind me of your flight details, and is Clarissa on the same one? Dad and I are thinking of going back a day early but I know we said we'd give you a lift to the airport. Nothing to worry about, I'll explain when you're back. Lots of love."'

'Nothing to worry about?' Clarissa repeated. 'What does that even mean?'

'Tom's granny probably finally kicked the bucket. She's like a hundred and ninety years old.'

'Oh don't be a prick, Lal. At least mine's not a fascist like yours.'

I decided to make myself scarce when we got back to the house. I thought I could probably take a wild guess at what had gone down whilst we'd been away. None of it was any of my business, though, so when we got back and found Jenny and Bryan sitting at the table on the patio, I made my excuses about having a train the next day and went to go and pack my bag.

Much later, when I knew that the coast would be clear, I slipped out of the house and made my way to the beach. It was late enough in the summer now for the night to have a real edge to it, but the sea was as listless as it always was here. I sat on the cool sand and pulled my shirt tighter around me. I'd been watching the dark, unmoving mass of water for a while when I became aware of someone approaching me from the dunes. I wasn't surprised when it was him. He didn't speak at first, but I could feel the pressure of his eye contact like fingers pressing against the contours of my profile. I was the first to speak, because I wanted to challenge him.

'Julian showed them the photograph then?'

'Jesus Christ. Did he send out a bloody newsletter? Rent a town crier?'

I didn't tell him how I'd really seen it. I thought it was better not to alert him to the risk of sharing his email password, as it might be a useful thing for me to carry on knowing. I let the silence needle between us. It didn't make me feel uncomfortable any more.

'Anna left,' he said, finally.

'I'm really not surprised.'

He made the kind of smug grunt of protest that you'd expect from the sort of man who likes reading internet forums about the decline of masculinity. 'It was overdue,' he said.

'Right.' I wondered how easy it would be for me to walk away from this conversation and go to bed.

His gaze was still petitioning me to look back at him, and after a while he said, 'You know, you don't have to leave tomorrow.'

I didn't deign to reply. He carried on, oblivious. 'Now that Anna's gone, it would be easier for you to stay here.'

I dared to look at him then and saw that his face was deformed with a static, nauseating smile. He edged closer to me and I felt my stomach tighten. His jaw was unnaturally mobile and it occurred to me that he might even be high.

'I'm not even going to pretend to know what that means.'

He reached for my hand. 'Oh come on,' he whispered. 'You can't deny that there's some kind of electricity between us. We can both feel the tension.'

Strangely enough, at that moment I thought about my first job, in a supermarket. I was sixteen. I was in the walk-in fridge with my line manager, who was about Michael's age but not privileged enough to look so well preserved. He'd had a neck tattoo and a ratty ponytail slithering out of the base of his shiny pink skull. It was April, and the first straw-berries (bloated with water and artificially fragrant) had come in. I liked the way they made the walk-in fridge smell. My adolescent self was so sweetly romantic that I'd written diary entries about the perfume of the new season arriving at work. I was the kind of dreamy teenager who used to buy up all the reduced gaudy chrysanthemums at the end of my shift and fill my bedroom with them. My line manager, clutching his clipboard and wetting his lips with his tongue, had asked me to pick up a crate of strawberries from the floor, and as I'd bent over to get them (not bending my knees like they'd taught us on our first training day), he'd spanked me so hard my eyes had stung. I was too embarrassed to turn around. I felt my nose burn. I felt like my skin was greasy with shame.

'Off you go, Flirty Gertie,' he'd instructed breezily. 'They're for the promotion end on Produce!'

Michael placed my hand between his legs. 'This is how you make me feel,' he whispered in what was presumably an attempt at a bedroom voice. 'Doesn't that make you feel powerful?'

In a way, it did make me feel powerful. At the beginning of the summer, it probably would have made me feel powerful enough to be turned on by my own potency. I would have let him lean in and slide his clammy free hand underneath my shirt, and I probably would even have felt aroused by the heat of his breath on my earlobe. My sexy silver-fox artist boss, I would have thought. This is a rite of passage. I didn't feel that way any more.

'*I* make me feel powerful,' I said, and extricated my hand from his.

39

Michael

'I think we should move the action to Italy,' said Angela, her mouth, naturally rationed and stingy, attempting to blossom into mateyness as she spoke. 'This whole storyline about this military dictatorship? It doesn't work. The characters are all apathetic anyway, and to be honest, no one even remembers it. I think about Greece and I think about package holidays, you know? Scousers on planes. Those ugly high-rise hotels where they serve bacon baps at brekkie.'

'Plus you want to go and spend six weeks filming in Tuscany.'

'Oh *hardly*, Graham – East Anglia more likely. Anyway, I wasn't thinking *lush* Italy. I was thinking more Naples, or Palermo – you know, somewhere with a bit of Athens' grittiness? I think that would suit the character better. He's intrepid, right?'

I nodded, swallowing the dregs of my pint. *Intrepid*. I could live with that. 'I see what you mean. I'll work on it.'

She beamed with grating enthusiasm and I wondered how Jenny possibly coordinated working in the media with all these tossers. 'I'm so *excited!*'

Graham, the weedier half of the gruesome twosome, aped her every gesture, and I watched him with a sort of grim fascination. Angela clasped her hands together and raised them to her lips, and for a surreal drop of a second I thought she was going to say something like *namaste* and out-Primrose Hill even herself. Instead she attempted to make her eyes gleam and scaffolded her parsimonious gob into a toothless smile.

'Well! I've got to dash, gentlemen. I've got about fifty million slices of smoked salmon to roll into bloody nibbles for this party tonight.' A theatrical groan. 'I guess I'll see you both after the holiday, if we haven't all been eaten alive by a flesh-eating computer virus, or whatever it is my son tells me we're going to get. God, 2000. I feel *old*.'

Wondering if she always spoke like that, I slithered off my bar stool. Outside, I was swallowed by the thrum of public-school Henrys. London Bridge was swarming with them – a heaving, braying mass of pinstriped, sandy-haired chaos. Bank would be a nightmare, I thought miserably, and resented Anna with every grain of my being for choosing to live on the Central Line.

I slipped into automatic pilot the moment I got down into the press of mechanical bodies, and fought my way along the endless choking corridors.

'There are severe delays on the Hammersmith and City, District, Northern, Bakerloo and Victoria lines.'

Up and down those interminable spiral staircases.

'There is a good service on all other lines.'

Through the din of faceless ghost people, and up onto the diminishing squeeze of the platform.

Angela's words flashed through my thoughts and felt all at once like a judgement. *Apathetic.* People were always so quick to dole out accusations of apathy, and yet I doubted she'd be volunteering to go and make smoked salmon nibbles in a Liberian refugee camp any time soon.

I hobbled onto the train with the rest of the miserable ants, and closed my eyes. Italy. I could deal with Italy. She'd have liked to have gone to Italy. I felt a small twinge of pleasure as I imagined her silhouette re-created like a paper doll in Trastevere, or on a terrace on the Piazza Maggiore in Bologna; a two-dimensional figment in the cotton dress with the blue anemones, unfolding onto the scenery like a Christmas cracker crown.

'The next station is Holborn. Alight here for the British Museum.'

Holborn, Russell Square, Tottenham Court Road, Goodge Street. The kinds of places no one lived any more. A knot of stations around which I'd briefly built some semblance of a life with her.

I opened my eyes and felt the nerves around my throat contract. She was standing on the platform in the man's shirt and cropped trousers she used to wear for Jeremy's gigs, with her hair piled on top of her head. Hand holding a smaller hand – too small for me to see. Eyeing me confrontationally, with none of the gauche timidity of before. Eyes expecting answers.

But of course she wasn't – *they* weren't – and as quickly as they'd appeared, they were folded neatly away again into the surge of harried commuters.

40

Leah

I felt a bit numb, a little slower – dimmed – as I made my way up the lawn and onto the smooth flagstones of the patio. Above all I felt calm. I inhaled the perfume of the fresh marjoram one last time and savoured the damp grass smell for a second.

In the hollow of my room, I grabbed my bag and lingered on the view from my window – the suggestion of moonlight glinting off the ripples of the sea. It had all been predictably seedy in the end. I knew there was no way I'd get to Marseille by myself at this time of night, but I also knew that I had to be elsewhere, that I couldn't wake up here tomorrow morning. The idea of it impelled me to move forward, and to not stop and think about everything that had just happened.

My escape was going smoothly until the moment I reached the front door.

'Leah?'

I swore under my breath.

'Is that you?'

'Bryan?'

He was sitting on the sofa in the living room, flicking through an old copy of *Harper's* magazine.

'What are you doing?' he asked, eyes straying to my rucksack.

'Why are you awake?' I stammered.

'Where are you going?'

For all my impulse towards movement, I felt pinned now to the doorway where he'd caught me. All his agonising, well-intentioned concern.

'Stay there,' he said. 'I'm going to get my coat.'

We didn't speak much in the car, but then Bryan was so elementally non-verbal. He only spoke when necessary at first, to ask practical, useful questions.

'You're sure you have somewhere to stay?'

'Uh huh.'

'You've texted him?'

'Texting him as we speak,' I lied, reaching for my phone. I knew, at least, that Jérôme was working tonight; I'd been intending to just sort of glamorously pitch up at his bar like Ingrid Bergman.

'OK,' he assented, turning on the car radio.

The classical music station was playing a Chopin nocturne. I got into the rhythm of our non-conversation – I was even grateful for it. I pressed my head against the cool car window and floated in the hum of the engine, in the lilac haze of the motorway.

'You know, I'm sure that whatever happened, it wasn't your fault,' he announced, apparently from nowhere, his eyes fixed on the road.

'Oh, I don't know.' I shrugged. 'It was definitely partly my fault.'

Another five or ten minutes passed before he spoke again.

'Well you shouldn't feel bad about it, whatever it was.'

I watched him shift slightly in his seat, adjust the belt, laboriously check the petrol gauge, the speedometer, and tap along to the music on the dashboard. At last he said:

'You know. I've always known he was a twat. He's not a good man.'

Straight lines ahead of us, dwindling lights, arrows urging us towards Marseille, Martigues, Toulon.

'When Jenny was a kid, something really awful happened to her. She's from a big family – I'm sure she's told you that?'

The patterns of light from the road grazed his profile. Beams of orange, shafts of shadow, looping like a turntable.

'She had an older sister called Marion, who suffered from depression. Really bad depression. No one ever talks about her in the family any more; they've all just internalised this *huge* trauma . . .'

He craned his head to check the rear-view mirror. 'Marion killed herself when she was nineteen. She drowned herself. Jenny was with her when she did it.'

'Oh God . . .'

'And she never talked to anyone about it. *Anyone.* Marion ceased to exist in the language of the family. It was a different time,' he added, as if that explained it away. 'Then she met Michael at university, and when they'd been friends for a while, she told him all about it – I mean *really* opened herself up to him. Oh. Shite, almost missed the turning.'

The click of the indicator as he hung a right. 'Guess what Michael's first published work of fiction was about?'

'No . . .'

'Won a literary prize for undergraduates.' He laughed. 'That pretty much sums up how he feels about us all, in my opinion. We're just raw material for him.' He looked at me then. 'He'll get what's coming to him, though. You'll see. And Jen's not going to forgive him this time.'

*

Jérôme's face through the crowd. The row of white teeth when he realised it was me. A cigarette behind his ear like a builder with a biro. Bodies moving against each other.

Soaring. A middle-aged man putting 'L'Aventurier' on the jukebox. My shoulders going despite myself.

*

The following morning I woke up habitually early, long before Jérôme. I padded barefoot out into the kitchen, shafts of morning sun leaking in through the shutters and casting great geometric patterns on the terracotta floor. I put on a pot of coffee and went and opened them, throwing out light about the room. Out of habit, I suppose, whilst I waited for the coffee pot to rattle into life on the stove, I opened my computer and clicked in to Michael's email browser. I felt a pang of voyeuristic excitement when I saw that there was another email from *j.f.gresford*.

The first thing that opened on the screen was a new photograph. It looked as if it had been taken in the early nineties and was of a girl about my age. She looked a lot like Larry, and she was smiling at the person taking the photograph, twirling an empty wine glass between her fingers.

This is a photo of my god-daughter, Iris, who came to live with us for a few years in California when she was a student. After Christine (she abandoned 'Astrid' a long time ago) turned up at my mum's place, we took her in for a while. She went back to England with Mum just after Iris was born, and after the fall of the regime out in Greece, Dimitri ended up coming to the UK to finish his studies, which had, needless to say, been put on hold when he was arrested. He and Chris married in '77, and he was Iris's father as far as it mattered. They kept you out of it to protect her from the truth. I appreciate that it must have been difficult for you, but I hope you understand that I had a duty to respect their wishes.

When I didn't tell Jenny and Anna everything the other night – when I let them believe that you'd just abandoned Chris in Athens – I did it to protect your own kids. If they don't know what you did, maybe it's better to let them carry on believing that. You're their father after all.

Please don't bother trying to track Iris or Christine down. I told you when I arrived that I'd come here on the basis of an email from Jenny, and it's my turn to admit that I wasn't entirely honest. Me coming here was part of a long grieving process. Iris passed away two years ago, after a long battle with illness. You should know that she was a bright, vivacious and wonderful girl, and that she lived a happy life. You should also have the decency to respect her parents' wish not to hear from you. If you should decide otherwise, don't forget that there are still a handful of us who know what you really did. Anna kept talking about this new novel you're working on. I'm sure you wouldn't want any negative press.

Best,

Julian

Underneath was a link to an archived *New York Times* article. I opened it and read the first few lines:

> ATHENS, Jan. 9 – The military government that ruled Greece for more than seven years regularly inflicted physical and mental torture on its political prisoners, according to numerous accounts now being made public . . .

*

365

When I tried to open Michael's emails again later that day on the train back to Paris, I discovered that he'd changed the password for the account. I shut my laptop and watched the world flit by outside the window. Fields teeming with husks of dying sunflowers. Great craggy rock faces grazed with the *garrigue* and plunges of bottle green. Hay bales, church steeples and telegraph poles. Olive groves. I realised that I felt relieved.

Epilogue

Michael

'So you're aware of how a lot of people – especially the younger generation – are reacting to your new novel then?'

I was heartened to see that Joanna Pritchard hadn't aged well. She had that flabby, jowly look that a lot of middle-aged women get, and it made her red lipstick smack of desperation. She was dressed expensively. She'd had a good career. That this interview was taking place in a coffee shop (Scandinavian furniture, baristas in leather aprons, waxy philodendrons) made me suspect that her newspaper wasn't doing quite as well as it had been the last time we'd met.

'I believe they keep calling me an *old white man*, which isn't a thrillingly original observation.'

Joanna smirked.

'I'm rather hoping that they'll do me the honour of blanket no-platforming. Speaking engagements are such a drag.' I took a sip of my espresso. 'What did you think of the book?'

She seemed to concentrate very hard on her fingernails. 'Well, it's a best-seller already, and it's new. It's exciting.'

It was certainly exciting for my bank balance, which was fortunate seeing as Anna had decided to take me to the cleaners when she'd pitched up with the bloke my daughter affectionately referred to as 'the art sleaze'.

'What else?' I insisted.

Another of her trademark smirks. 'It's provocative.' She shrugged. 'In my opinion, *too* provocative. A lot of the content is interesting, but it just gets lost in all the politics, which frankly sometimes border on weird. I kind of got the impression that you were just trying to piss people off.'

I was bored of this question. 'It would seem that one can't help it these days.'

'It's funny you should say that, because that's exactly what you said the last time I interviewed you – although last time you were pissing off quite a different audience.'

Bitch. I attempted to look puzzled. 'You've interviewed me before?'

Joanna momentarily looked like I'd leant across the table and slapped her smug little face. 'It was a long time ago,' she sniffed when she'd regained her habitual air of superiority. Evidently still smarting somewhat, however, she asked: 'How does it feel to be the unwitting darling of the alt-right?'

I thought about my divorce, I thought about how easy it had been to buy Bryan and Jenny out of the house in Saint-Luc, and I thought about all the drinks I'd buy the pretty twenty-three-year-old editorial assistant at the party my publishers were throwing for me tonight.

'I think I'll manage to bear it.'

Acknowledgements

To Charlotte, my wonderful agent, who believed in this book and in me as a writer long before anyone else did. To Desperate Literature in Madrid, and especially to Terry, Charlotte, Rob and Emily: without the Desperate Literature Prize this book would probably still be an abandoned manuscript gathering dust in the proverbial bottom drawer.

To my brilliant and forever hilarious editor Amy, with whom it was a total delight to work, and to everyone at Tinder Press who has helped make this book what it is. To Antonia, who is not only the best PR going, but has also been so supportive throughout the weird and wonderful journey of publication. To Yeti for the striking and badass cover, and of course, to Jane and to Vicky. My head is still spinning that any of this is real. Thank you for all of your hard work and for having faith in *Voyeur*, and in me.

To everyone at Andrew Nurnberg Associates who has worked so hard for this book, and to Anna who kindly gave it the once over before it was sent off on submission.

To my first readers: To Fiona, my mother, who read this when no one else knew it was being written and who, along with my father, Richard, instilled the compelling power and dizzying delights of books in me from day one. To Jess – my soul mate – without whom this book would never have even been conceived. Thank you for all the gorgeous chaos. To Jaimie, whose killer feedback at the beginning was instrumental. To Kate, who has inspired me and shared her (endless) wisdom and friendship right from the start – I wish Valtaro's were still around so we could celebrate there. To Jess A whose insight and support made this all seem possible. To Chris, who was not only a first reader, but who has also scooped me up out of every melodramatic meltdown for the past decade.

To Adam, who sat down and had a drink with me and gave me hope and advice when the ten thousandth literary agent had rejected the manuscript. To Madeleine who kindly read a very early draft and gave invaluable feedback.

To Dimitris, one of my favourite regulars at the café where I worked when writing this book. Dimitris saved the latter part of *Voyeur* when we got talking about the military junta whilst he waited for his double espresso at the counter. Thanks also to his father, and to his father's neighbour in Athens who gave me some insight into life there in the 1960s. I owe you all a lifetime of coffee.

Huge thanks to Kyveli and to Phoebus for Greek translations and for making sure I didn't make any glaring mistakes with regards to writing about their homeland. Special thanks to Feev for the music, and for showing me Athens for the first time. A thousand thanks as well to Antoine for patiently trawling through all my French mistakes. I'm sorry that after all of our time together my grammar in your glorious language is still a total shambles!

To all the other people who left their trace on this book: Sandra, Siobhan, Elle, Steph, Cameron (the original maker of collages) . . . to all of the people I worked with at Bob's whilst this was being written, and especially to Mustafa – I always send my love. To the regulars at the Bastringue, upon whose glorious terrace much of this book was conceived after one too many negronis. To the English Department at Ysgol Brynhyfryd, and to Eileen and Bethan – the first people who ever told me that writing was a thing I could do. To my grandmother, who I hope will see this somehow and know that she was the one who taught me that art was a possibility. To all of my friends and family who put up with me, and whom I love beyond words.

Above all, of course thank you to Jan. My love – I'm so happy I could pass out.

Read on for a special extra chapter,
when back in 1974 Michael realises his secret
might be about to come out . . .

1974

The party was interminably dull, but I was hardly going to leave given that the booze was abundant and that the whole farce was being thrown in my honour. It was at Sappho's palatial flat just off Cheyne Walk, which honestly wasn't a part of town that I was particularly fond of. We'd been seeing each other on and off for the best part of the year. She was convenient because thanks to certain bohemian aspirations, she didn't begrudge me the 'off' parts as other girls would. She was also frighteningly well-connected and, above all, rich, which as my income had been patchy when we'd first met, had been an immensely appealing character trait. Saph wasn't the sharpest tool in the shed, but she was good at *appearing* to be bright due to the small fortune that her parents had forked out on her education. She knew the names of all the right books – even if she hadn't read them – and she was infuriatingly adept at flitting casually between various European languages. One of her more galling affectations was that she insisted on calling me *Michele*, as if I were some kind of closeted Italian; and I don't say that lightly, as she really did have a whole arsenal of galling affectations.

The party was an anniversary of sorts. It was a year to the day that I had published a review in a small but respected, taste-making literary magazine that had entirely altered my career – and by altered, I mean established altogether. It was of a debut novel that happened to have been written by one of the most popular and vacuous female newspaper

372

columnists in the country. My detractors called it gratui-
tously nasty. My pious schoolmistress sister, for example,
sent me a letter from whatever boring village in Cheshire
she'd elected to live in, telling me that if one didn't have
anything nice to say, it was better not to say anything at all.
Even her handwriting was undersexed. Apparently though,
more people than I'd expected on this foetid, pearl-clutching
little isle actually had a sense of humour. I'd made myself a
reputation in one fell swoop. People wanted to talk to me
at parties. My opinion was all at once sought after. Mincing
arts editors from national newspapers suddenly wanted
to take me out for lunch. One, snivelling over his plate of
chicken supreme à la forestière, told me that he thought I
really was the 'perfect, picturesque poster boy for the youth
in revolt'. It was with him that I took up a job, and for the
first time in my life, began to acquire both money and status.
The logorrheic Labrador of a columnist who had effectively
launched my career was called Sybil Longford. Sappho
had made up the invitations as ones to a *soirée* celebrating
Sybil's career. Saph had such criminal amounts of expend-
able dosh that she'd even gone to Hatchards and bought
multiple copies of the first novel in question, piling them up
around the flat for people to openly mock. I'd drawn the
line at her tedious friends requests to sign them. Like most
literary types, they fed off other people's disasters.

I was on about my fifth or sixth *Sybil Sinker* – naturally
the party had themed cocktails – when Clara Stanton
pitched up. Sappho had returned to the drawing room with
a face on and sighed, 'it wasn't my man at all – it's my
brother and some new girl of his'. Her *man* was of course
her drug dealer. Talking like a Velvet Underground song,
rather than the *Tatler* fixture that she actually was, was yet
another vexing habit of Sappho's. 'I suppose I ought to get
them a drink,' she sighed, 'you talk to them.'

The brother – Horace, Heraclitus, Christ knows – dumped his tatty Mick Jagger mink on a chaise longue, and crossed the room without so much as acknowledging me. I was glad; and when I clocked that the 'new girl of his' was Clara Stanton, I could hardly believe my luck.

'Hello darling,' I said, kissing her cheek, letting my palm graze the small of her back. 'It's been forever.'

She stiffened. 'Hasn't it.'

I stepped back to take her in and registered her facial expression, which was about as cold as the tone of her voice had been. What could I possibly have done to offend Clara?

'You want one of these?' I said, shaking the ice about in my glass.

'What's one of those?'

I shrugged. 'I'd rather not know. All of the booze that Sybil considers to be part of her personal brand apparently. Lillet. Campari. Hemlock . . .'

'I'll have whatever's going I suppose. Lord knows I could do with a drink.' She was looking past me, clearly scanning the room for anyone else that she might know.

'Christ Clara, I almost get the impression you're trying to get rid of me.'

She finally smiled. 'Well aren't you astute?'

About an hour later, after *Sybil Sinker* seventeen or thereabouts, I found myself in a conversation with the ghastly brother. 'So you're a friend of Clara's from Ox, I gather?' he drawled, puffing on a clove cigarette like some old queen.

'How did you two meet?' I asked.

'In New York actually,' he simpered, as if the fact of having been in New York was some kind of achievement. 'She was working on a paper over there and we met through an old school pal of mine. You might know him too actually. Julian Gresford?'

My throat contracted 'Vaguely. Hardly. A long time ago.'
I downed the rest of my drink. My hands, I noticed, were
trembling. How unpleasant. 'How is Julian these days?' I
asked, trying to smooth out my voice. I heard myself ask the
thing that I really wanted to know. 'Got a girl on the scene?'

The brother raised his eyebrows. 'A *girl*? How well did
you know Gresford?'

So she wasn't with him at least. She, they, who knew. The
point was that Astrid wasn't living with Julian. Sappho's
idiot brother wouldn't have missed a knockout like Astrid.
And another thing, I tried to tell myself as I made for the
drinks cabinet having escaped his clutches; Idiot Brother
seemed completely unaware of Jules and I having any kind
of past together. So surely Jules couldn't have been talking
about it. He wasn't telling people about what had happened.
I kept repeating it to myself as I ransacked the cupboard for
scotch. He wasn't telling people about what had happened.
It was only when I'd poured out my whisky (Sappho always
had the right brand) and had lit a cigarette that it occurred
to me why Clara might have been so frosty when she'd seen
me. The horrifying thought bloomed in my mind. I could
feel it press at my temples, at the sockets of my eyes. The
noises around me became indistinct. I closed my eyes. I felt
nauseous again. If Julian had told Clara, who else might he
tell? Who else might he already have told? In the nebulous
din – voices, music, glasses clinking – I picked out Saph's
braying laugh. She was reading an extract of Sybil Longford's novel. I imagined the gleeful column that Sybil would
write when what had happened in Greece became public.
I was going to have to get very, very drunk.

After several painful hours, I managed to catch Clara as she
was making to leave. By this point, I was also quite high,
and chemical confidence propelled me towards the hallway,

where she was putting on her coat. I felt disembodied as I readied myself to face her. I pushed the front door closed with my hand, barring the exit. 'Clara, sweetheart. I know why you're being like this, and it's important that you let me explain my side of things.'

'Mick,' she said tersely.

'No. Listen. You have to hear me out. You know what Julian's like. He's a bloody fantasist. I'm not going to stand for it.' I heard myself hiccup. This wasn't quite as dignified as I'd been intending.

'Julian? What on earth has Julian got to do with any of this?'

'I'm sorry?'

'Oh God. It's so like you to blame someone else isn't it? You really think I'm not being chummy with you because of something Julian said? You really think I give damn about Julian of all people?'

I blinked. I felt my palm fall from the door. She seized the opportunity to grab the handle.

'Michael,' she said, 'the last time you spoke to me I wasn't wearing any clothes. We'd just been so intimate that my skin still smelt of your vile bloody cologne.' She sniffed, and smiled graciously, 'Thank God you've grown out of that.' As she stepped over the threshold she said, 'Not even a 'phone call. And by the looks of this tacky party, you've still got no form, have you?'

As her figure disappeared along the bright, carpeted corridor and down the gleaming, pristine staircase, I felt a surge of electric relief. I could have laughed. Back in the drawing room, I picked up one of the copies of Sybil Longford's novel. Cresting the euphoria, I cleared my throat, and when the people around me stopped talking to listen, I began to read aloud.